"YOU GIRLS ARE HEADING WEST
WITH YOUR HEADS
STUFFED FULL OF DREAMS,

and you don't know what the hell you're getting yourself into," Dan Tallant raged. "There's a shortage of women in Texas. I should know. You'll find out you'll have to pay a price—"

"And I'm willing to pay a price right now," Tamsen snapped, her eyes narrowed. "For some horses. Whenever you're ready to get down to business."

"Are you now?" Tallant snickered. "The merchandise looks good, what I can see of it." He came toward her. "Maybe we can make a deal then." His voice was caressing as he reached for her.

"You're wrong," she whispered, "I didn't mean . . ."

Books by Aola Vandergriff

Daughters of The Southwind
Wyndspelle
The Bell Tower of Wyndspelle
Wyndspelle's Child

Published by
WARNER BOOKS

DAUGHTERS
OF THE
SOUTHWIND

Aola Vandergriff

WARNER BOOKS

A Warner Communications Company

WARNER BOOKS EDITION

Copyright © 1977 by Aola Vandergriff
All rights reserved

ISBN 0-446-89230-0

Cover art by Adrian Osterling

Warner Books, Inc., 75 Rockefeller Plaza, New York, N.Y. 10019

W A Warner Communications Company

Printed in the United States of America

Not associated with Warner Press, Inc. of Anderson, Indiana

First Printing: April, 1977

10   9   8

Contents

Book One
    McLeod's Daughters   9

Book Two
    Madame Franklin's Parlor
        For Gentlemen   197

Book Three
    Castle In Spain   399

DAUGHTERS
OF THE
SOUTHWIND

Book One

McLeod's Daughters

Chapter 1

St. Louis, at the confluence of the Missouri and Mississippi rivers, long known as the Gateway to the West, was booming that late summer of 1848. For years, the city had served as a marketplace, a supply depot for the frontier. Now, the first ranks of gold-seekers had arrived, heading toward California. And with them came the speculators, the gamblers, those who would live from the sweat of the miner's brow.

Prices soared. The inns were filled with folk delighted to leave the discomfort of their covered wagons for a while, forsaking pioneer life for a good hot meal, a real bed, a bath. Down on the waterfront, the Manuel Lisa Warehouse, built by a Spanish fur trader, used by John Jacob Astor for storage, housed a sailmaker in its loft. But now his needle was turned to other uses, the mending of tarpaulins and wagon covers.

On the outskirts of this great city, where politicians in their frock coats and tall hats rubbed shoulders with feral-smelling woodsmen in their fringed jackets and leggings, covered wagons bloomed like a vast sea of mushrooms. Each day, a new train left, moving west.

It was here that the McLeod family was stranded. They had left their home in Pennsylvania with two wagons, each drawn by a span of fine oxen. They carried a cargo of agricultural implements they planned to sell in the new state of Texas. Scott McLeod, former farmer, father of three motherless daughters, now fancied himself a business man.

Offered a fair price for his oxen by a fellow traveler on the trail, McLeod, trusting in his newfound talents, sold them, contingent upon arrival in St. Louis. There he would move his family and supplies down the Mississippi by boat to a point where he planned to purchase new teams and strike out across country to Texas.

McLeod learned too late that the cash he had received was only a pittance now that the gold fever was fermenting. The oxen could not be replaced at a price he could pay. And everything that would float on the river moved back and forth between industrial centers, carrying equipment bound for California.

Except for a few stout German farmers heading for Oregon, all wagon trains seemed destined for California. His only chance, if he should find horses or oxen, was to join a group moving along the Santa Fe Trail, and break away. Texas it had to be. McLeod was not one to change his mind.

Trapped in the confines of the wagonyard, McLeod met a kindred spirit, a funny little Englishman, William Winston Wotherspoon, better known as Dusty. Dusty, who was well acquainted with the West, was eager to return, and his tales of Texas were as prodigious as his thirst.

"You'll want to go to Magoffinville," Dusty would say, passing the bottle he always carried with him. "Now that's the place! Say, did I ever tell you—?"

Wagon trains came and went. Still the McLeod wagons sat. Dusty's, too; one of his horses had contracted a colic; one wheel of his worn vehicle moved at an impossible slant. The two of them, Scott and Dusty, drank and dreamed away.

Then Scott McLeod came down with Missouri fever. As he lay on his pallet in the wagon, out of his head at times, shivering with ague, his daughters reacted each in her own way. Emmeline, the eldest, rarely left his side, conscientiously nursing her charge. Tamsen, the middle daughter, tended to the chores and took the responsibility for her family's welfare on her slender shoulders.

Arabella, the youngest girl, fretted. She wasn't accus-

12

tomed to inactivity, but her efforts to find some excitement were always foiled by her sisters.

I'm sick of just sitting here, Arabella thought on one sunny morning. And I'm sick of people being sick! The day had dawned bright and blue, and she'd got up early to watch the mists rising off the river. How she longed to go to the docks! The river fascinated her with its colors—turgid yellow water, the gray-blue shoals beneath it that spelled danger, the limestone bluffs above.

Even more so, she liked the people; the roustabouts and stevedores; the black men, shirtless, rippling muscles in the sun; the fancy ladies who came out in early evening, twirling their parasols, lifting their skirts to show a well-turned ankle.

Arabella lifted her own skirt, experimentally, and whirled in a little dance. The men had been nice to her the time she had slipped away and gone there alone. Tamsen didn't have the right to be so nasty about it! They had called her Sis, and when she sang and danced for them, they'd thrown coins. She still had those coins, wrapped in a handkerchief and hidden in the chest where her things were kept.

Tamsen and Em were talking about how much they needed money this morning, and she'd been tempted to offer it to them. But they'd try to make something bad out of what she'd done to earn it. For the first time, she wished, forlornly, that she was back home, that cranky old Mrs. Goodson, the housekeeper, was still around. Her sisters were always watching her here. At home, she'd had more freedom. Why couldn't Tamsen and Em realize she was a grownup, now? Almost fifteen! And she'd bet she'd already kissed more boys than either of them!

What had happened to them? Her green eyes narrowed as she thought about their problems. It was so much fun in the beginning, starting out on their great adventure with such excitement that even the hardships of the trail were easily ignored. Even Tamsen had been

13

bearable, less bossy. It was this long wait here getting on everybody's nerves. If they could just move on . . .

But to move, they needed horses or oxen. Papa had been unable to find them. And now he was sick.

Arabella remembered seeing a corral where the owner rented space to newcomers for their horses. She'd never seen such horses before, huge animals, with hooves like dinnerplates. They would do so nicely.

Had Papa approached the owner? If not, someone really should. She might go and ask the man. Tamsen had forbidden her the docks, but she'd said nothing about the corrals.

Well, why not? Maybe she could make a deal for those horses. Surprise Papa!

She cast an eye toward the McLeod wagons. Tamsen, bent above a fire, was stirring something. Probably soup for Papa. Lifting her skirts, Arab ran like the wind. When she reached the corral, she vaulted over the top rail in a flash.

Dan Tallant's first thought of the morning, as usual, was to check his stock. They were draft animals, purchased with an eye toward pulling heavy mining equipment into inaccessible regions. The horses were a part of his cover—necessary to the new identity he intended to assume when he reached California. They were to serve as his introduction into certain circles.

As he walked toward the corral, he saw what he thought to be a child mount the fence and disappear into the enclosure. Tallant began to run, swearing under his breath. He, too, leaped the fence and, grasping the offender firmly about the waist, pulled her toward him.

"Get out of here," he ordered, as he held the struggling girl. "You have no business here!"

"Leave me alone!" Arab yelled, kicking backward, connecting with his knee.

Grimly, he carried the girl, spitting like a cat, to the fence. There, he turned her around to face him and sat her upon the top rail.

"Good Lord," he said, as she narrowed green eyes at him, "I thought you were a kid."

14

"Well, I'm not!" The girl's haughtiness could have graced a queen. Tallant was torn between anger and a desire to laugh.

"Whoever you are," he said, firmly, "you have no business being in this corral. I'm Dan Tallant, and I'm responsible for these animals. Do you realize what might have happened if one of them had stepped on you?"

The green eyes had widened. A practiced smile touched Arab's lips, a dimple flickering enchantingly in her right cheek. "*You're* Dan Tallant? I thought you'd be an *old* man."

Despite himself, Dan felt the magnetism of the girl's charm. God help me, he thought, amused. God help any man this girl has designs on. Her eyes were pools of innocence, but she was definitely one of those who are born knowing.

"And what gave you that idea?" he asked, levelly.

"Oh, I don't know. Maybe something Dusty said."

"Dusty? Old Wotherspoon? I've seen him around. Ah, I know! You're one of the McLeods. You have two beautiful sisters!"

Arabella's face twisted sourly. "Em's beautiful, I guess," she said, grudgingly. "Tamsen's just bossy."

"Then Em's the dark one? Little, with long black hair?" Tallant flushed. He'd refused to admit, even to himself, that he'd watched the girl at her campfire from a distance.

"That's Tamsen." Arab shook her red curls, and decided to change the subject. "And I'd like to buy some of your horses."

In her effort to persuade him to sell her father the horses, the whole story came pouring out; how, after their mother had died, they'd left their home to fulfill Papa's dream of moving to Texas; how Papa had sold their oxen on the trail and, now that he was sick, they could go no farther. Tamsen, she said, thought when they got to Texas, Papa might not drink so much. And it was Tamsen's idea that Em would be happier somewhere where everybody didn't know she'd been jilted. But of course Tam's real reason for wanting to move

15

was that she didn't want to marry Will Franklin and be a farmer's wife.

Tallant listened, a little dazed by the amount of information being heaped upon him. Apparently the tiny dark girl he'd admired—Tamsen, was it?—was the ramrod of the outfit. He jumped a little as Arab stopped abruptly.

"How much?" she said.

They were back to the subject of horses. "I'd like to sell them to you," he told her, regretfully, "but they're already contracted for. That means they've been sold— to some people in California. I'm just seeing that they arrive safely."

Arabella was sick with disappointment. "I was so looking forward to getting to Texas. We're going to be rich, you know, when Papa sells his supplies. Tamsen says we'll have pretty gowns and go to balls, give parties—"

Dan thought of the Texas he knew. Three girls, a sick father—Good God! There ought to be a law that would send them home!

"Miss—"

"Arabella," she offered. "Arabella McLeod, but everyone calls me Arab."

"I want you to take a message to your father for me. Tell him he won't like Texas. It's no place for ladies—" he turned her hands palms up—"ladies with lily-white hands. And it's no place for folks who aren't strong. Once you're there, it'll be too late to turn back, too late to quit. So it might be a good idea to go back where you came from. Will you tell him that?"

"I guess so," she lied. Now her only desire was to get on her way. This man was interesting, but he was too old for her. He was older than Em, who was twenty. And she must still find teams for the wagons. She repressed the urge to clamber down, an age-old instinct telling her to appeal to the stronger sex. She dimpled at him once more. "Will you help me?"

"For a kiss!"

Putting his hands about Arabella's small waist, he

16

swung her, giggling, into the air. Then, evading the pouting, proffered lips, he touched her cheek gently with his own.

That's not the way it appeared to Tamsen as she hurried across the packed earth toward them. When she came up to Arabella, Tamsen took the younger girl firmly by her arm and turned to give the dark stranger a withering look.

"Arab," she moaned. "Oh, Arab, how could you!"

"But he's *nice*," Arabella said, defensively. "He can't sell his horses, but he gave me a message for Papa."

"And what might that be?" Tamsen was still angry, but there was a question in her eyes.

Arabella stammered as she recalled the content of Tallant's message. Tamsen might take what he'd said seriously. "He said . . . he said to tell Papa we ought to go back home. That Texas . . . Texas is no place for lily-livered ladies, or for quitters like us."

"Well!" Tamsen gasped. "Indeed!"

Arabella suppressed a smile. She had managed to turn Tamsen's anger in another direction. They'd never think of returning to Pennsylvania now. "I tried to buy his horses," she explained, "but he won't sell any. I guess men don't want women on their old wagon trains."

"We don't need his horses," Tamsen said with determination. "We'll find a way!" But as they approached the wagons, so long immobilized, she felt a quiver of uncertainty.

The feeling was still with her as she walked toward the fire where Em was dishing up some broth for the sick man in the wagon. Tamsen had really been the one who persuaded her family to undertake this venture. Now they were stranded here, and Papa was ill. The reasons she had given herself were good ones; Papa had always wanted to go to Texas, and then Em's beau married someone else. Arabella was getting to be a handful, getting talked about with all her pranks.

But were those her real reasons? Could it have been because she wanted more from life than Will Franklin and his Pennsylvania farm had to offer? She thought of

17

the dull kisses he had forced upon her and shuddered.

Em looked up from the pot of soup that boiled above the campfire, her pretty face flushed pink beneath the soft golden-brown hair that fell in curling tendrils. "Tamsen. Did you find her?"

"I found her." Tamsen described the circumstances of Arab's latest escapade.

"You worry too much, Tam," Emmeline McLeod said, gently. "She's just a child. I don't think the man intended any harm."

To Em's amazement, Tamsen's eyes brimmed with tears.

She brushed them angrily away. "I'm sorry, Em. I don't know what's got into me. I was hateful to Arabella just now. And so mad at that man, I felt like hitting him! Everything's going wrong, and I feel so responsible!"

That was the trouble, Em thought, taking the small, work-worn hands in her own. Tamsen's head was bowed, and the back of her neck, where the hair swept upward in two raven wings, looked so young and vulnerable. Somehow, since Tamsen felt responsible for all of them, they had let her bear the brunt of the family decisions. Papa was lovable, but a weak man. Em had a delicate constitution and a rather passive nature. Arab, dear scatterbrain that she was, rarely thought of anything except her own impulsive desires.

They had all depended so heavily on Tamsen, even when she was a child. Papa had named her Tamsen, for Thomas, when he hadn't had the boy he wanted. He referred to her as his "good right arm."

But she wasn't a boy! She was a girl, a beautiful, dark-eyed small girl, who deserved pretty clothes, laughter, good times . . . *Perhaps it is time*, Em thought, *for me to make some decisions!*

"Tamsen," she said, "let's go back home."

Tamsen's head jerked up. Em had voiced the thoughts in her own mind. But now that they were out in the open, they sounded ridiculous. Go home? Quit? The message Arab had delivered still rankled. They would

18

get to Texas, somehow! Once there, they would sell their goods and buy a decent home. Em would find some nice, cultured young man. Papa would stop drinking. And Arab would become a lady—she'd picked up her rough ways from the people surrounding them. In Texas, that would all change. No, Tamsen told Em, they were not going to give up now.

The chance to cultivate Arab's manners came sooner than Tamsen expected. As she crouched stirring the stew that was to be their evening meal, she heard Dusty's voice. He always just happened to drop by to visit Papa at mealtime.

Tamsen left the fire and hastened to the rear of the second wagon where the invalid's bed was surrounded by boxes and crates of supplies. If that odious little man had brought Papa a bottle again—

She halted in shock at Dusty's appearance. The grubby clothing he normally wore was replaced by an ancient suit. His scraggly mustache had been clipped, disclosing two missing front teeth as he smiled. Atop his graying poll was something that resembled a hat. In one hand, he carried an elegant walking stick.

"D—Dusty?"

Dusty bowed elaborately, "My lady, I would like to present my good friend, Lord Newby, late of England, for some time a member of society in this charming city; soon to set forth on the trail to our incomparable West. Your Lordship, Miss Tamsen McLeod, fairest of the fair, a blossoming beauty."

Tamsen turned toward the newcomer. Lord Newby was a slender, rather colorless man, with amusement in his small, twinkling eyes. When the flustered girl extended her hand, he bent above it in a courtly manner.

"Charmed."

And he meant it. He'd just met the gracious Em, a creature done in pastels, and Arabella, a little baggage if he ever saw one. But there was something in this girl that intrigued him. She was small, to be sure, and that dowdy dark dress did nothing for her. Her face, flushed with firelight, had a Madonna-like beauty that was deceptive. There was something more than surface loveliness here. This girl had a core of iron.

He found himself speculating on how she would appear in another setting.

Papa invited the gentlemen to dinner, much to Tamsen's consternation. There was so little to serve, but Tamsen went about her preparations with resignation. Spreading her good shawl over the stump that served as makeshift table, she felt a twinge of regret that her mother's good dishes had been left behind. Yet Lord Newby accepted his tin cup of soup with a savoir-faire that made it seem worthy of a banquet, and she found herself at ease in his presence.

"Your father seems quite ill," he said, with concern. "Has he seen a physician about his health?"

Tamsen lowered her gaze. She could hardly tell him that they knew no one here, that there was not enough money for a doctor.

"It is just the fever," Dusty put in, rescuing her. "Nothing to be done for it. He has a bevy of pretty nurses," he bowed to the girls, "and whisky has wonderful curative powers for his ailment. Besides, these chaps here with their fancy offices know nothing about medicine. The good doctors are out West. Did I ever tell you about Doctor John Marsh?"

He launched into an amusing anecdote about a man who went West with only a Bachelor of Arts degree, married an Indian woman, and took up the practice of medicine with great success. His story brought a flurry of interest and, thus encouraged, he brought forth tale after tale of the West, fortifying himself after each story with a drink from his bottle. Finally, he reached an emotional, confidential stage, telling the true reasons for his wanting to return to Texas.

There was a woman, a true lady, more beautiful than the sun or the stars. Tears filled his eyes as he waxed eloquent in regard to her beauty. True, they had quarreled and parted, but he was certain she was waiting for him. His incomparable Nell.

Tamsen was torn between laughter and pity as he talked on about Nell and Magoffinville, the place he hoped to find her. Was there truly a woman who loved this little man who had been a thorn in her side since Papa met him? She looked at his round crinkled face, with its red-veined complexion; at the wispy mustache above a mouth that revealed missing front teeth; at his bleary eyes, now dimmed with tears of emotion. It could not be!

He took another drink and gave a hiccupping sob.

"I believe our friend is about ready to retire for the night," Lord Newby whispered to Tamsen, a wry note in his voice. "Though I do enjoy hearing his tales of the West." He stood, helping Tamsen to her feet.

"I must return to my hotel," he said. "And I would like to repay your fine hospitality. I would be most honored if you would allow me to invite you to dine with me."

He named his hotel, the most popular and expensive place in St. Louis. Tamsen's eyes widened. She had heard of this establishment with its silken draperies and deep carpets, but had never dreamed that she would enter its doors. Oh, how she would love to dine there!

But why had he invited *her*? Why not Em, who looked so lovely tonight? She had put herself forward, somewhat, in an effort to be hospitable, but it would be terrible if he thought she had an interest in him! And that idea might be enhanced if she agreed to have dinner with him alone.

Was it even proper? She looked at Em, at Arab. They were both nodding for her to accept. Well, she would, for all of them!

"Thank you," she said quickly. "I'm sure we'd find it enjoyable. What time would you like us to be ready?"

Lord Newby was nonplussed, but only for a moment. "Tomorrow at seven," he murmured, bowing over her hand. "I shall be here with my carriage. I feel fortunate to be able to escort three such lovely ladies."

He hid a smile as he left. He'd gotten what he deserved, an old stick like himself daring to be captivated

21

by a dark-haired young beauty. He'd have to get his pleasure watching three beautiful creatures have a good time.

The next day, the McLeod girls rushed about in a flurry of preparation. Tamsen worked feverishly at altering an old blue silk for Em. Arabella had unpacked a pale yellow dimity. Ruffled and high-necked, it was quite suitable for a young girl.

"What are you going to wear?" Em asked.

Tamsen pushed back her hair from her face, dewed with perspiration in the humid evening.

"I thought my navy serge. It's held its press well—"

"You will not! You'll wear that red dress Arab outgrew! And I will do your hair!" When Tamsen shook her head, Em said, "Then I will not go!"

Tamsen capitulated, secretly gratified at Em's insistence. Later, after she slipped into the gown, she sat quietly pleased as Em arranged her hair in an elaborate style.

"There! You look beautiful. Tam, don't you think Arab could have her hair put up? This once? After all, she is almost a young lady, and she seems upset—"

Before Tamsen could answer, there was a sound of carriage wheels and Lord Newby had joined them. As he greeted the two young women, his gaze, brushing Em in appreciation, stopped at Tamsen's glowing beauty.

"My word," he said, unsteadily. "My word!" Then his eyes widened in surprise.

Arabella, descending from the canvas wagon, was a vision of young womanhood. She had put her hair up and her neckline down. All girlish ruffling had been removed from the dress. About her throat was fastened a length of brown ribbon that emphasized the pearl-dusted flesh of her young breasts which rose provocatively from the gown.

Tamsen opened her mouth to speak, then closed it again. It would not do to call attention to Arab's rebellion before their host. But somehow she felt a sadness deep inside at Arab's determination to become an adult—like a forced flower.

Lord Newby moved forward to offer his hand to her little sister. "I must repeat," he said, smiling, "I am a lucky, lucky man, to be able to entertain such charming companions."

In the carriage, Arabella used her newfound assurance to flirt outrageously. Lord Newby repaid her efforts with gallantry, treating her as he would a precious younger sister. At last, Tamsen was able to relax. Even her concern for her father, who was left behind in Dusty's dubious care, faded as they drew up before the magnificent facade of Lord Newby's hotel.

As they entered, deferential black-clad waiters scurried to find a table at Newby's command. Dazzled by the glitter of crystal, the wealth of lush carpeting beneath her feet, Tamsen watched Em, who behaved as if she had been born to such luxury.

Em would live like this some day, Tamsen vowed to herself. Em—and Arabella. For her little sister did not seem out of place in this atmosphere. Indeed, she seemed dressed appropriately, considering the other women in the room. Tamsen's heart swelled with love and pride.

When they were seated, their host ordered wine and translated from the French menu. "They have lobster here," he informed them. "The only place one can buy them. They are brought in live—"

"I suppose they are frightfully expensive?" Arabella attempted a tone of bored sophistication.

A smile touched Lord Newby's lips. "Oh, quite."

"Then I'll have that."

"Arab!" Em and Tamsen gasped in unison. The girl looked sulky.

"If it's the money," she said, haughtily, "I can pay for it."

Drawing a handkerchief from her bosom, she spilled coins onto the table. Before her startled sisters could rally, Arab's expression changed. "Look! There's somebody I know! There's Dan Tallant! Over there with a lady!" She turned to Lord Newby, eagerly, "Can't we ask them to sit here, with us?"

Newby looked uncomfortable. "I know Tallant," he said, "and I should be happy to do so, except for his companion."

"She is very beautiful," Em said.

"I know. But she is not a lady. In fact, she has a most—most unsavory reputation. Notorious."

Arabella's eyes glowed with excitement. "Oh, please *do* invite them! I've never known anybody like that!"

"For myself," Lord Newby said, his face red, "I do not mind. But your sisters might."

"They wouldn't! Would you, Tamsen? Em? My goodness, it isn't like she has anything catching."

Her voice had risen. Tamsen, fearing it would carry, placed her hand over Arab's. "The table is small. There isn't room—"

It was too late, Dan Tallant had turned and was smiling in their direction. Tonight he looked different—almost like a gentleman—dressed in a well-tailored suit, his unruly hair subdued. Perhaps her first impression of him had been wrong, Tamsen thought as Newby crossed to speak with him.

Lord Newby directed the waiters to set two more places at his table, and Tallant moved to join their group. He introduced the lady on his arm as Madam Sainte, bowing as he was presented to the three young women, Tallant gave Arab and Tamsen a quick sardonic smile. Tamsen's color flared as he seated himself beside her, his virile presence upsetting her somehow.

Dan Tallant, too, was moved by emotions he did not wish to admit. He had received rather a jolt when he turned to meet Tamsen's eyes. From the way she looked at Madam Sainte in horrified fascination, he assumed some remarks had already been made about the lady's character. Something about Tamsen made him want to explain to her that this was not a pleasure outing, but business.

Why should he care what she thought of him? Actually, he did not know the girl. True, he had admired her from afar, and now, close to, she was even more appeal-

24

ing. The big dark eyes she turned on him were like shadowed pools in which a man might drown.

But not Dan Tallant! His only interest lay in convincing her that the family should return to Pennsylvania—for the sake of them all; the little scamp who had been in the corral, the older sister who truly looked the part of a lady, and this dark beauty next to him.

"I suppose Miss Arab gave you my message?" he inquired.

"She did."

"I hope you considered it seriously. Returning home, I mean. With your father ill—"

"My father's health is improving." Tamsen's voice was cold. "We intend to go on."

He lifted his glass. "A toast to Texas, then," he said, but he was still considering ways to convince this stubborn girl that she was wrong.

Tamsen lifted her glass. "To Texas."

The wine was cooling, fragrant after the humid heat of the day, and she allowed the waiter to pour her another. A few minutes later, she felt Dan Tallant's knee pressed against her own. Her face reddened, and she turned an icy stare on him.

He caught her expression, wondering at it as he conversed with Lord Newby. When he received another outraged look, he dropped his napkin, purposely. Leaning down to retrieve the napkin, Tallant looked under the table where he found the culprit. The table was supported by a pedestal, carved ornately with a lion's head. Evidently Tamsen had moved so that the lion pressed against her skirt.

Tallant grinned to himself, knowing what the girl thought.

Oh, why didn't he take that—that woman, and go, Tamsen wondered. It had been such a lovely evening before the couple joined them. There! That touch again! Aided by a third glass of wine, Tamsen's temper boiled over.

Drawing her foot back, she kicked out hard.

25

The quaking of the table and rattling of dishes drowned her low moan as she came in contact with the solid pedestal. The others, her sisters, Lord Newby, Madam Sainte, jerked in surprise.

"I'm sorry," Daniel Tallant said, smoothly. "Clumsy of me."

Tamsen, nursing her hurt foot, was angrier than ever. He had known all along what she thought.

She had another glass of wine.

Before long, it didn't matter to Tamsen what had happened, or even that Dan Tallant was there. The evening became a blaze of light and color. The crystal chandelier overhead seemed to spin, and the room became too warm. Tamsen could hear Arabella growing giggly, but she couldn't bring herself to care. In the morning she would only recall the strains of soft music, Dan Tallant leading her in a graceful waltz, the mirrored images of the two of them meeting as they dipped and whirled, his face near her own growing until it filled the world. . . .

"I want you to meet me, tomorrow," he whispered. "There's something I'd like to speak to you about."

She remembered that he'd kissed Arabella, that he'd come here tonight with a fallen woman. She recalled the message Arab had given her, fuzzily.

"I—I don't think we have anything to discuss."

"Perhaps not." Were those dark eyes mocking her again? "But if you change your mind, you will find me at the Elkhorn Bar. All day."

Finally, it was time to leave. Tamsen stumbled a little on the way to the door, and Tallant caught her arm. His fingers seemed to burn through the material of her sleeve.

"Are you all right?" Em asked with concern.

"Just fine," Tamsen said, regally.

The trip back to the wagon in Lord Newby's carriage cleared her head a little. Lord, how her foot hurt! She thought of the meeting Tallant had suggested. Did he think she would come running to a man who would be

26

seen with someone like that Sainte woman? But what if he had decided to sell them some of his horses?

"I like lobster, even if it is funny-looking," Arabella was telling Em. With a jolt, Tamsen recalled the money Arab had dumped on the table in the hotel. Small coins, but so many. How had she come by it? She rubbed her forehead to clarify her thoughts. Lord Newby was speaking to her.

He would be leaving in the morning, though he was concerned about starting his trip so late. He feared winter would arrive before he reached his destination. Again, Tamsen thought of Tallant's horses. The McLeods dared not be winterbound here. They had not enough funds to survive.

When they reached their wagons, the girls said goodbye to Lord Newby and thanked him for an exciting evening.

As Lord Newby lifted Arabella from the carriage, she favored him with a drowsy smile. "I had one bloody good time," she said, borrowing a word from Dusty, "even if it did cost a lot."

The party dispersed on a happy note. It had already become a magical evening to look back on, a fairy-tale evening, touched with enchantment. Young Tamsen, Lord Newby thought, had been the most enchanting of all.

"I'm an old man," he said softly when Em and Arab had left them. "I can think of only one thing I'd like to carry with me on my journey. The memory of a kiss—"

Tamsen stood on tiptoe to oblige him and then whirled off to bed to relive the exciting evening once more before she fell asleep.

Chapter 2

The next afternoon, Tamsen, dressed in her most demure dark gown, and wearing a bonnet that hid her features, walked along the dock front. She felt awkward and uneasy amidst the noise and hubbub that filled the area. The good thoughts of this morning had deserted her, and her courage was failing.

Somewhere along here, she knew, was the Elkhorn Bar.

It had all seemed so simple this morning over breakfast. The girls had been bubbling with descriptions of their wonderful night out, and Papa, feeling better, out of bed for the first time, had been an appreciative audience. So, Tamsen had mentioned her conversation with Tallant—saying only that he wished to discuss something with her, not where.

Papa was excited. Maybe the man would sell them some trail animals after all. Or perhaps he knew where there were some to be purchased. Scott McLeod bemoaned the fact that he was still too weak to be up and about.

Tamsen said she would go on the family's behalf. For in the night, she'd done some thinking. What did she have against Daniel Tallant, anyway? The scene she saw at the corral when he kissed Arabella? That was just an impulse, perhaps Arab's. The man apparently had a lady friend. Well, not exactly a lady, but that was surely his affair. As to his insulting comments about their going home, Arab could have been in error. The girl wasn't above embroidering the facts of a conversation if it suited her.

28

Now, though, Tamsen was beginning to feel faint-hearted. The noise as roustabouts heaved cargo to the dock, half-naked, gleaming in the sun, was tumultuous. Rouge-cheeked ladies leaned on parasols, languidly, in converse with these roughest of men. There was a smell about the place, a smell of sweat, too-strong perfume, and an animal scent she could not define.

But she must see Tallant. She had talked with a wagon master this morning. He told her that all trains must leave within the week or plan to winter here. That was what she must keep uppermost in her mind.

Stepping around a drunken river man, she saw the two-story, jerry-built house. A painted woman leaned from an upper window, sleazy robe slipping from her shoulders. Tamsen frowned. A rooming house? She thought he'd said a bar. But it was the right place. A sign creaking from a post over the door read *Elkhorn*.

Summoning her courage, Tamsen opened the door and stepped inside.

She found herself in a huge room, dimly lit and smelling of beer, sweat, and urine. A saloon, without a doubt. She paused for a moment to adjust her eyes to the building's interior, hoping to see Dan Tallant and beckon him outside.

Directly before her was a long bar of heavy, weathered dark wood. In the shadows to her right, she could make out a number of round tables. At some of them, men slept, bearded faces cradled on their arms amid a scattering of cards and poker chips. To her left, a stairway rose to mysterious upper regions.

As she stood blinking in the dimness, a figure broke away from the bar and slouched toward her. Dan Tallant? No, this man wore a hat pulled low over whiskered features.

"Looking for somebody?" he asked. Before she could answer, he leered at her. "Will I do, honey? Give us a kiss—"

His whiskey-sodden breath seared her face, and she shuddered away as someone caught at his shoulder, wheeling him from her. "Forget it, Jack. This is a lady. She's here to see me on business."

Tallant! She hadn't thought she'd be so glad to see him, ever! Then the scene before her began to penetrate. The two men were eyeing each other, on the verge of coming to blows. Others were leaving the bar, coming toward them. A group of armed, drunken, grinning men, spoiling for a fight.

"No," she whispered, "oh, dear God, no!"

But the impasse was broken, and the man backed away when he saw Tallant's face. "Business, huh?" He grinned at Dan. "Be my guest." Then, "Sorry, lady. No offense."

Tamsen offered a weak smile in answer to his apology, then stiffened as her rescuer led her toward the stairs. Perhaps he had an office up there, but she would prefer to deal with him outside. Sensing her reluctance, Dan Tallant tightened his grip on her arm.

"Don't be a little fool. Move! Or do you want to start a brawl? Get somebody killed?"

After one backward look toward the hushed room filled with watching eyes, she followed along, meekly.

At the top of the steps, he knocked at a door. A woman shrilled in answer, and a man's deep voice growled an obscenity. "Occupied," Tallant stated, moving to the next. He opened the door and waved her inside.

It was not an office, but a bedroom. His room? She looked at him, wide-eyed. From the next room, through the paper-thin walls, there was a creaking sound followed by an excited squeal, then a giggle.

"Oh, Lord," Tamsen whispered. "Oh, Lord!"

This place and what it stood for had become clear in her mind. A traveling minister had preached about the fleshpots of the city, places where women sold their bodies, using ugly words like fornication and adultery. In the sleepy little Pennsylvania hamlet, such goings-on seemed unreal, as far away as heaven or hell. But it was true. Here and now. And Tamsen was trapped in the middle of it, in a room such as the preacher described—with a man blocking the exit.

Tearing her gaze from the dark eyes that mocked her, she made a pretense of studying the room, looking at the enamel bedstead with its sagging springs, quickly averting her attention to a white china jug and basin, the single chair. And here, again, was the scent of sweat and heavy perfume, that animal scent, intensified.

She's scared, Daniel Tallant thought. She knows what this room is. And maybe I'll have to scare her some more. But first he intended to try to hammer some sense into that lovely, stubborn head.

"Why did you bring me here?" she asked, in a small voice. "We—we could have talked in the wagonyard."

"But I wanted to talk to you in private. And I wanted you to get a good look at this place."

Tamsen's heart was beating too fast, her mouth was dry, and her brain was obscured in a mist of terror. The presence of the man who stood before her was so formidable, she had to fight to keep her senses.

"Anything we have to say can be discussed in a public place," she said. "And I do not care for our present surroundings."

"I didn't think you would," he said, with a twist of his lips that might have been a smile, had it reached his eyes. "But I thought you might want to look over the kind of life you've got ahead of you."

Her head jerked up in shock. "I have no idea what you're talking about!"

"No, I don't imagine you do. You girls are heading west with your heads stuffed full of dreams. And you don't know what the hell you're getting yourself into! Pretty gowns, balls!" He repeated Arab's words. "*This* is what the West is like. It may change someday, but right now, it's like this. Is this what you want for your sisters?"

Her anger faded before the temper that blazed at his presumptuousness. "You're lying," she said. "Papa says—"

"Papa says!" Now he was mocking her. "If I thought

31

your father was the driving force behind this petticoat caravan, I'd talk to him! But I know better! Your old man drinks, he's sick and weak, and just as full of hare-brained notions as the rest of you! He hasn't bothered to find out what he's letting his daughters in for! There's a shortage of women down there. I should know. You'll find out you'll have to pay a price—"

"And I'm willing to pay a price right now," Tamsen snapped, her eyes narrowed. "For some horses. Whenever you're ready to get down to business."

Her voice faltered as she realized how her words sounded. The anger left his face, a lazy, mocking expression replacing it as he looked her over in a way that made her burn with embarrassment.

"Are you now? The merchandise looks good, what I can see of it." He came toward her, cat-like, and she shuddered away from the intent in his eyes.

"Maybe we can make a deal, then." His voice was caressing as he reached for her.

"You're wrong," she whispered, "I didn't mean—"

His mouth came down on hers, and for a moment, she was too shocked to struggle. Then he led her toward the bed. A rough hand reached under her chin, untying the strings of her bonnet. Her dark hair tumbled down. The buttons of her high collar gave way beneath his hand.

"Let me go," she raged. "Damn you! Oh, damn you! Let me go!"

Releasing her, he grinned down at her tearstained angry face. "Such language!" he drawled. "Well, make up your mind! Do you want horses at *my* price? Or not?"

"I don't want anything from you," she panted. Turning, she ran through the door and down the stairs to stop short as grinning figures turned toward her.

"Look at that," a man leered. "Must have been *some* business Tallant had in mind. Could use some of that myself."

With a strangled sob, Tamsen fled from his reaching hands, out into the sun.

From an upstairs window, Dan Tallant watched her

go, his dark eyes a little sad. Wondering at his own state of depression, he tapped at the paint-shaling sill with restless fingers. He had made his point. Unless he guessed wrong, the girl would pack up her family and turn tail toward Pennsylvania. Let the little Arabella practice her wiles on someone civilized. Back there, she'd stand a chance, but not in Texas. The other girl, Emmeline, belonged back east, too. She was the type to wither and fade like a flower in harsh circumstances.

Not Tamsen, though. He grinned wryly as he fingered a scratch her clawing nails had left. Tamsen could take care of herself. She was his kind of girl, with lots of courage and nerve. Maybe it was a good thing she'd *had* so much fight in her. When he'd put his hands on her, he'd found himself carried away on a tide of feeling that was damned hard to reverse. For a moment, he found himself wishing he didn't have a job cut out for him in California, that it didn't require him to be a loner—

He frowned down from the window, hoping Tamsen would be able to get back to the wagonyard without too much trouble.

Tamsen was having difficulties. Before, somber-clad, with a concealing bonnet, she had arrived at the Elkhorn safely enough. But now, her cheeks flaming, black hair tumbling down, dress disheveled, she was an object of interest.

"Where you going, sweetheart?" a big man called good-naturedly. It seemed the dock area was one mass of insinuating voices and reaching hands. Tamsen ran until she could no longer breathe. Somewhere she had taken a wrong turning. She was lost.

Crouching beside a building built partway into the limestone cliffs, she tried to straighten her dress, arrange her hair. Somehow, she must regain the appearance of propriety.

Then she heard a familiar voice. Slowly, recognition jarred her.

Arab! Arabella, singing! And beneath the girl's pure tones, the low growling approval of men's voices accompanying them.

33

For a moment, Tamsen thought it was part of her nightmare, that she was dreaming. Then the huddle of men on the wharf before her parted so that she could see.

It *was* Arabella! Dancing! Her skirts whirled, showing her ankles, the lace on her underthings! She was singing some awful, common song.

"*I'm a good girl*," she sang, "*Not a bad girl*." She waggled a warning finger. "*So don't let your eyes roam*." Then her hip jutted out in one direction, provocatively, "*But you can follow me home, boys*," the other bumped to one side, petticoats flying, "*You can follow me home—*"

Oh, dear God!

The song ended and the wharf exploded in a shower of coins.

Tamsen sagged weakly against the building, recalling the handkerchief Arab had carried the night before—the coins it had contained. This was how the money had been earned. This was not Arab's first performance at the docks.

Numbly, Tamsen watched the laughing Arabella scramble for the money. Then, with a seductive wave, her sister raised a hand in farewell. "I have to go."

"You can go home with me, Sis," one of the grinning men called.

Arabella made a rude sound, but blew a kiss as she turned to run away.

I should have gone out there, Tamsen thought. *I should have broken it up! Dragged her home.* But she knew those would be the wrong tactics. Despite the girl's behavior, she was an innocent. Arab could not possibly know what effect she was having on those ruffians! Best to pretend she didn't know about it, Tamsen thought, and to get away from this place as soon as possible. Here, Arab would not remain an innocent for long.

Fortunately, Dusty provided the solution to her problem. He returned to the wagons that very night, teetering with drink, to announce he'd won a string of horses in a poker game. They were ancient nags, army rejects,

34

their circled *US* brands vented. There were only ten of them, and it took twelve to draw the ponderous McLeod wagons, but Dusty had an idea.

His own wagon wasn't in good shape. He didn't relish riding horseback all the way to Texas. He would leave his vehicle behind, add his horses to those he'd won, and drive one of their wagons in the sick man's place—if they would head for *Magoffinville*.

A pause followed his pronouncement; then Tamsen burst into tears. She threw her arms around the little reprobate she'd once disliked because of his bad influence on Papa.

"Dusty," she cried, "you're the answer to a prayer! I love you!"

"By Jove," Dusty mumbled, flushed with pleasure. "Well, my word! It's the least a man can do for his good friends." He blinked watery eyes filled with alcohol and emotion. Then, turning to Scott McLeod, who had left his bed to take the evening air, Dusty drew a bottle from his pocket.

"I brought along a little something to celebrate."

Even the sight of Papa drinking could not dampen Tamsen's spirits. Soon they would be on their way.

Chapter 3

In less than a week, the McLeod wagons rolled out with the last scheduled train for the year, heading for Independence. The yard they'd left behind was nearly empty. Only the more timorous souls chose to winter there and wait to get an early start in the spring.

After two days on the trail, however, the McLeod family lost its exuberance and settled in to endure. The wagons rolled smoothly across the grasslands, stirring clouds of butterflies, sometimes hub-deep in early fall flowers, but the humid heat of the river traveled with them. There were swarms of biting midges and occasional snakes that set the old nags dancing, tangling their harness; gopher holes, concealed in the matted, browning vegetation, added yet another hazard.

If these were her only worries, Tamsen thought, lifting one blistered hand from the reins to mop her sunbrowned face, it wouldn't be too bad. But why had Dan Tallant chosen to join this particular train and plague her?

Her eyes darkened as she thought of his hypocrisy. Both nights out, he'd come to the wagon to ask about Papa's health. All the time, he'd looked at her as if daring her to speak of what had taken place in the Elkhorn Bar that day. And he was so mannerly toward Em! Complimenting her! And last night, he helped Em from the wagon when they stopped.

Did he think Em would be an easier mark than Tamsen?

One of the horses stumbled, getting out of step. Tamsen swore under her breath, sawing at the reins until order was established once more. A clatter of hooves sounded over the melee, and Tallant's wrangler, young Mike Dunnevant, reined in beside her.

"Saw you was having trouble, ma'am. Thought maybe you could use a hand."

Tamsen felt hot and cross. Why was it that Tallant and his henchman only saw what she did wrong, not what she did right? She tried so hard, and she was so tired. There was a trace of exasperation in her tone as she said, "Thank you, I can manage quite well."

He touched his big hat and rode away. She watched him go—a giant of a man in his early twenties—grudgingly thinking that he was good-looking in his way. Blue-eyed, pink-cheeked, he had a swaggering shyness. Everything about him was outsized, including his capacity for liquor. He, too, was beginning to present problems.

Dunnevant was the one who kept Dusty supplied with his eternal bottle. From Dusty the bottle eventually found its way to Papa. Also, Tamsen had seen Arabella flirting with the man from time to time. It bothered her.

Her mouth curved in a wry smile. It was time to be honest with herself, she decided. No matter what, Papa would drink and Arab would flirt. It had nothing to do with Mike Dunnevant. Her irritation at him stemmed from something in herself, her knowledge that here was another watching pair of eyes, waiting for her to give in and ask for help because she was a woman. And she did not intend to fail.

Her determination stayed with her almost all the day. The last hour, however, was torture. Her eyes felt hot and gritty, and her hands were blistered from the reins. When the wagons halted in a grassy area for the night, her slim shoulders slumped in relief. Another day was done. How many miles? Ten? Twelve? And so many yet to travel. Perhaps, with time, the driving would become easier. Em could not drive for any length of time; she was too delicate. And the irrepressible Arab would finish off these poor old nags if she were allowed to sit at the reins.

Tamsen unhitched the horses, freeing them to graze, giving each a sympathetic pat. *They're worn out,* she thought, *like me. If only Papa were well enough to help!*

But Scott McLeod had chosen this night to have another setback. Em was in the wagon beside him, covering him with blankets to keep away his chills. Arab had slipped away to explore their new campground. Wearily, Tamsen gathered chips and firewood. Dew-damp already, the fire sputtered, smoked, and refused to burn.

Tamsen's eyes filled with tears. Papa needed something hot to drink. This was a perfect ending for a hellish day!

As Dan Tallant approached the willowy figure bending over the smouldering campfire, he was thinking about how small she was, how defenseless she looked, and wondering what drove her to her efforts. She should go back to civilization, marry some man who'd put a decent roof over her head, cherish her. They were only two days out. There was still time. He would see the family back to St. Louis himself—catch up with the train later.

Maybe if he apologized for the scene at the Elkhorn, explained that he had done it deliberately, he might be able to reason with her. He felt a pang as she raised her face at his approach, and he saw the glitter of her tear-wet cheeks.

"Let me do it," he said, huskily. Dropping to his knees, he had the fire blazing in no time. She stood silently by until he rose and turned to face her.

"That'll do it, I think," he said.

"I suppose you're expecting payment?"

"Now, wait a minute. You've got me all wrong. I've been wanting to talk to you. To explain."

"There's no need for explanation." Tamsen's voice cut through the sound of crackling flames like ice. "I believe I understand you very well."

His face hardened, the firelight giving him a dark and sinister look. "I was only trying to help," he said, shortly.

"And I am trying to tell you we don't need your assistance. All we want is to be left alone!" Her frigid composure slipped as she met his gaze. "For God's sake, why do you keep interfering? What do you want from us?"

Tallant fought down his own fury. He had never been so tempted to grab a woman and shake her until her teeth rattled! He had tried to make amends, and if she wanted to be stubborn and bullheaded—mess up her life—then let her! He shrugged and gave her a mocking grin.

Tamsen's eyes were hot with anger. "Please go."

She watched him walk away with his long, lazy stride. She had never despised anyone so much in her life— unless it was herself. For, since that day in the Elkhorn Bar, she'd been plagued by dreams. Dreams in which she'd gone into his arms, willingly, in that awful room!

She whirled at a sound. Em had come from the rear of the wagons, in time to witness his departure.

"Papa's better." A worry-frown crinkled her smooth brow as she looked after the retreating figure. "That was Mr. Tallant, wasn't it? Shouldn't we have asked him to supper? He's been so kind to Papa."

"We're running low on supplies," Tamsen said, shortly. "We can't afford guests."

Em was quiet for a moment, taking note of Tamsen's flushed face and the anger in her eyes.

"Tamsen, why do you dislike that man so? I can't help noticing. Has he been forward? Is there something you haven't told me?"

Tamsen turned, lifting a kettle of water to the fire. "He's trash, Em. I don't want him around."

"Oh, Tamsen, I don't think—"

"That's the trouble with you, Em! You don't think! Do you remember seeing him in the hotel that night? The woman he was with? Doesn't that tell you anything? And believe me, Dan Tallant doesn't do favors out of the goodness of his heart! Not for any woman, he doesn't! He expects something in return!"

"Tamsen!" Em's face was pink. "What a dreadful

39

thing to say! I'm not saying Dan Tallant's a saint, he's a man. And he certainly has a right to choose his own companions. I'm sure he wouldn't force his attentions on a woman."

"Indeed!" Tamsen's cheeks were blazing with a blush she could not control. That day in the Elkhorn, was there anything less than circumspect in her behavior? Had he been able to guess the wild thoughts in her mind? Sense how her pulse was pounding at being alone in a—a place like that—with a man?

"Indeed!" she said again, weakly.

A giggle from the rear of the wagon, followed by a man's low chuckle, brought Tamsen back to her senses.

Em and Tamsen rounded the canvas-covered vehicle to find Arab seated on the lowered tailgate. Her skirts were hiked a little to display a modest amount of shapely ankle. Before her, and enjoying the view, stood a none-too-sober Mike Dunnevant.

"You're just saying that," Arabella said, coyly, as her sisters converged upon the scene. "I'm sure you've known lots of girls prettier than me."

The sight of Em and Tamsen interrupted his laughing protestations. His cocksure attitude degenerated into confusion as he bowed, first to one, then to the other.

"Good evening," he said, "I just come by to see if you folks needed any help. Didn't have nothin' better to do—"

"But Arabella does," Tamsen said, firmly. She pulled the reluctant girl around to the fire, leaving Em to make polite excuses. She said nothing, but Arab, sensing that Tamsen was upset, willingly turned to for once, peeling potatoes, dishing up the food, and finally washing out the tin utensils from which they had eaten.

"I think," Arab said at last, "that I'll go to bed."

"At least we know where she is," Tamsen said, glumly, after she had left them. "Em, what are we going to do with her?"

"Don't you think you're being too hard on her?"

"I don't know," Tamsen whispered. "But, oh—Em, she's so innocent. She doesn't know what she's doing

40

when she sets out to attract men the way she does. And she can't seem to help her behavior. I think she was just born that way."

"I don't know," Em said. "Maybe that's not such a bad way to be."

"Em!" said a scandalized Tamsen. But when she looked at Em's expression and caught her own sanctimonious tones, she had to laugh. Suddenly, they were both reduced to giggles. They threw their arms around each other and, their worries forgotten, they settled down to a long intimate exchange.

The sky was heavy with stars; it was a night for romance. Em felt it, too, Tamsen thought, looking at her dreaming features, white with moonlight.

"Em, do you ever think of George—and wish things might have been different? I mean, does it still—hurt? That he married someone else?"

Emmeline was quiet for a moment; then she laughed, softly. "Tamsen, I'm going to tell you something I wouldn't tell another soul. Yes, I think about George Harper, and it does hurt sometimes. But not for the reason you think. I—I wanted a home and children. But I guess I didn't want George. One night, about a week before the wedding, he became most . . . most ardent, and I found I couldn't stand him. He didn't leave me at the altar. It was the other way around."

"And you let everybody think—oh, Em!" Tamsen began to giggle again, Em with her. When they finally sobered, Em asked, "Tamsen, do you think there's anything wrong with me? You remember Cassie Breedlove?"

Tamsen did. Cassie was a masculine sort of woman who wore boots and overalls and farmed alone. Mean people laughed behind her back and talked about her in whispers. And here was delicate Em, worrying that she, too, might be lacking in femininity, just because she found the attentions of dull George Harper unappealing.

"Now that you've confessed to me," Tamsen said, smiling, "let me tell you how I felt about Will Franklin." Her story was much the same. They talked on into

41

the night. And at last, Em said, "Tamsen, what do you want out of life?"

"I'm taking one day at a time," Tamsen told her. "Right now, my only goal is to get us to Independence."

Within a few days, Tamsen had achieved that goal. The wagon train reached Independence and moved on. The weather held as they traveled through the meadows and woods that marked their way to the next goal, Council Groves. Dusty, who had traveled this route in the rainy season, when wagons were mired to their hubs in the rich black soil, told them how lucky they were.

The earth was fertile and starred with flowers. From the wagon seat, Tamsen looked over the countryside and yearned to walk among the flowers and streams. So, it seemed a blessing one afternoon when the train paused early for repairs, and Tamsen was able to suggest a walk to Arabella. Em declined, preferring to remain with their father.

It was an inspired idea. Arab, kept at short leash since the Dunnevant incident, had been sulking. But as she wandered with her sister across the blooming meadows, her ebullient spirits returned. Tamsen, too, felt as if the weight of the world had been lifted from her shoulders. The off-lead horse of the span she'd been driving was winded. A rear wheel of the wagon creaked ominously despite generous applications of grease. Supplies were rapidly diminishing. But here, beneath the blue sky, woolly puffs of clouds adorning it, she felt happy. Carefree.

Best of all, Tamsen and Arabella were friends again. It was a good feeling to wander as they willed with a whole afternoon to while away, no chores until the evening.

"You look tired," Arab said finally. "Maybe you'd like to rest awhile."

Tamsen had not felt weary, but the girl's words were a reminder of all she had endured. It was good to sit down, her back against a sun-warmed stone that eased the ache of her shoulders. Drowsily, Tamsen watched Arabella wander in the fields, arms full of flowers. Then, with only the drone of bees in her ears, Tamsen drifted into sleep. A sleep that was honey-warm and dreamless.

A sound brought her upright.

She shook her head, still sleep-fogged, trying to orient herself to her surroundings. What was she doing here? Then she remembered. Her relaxed state had been penetrated by a scream. Arabella! It was Arab's voice she'd heard. Tamsen leaped to her feet.

Emerging into a rocky clearing surrounded by a small grove of trees, she saw her. Arab was struggling in the arms of a man whose size identified him as Mike Dunnevant. Dear God, what was he doing? Tamsen heard his drunken laughter as Arab screamed again.

Tamsen began running.

Reaching the grappling pair, she caught at Mike Dunnevant's arm. He brushed her off, much as a bear would absently remove some small attacking nuisance. Tamsen fell backward. Angered, Arabella bore in to attack.

"Leave her alone," she shrilled. "You—you big clod! Leave my sister alone!"

Still tipsily oblivious to Tamsen's presence, Dunnevant reached for Arab once more. "You come here, little darlin'," he laughed. "I didn't come out here to play games—"

He swept the girl up in his arms, giving her a bear-hug that made her squeal.

Tamsen, half-dazed, got up from the ground, holding a large stone in both hands. Raising it high above her head, she brought it down hard. There was a thudding sound as it connected with Mike Dunnevant's head. Slowly the big man sank to the ground. Arab fell away as he released her, stunned at the thin flow of blood that stained Dunnevant's blonde mane.

"Tamsen," she whispered, "oh—!"

But her sister had dropped to her knees beside the fallen man, frantically searching for a heartbeat. The stone hitting his head had made such a horrid sound. Was there a beat in that massive chest? Or was it her own that throbbed through her, sounding in her ears?

"Oh, my God," Tamsen moaned, "my God!"

"Is he—dead?"

"I don't know. I never saw anybody dead before. But I think so. He—he isn't moving."

"Oh, Tam!"

Tamsen rose. As if by mutual consent, they joined hands and began to run, back to the haven of the wagons.

Once there, they managed to conceal most of the damage to their persons. They washed the blood from Tamsen's hands and straightened their disheveled hair. Then they busied themselves with preparations for the evening meal, carefully skirting any mention of their afternoon to Em.

Em was concerned. They both looked so pale. She chided herself for not having noticed before. But she had been so busy with Papa. Worrying that they'd been skimping their rations, she tried to press some dried fruit on them. But neither Tamsen nor Arab could swallow, thinking of what lay in the grassy, flower-studded meadow.

It wasn't until full dark, when Em had gone off to check on the sick man, that they could talk about the dreadful deed.

Arab burst into uncontrollable weeping. "I can't stand it, Tamsen! I just can't! It was all my fault—"

Tamsen put her arms about the shivering girl. The knowledge of what she'd done lay like a sickness inside her. She sought frantically for justification. "He was drunk, honey. Even so, there was no excuse for attacking a girl your age—"

Arabella shook her red curls, shedding fresh tears. "But you don't understand, Tam. I told him where we were going, that I'd try to sneak off and meet him. He thought I wanted him to . . . to . . . ! Then I got scared. I didn't know he'd been drinking. He's really nice, Tam. I mean, he was."

"But to carry on with a fourteen-year-old—"

"I lied," Arab said, dully. "I told him I was eighteen. It's my fault."

44

Arab's flirtatious ways had finally caught up with her, ending in disaster. But, Tamsen felt, Arab must not carry the burden of guilt. She was so young.

"No, Arab. I did it. I was the one who hit him. I killed him."

They were standing before the cookfire. Around them, the night had grown still. The silence was shattered by a ululating sound in the distance, a coyote's howl, raised to the moon.

"My God!" The words burst from Tamsen as a new horror entered her mind. She saw her dread mirrored in Arabella's eyes.

"We can't just leave him," Arab whimpered. "Oh, Tam! Animals! I couldn't bear it!"

"Then we will have to bury him."

Tamsen and Arab jumped as the voice came from behind them. A white-faced Em swayed there, clutching at the wagon for support.

"I heard," she said. She looked at the circled wagons, at the campfires dying down. "We'd best wait a little while. Tamsen, Papa's sleeping. Can you reach some of his spades? We'll each need one."

Even in the dusk, Tamsen could see Em's delicate features set in a new determination. "No, Em, this is none of your affair," she said. "We can handle it."

Her once tractable sister was adamant. "We've got to bury the man. It's the Christian thing to do. Besides," she added, logically, "somebody might find him and ask questions."

Arab's hysterical giggle at Em's comment was silenced as the other two frowned at her. Nervously, they settled themselves to wait. Time dragged interminably before the campground quieted. Then, three white-faced wraiths in dark dresses rose and slipped out into the night, pausing at the barking of a dog, at the sound of a man's voice raised in alcoholic dissonance. Once over the gentle rise of the hill, Tamsen unsheathed the lantern she carried.

Now the problem was to find Mike Dunnevant's body. With a cry of recognition, Tamsen located the place

45

where she'd been napping that afternoon. Leading her sisters toward the sight of Arab's struggle with the big, laughing man, she uttered a silent prayer: "Let there be nothing there. Let him be gone. Please God, let it all have been a dream—"

Her prayer went unheard. Mike Dunnevant's body still lay as they'd left it. Sprawled on his back, his pale face showed the dreadful head wound. At Em's gasp, Tamsen quickly turned the light away.

"We'll dig here."

Keeping her back to the thing that lay on the ground behind her, Tamsen set her foot to a spade. It grated on stone.

After an hour or more of digging, Arab weeping all the while, the girls gave up. Tamsen straightened her back and took a deep breath. "We can't dig any deeper. And we can't move him very far. He's too big. We'll have to leave him where he is, or," she indicated the shallow hole, "roll him in here and cover him with stones."

Arab shuddered. "I couldn't bear to touch him," she said, her voice quivering. Tamsen's heart turned over. Arab looked like a little girl who had been punished beyond her endurance.

"We don't have to touch him," Tamsen assured her. "Look, we can slide the spades beneath him and use them as levers. Just roll him."

The plan worked. But as the body turned, flaccidly, face down, Tamsen thought of something else. She knelt, gingerly going through the man's pockets.

"Tamsen! What are you doing?" It was Em's voice, taut with horror.

Tamsen looked up. "Seeing if he has any money. He won't need it, and we do! We can buy fresh supplies in Council Grove."

Em said nothing, and Tamsen continued her search under disapproving eyes. She patted a bulging pocket, pulling out a bandana. There was something else. She slid her hand inside, her fingers closing on a clasp-top, worn coin purse.

46

"Get the hell out of there!" The bull-roar rocked her back on her heels. She went sprawling backward in the grass as the bloodied corpse sat up.

"Good God," Mike Dunnevant growled. "Can't a man sleep it off without some idiot woman jackrolling him?" He put a hand to his head and moaned. "God! What hit me?"

There was only a rustle of petticoats for an answer as Emmeline McLeod fainted quietly away.

Chapter 4

Though the sisters were chastened by the incident, especially Arabella, who was for a while the epitome of girlish purity, Mike Dunnevant seemed to bear them no ill will. He was ready to admit he had been at fault. Besides, there was something about the situation that tickled his funnybone. He got a kick out of answering questions regarding his battered appearance.

"I ran into a couple of wildcats," he would say. If the listener expressed doubts, he'd amend it. "I ran into a rock."

Too, he'd felt ill at ease with Tamsen and Em, regarding them as real honest-to-God ladies. The ladies had spunk. He liked that in a woman. And, the tender loving care he received—after they'd tried to bury him, of course—had made the whole thing worthwhile. He was kind of glad it had happened.

Dan Tallant watched, puzzled, as the young man visited the McLeod wagons, usually carrying gifts. A brace of rabbits. A haunch of venison. And he began to wonder if big Mike was sweet on Tamsen.

For some reason, this bothered him. He liked Dunnevant, who was two-fisted, a hard drinker, and a good rider. He'd hired him on a hunch in a St. Louis bar. But Mike wasn't for Tamsen. Or any of the McLeods, for that matter. And who could guess his intentions? Dan decided to keep an eye on the situation.

The wagon train reached Council Grove, where a resident blacksmith was available to make repairs. The Smith with no formal learning but much practical experience of medicine, examined the two ailing

McLeod horses, and he also took a look at Scott McLeod. In his opinion, none of the three would last very long.

Tamsen, angered at his blunt diagnosis, placed no credence in his words. She was sure that everything would be all right when they were once more on the trail. The journey had been a lucky one thus far. Miraculously, the weather still held.

The good weather helped to influence the decisions made by the leaders of the wagon train about the route to be followed thereafter. The first part of the journey was almost over. The second part would begin at the river crossing west of the Big Bend on the Arkansas. Here the trail forked. One way led across the ford on the Arkansas River, through the desolate, arid Indian-infested Cimarron desert, then to the grass and cedars east of Santa Fe.

The alternative route was to follow the Arkansas River westward to Bent's Fort, an adobe stockade, the leading trading post of the American Southwest. There they would find better water, the opportunity of trading for supplies, and less danger from Indians.

The train was split by the decision. In the end, the Indian situation tipped the balance. If the weather was still fair when they reached the Big Bend, Fort Bent would be their destination.

Dusty chafed at the decision. The Cimarron trail was shorter, he thought. He would be with his beloved Nell all the sooner. But the trails all merged at Santa Fe. And from there, one only had to follow the Rio—to Magoffinville.

The train, reorganized for protection against marauding Indians, moved out. The atmosphere was different now, more tense. Tallant and Dunnevant took turns at guard and were less frequent visitors at the McLeod wagons. Though Tamsen told herself she preferred things this way—that she did not want a man of Dan's caliber visiting Em—she felt a hollow ache of loneliness. Em and Arab, too, were affected by the monotony of the trip—wagons rolling endlessly each day; the only excitement a broken wheel; the Perkinses' baby having croup; a horse stepping into a gopher hole, breaking its leg, having to be shot.

They reached the Big Bend of the Arkansas. The weather still held. The party turned toward Bent's Fort, with its rougher terrain. At Bent's Fort, the mountainous route would turn south through the Raton Pass to meet the main trail.

Though the days were beautiful, dawning crisp and clear, sun-warmed in the afternoons, this section of their journey was fraught with mishaps. It was not uncommon to see a wagon lose a wheel and slew across the pathway of the others, sometimes dragging horses to their haunches in a screaming melee. Indians were sighted, but only at a distance. Men stood guard at night, rifles at the ready, tight-lipped, watching for danger.

Two of Tamsen's horses began to heave. Wind-broken, Dusty said. They were unhitched and tied to the back of the wagons to follow after. The wagonload of possessions was lightened so the remaining animals could draw it. The girls shed tears as their precious keepsakes were piled beside the trail to be left behind.

"It could be worse," Dusty informed them, gently. He pointed out a small rock mound, with a marker made of crossed sticks that leaned askew. Tamsen felt a cold chill at the back of her neck at the thought of what other travelers had had to leave.

Supplies were short and tempers were shorter as tired people, tired animals, and tired wagons neared Bent's Fort. Spirits lifted a little when the train stopped for their last night on the trail before reaching the post.

Tamsen, wearily tending the cookfire, looked up to see Dan Tallant approach. Despite herself, her heart speeded up. He had not been around for three or four days. She almost got up to meet him. The impulse was deadened as she saw that Em and Arab had already done so. Laughing, an arm about each of the girls, Tallant came to the fire.

"Well, you've been quite a stranger," Tamsen said, flustered.

"A situation I'm most happy to remedy."

"I'm sorry I can't invite you to supper with us, but—" Tamsen indicated the sparse kettle of potatoes and jerky readied for cooking. "As you can see, our supplies are low." There! That should block Em's attempt at hospitality, sure to be proffered.

"I came to give you an invitation," Tallant said with a grin. "I've been off hunting, and with good results. Tonight, we're going to celebrate. All the fresh meat we can eat. A fiesta." He gestured toward preparations for a bonfire in the center of the circled wagons.

"Fiesta?" Arabella asked curiously.

"A party. A dance," he explained.

"Oh, Tamsen! Oh, Em!" Arab couldn't contain her excitement. The face beneath her red curls was bright with anticipation. Em, too, wore an expression of wistful wonder at the thought of having a good time. Then the light went out of her eyes.

"It sounds wonderful," Em said. "I want you and Tamsen to both go, Arab. I'll stay with Papa."

Tamsen, who had been momentarily transported into another world, a world in which there would be laughter and dancing and an excuse for wearing a pretty gown, came down to earth again. "Don't be a goose, Em," she said, tartly. "You're going. I'll watch over Papa. Do you think I'd feel like a party, after driving a team all day?"

Em's eyes looked wounded. "I've asked to spell you off, Tam. I will, you know, gladly—"

Tamsen hugged her. "I didn't mean that the way it sounded. It's just that I don't want to go."

"If it makes any difference," Tallant said, coolly, "Mike Dunnevant will be there."

Tamsen forced a radiant smile. "Now you are tempting me," she said. "But the answer is still no. I will be with Papa in the wagon, should Mike decide to drop by."

Dan Tallant turned from her, said his farewell to Arab and Em, and walked away.

Finding it futile to try to talk Tamsen into going, Em and Arab fled to the wagon and reappeared in the

51

gowns they'd worn for their dinner with Lord Newby. Tamsen didn't make a fuss about Arab's bared shoulders. The girl had been more sedate, of late, and Tamsen only hoped she'd enjoy herself tonight. Em, too. Em rarely left the wagon, staying close by their father's side.

She did mention, with a look at the sky, dull now, heavy, but still warm, that it might be wise to take shawls.

After they had gone, Tamsen stood staring in the direction of the bonfire, her body yearning toward the music of guitars and a concertina. She could have asked Dusty to stay with Papa for a little while and taken turns.

But now it was too late. Pouring the broth from the stew into a tin cup, she carried it toward her father's sickbed.

Scott McLeod came to meet her. He was fully dressed, his clothes hanging on his emaciated frame. But there was a tinge of red along his cheekbones, and his eyes were very bright. From excitement? Whisky? She could smell it on his breath. He had his fiddle in one hand.

"Papa, you shouldn't be out of bed!"

"Hell," he slurred, "I'm not sick. And I'm going to the party." He put her to one side, gently, and headed toward the bonfire, weaving as he went.

Tamsen looked after him, worriedly. Should she stop him? Force him to return to the wagon? He did seem much better. Maybe it would be good for him. A warm wave of anticipation rose within her as she thought of the red dress she'd worn in St. Louis. Her feet moved in the pattern of a dance, her weariness leaving her. She felt light as a cloud.

For with Papa at the party, there was nothing to keep her here. She would go to the party and she would dance all night! Wouldn't Mister Daniel Tallant be surprised!

Music sang in her ears as she slipped into the gown that fitted her so snugly in all the right places, the gown that would swirl when she danced, like a flame.

52

Scott McLeod was partially responsible for that music. Drunk or sober, he'd always been able to out-fiddle anybody in Pennsylvania. Tonight he was doing himself proud. Em had given him hell, of course, which was what he'd expected, but he'd put his foot down and she'd given in. She was a good daughter.

He smiled at her now as she came toward him, his heart swelling with pride at the thought of his three lovely girls. Not bad for a rawboned, red-headed Scotsman to sire. Arab was more like himself, he supposed. She had his coloring, anyway, but it was transformed into a beauty he'd never had. Em was a combination, no doubt, with her soft gold-brown hair, her fragility. Tamsen was her mother all over again, tiny, dark-eyed, yet with something the other girls didn't have. Gumption, he guessed. Yes, that was the word for it. Gumption.

"Having a good time, daughter?" he asked Em.

"Wonderful!"

Em sank down to the log next to her father. Her pale complexion was shell-pink with happiness and the exertion of the dance. Dan Tallant was a good dancer and an attentive companion. It had been wonderful to dip and whirl to the music. She felt so unfettered, so free.

And part of that music had been Papa's. She smiled at him now. "I'd forgotten how well you played," she said, gladdened by the pride her words seemed to arouse.

"Going to play a lot when we get to Texas, girl. Sing and dance all night. Really kick up our heels, once our fortune's made."

"Are you sure Tamsen's coming to the dance?" Em asked. "I wonder if I should go look for her?"

"Let her be. She'll come if she wants. Go have yourself a good time, honey. You and Arabella——"

Em's eyes sought the yellow dress that marked Arab in the crowd. This time, a Spanish tune was playing, guitars strumming blazing chords as the wagon people entered in, some awkwardly, some with ease.

Em found Mike Dunnevant's huge figure. He was

standing on the sidelines, glaring angrily at someone. She followed his gaze. Dan Tallant and a girl in a red dress. They both stood still, Dan evidently demonstrating the steps of the dance. Em frowned, trying to see the girl's face, but it was hidden.

Then the two moved out, the man's long legs moving expertly, the girl a swirling, graceful blur of color. Em stood tall to see better.

The music quickened its tempo, and panting couples dropped out. At last, there were only the two. At the final chord, Dan Tallant bent his partner backward, her long hair flying about them as he twirled her around.

Tamsen!

"You're beautiful when you smile," Dan Tallant whispered, under cover of the applause that came from the onlookers.

The spell of the music had left her. Tamsen was only conscious of Dan Tallant's nearness, a nearness that turned her weak and made her knees tremble.

"Was I smiling? I suppose, in the excitement of the dance, I forgot who my partner was! Oh, there's Mike—"

Dan's fingers caught her arm, holding her back, "You're beautiful when you smile, you have the body of a temptress—" She shivered at his words, at the look in his hot eyes, and then he continued, "The soul of an old maid." He added, viciously, "And the disposition of a bitch!"

With a muffled word that might have been an oath, Tamsen jerked free. She ran across the firelight to big Mike Dunnevant. The look of anger left Mike's face and, as the music started, he led her into the dance. "I was looking for you," she said, fervently. "The only reason I came was to dance with you."

His blush reflected the glow of the fire. But soon Tamsen was claimed by another pair of arms, and another. Old men, young men, married and single. Before this evening, the McLeods had kept their distance from the other members of the train. But as Tamsen's

54

gown swirled to show a pair of shapely ankles, more than one female voice was heard to comment sourly that it was just as well the McLeods would leave the train at Santa Fe.

The soul of an old maid, indeed! Every pair of masculine eyes told Tamsen differently, and it was a heady feeling. Mike, dancing with Arab, sent her a rueful look. But Arab looked blissful. When Tamsen saw Em, she was touched by an odd pang of something she didn't recognize. Em was dancing in Dan Tallant's arms.

Em, too, felt a pang. She saw Dan's angry eyes as he observed Tamsen's actions, and sensed the tension in his body. A new knowledge grew in her mind—a knowledge that both gladdened and saddened her.

Em was not in love with Tallant. She knew that. Yet she liked him and had assumed that she was the reason for his visits to the McLeod wagon. Now she knew differently. Poor man, he probably didn't know how he felt about Tamsen, himself.

After her first brief glimpse of Dan and her sister together, Tamsen threw herself into a fiesta mood with renewed fervor. Dizzy with excitement and exertion, she did not feel the weather change; the cold blast of air that changed the warm mist into a fall of icy droplets. She didn't hear Scott McLeod's playing falter and finally cease.

During a lull in the music, she began to shiver. Looking across the fire, its flames spitting and hissing in the dampness, she saw that her family had gone. Em, Arabella, Papa—even Dusty was nowhere to be seen.

She gathered her skirts and ran for the wagon. There she found her father shaking with chills as the others rubbed his blue-tinged body with warm water and whisky.

That night, Scott McLeod came down with pneumonia.

He was feverish and raving when they pulled into Bent's Fort. Tamsen and Em took turns sitting with him, trying to conceal the seriousness of his condition from Arabella. So Arab, at the reins, was first to catch sight of the Fort itself.

Bent's Fort was situated on the northern bank of the Arkansas, on a low, level bluff of prairie that sloped gradually to the water's edge. Built of adobe, in the form of a hollow square, circular towers rising from two corners, the fort looked like a castle to the girl.

A cold rain slanted gently at their approach. The wagons circled for the night. Dan Tallant came hurrying to the McLeod wagon accompanied by a man in uniform. A military surgeon, waiting for the regiment he was to join.

The man, Major Codbee, was an unprepossessing gentleman, a bit shifty-eyed and unkempt, his mutton-chops untrimmed. Tamsen viewed him with distrust as he pushed and prodded at the sick man, shaking his head, talking in terms of purgatives and leeches.

"He's not fit to go back on the trail," he said. "You'll have to winter here at the fort, get him settled into one of the rooms—"

Before Tamsen could speak, Tallant was agreeing. "I'll go make arrangements. You're right. He shouldn't go on."

"You're both wrong," she said, shakily, twisting her fingers in her agitation. "He's *going* on! We can't stop now!"

"But the trip would kill him!" The surgeon's face was choleric.

"He's not going to die! Do you hear me? He's not going to die! Now clear out of here, both of you!"

The two men climbed down from the wagon, and Tallant turned to look at her as she stood framed in the canvas opening. He seemed to study her for a long time. Then he said, "Someday, Tamsen, you'll learn there are some things you can't control. I'd advise you to consider that, before you act."

"You'd like to see us fail, wouldn't you?" she spat at him. "You'd like nothing better than to see us turn around and go home!"

"You're quite right," he said, somberly. "I would."

The next day, Tamsen entered the trading post through the large gate that led into the square. Around the square were a number of small rooms occupied by traders and employees. One door stood open. Tamsen could see its clay-washed interior, no bigger than a cell. And this was the kind of place they'd suggested Papa spend the winter in—when he might be enjoying the Texas sun! She shuddered.

In the center of the square was a press for packing furs, and three large rooms. One was used as a store, another as a council room, the third, a common dining hall. Tamsen felt a little weak at the delicious odors emanating from the last building. Lately, she'd been pleading little appetite in order to conserve their food, which was almost gone.

She went to the store, where she purchased a small sack of flour and a bag of dried beans. She wavered between tea and coffee. Papa dearly loved his coffee in the mornings, but tea might be better for him. A bit of jerky for broth, a slab of fat bacon, in case he improved soon.

"Is this all?" the trader asked.

"We're still quite well supplied," she lied.

She returned to the wagon, having spent the last of her money, as well as Arabella's coins.

The next day, the wagon train, refreshed and resupplied, moved out on the last leg of their journey. As he had done all through their journey, Scott McLeod seemed better one day, worse the next. He seemed much improved as they reached the Raton Pass, and the girls were in agreement that it had been well to continue on.

At the pass, however, trouble struck again. The teams on the light wagon could not pull the grade. Reluctantly, Tamsen added the two windbroken horses to the vehicle, and their combined strength made the difference.

But at the top of the pass, one horse went down, taking the other with it. They both struggled to rise, heaving, bleeding from mouth and nostrils.

Dusty untangled the dying animals from their harness and waved Tamsen on. As the remaining horses maneuvered the wagon easily on the downward slope, Tamsen heard a shot. Another.

She thought of what the blacksmith at Council Grove had said. None of them will make it. He had been speaking not only of the animals, but of Papa. But he had been wrong. Papa was going to make it! Last night, he'd seemed so well!

The improvement had been a temporary one. By nightfall, Scott McLeod was feverish and delirious again. The rasping of his breathing rose and fell in labored monotony. Em and Tamsen worked over him all night with poultices and plasters.

"M-m," he kept muttering. "M-m-m."

"I think he's trying to say 'Martha,' " Em whispered. "He's thinking of Mama!" Her eyes and Tamsen's met in a fearful surmise.

His condition remained unchanged as the wagon moved on.

That night, his cheeks didn't blaze with fever. He seemed cooler to the touch. Tamsen was delighted, though Em was still concerned. "He has a blue look around his mouth . . . and the pupils of his eyes . . . Tamsen, I think he's worse."

Tamsen's heart turned over, but she scoffed at Em. "He is better, you'll see," she said, then bending over the sick man, praying her words would penetrate through his coma-like state, "Papa, we're almost there! Do you hear me? We're almost to Santa Fe! And then Texas!"

Leaving Tamsen to sit with him, Em climbed stiffly down from the wagon-bed. Leaning against the wagon, hands covering her aching eyes, she did not see Dan Tallant as he approached.

"How's your paw?" he inquired.

Em jumped at the sound of his voice, then burst into tears. He took her in his arms, soothing her, raising her flower-like face to dry the tearstained cheeks. "Don't, Em," he whispered, "oh, don't!"

58

"Papa's going to die." The statement quivered in the air between them. And saying it, she knew it was true.

"I know," he said, holding her shuddering frame more tightly, "I know."

This was the scene Arabella came upon as she rounded the wagon. She ducked back out of sight to consider it, thoughtfully. Tamsen thought Tallant was a son of a bitch. Arab didn't think so, but Tamsen was so often right. He was hugging Em, right this minute. Had he done something to make her cry? Em had been hurt once, jilted by that stupid George Harper! Somebody just ought to ask Dan Tallant about his intentions! It should be Papa, by rights, but Papa was sick. As Arab climbed into the wagon, settling herself into her little nest in the crowded area, a plan was beginning to evolve in her head.

The next morning, just before dawn, she dressed quickly and hurried to where Daniel Tallant slept beneath his wagon. Ducking her head, she crawled to his side and touched his face with her hand.

He sat up. "What the hell! Arab!"

"Shhh," she said, "I have to talk to you." She stated her errand, peering suspiciously as the blanket that covered him appeared to shake. Was he laughing at her?

His voice, when he spoke, was a little muffled, but deadly serious. "I appreciate your concern for your sister, Arab. And you were right to come to me. I'm very fond of Em, but only as a friend. She was unhappy about something else, and I tried to comfort her. Believe me, I respect her. I'd do nothing to hurt her."

"I didn't think so," said the exuberant girl. "And I think Tam's all wrong about you! Oh, Dan, I just *love* you!" She threw her arms about the startled man and kissed him.

Crawling from beneath the wagon, she raised her head to find herself looking straight into Tamsen's face. Tamsen looked so queer, her mouth pursed up like that, her eyes huge and round, her face white as if she might be going to faint.

"Tamsen, I was just—," Arabella began, defensively.

But the change in Tamsen's expression stopped her. Her face seemed to break up, to shatter like a piece of fragile glass. "Arabella," she said, in an awful-sounding, hollow voice.

"Arabella, Papa's dead."

Chapter 5

The sky was heavy and the falling snow, rendered the Sangre de Cristo range above them invisible as Scott McLeod was laid to rest. Only an hour was allotted for the digging of his grave and a brief service. The brooding weather allowed no time for grief. The train had to move on.

Tamsen was surprised as she returned to her wagon to find Mike Dunnevant waiting. Dan Tallant's orders were that he should offer his services as driver in Tamsen's place. The big man shifted from one foot to another, embarrassed in the presence of the family's sorrow. For the past several weeks, he'd made himself conspicuous by his absence, having a typical healthy male's dread of being around sickness.

Tamsen refused his assistance and took her place at the reins. The wagons moved out. Tamsen could hear Arabella's sobs above the crying of the wind, Em's gentle tones as she tried to comfort the girl. But Tamsen's only tears were due to the wind-borne sleet that clawed at her face with icy fingers—a cold she did not feel, for she was numb.

At length, the horses under control, she felt in the pocket of the gown beneath her wrappings, seeking the little Bible she'd found among Papa's things. Between its pages was pressed a sprig of forsythia, still retaining its color, though it now had the papery, straw-scented texture and smell of a preserved flower.

She knew where this sprig had originated. The bush grew by the steps at the front veranda. Her mother had planted it, but she had not lived to see it bloom.

The dried blossoms brought back a flood of memories. She and Em had played on that porch as children. And later, Arabella. George Harper had courted Em there, in the big wooden swing. And she had had her turn there, with Will Franklin.

A sudden nostalgia rose inside her, making her hurt. She hurt for the days that were past and could not return. The smell of grass, new-scythed, the taste of lemonade on a summer evening. Papa, leaning against a porch column, spinning his tales of Texas, of how he could strike it rich, in a new country.

She had been the one who talked them all into leaving. Tamsen knew that, as sure as she knew anything in this world. Papa was a dreamer, not a doer. He would have been content just to talk about going to Texas. It was she, Tamsen, who concocted the plans for the move. *Why*, she wondered dully. Why?

She had told herself it was because of Em, who had to face a gossiping neighborhood when her intended married someone else. She was convinced Papa drank because he had never fulfilled his dream, that Arabella deserved a better life than some country bumpkin could give her.

But had she really considered them—Papa, her sisters? Or did she insist because she was the one who wanted to get away?

Wanted what? Not this! Oh, dear God, not this! Papa dying, this weather, her team faltering, supplies diminishing. What was to become of them?

With a kind of horror, she stared ahead into the swirling snow.

Behind her, Dusty was immune to the cold. He had fortified himself copiously with spirits to help him forget his sorrow. Scott McLeod had been his good friend. Despite his drunken tears, Dusty handled the horses well. It was only when he was stone sober that he couldn't drive a straight line. Rubbing his bleary eyes, he tried to put Scott's death from his mind. The girls had each other, he thought, woefully. It was he who needed comforting.

He needed Nell, his Nell, who waited in Magoffinville.

When they stopped at nightfall, Tamsen finally gave way to weeping. Again, it was Em who offered her solace. Going west had been Papa's dream. And wasn't it better to die, if one had to, going toward a dream?

Tamsen's guilt feelings were not relieved. The Bible in her pocket, with its pressed flower, weighed on her conscience. She finally put it into the chest containing her things and closed the lid.

The next morning dawned fair, and the train set off once more. Horses and oxen struggled through drifted snow, eyes wide and nostrils distended. The train made little headway that day and the next. The weather slowed it to a plodding pace. As time passed, Tamsen watched her teams weaken and become rib-thin.

An estimated two days out of Santa Fe, which had become a Mecca to the travelers in their misery, Dan Tallant approached Em with a proposition. It was clear the McLeod horses wouldn't make it to Texas, perhaps not to Santa Fe. His idea was, with Scott McLeod gone, that they should borrow his horses and continue to California. Tallant would act as their protector and see that they were set up comfortably on their arrival.

Em, buoyed by the prospect, went in search of Tamsen.

Tamsen heard her out, the self-guilt she'd been feeling slowly turning into anger. She'd been out of her mind! It was Dan Tallant who was responsible for their plight, not she! She'd gone to him in good faith to buy his animals. He'd countered with an indecent, impossible proposal. With good horses, the trip would have been far easier; they might have left a day or two earlier.

Now he had offered the animals to Em. What price did he expect *her* to pay? It had been his idea to hold the fiesta where Papa caught pneumonia. And—her eyes widened as a picture flashed belatedly into her mind—Arabella! She had come crawling from beneath the wagon where Dan Tallant lay rolled in his blankets

63

that dreadful morning! What was she doing there? A fourteen-year-old girl! What kind of monster was he?

"Where is he now?" she asked, her voice flat.

"Waiting at the fire." Em looked at her, worriedly.

Dan turned at Tamsen's approach. "I've been wanting to offer my sympathy—"

"We don't want your sympathy," she said, her voice steady and filled with hate. "We don't want your horses, nor your charity. We don't want anything to do with you or your kind. Keep away from our wagons—away from Em and Arabella. That's all I ask."

He bowed, but without mockery. "Glad to oblige. It might please you to know I'm leaving the train, riding to attend to business in Santa Fe. I'm leaving Mike with the horses should you change your mind."

Then he was gone.

There was a chuckling sound behind her, and Tamsen whirled to see Dusty. "By Jove," he said, "I wouldn't have missed that for anything!"

He had listened to Em's tale of Tallant's offer, and had been stricken with fear that Tamsen would take him up on it. California was a long way from Texas, and he would have been in a quandary. He'd begun to fancy himself as the girls' protector and would have felt himself bound, as a gentleman, to see them to their destination.

That their destination might be other than Magoffinville was a thought too dreadful to face. Yet Tamsen had settled that, and quite well. He admired the girl's spunk!

Then the smile that revealed his two missing teeth gradually faded as he remembered his other errand. The lead horse on the second wagon was down and floundering. Another didn't seem too well. Perhaps there was no choice! Timorously, he conveyed his news.

Tamsen burst into tears.

"It isn't fair," she wept. "Tallant knew it, or he wouldn't have chosen this time! Oh, Dusty, we can't be obligated to him! I can't tell you why, but we can't!"

Dusty averted his eyes from her tearstained cheeks, tugging at his straggly mustache. "He did say he was riding into Santa Fe? Leaving Mike Dunnevant to bring his horses in?"

"Yes."

After a moment's pause, he said, "I can go visit the lad for a while. Suggest a few drinks—"

Tamsen stared at him, holding her breath. Did he mean . . . ? Then, at the mischievous grin touching his lips, she threw her arms around the little man.

"Dusty, you devil! I love you!"

Dusty returned to his wagon to watch until a spirited horse with its lean rider thundered off into the night. Then, bottle in hand, he set off to find Mike Dunnevant. What had been only an idea had become a plan of action. Dusty had never been a horse thief before. But the hug he'd received was worth any consequences. It had felt wonderful. Though the girl was skinny, of course, not well-rounded and comfortable, like Nell.

"Cheers, my friend," he said, squatting on his heels beside the big man, already in his bedroll. "I could do with a spot of company. Never cared to drink alone."

In the meantime, Tamsen, dressed in Dusty's additional set of trail garb, shivered as she waited, wondering how long it would take. At last, freezing from inactivity, she climbed into the wagon, intending to get her blanket—only to face the business end of Papa's gun.

"Stop right there!" Em's voice quavered. Then, "Tamsen! What in the world!" She sounded scandalized. "I thought you were a—a thief lurking about out there! And in men's clothes!"

"Please, Em! It's . . . a secret. Go back to bed, and don't disturb Arab. Please! No matter what happens!"

In a short while, Tamsen saw Dusty weaving toward her over the snow. "He's out," the man said in an admiring tone. "Never thought he would make it. By Jove, it took my bottle and two of his!"

One by one, she and Dusty fastened halters to the

huge, docile beasts, leading them to the McLeods' wagons. At each trip, Tamsen paused to inspect the recumbent Dunnevant. "Is he still sleeping, Dusty? Do you think he'll stay that way?"

On the last foray, she broached the subject of supplies. Dan Tallant was apparently not wanting for money. He would be able to restock at Santa Fe. Supposing they took a little food from his wagon . . . not enough so that it would create a hardship.

Dusty nodded. "We'd be doing the chap a favor, lightening the load a bit."

Taking horses was one thing. Stealing supplies was another. Tamsen looked guiltily toward the slumbering Mike. "Do you think he's still asleep?" she began, again, "Do you think—"

"For God's sake," Mike Dunnevant growled, "why don't you tie me up?"

After their initial shock at finding the man had been playing possum, observing their secretive movements with amusement, Tamsen and Dusty agreed it would be a wise move. Tying him up would absolve Mike from all blame. Though it had been his own idea, Dunnevant was a recalcitrant subject. It suited his humor to be a dead weight, to pretend he was still in a drunken stupor. The process of binding him—not too tightly—took almost half an hour. The joke was beginning to wear a little thin, Mike thought glumly. Why the hell didn't they hurry? At last, trussed ineptly but securely, he watched them leave with the last of their purloined supplies. They would soon be on their way.

He would miss them. The McLeod girls, and old Dusty, too. But right now, the liquor he'd consumed was catching up with him. All he wanted to do was sleep.

Securing the horses and supplies had only been the beginning of their problems. The collars and bridles that served the emaciated teams would have to be adjusted to fit the larger draft animals. Tamsen fumed as she struggled to change the position of buckles on leather that had lost its pliability. Her frozen fingers were bleeding by the time they were able to back the two wheel-horses into the traces.

Dear God, they must leave before dawn! And they had yet another hurdle before they were clear of camp. There would be a guard on the outer perimeter at a spot they must pass in order to head toward their destination.

Again, Dusty had a plan. When the animals were in position at last, he went to carry it out.

He knew the man on guard duty. Will Hargis was an honest man, and could not be bribed. But he was a notorious jokester and had been put off by Dan Tallant's comments that his idea of good fun was not acceptable on a wagon train. And Dusty had a fantastic story to tell him.

The McLeod girls, sweet, delicate young things that they were, had taken Mike Dunnevant at gunpoint and tied him up. Dusty elaborated on the humorous aspects of the situation—the gigantic man beset by a bevy of fragile femininity. He chuckled as he told it, and Hargis was grinning like a monkey when he finally paused.

"Get on with it, man. Why'd they do it? He get out of line with one of the girls? They gettin' even?"

Dusty feigned a convulsion of laughter. "No," he wheezed, "this is the amusing part. Jove! You will never believe this! They," he wiped his streaming eyes, "they are stealing Tallant's horses! They're breaking away from the train, going to Texas. The little ladies are horse thieves! And it serves Tallant bloody well! The whole train will be laughing—"

What a joke on Tallant! On Dunnevant! The joke seemed even funnier as Hargis sipped from Dusty's bottle.

"The problem is," Dusty finally confided, "they've got to come along this trail. I suppose you'll have to stop them. Pity."

"I got some business to do out in the weeds," Hargis said with a wink. "Won't even see 'em as they go by.

By God, I can't wait until mornin'! Tallant'll be fit to be tied!" He guffawed and slapped his knee.

Tamsen was waiting in the darkness at the edge of the clearing. Her heart leaped as Dusty told her the results of his conversation. Together they hurried back to the wagons. Tamsen crept inside. Em and Arab were sleeping, thank God. She withdrew and climbed to the wagon seat, taking up the reins.

Em was not really asleep, but pretending to be, her mind whirling with wild speculation. Lying wide-eyed, she had listened to the sounds of horses being hitched, heard the stamping and snorting of large, healthy animals. Later, Em sneaked out to see for herself. The beasts bulked huge against the night sky, and with a sickening plunge in her breast, she recognized them. These were Tallant's horses. There were no others like them on the train.

Now she felt the wagon begin to move. Arabella turned and murmured at the sway of the vehicle, and Em put a comforting arm across her. Whatever was happening, she must put her trust in Tam. But how did she come by the horses? She thought of Tamsen's dislike of Tallant, her refusal to become obligated to him, since, as she put it, he wanted something in return.

Tamsen wouldn't! Or would she? Tam was so many people inside that small frame! Gentle but stubborn; vulnerable, yet tough in a way that Em could never be. And she wanted things, for all of them, the things they would find in Texas—

Em was suddenly afraid.

In the morning, she learned that Dan Tallant had changed his mind. He'd loaned them the horses for the remainder of their journey. When they reached Magoffinville, the animals would be handed over to one of his agents for delivery to California.

The story sounded plausible, Em thought as she studied the bland faces of Tamsen and Dusty. When they explained that their haste in leaving the train was due to the necessity of catching Tallant's agent before he left on his westward journey, it began to make some sense. But the reason for moving through Santa Fe in the darkness of the following night, Em failed to understand. She did not know, as Tamsen did, that the owner of the horses slept behind one of the shuttered windows of the old Spanish town.

Chapter 6

The journey from Santa Fe was an exhausting one, filled with perils that did not materialize. Along this trail, there was always danger of Indian attack. The travelers knew nothing of their temper at this time. They were hostile at best. Dusty spent the evenings at the cookfire, regaling the girls with tales of past atrocities. As they stood guard in pairs, each cactus, thorny mesquite and yucca plant took on terrifying human forms in the darkness.

Finally, Dusty learned, from an Indian traveling with his stolid squaw that more bountiful hunting prospects had lured the red men south and west. They were safe unless they met a ragtag band of marauders. They were able to sleep at last.

They moved on as the weather turned unseasonably cold. Tamsen shivered at the reins. The cold was a boon, Dusty pointed out, since they must follow the sandy bed of the Rio Grande. A sudden thaw in the mountains behind them could turn the river into a raging torrent. Looking at the snake-like trickle, frosted at its edges, Tamsen could not believe Dusty's morbid statements—that it would be possible for a wall of water to sweep down upon them, tumbling the wagons ahead of it like children's toys.

The girls lived in fear. They were never warm. Supplies were running low, and Dusty was unusually silent. Still, ahead of them was Texas, waiting for them, leading them on with its promise.

But Texas failed them, too.

It's the same river, Tamsen thought as she walked

with Dusty through the cantina district at the edge of Magoffinville, except dirtier. The sewage from the shabby adobe structures was dumped directly into the Rio Grande below. The sights and sounds here were reminiscent of the Elkhorn Bar on the docks in St. Louis. But the smell was intensified.

"Well, here we are," Dusty said, pausing before one of the unprepossessing buildings. "This is Nell's place. She will help you, if anyone can." He looked a little pale, unsure of himself as he gestured toward the swinging doors, as if he weren't too certain of his own welcome.

Tamsen hesitated at the thought of entering the cantina, but all other avenues were closed. Their supplies were gone. She could find no means of earning a living. The farming tools that were to have made their fortune were not needed here. It had all been a dream.

Dusty had taken them directly to a place nine miles out of Magoffinville upon their arrival, to an adobe sheepherder's shack he'd guessed might be unoccupied. It was, and there was evidence the sheep had shared the structure along with the herder. But it was a house. A welcome sight after the long days on the trail. There was a well, though it contained brackish water. The girls set to cleaning the place, fixing tarpaulins over the yawning windows to keep out the chill wind.

The shack had been a distraction to keep the McLeod sisters from learning the truth too soon, that there was no place for them here. Dusty had kept it from Arabella and Em, but had gone to Tamsen with a guilty, hangdog expression. The people here were not farmers, he mumbled, but rather cattle or sheep men. It might not be wise to mention farm tools, at least until the area attracted more settlers.

Tamsen went white. "You let us come here, knowing that? You didn't tell Papa?"

"I did, but the man refused to listen. He was certain things would improve. He may have been quite correct in his assumption." Dusty eyed the ceiling, virtuously.

Tamsen went to the door, looking at the soil that sur-

71

rounded the adobe structure. Desert-like, with sparse winter vegetation, it bore no resemblance to the rich loam of the farming country at home.

"Then I shall have to find some work. We must have some kind of income. I can do housework. I'm accomplished with the needle. Tomorrow, we'll go into the city—"

Dusty looked even more guilty. "I'm afraid there's a bit of misunderstanding there, too—about Magoffinville. It's not exactly what you'd call a city."

It certainly wasn't, Tamsen thought now, trying to steel herself to meet Dusty's Nell. Magoffinville was nothing like she'd dreamed it would be. A dusty village with hard-packed streets, situated north of the Rio at the foot of Franklin mountain. There were about seven hundred permanent residents. In addition, it had a roving population of soldiers from a new garrison situated nearby, cowhands and drifters who had infiltrated the area following the end of the Mexican War.

Tamsen had spent the day seeking work, and in vain. By the time night fell—the sun having tumbled from the sky in a blaze of color—Tamsen's spirits had fallen, too. There was no demand for farm tools, as Dusty had said. And Mexican labor was cheap here. The few officer's wives who accompanied their husbands to the new garrison had brought along their own servants. A small community of camp followers served as laundresses and seamstresses for the military post. There was no work for Tamsen anywhere.

Dan Tallant was right in his warnings. That probably irked her more than the discovery that she had no way to earn a living for herself and her sisters.

Then Dusty had suggested that they talk to his Nell. He'd been wondering how he could induce Tamsen to accompany him. It would be easier, somehow, with a third party present. He was a sensitive man, and Nell was so charmingly unpredictable. Sure that Nell would have a solution, he led Tamsen to a cheap cantina in the red-light district.

Sensing Tamsen's reluctance to enter, Dusty beckoned her to a gate at the side of the structure. "We can go right into her office from here," he said, opening it. They entered a courtyard of sorts. Once it had seen better days, apparently having been a walled garden. Now the fountain in its center was broken, the vegetation that once ornamented the place long dead. The place was malodorous and grim beneath the late afternoon sun.

From the cantina wall that formed its perimeter, two balconies sagged below shuttered windows. Dusty took a deep breath and squared his shoulders, then knocked at the door. The slab door hung a little awry, not quite fitting the warped frame.

"What the hell you waiting for?" a voice boomed. "Come in!"

Dusty ushered Tamsen through the door and followed her, nearly stepping on her heels as she stopped stock still at the sight of the woman before her.

An elephantine figure with its bulging curves squeezed into a gown of turquoise velvet, dripping with Mexican turquoise and silver, peered at Tamsen from small, shrewd eyes above garish painted cheeks. "Well," the woman boomed, "what the he—?" She stopped as she caught sight of Dusty. Tears dimmed her eyes as she looked at him for a long moment. Then the small eyes disappeared in an expansive smile.

"Dusty," she roared. "Dusty! You misbegotten, whisky-soaked little English sonavabitch! Where the hell did *you* come from?"

Tamsen was barely able to get out of the way as Nell moved toward Dusty with a speed that belied her mountainous frame. Then he was clasped to the immense bosom like a child.

Tamsen, forgotten, turned to study the wall.

The touching scene was brief. It ended with Nell giving Dusty a resounding whack on the back that sent him staggering.

"Let go, you damned old fool," she bellowed, affectionately. "Now, let's get down to brass tacks. Whattaya want? Whatcha doing here? Who's this?" She jerked an

73

intimidating thumb in Tamsen's direction.

In a few words, Dusty outlined the story of the McLeod girls, describing their situation. All the while, Tamsen stood quietly miserable under the woman's scrutiny.

"You know I don't own this place any more," Nell said, thoughtfully. "Belongs to Pete Martinez. I only run it." She pulled at her underlip, smearing the paint a little. "But maybe I could put her on." She scowled at Dusty.

"She willing to work upstairs?" Then, at the little man's pained expression, "No, I reckon not."

The furious scowl turned on Tamsen. "You do anything? Sing?"

"A—a little," Tamsen stammered, overwhelmed by the force of the woman's personality. The gimlet gaze moved over her, head to foot.

"What about getting along with the boys?" she barked. "Can you smile? A little pat on the fanny never cost nobody nothing! Can you remember that?"

"Ye-es."

Dusty's face was furiously red. "For God's sake, Nell, can't you see this girl is a lady?"

"Shaddup," Nell snapped. "I allus say, you can't judge a book by its gawdamn cover. Leave this up to me, you little shrimp! I got me a hunch. . . ."

Tapping her teeth with a long, painted nail, she looked Tamsen over once more, then went out to the hall.

"Katie," she shouted, "drop whatever you're doing! I don't give a damn what his name is—get down here, on the double!"

Tamsen was dressed by the helpful hands of an Irish girl whose appearance she'd hardly noted in her own nervousness. Soon, she stood before Nell, waiting as the big woman studied her. Tamsen wore a crimson gown left behind by one of the girls who had gone off with a wealthy man. The change of costume made an amazing transformation in the girl. Cut low, it bared slender but seductive shoulders and the swell of a provocative bosom. The waist, cinched tightly, could be spanned by a man's hands. The full skirt was long in back, its front slit to the knee to reveal a tempting length of leg when Tamsen moved.

I can pick 'em, Nell thought with satisfaction. The girl looked the part. The important thing was how she would behave.

She shoved Tamsen toward the door that led into the cantina. The early crowd was coming in, and now she'd find out if her hunch was right. "Give 'em a song and dance," she ordered, "an' then circulate some. Ain't saying you got the job. Ain't saying you ain't. It's up to you." Then, as an afterthought, "Wiggle your butt some. It ain't ossified! Now, what you going to sing?"

Tamsen searched her memory. What kind of song would be suitable for a place such as this? She closed her eyes. Engraved on her mind was a picture of Arabella, dancing on the docks. She would never forget the way the girl had moved, so suggestively, nor the words to that awful song they had learned from naughty schoolboys so long ago.

As Tamsen whispered the words from the refrain, Nell's eyebrows shot upward and she grinned. Then the big woman moved ponderously into the cantina, whispering something into the ear of a man with a guitar slung over his shoulder.

The guitarist played a few chords and then looked expectantly toward the door behind which Tamsen waited, frozen with fear. He repeated them. Finally, she moved out into the room to face a sea of watching eyes.

"Look at *that!*" a man's voice exclaimed. Another chimed in, "Ay! *Qué linda!*"

A pause, then the chords began once more.

"Think about the men," Nell had admonished. "Think about the effect you're having on them."

But Tamsen could not. All that touched her mind was fear of failure. The larder was empty in the adobe shack. And Em had developed a cough. All that was important was that this was a job! Work for which she would be paid—if she could handle it.

The thought galvanized her into action.

Raising her arms, holding them palms up to her audience, she moved into the room that smelled of beer —and of men. As she reached the center, she summoned her voice. It did not come, but the music, the sound of her trying, was drowned in a wave of rowdy applause.

The guitarist began once more, and this time, Tamsen's voice came easily. It was not like Arabella's, clear, sweet, and true. Tamsen's voice was oddly husky, with occasional little breaks. It suited the sultry words of the song she sang. She found her body moving of her own volition.

"I'm a good girl," she sang, saucily, "not a bad girl!" An admonishing finger. "So don't let your eyes roam. But you can follow me home, boys," one hip moved to the side, beginning an uproar, "You can follow me home!" The V of her skirt parted to reveal slim, enchanting legs as she sang all the verses she could remember.

The song over, Tamsen was deafened by shouting male voices. "Do it again!" "*Màs! Màs!*" There was even a cockney accent far from home. "Blimey!"

Tamsen stood for an instant, wanting to run. Then she remembered Nell's words. "Circulate some." She moved among the men, her lips still curved in a seductive smile as she evaded reaching hands with a pat on a head here, a kiss on the cheek there. . . .

"I've done it," she exulted. She was a success!

A big man who smelled of horses and sweat grabbed at her slender waist and lifted her onto the center of a table. Other men crowded close.

Looking down into leering faces, she was frightened. Then, clasping her hands at her breast, she began to sing.

This time it was an old song she had heard her father sing. A ballad of a boy who had left home, gone wrong, and returned to find his mother dead—before he could ask her forgiveness.

As she sang, she thought of home, herself, of Papa,

of what Mama would think to see her daughter in a place like the cantina. Her voice broke on a note, but she went on to sing to the end.

When she finished, her eyes were filled with tears, and she looked down to see her tears reflected in the eyes of the rough men around her. There was a hushed silence, then a soft "*Qué linda*" that ended with a sigh.

"Blimey," said a cockney voice, "she's a bloomin' lydy!"

I've done it, Tamsen exulted. She stood straight, flooded with a strange sense of power. Then, blowing kisses with both hands, she signaled to the man who had placed her on the table. He lifted her down with reverent hands, and she danced, confidently, back to Nell's door.

Inside, barring her path, was a tall, dark-bearded man. He looked her over with cold, reptilian eyes, then stepped out of her path, with a curt nod to Nell as he left the room.

Nell breathed out with a whoosh of relief. "That was Pete Martinez, the owner of this joint," she said. "He thinks you'll do—when you loosen up a little. Now, get out of that gawdamn dress and we'll talk a little business."

"Business" consisted of warning her against the cantina-owner. Nell hadn't liked the way he gave Tamsen the once-over. Her advice was to be nice to him, in order to keep her job—but not too nice. Tamsen's hours were to be from sundown to sunrise, or until things quieted down, whichever came sooner. And it would be a good idea to keep her home life and her work separate, just to be on the safe side.

Nell pulled a piece of paper in front of her. "Now," she said, "what name do you want to be known by?"

"Do you mean—just invent one?"

At Nell's nod, Tamsen thought for a moment. "Poppy," she said, finally. "Poppy Franklin," she finished, recklessly borrowing Will Franklin's last name. A sardonic smile crossed her face at the thought of stuffy Will, if he could see her now.

As she and Dusty rode homeward through the night, Tamsen planned for the future. Tomorrow she would have Dusty dispose of Tallant's horses. He'd said he had contacts here who would ask no questions. They'd be able to live on the proceeds from the sale until she drew her first pay.

But Arab and Em must not know what she was doing. She would tell them that she'd found work at a dress-making establishment. One where they used *machines*. Since they had a large volume of business and few machines, it was necessary to work an additional shift. Therefore she would be doing night work. After all, it would only be until she found something else, something more respectable.

Respectable or not, she thought back over the evening with a guilty satisfaction, seeing herself as she'd looked in that gown, hearing the words of masculine approval. "Ay! Qué linda!" She wondered what that meant. She would find out.

Her singing and dancing, too, had been well received. She felt she'd held her audience in the palm of her hand. Was that how Arabella had felt, there on the docks?

She pushed the thought away. Arabella would be able to grow up respectably. She would never allow Arab to appear in a place like the cantina. Tamsen was there only because she had to be.

Dan Tallant had called her an old maid! Unable to control the smile of pride at her evening's accomplishments, she spurred her horse on to reach Dusty's side. He had imbibed freely, and as he rode, he sang a series of bawdy barroom songs.

Tamsen listened closely. She must add to her repertoire.

Chapter 7

Thus began the double life of Tamsen McLeod.

For the first week, she was nervous and jumpy as she approached the cantina, wondering that she had even considered such an occupation. Yet once within its doors, she lost her concern. She was not Tamsen McLeod, the responsible sister. She became Poppy Franklin in thought and in action.

Business boomed as men straggled in from other haunts to see "the new girl." Tamsen handled their rough attention with an expertise that surprised her. And the big man who had lifted her to the table that first night was always there. He had become her self-appointed protector. His name was Cal Tuttle, he was a rancher, and there was an air of affluence about him, despite his Western garb.

"You don't belong in this place," he said to her, quietly, one night. "You need a nice little setup, all your own."

She had heard the same words from several of the other customers, but Cal Tuttle was different! A big man, steady, evidently well off, surely he meant something else by his little speech. Maybe he could see through the Poppy Franklin facade. He might even have marriage in mind! She did not love him, but, oh, to find a decent home for herself and her sisters. . . .

The guitarist began to play and Tamsen rose from the table to join him. It was time for her to sing. But Tuttle reached out a large hand.

"May I see you home tonight?" he asked, with urgency. "There's something I'd like to discuss."

Tamsen looked at him, seeing clear gray eyes with sun wrinkles at their corners, brown hair above the tanned face, hair that was sun-streaked with a touch of gray. It would not be night when he saw her home, but early morning. There would be explanations to make to Em and Arab. She dared not risk it. But perhaps if she explained her situation to him. . . .

"I'll think about it," she promised him. Then she danced to the guitarist's side and sang a love song especially for Cal.

Immediately after her numbers, Tamsen was summoned to the back room where Nell presided. The big woman looked at her sourly.

"Saw you shinin' up to Cal Tuttle," she said. "Don't like it a gawdamn bit. Figgered I'd better tell you to watch your step."

Tamsen stared at her incredulously. Was the woman trying to tell her with whom she could flirt? It was none of her business! "For God's sake, Nell," she said angrily, "I haven't done anything but talk to the man, treat him the way you told me to treat the others. Did you think I was planning to go upstairs with him? Like Katie? Carmen? Maggie? Do you tell them who they can—"

"Thass business," Nell grunted.

"Well, maybe this is business," Tamsen flared. "Mine! I only work here. You can't run my life."

"Hell, no," the woman growled. "I can't do that. But I can decide if you're going to work here. You get outta line, and I'll tie a can to your tail so fast you won't know what hit you."

The two glared at each other until Tamsen finally lowered her eyes. It was blackmail, but she needed her job. She would have to appear to give token compliance, at least until she could find something else to do. Then she would see Cal Tuttle any time she pleased. She reentered the cantina, her brow furrowed in thought. Why would Nell take such a stand? Did she fear the big man might have serious intentions? That she'd lose her new star?

And that was what she was—a star. She could sense the customers snapping to attention when she walked into the room, could fairly feel the electricity of their emotions. Smiling, now, she signaled the guitar player and held out her arms to encompass them all, as she sang their favorite song.

"I'm a good girl, Not a bad girl—"

They loved her and she loved them. Not as Tamsen McLeod, but as her other self, the self that loved the noise, the gaudy glitter of the cantina, the adulation. Here, she was *someone*.

Her new attitude toward her work surprised Tamsen. She reminded herself that she'd been threatened with the loss of her job, a job that meant food and shelter for her family. Perhaps, for a moment, her fear of being out of work made the cantina seem more glamorous than it really was. The last thing she wanted to be was an entertainer in a place such as this! She was tempted to defy Nell, anyway.

Yet, when Cal Tuttle pressed once more to accompany her home, she dissembled. "Not this time," she smiled at him, touching his cheek with a teasing forefinger, feeling his taut facial muscles quiver at her touch, "but perhaps another night . . ."

Dusty was waiting for Tamsen in the gray dawn, as usual, except this time the little man was sober. Though Tamsen was gratified at his condition—Dusty normally drink-sodden was token protection—she felt a twinge of fury. Dusty's sobriety would be due to Nell. She'd deliberately kept him this way to serve as spy. Tamsen felt like a prisoner under guard as they rode to the small adobe, which seemed to be more distant every day.

Despite Nell's strict rulings, Tamsen began to bloom. At home she felt the weight of responsibility, but at the cantina with Cal Tuttle's attentions and the admiration of the clientele, she was thriving as Poppy Franklin. Her sisters couldn't help seeing how much she'd changed. Em was pleased that Tamsen seemed happier, but Arab's green eyes glinted with envy.

"Tam makes me sick!" she said, candidly. "She

doesn't care about us at all! She goes to Magoffinville every day, and we haven't even got to see what kind of a town it is! It makes me mad! She's not stuck out here like we are!" She gave the interior of the two-room adobe a hating look. "In this hole!"

Em put her sewing down. "You stop talking like that! Right now! Tamsen's working! When I think what we owe her! If it weren't for this cough——!"

"I could work, too," the girl said, sullenly.

Em began to laugh. "Look at those stitches," she said, in good humor. "You've skipped a place! Left a hole big enough to throw a cat through! *You* want to be a seamstress."

Arabella flushed, then joined in the joke on herself. "I guess not," she admitted. "But I'm not going to stick around the house all day like Tamsen said." She rose. "I'm going to take a walk. Want to come with me?"

Em sighed. "No, I'll finish this." She held her sewing closer to the light that helped little in the gray of early twilight. "But don't go too far. And be back in this house before dark."

Em was just as bossy as Tamsen, Arab thought, sulking a bit. The day had been a warm one, a false spring, though bits of green were beginning to show on the desert land. Yet she had been kept in, tending to household chores—to spare Tamsen, Em had said. And now Tamsen had gone to work—in a place that had assumed the proportions of a metropolis in Arabella's eyes. Arab, at least, should be able to see what was over the rise of the nearest hill!

She lifted her face to taste the breeze, cool but with a promise of spring. Dusty had promised that soon the desert would come alive with all manner of baby things. Quail, doves, rabbits, roadrunners. She couldn't wait.

Lifting up her skirts, Arab began to run.

Em finished her work and rose, rubbing her back. The work was so tiring. She didn't see how Tamsen could manage to stitch all night and still be so fresh in the morning. She stepped outside. It was still light, but the sun was setting in the west. The one thing she loved here was the sunsets, more colorful than any painting. She watched for a moment, then forced herself to re-enter the house. Tamsen had eaten before she went to work, but Em and Arab preferred to wait.

Em busied herself with their evening meal. She made coffee from the cracked, browned-in-the-oven wheat that often served for the brew. There was so little real coffee left, she worried, and it should go to their bread-winner, Tamsen. Moving the coffeepot to the back of the wood stove—a cranky cast-iron thing—Em set a skillet of bacon to frying.

Very little meat, she thought gloomily. Mostly grease. Perhaps she should make a water gravy, though Arab detested it so. Still, it was filling.

Lifting the shriveled bacon to a plate, she stopped, listening. Often the wind cried about the house at night, but this was different—almost human—

Arabella!

Em ran to the door and threw it open. Arab was running, screaming, her skirts held high as she skimmed like a bird across the desert prairie. Behind her were three figures, running easily in pursuit.

Dear God! *Indians!* Em's knees went weak.

Then Arab was through the door, across the room, ducking beneath the table that was spread, for lack of a cloth, with the remains of an old sheet. Em tried vainly to close the door against the girl's pursuers, but failed. It was pushed open, and she was pressed against the wall behind it. Then the Indians were in the house. One bent over to lift the table cover and caught hold of Arabella's red curls!

Em moved like an avenging fury. Snatching up the skillet of hot grease, she poured it on the posterior of the crouching youth, then turned to face the others and flail out at them with the emptied utensil.

Arab's attacker, who had clapped his hands to the seat of his breeches, was dancing in pain. The other Indians jabbered in a heathen tongue, and then they both burst into laughter. Leaving his partner to usher the injured youth outside, one Indian tried to compose himself. With a stern expression that kept slipping around the edges, he pointed to his chest, then raised one hand.

"I think they want to be friends," Arabella said, peeping from beneath the table cover. "I think he means—"

"I don't *care* what he means," Em said, furiously. She advanced on the Indian with her upraised skillet. "Out! Out!"

Leaning weakly against the door, now barred and in place, Em could hear the Indians leaving, still making odd gobbling sounds of laughter.

I'm going to faint! she thought, dazedly. *And I must not! I must not!*

She pulled herself upright with an effort. "You know," she said to Arabella, "our supper's ruined. There isn't any grease for gravy."

But Arabella wasn't listening. Her face was shining with excitement as she loaded Scott McLeod's gun. "We've got to be ready when they come back," she said. "They won't come at night. Dusty says they always attack before dawn—"

Tamsen saw no sign of Indians as she returned on the long journey from the cantina. She had other things on her mind. Tonight had been reasonably quiet, and Nell had closed up early. It somehow seemed to strike at Tamsen's pride. Perhaps she was no longer the main attraction in Magoffinville. She wondered if the cantina's clientele had gone elsewhere. Nell had assured her that such nights sometimes occurred, but this was the first time she'd seen it.

Loaded to the gills, Dusty swayed on his horse, mumbling bits of poetic fancy regarding Nell. Well, Tamsen wished Nell had him! Somehow, when they reached the adobe, she'd have to guide him into the shed. Then she faced another problem. How to explain her early arrival to the girls. It was barely three o'clock!

A machine broke down. That was it. *Her* machine.

Reaching the adobe at last, she managed to coax

Dusty off his horse. Then she led him to his shack, irritated at the way he stumbled and crashed into everything. It would be so much simpler if the girls didn't wake up.

Tamsen left Dusty comfortably situated on the pile of horse blankets that served as his bed and rounded the adobe, walking softly, the feather bobbing gently on her hat.

Inside, Arabella took a deep breath and squeezed the trigger on her father's gun. The night was blasted with noise and a glancing of flame.

Arabella picked herself up off the floor as Tamsen picked herself up off the ground. Green eyes met brown ones as Arab stared through the curtained window. Tamsen's eyes were blank with shock, Arab's filled with horror.

"My God," Arabella whispered. "It wasn't an Indian!" Then, as an afterthought, "But I sure shot the dickens out of Tamsen's hat!"

Terrified at the girl's story, though unable to believe Em's part in it, Tamsen insisted on rousing the drink-sodden Dusty. Plied with coffee—real coffee—he finally became sensible enough to inform them that he didn't think they'd been in danger, that there would be no wild Indians this near Magoffinville, especially with the new garrison stationed here.

The girls placed no credence in his explanation. They watched by the windows until dawn. Em was frankly frightened; Arabella, now that her first fears were over, was rather hopeful that the adventure hadn't ended. Tamsen mentally chastised herself for having exposed her sisters to danger. She would have to move them closer to civilization somehow. She thought of Cal Tuttle.

The Indians had not gone. They came back later in the day. The girls, peeping through the tarpaulined windows, watched them talking to Dusty, laughing, gesticulating. Dusty laughed, too. Soon he led them toward the house.

They entered to face a trio of frightened girls, huddled close together for protection.

These were friendly Indians, at least for the moment, Dusty explained. They were Mescaleros, down for trading at Magoffinville. Last night, they had meant no harm. They'd seen Arabella and, wondering at her red curls, followed her to inspect her hair more closely. They had admired Em's courage.

The leader stepped forward, holding out a necklace of turquoise and silver, a medallion of sorts. He proffered it to Em with great dignity.

"Take it," Dusty told her. "It is a token of admiration for your bravery."

Em accepted the gift gingerly and placed it around her neck. The Indian smiled, pointing to his chest and raising his hand in that odd salute as he'd done before. Then they were gone. The two older men were mounted bareback on small spotted ponies. The third, the injured youth, evidently preferred to walk alongside his horse.

All was well, since it had ended well, Em tried to assure Tamsen. But Tamsen was sunk in her new worries. What if they had not been friendly Indians? What if they should decide to return?

"It's Arab's fault for going so far afield," Tamsen said to Em, stubbornly. "You should have kept her here in the house! Then none of this would have happened! A fourteen-year-old girl—"

"Fifteen," Em reminded her, gently. "And you can't keep her hidden forever, Tam. She's a pretty girl, growing up. She needs friends, companions. She was talking today about finding some work to do to help out."

Tamsen stared at her, face white. "And what can she do? Would you want her to work in a cantina—a bar?"

"Good heavens, no!" Em, too, was pale, her eyes filled with horror at the thought.

Tamsen felt a sickness at the pit of her stomach. She had justified her job to herself, but it seemed so different through Em's eyes. It would only be for a time, she assured herself. Only for a time. But meanwhile she must find a way to solve Arabella's problems.

The next night, she borrowed money from Nell and purchased a rickety buggy. On Sunday morning, she would drive her sisters to church, to the services held in an empty warehouse at the edge of town. There would be little chance of being recognized, she thought wryly. The cantina's customers consisted of a rough element, not exactly religious types. After a wild Saturday night, they would all be sleeping it off.

Tamsen McLeod, in a mourning veil and a sedate dark Sunday gown, would bear little resemblance to Poppy Franklin, lady of the night.

"I don't see why you have to dress like that," said Arabella, demure in her ruffled dress. Em, too, cast an uneasy look at Tamsen. Em had chosen to wear a blue challis with bonnet to match. Papa had never liked mourning, yet she felt Tamsen should dress as she thought best.

They entered the warehouse church a little late. The swelling sound of a familiar hymn filled the air. It brought tears to Tamsen's eyes, and she was grateful for the veil as they took their places in an empty row of benches in the back. How good to hear the hymn that was one of Papa's favorites! How wonderful to see families seated together in worship, united, as the McLeods had once been.

Tamsen turned as Arabella stirred beside her. The girl was leaning far forward, her eyes meeting those of a clean-cut-looking boy in the opposite row. Tamsen smiled, indulgently. It would do no harm for her to meet someone of good upbringing who was a member of the church.

Pulling her veil to one side, Tamsen surveyed the boy's family. Two little girls, three boys, a work-worn but nice-appearing mother, a baby in her lap. And the father—

Tamsen gasped as she looked straight into Cal Tuttle's horror-stricken eyes.

"Today," the minister exhorted, "I wish to speak on brotherhood. We must pray for the souls of the fallen, those who have bowed beneath the weight of vice and of drink, those who are doomed to hellfire everlasting! For in the eyes of God, all men are the same. . . ."

"All men are the same," thought Tamsen, her fists balled tightly in her lap. "All men are the same!"

Chapter 8

After the service, Tamsen wished only to escape, but that proved to be most difficult. The congregation was determined to give them a welcome that would assure their return. Among the most eager and friendly was Elizabeth Tuttle, Cal's wife. The big man stood by, red-faced, as his wife steered the girls through a series of introductions.

He won't tell on me, Tamsen realized, as long as I don't tell on him!

She did have a bad moment when Em mentioned something about the dressmaking establishment where Tamsen worked. The woman frowned. "I hadn't heard of it." Then, "But of course, we live out on the ranch—and I make my own things." Mrs. Tuttle issued an invitation for the girls to visit. Tamsen gave an evasive answer and turned the subject to something else. She did not wish to accept the woman's hospitality—nor to have to return it.

The ordeal over at last, Tamsen turned the buggy toward home, in relief. As they bounced along the rough road, Em mentioned shyly that one of the gentlemen, a Major Arbuthnot from the nearby garrison, had asked permission to call later in the day.

Tamsen remembered the man. Large and softly rotund, with billowing mustache, she had secretly regarded him as pompous and a little boring—his attendance at the small church was evidently a concession to a lack of other social life. But she had seen his eyes on Em. Em could do worse, she thought. The man was dull, but maybe that was an attribute. He wouldn't spend the night in cantinas when he had a wife and family at home!

When they reached home, the sisters went into a flurry of preparation for their visitor. Dipping deep into their larder, they fairly decimated their food supply. They tried to approximate a company table, bemoaning the loss of the civilized articles that had been their mother's, the things they'd been forced to leave behind on the trail.

The Major didn't seem to note the lack. He spent the evening talking about himself, bandying the names of well-known people he'd met, pausing only to see if his audience was dutifully impressed.

"Whew," said Arabella, the moment the door closed behind the man, "I'm glad that's over!" Em, pink from the knowledge that Arbuthnot's eyes hadn't left her all evening, agreed. But Tamsen said, "I thought he was quite nice. So well-bred, don't you think?"

Dusty, angered at being overshadowed as far as conversation was concerned, and suffering from an enforced dry spell as well, took his bottle from his pocket.

"I think," he said, succinctly, "the chap's a bloody, boring, pompous jackass!"

With that, he left the room.

Tamsen returned to work the following night, still raging inwardly at Cal Tuttle's perfidy, wondering if he'd dare to show his face again.

He did not. And for the first time, she knew how much she had come to depend on him. When Cal was present, the cantina's clientele had more or less regarded him as her protector. He was a big man physically, but even more importantly, he was influential in the area. He had a big ranch.

As the nights passed, Tamsen sensed that the rowdies who frequented the place were becoming more difficult to control. Hands grasped at her skirts, and obscenities were murmured in her ears as she whirled away. And Pete Martinez, the cantina's owner, kept watching her with cold, reptilian eyes.

One night Nell called Tamsen into the back room and presented her with a small, flat, deadly-looking weapon. "You better start packing this," she said, matter-of-factly. "Keep it on you. May need it if one of them sonavabitches starts something."

"I can handle them," Tamsen said stiffly.

"Bullshit!"

Nell turned her back rudely, and Tamsen knew she was dismissed.

Katie showed Tamsen how to use the little gun and how to make a pocket for it to conceal it in her skirts. "Better practice some," Katie told her.

Tamsen studied the girl, wondering as she had so many times why she plied her particular profession. Sorrel-haired, her pixie face dusted with freckles, and with her wide, honest grin, the girl just didn't seem the type.

Katie Ryan smiled now. "You're wondering why I do what I do, aren't you?" she asked. Tamsen blushed. "Well," the small Irish prostitute said, gamely, "there's some that like it, and some that don't. I like it. And if you don't, you'd better learn to use that thing." She pointed to the gun.

Tamsen hugged Katie. For some reason, she had become quite fond of Katie, and of Carmen, one of the other regulars, the pretty Mexican senorita whose beauty was marred by a missing front tooth which had been knocked out by an amorous customer. Fond even of Maggie, flat-footed, phlegmatic Maggie who washed the glasses—and went upstairs when a man was desperate and there was no one else available.

"Thank you, Katie," Tamsen said. "I'll carry the gun, because Nell told me to. But I'll never need to use it."

Only two nights later, however, the need for the gun arose. Buck Farnum, a drifter from out of town, had been frequenting the cantina for about a week. *Dangerous*, Dusty termed the young man. Dangerous because he fancied himself as a gunslinger.

For the first few nights, Farnum had joined the bragging at the bar, boasting of being associated with a gang of notorious outlaws. Then his boasting took the form of taunts as he tried to goad other men into draw-

91

ing their guns. His efforts ignored, he retired to a corner table where he sat drinking steadily, his eyes on Tamsen.

Once, as she passed his table, he caught at her arm with a drunken invitation to go upstairs.

She smiled and shook her head as she pulled away. "I only sing here," she said, "Perhaps one of the others?"

He made a flat, ugly sound. "Don't give me that! You're all alike. Name your price. I've got the money." Reaching into his pocket, he drew out a handful of gold coins. He was still counting them out on the table as she walked away.

Nell, who was watching as usual, saw the incident and the fury that blazed in the scorned man's eyes. In the early dawn as Tamsen prepared to leave, dressed once more in a sober gown, Nell delivered a word of caution. "That Farnum feller ain't no man," she said. "He's a gawdamn snake. Better keep yer eyes peeled fer trouble. Ain't no tellin' when he'll strike."

Despite her feeling that she could handle any situation, Tamsen wes nervous and jumpy on the long ride home. She could see that Dusty was worried, too. Sliding her hand into the pocket of her cloak, she found the little gun. From now on, she would carry it at all times —just in case trouble did arise.

Buck Farnum was a drifter, she thought. Perhaps he would leave town soon. How she wished that he would.

But he did not. The next night, he was there at the same corner table, his eyes fixed upon her every movement, making her feel somehow unclean. She could feel the tension in him growing, tightening, like a coiled spring.

At home, her own nerves must have shown in her face. "You're working too hard," Em said. "Tamsen, this isn't fair. I should be doing my part."

"Then who would look after Arab?" Tamsen asked. "No, Em. It's better this way."

But the conversation brought on a spate of questions about the place where Tamsen worked, and Tamsen had to invent a big warehouse, imaginary machines, find names for her co-workers. After all, she could hardly say that she worked in a cantina and that her frazzled nerves were due to an outlaw's insistence on taking her upstairs to bed.

The set-to with Buck Farnum came on a Saturday night. Tamsen had just finished her song when he grabbed her roughly from behind and shoved her toward the stairway. For a moment, she went with him, quietly trying to talk him sober. "It's against the rules—Buck?—Is that your name? Now, if you'll go back to your table, I'll have a bottle brought to you, compliments of the house—"

He shook her as she resisted him at the foot of the stairs. "Don't pull any of that crap on me! We're going up those steps, and then I'm going to—!

As he went into the obscene details of what he had in mind, Tamsen tore away from him, but he reached out and caught the bodice of her gown. She heard the material tear. Then she was in his arms and struggling. From the room behind them she heard a low, angry growl as her plight came to the customers' attention.

Buck Farnum stiffened, then threw her from him. She fell on the uncarpeted steps. Half-dazed, she sat up to see the gunfighter, both guns drawn, turn to face the room full of men.

This was what he had wanted, she thought, dizzily, to stir someone into a confrontation. She recalled Dan Tallant's words, *"Do you want to start a brawl? Get someone killed?"*

"Come on," he jeered. "Who's first? Me and the girl are going upstairs. Anybody want to make something of it?"

She saw the faces of men she'd come to know and like. Young Charlie Spring, just a kid, only fifteen, but wearing guns, his hands poised. Duke Burton, seventy if he was a day, old and slow. Bert Sproul, Toby Parker, Carney Hamm—

"Don't," she whispered at the expressions on their faces, "oh, don't!"

In the back room, Nell and Dusty had heard the

commotion but paid little attention. It was the stillness that finally got to them. They looked at each other and saw the same thought in each other's eyes.

Trouble!

Nell hurried to the door, Dusty on her heels. At her muttered oath, he peered around her bulk to see Tamsen lying across the steps, her gown torn, Farnum standing over her.

"My word!" he said. He should do something! Nell kept a gun in her desk, but he'd never learned to handle one properly—

Farnum's gaze had fastened on young Charlie Spring. "You," he said, "you gonna try to stop me? Or you?" He glared at Duke Burton, with his trembling hands. "None of you got any guts?"

"I have," came a voice from across the room. "Put them gawdamn guns down an' get th' hell out of here!"

Nell!

"Only one *man* in the room, an' he's a lady! Well, you going to make me, fat lady?" The gunman gave a nervous giggle. "Maybe I could help you out a little, sweetheart. Shoot off a few pounds."

The insult to his beloved was too much for Dusty. He wriggled around Nell and positioned his slight frame before her enormous figure like a small fighting cock. "I say," he barked, his fists in a fighting position, his wispy hair standing on end, "that's no way to talk to a lady! I demand satisfaction, sir! Come out from behind those guns and fight like a man!"

Buck Farnum was taken aback, and the gun he'd leveled at Nell wobbled in his hand.

Tamsen seized the rail to regain her footing. One hand dipped into her skirts and came up with the pistol Nell had given her. She pressed the muzzle to the gunman's back.

"Drop your guns! Now kick them away!"

Buck Farnum complied.

She walked him to the door, where he turned to face the jeering customers of the cantina.

"You can't do this to me. You can't treat Buck

94

Farnum this way and get away with it! Ain't no damn prostitute in the world that can!"

He didn't have a chance to repeat his threat. Tamsen fired at the floor at his feet. He jumped, whirled, and was gone into the night.

Tamsen turned to acknowledge the applause in the room with a heady sense of victory. It was only when she saw Pete Martinez's eyes and what lay within their depths that she realized her gown was torn. His gaze touched her ripe curves and she stood hypnotized for a moment.

Then, catching up a coat a man had draped over a chair, she wrapped it around herself and hurried to the back room where she collapsed in Nell's arms.

"Wouldn'ta missed it fer nothin'," Nell said. "Guess I ain't never been so gawdamn proud in my whole life."

Tamsen lifted her head to acknowledge her praise, but Nell was smiling fondly at Dusty. "Look at th' little shrimp! Couldn't fight his way outta a paper bag, but he stood up t' that sonofabitch!"

"Guess I told him," Dusty bragged.

"You sure did," Nell said, fondly. "You sure as hell did!"

That night, Nell loaded the girls into a buckboard and followed Tamsen and Dusty until they were safely out of town. The vehicle bristled with guns. Her efforts at protection were not needed. The following day, they learned Buck Farnum had left town in a hurry, though he swore he'd return.

"And that," Nell snorted, "is a lot of bull!"

Pete Martinez, however, managed to catch Tamsen in the back room of the cantina, alone. He showed his teeth in a cold grin that made the girl's skin crawl.

"You did good last night. Pretty damn good, I think. You're my kind of woman." He poked her in the midriff, and she tried not to shrink from him. "And you like your work, sí? You like to work here?"

"Yes," she whispered.

"We talk about it sometime, then. Up there, no?" He pointed upward and she thought of those rooms in the

Elkhorn Bar, soiled shoddy cubicles with metal beds, pitcher and bowls, the scent of perfume and passion stale in the air.

Then, with a meaningful look, he was gone. There had been more than an invitation in his words. There had also been a threat. As if she would have to be nice to him if she wished to keep her job.

The first soft chords of a guitar began, and Tamsen ran out into the room, a bright smile fixed on her lips, embracing the audience with her arms. But her mind whirled frantically as she sang, making the sultry seductive movements that drove her watchers mad. She could not lose this income! Dear God, what would they do without it?

She thought about it the rest of the evening, and on the ride home. She would just have to play a cat-and-mouse game, that was all. And she must encourage Em to be nice to Major Arbuthnot. He was their only hope. If he and Em were married, she was certain he would care for Arabella. She, Tamsen, could not accept his charity, but she would be free of responsibility, free to—

To do what?

She put her hands to her aching head. Would life ever be without problems? For a time, things had seemed to be improving. Em seemed happy. Arabella, too, had seemed to bloom with the springtime, no longer the rebellious girl she had been. It was difficult for Tamsen, sitting in church, knowing what she knew about Cal Tuttle—though his attendance had been sporadic, she'd noted. Still, by taking the girls to church, letting them get to know people, her gamble had paid off—

Arabella was happy. As far as she was concerned, going to church and meeting the Tuttles was the nicest thing that had ever happened. When young David Tuttle approached her after church, she'd managed to intimate that though her old-maid sisters didn't exactly approve of boys, she did not share their opinions. She often took walks, she mentioned casually, in the mornings when Tamsen slept and Em was busy with the household chores.

Young David was enchanted, bemused by the slanting green eyes, the flashing dimples. Heretofore, his only experience with a girl was with the daughter of a neighboring rancher, a girl who was rawhide-tough, and completely without artifice.

David could not get away often, since his dad had set him to repairing fences, but there had been three meetings to this date, and he had dreamed a lot. Arab, with her inborn knowledge, kept each meeting just a bit short of fulfilling those dreams, thereby intensifying them.

This morning, Arabella had hardly been able to wait until Tamsen was abed. She had to keep her head down to hide the sparkle in her eyes from Em. And finally, when Em was busy with the dishes, Arab found her chance to escape. She fairly danced across the terrain, avoiding cactus, the prickly spikes of yucca, the bristly bunch grass that camouflaged holes made by kangaroo rats—so easy to catch a toe in and be flung sprawling.

When she reached the spot where young David waited, her cheeks were rosy from running, the red curls had tumbled around her shoulders, and her green eyes were alive with laughter.

David thought she was surely the most desirable creature in the world!

As they wandered, hand in hand, each electrically conscious of the other, David reflected on his father's attitude toward the McLeod girls. He'd heard him tell his mother to be wary of pressing her friendship with them. Oh, they appeared respectable enough on the surface, but he'd heard hints that their morals were not all they were supposed to be.

That had to be a lot of hogwash! Arab's sisters were prim and proper past all belief. Look at the way they treated Arabella! And Arab was an angel, straight from heaven. Ruefully, he wished she were a little less angelic. The chaste kiss she'd given him upon meeting had set his pulses to pounding, desire coursing through his body until he found his emotions difficult to control.

"Arab," he said, and his voice trembled a little, cracking in that way he hated. "Arab—"

But the girl was off and running. "Look," she cried. She had found a bird's nest in the grass. In it were two small, jewel-like eggs. The mother bird floundered in the brush at a distance, pretending to be crippled to draw the attention of the human invaders from her nest.

Arabella did not touch its contents, merely knelt to study the nest with rapt wonder. David, watching her, ached with wanting. The fact that it was spring, that his feelings were influenced by their romantic surroundings —the blue skies above, long swelling reaches of greening desert—did not occur to him.

He only knew he desired this girl. That he must have her.

The bird's nest forgotten, Arabella flitted on to new miracles; a cactus bloom, dew-sparkled; a hawk wheeling ahead in slow, lazy grace; the blue of the mountains in the distance, turning to rose with the morning sun.

"It's all so beautiful," she breathed.

He put a tentative arm around her, and she did not draw away.

"Arab," he asked hoarsely, "are you happy here?"

She flashed him a startled look. "Of course! Now that I've met you," she amended.

He gulped. "Then would you—would you *marry* me?"

"And stay here? Oh, no, I couldn't!"

He winced at her blunt statement, and she put her head against his shoulder, contritely. "It's not you, David. I love you. But I couldn't be a ranch wife and get old and tired. I want to live in a beautiful house someday—like a castle. And wear beautiful gowns and jewels."

She whirled away from him to pose, haughty as a queen, then dipped a graceful curtsey.

"But that's someday, David." She dimpled at the crestfallen boy. "It doesn't have anything to do with now! Come on—catch me, if you can!"

Laughing, she began to run and David followed her.

As she tripped, he reached out to grab her and both of them went down. The boy found himself entangled in skirts, clasping a delicious bundle of warm, scented flesh. His mouth sought hers and found it. This was a different kind of kiss than he'd had before, a kiss with promise and a fire that sent his brain reeling.

Arab, realizing things had gone a little too far to suit her, squirmed away. Her skirt, caught beneath the pressure of his weight, ripped a little at the waist. He's so awkward, she thought, with a trace of irritation. The man of her dreams would never behave in this clumsy, frantic, fumbling way!

Then she was on her feet and running back to the house. "I have to go now," she called back to him. Elusive as a will-o'-the-wisp, she was gone, leaving him standing alone beneath the blue sky, disappointed, but savoring a promise of things to come.

Arab, too, was somewhat disturbed. She had liked the feeling of his arms, the knowledge that she had aroused the male in him. Yet to her, it was a kind of game. A dangerous game in which she must not lose the upper hand.

That night, young David Tuttle dreamed of a ranch house, all his own. And the woman who turned to him in the kitchen, face flushed with heat and eyes alight with love, wore a crown of red-gold curls.

Arabella dreamed, too, but she did not dream of David. She dreamed, instead, of castles, jewels, and kings.

Chapter 9

Late one Saturday night in spring, Dan Tallant rode into Magoffinville. The cantinas were going full blast. And across the Rio, El Paso del Norte and its sister communities, Ysleta and Socorro, seemed a twinkling string of lights that reflected the stars in the night sky.

Travel-weary, dusty, covered with a few weeks' growth of beard, Tallant dismounted stiffly before a small, shabby Mexican casa. Reaching into his saddlebag, he removed an oilskin-covered packet of papers and thrust it inside his shirt. Then he knocked at the warped paintless door.

The grizzled Mexican gentleman who opened the door gave a shout of delight. *"Hola! Hola! Señor Dan! Bienvenido a esta casa!"*

Turning, Miguel Chavez called the rest of his family, "Abuela! Mamacita! Maria, Consuela, Trini, Jose—"

The room filled with people, newly wakened from sleep, all uttering cries of welcome. The youngest child, born since Dan's last visit, clung to his father's legs, hiding his face, shyly.

Dan went from one to the other, pausing before the little white-haired grandmother the longest as she reached to touch his cheek. *"Dios nos ha oido,"* she said, slowly, *"Eres una benedicion de Dios!"* The words were like a blessing.

Then he moved to Trini, the oldest son. There was a new gruffness to the boy's voice as he asked, *"Qué tal?"*

"Very well," Dan smiled. "Everything is going very well with me." He turned to Maria. In these last years, the girl had become a woman. A lovely one at that.

100

"Bienvenido," she said, shyly. *"Qué gusto verle."* How nice to see you—but she had chosen the formal version. Dan smiled to himself. So that was how it was going to be now!

"Come now," he said, "don't tell me you've forgotten how to speak my language!"

"No, Señor Dan." She ducked her head, unable to meet his laughing eyes.

A short time later, Dan scrubbed his lean, brown body in a washtub in the shed. His return to this friendly house had created a fiesta-like atmosphere. At that moment, the women of the household were preparing a feast of enchiladas, frijoles, and empanadas, to be washed down with cerveza. The men would bring out their guitars, invite the neighbors in, and want to dance all night.

He frowned. He would have to leave the festivities for a little while. He hoped it would not dampen his friends' spirits. But he must deliver the packet and discover when his contact would arrive with his new instructions. He hoped it would not be long. Maria's eyes were soft when they rested on him, and he could afford no involvement. Yet he could not hurt her. This family had been too kind to him in the past.

He changed into his other traveling clothes. Those he had worn would be washed and mended by loving hands. Then, trim in his faded Levi's, the oilskin packet thrust beneath a worn plaid shirt, he returned to the casa.

After an hour or two, he left, promising to return as soon as he could. They did not question him. That was another thing he liked about these people. They had always taken him just as he was.

After his long grueling ride on horseback, Tallant preferred to walk, savoring the night air with its mingled scents of blossoms and human habitation. Reaching the hard-packed road that fronted the cantina section of Magoffinville, he paused, listening to the laughter and noise that emanated from the batwing doors. It was like coming home. He grinned to himself.

101

Katie was in for a surprise!

He stepped inside the cantina and looked around for a teasing, freckled face, a tomboy grin. His eyes searched the room, recognizing Maggie and Carmen; there was a dark-haired new girl in red whom a chortling, tipsy cowboy had just tumbled into his lap. His gaze moved on, then returned. There was something about the new girl that tugged at his memory, something hauntingly familiar. . . .

Warding off the cowhand with a hug, Tamsen stood up and moved across the room in a graceful, side-stepping dance that enabled her to escape outstretched hands. She reached the guitarist's side and whispered something in his ear. He struck up a lively tune. It was a funny, bawdy little melody, and Tamsen made the most of it. Her husky voice broke, tantalizingly, resumed again, and her eyes grew slumbrous and dreamy.

Then, all at once, they opened wide. She stopped dead in mid-movement as she saw Dan Tallant's face. She seemed to shrink. A groan ran through the audience, a ripple of disapproval.

I've got to go on, she thought. *I've got to!*

She completed her act, casting desperate eyes at the closed door that led to Nell's room. If only the big woman would appear! Dusty! Maybe, if she danced in that direction, she could suddenly fling the door wide, go through it and out into the courtyard.

But as the last chords ended, a hard hand closed over her arm. She felt all of her strength leave her at Dan Tallant's touch.

"We're going to have a little talk." His tone was mild, but she knew it was deceptively so.

"Let me go," she whispered, fiercely. "One word from me, and this crowd will tear you to pieces!"

"And one word from me, and you'll be prosecuted as a horse thief. Do you know what that means in this part of the country? It means your life won't be worth a plugged nickel!"

Tamsen closed her eyes weakly. "All right, say what you have to say."

"Not here." He drew her toward the stairs. "Smile," he hissed. "Smile, damn you! Look like you're coming of your own free will. I'm sure you've done it many times!"

Tamsen smiled, inclining her head to one customer, giving a wave of a hand to another. On the steps, she felt many eyes follow her. Poppy Franklin might have been considered only a singer and entertainer before, but this gave the lie to it. From now on, she'd be considered fair game.

Dan Tallant seemed to know his way about. Opening a door, he bowed as he ushered her inside. Then, closing it behind him, he shoved her roughly into the room.

"First, where are your sisters?" he asked, calmly, though his mind was seething. "I hope you aren't going to tell me they work here, too!"

Tamsen moved behind the single straight chair, as if it offered protection against the scorn in his eyes. She held tightly to the back of it, her knuckles white.

"You've made a mistake," she said, her chin high. "I—I'm Poppy Franklin. I—I don't know what you're talking about. Perhaps, if you would explain—"

He jerked the chair from her grasp and set it behind him. "Stealing's one thing," he said, brusquely. "Lying's worse. All right, I'll find them. And when I do—"

"Please," Tamsen said, "oh, please!" She turned away from him, her hands to her face.

Dan waited, fighting the urge to soften, to relent. Damn it, the girl looked so small, so helpless. But he had reason to know better. She was willful, stubborn, and ornery as a mule. How many nights he had dreamed of her! Of the way she had stood over the fire on the trail, her dark hair hanging down. Despite the fact that she'd stolen his horses, he'd longed to find her to make sure she and her sisters were safe and cared for. His conscience had bothered him, and that was something rare for Dan Tallant. Rare and most uncomfortable. He'd had an idea the McLeod girls were something special, different from other women he'd known. Ladies. And now, to find Tamsen like this!

"Tamsen!" He took a step toward her, and she turned to face him, back to the wall, fingers spread to support herself.

"All right," she said flatly, "I lied. But I'm Poppy Franklin—the name goes with the job. Arabella and Em don't know what I'm doing. It was the only work I could find. If you tell them, I'll kill you."

He struggled against a wave of pity. Tamsen McLeod wasn't one to do anything she didn't want to do. He looked at her now, the skirt of the velvet gown fallen back, one gartered leg bared almost to the thigh. His face hardened. "You mean you don't want me to tell them and spoil your fun? Is that it?"

She met his blazing eyes with an effort. "No, you're wrong."

"Am I? You've found your niche, haven't you? All that high and mighty talk! You're nothing but a common—"

He stopped. A common *what?*

Tamsen looked about her at the sordid room. The bed had been used recently and was still rumpled. The lamp, its dim globe sooted, made flickering shadows in the room. At the window, a crooked shade hung raggedly across it.

She knew what he thought. "Let me explain—"

"Explain! Let's start with an explanation about horses! Tell me how you started your career of crime! And maybe you'd like to know how you made a laughingstock out of me! In addition to costing me thousands of dollars out of my own pocket! The money that went into buying those horses was not mine!"

"That's not true," she lashed at him. "We only got three hundred for the lot!" Then she caught herself. The words were an admission of guilt, and she could not take them back.

"Of course you did." His face was weary. "What did you expect? I imagine you dealt with some untrustworthy character, someone who promised to take them across the border and let them disappear into Mexico. Am I right?"

Tamsen was silent.

Tallant felt a sudden, unreasoning fury at the thought of those magnificent beasts given into alien hands, mistreated, perhaps, uncared for. Stolen so the girl could come here, to *this*.

"I offered you those horses once—for a price." His lip curled. "Now what I offered to trade for is used merchandise. Still, I suppose something is better than nothing. It isn't as though it's anything you'd miss."

The wall was behind her. Tallant was between her and the door. "I'll pay you," she blurted. "It will take a while, but—"

"You put a high price on your services. I'm leaving before long. You couldn't handle *that* many men. And I know better than to trust you. I'd better cut my losses while I can."

He came toward her, laughing, the devil in his eyes.

She drew her deadly little gun.

He laughed again. "What you have to protect, I cannot imagine," he mocked. "I could take that away from you, but it isn't worth it. You might get hurt. I'm going —this time. But I'll be paid for those horses. And at my price. And maybe I'll just collect when you least expect it!"

The pistol wavered as she thought of the trouble Dan Tallant might cause her. He could go to Arab, to Em, with the truth about her occupation, expose her as an entertainer in a cantina—and God knows what else, the way the man's mind worked!

As if sensing her thoughts, he said, "I'm not going tattling to your sisters, if you're worrying about that. Why should I cause them grief? But I'll be around. You can count on that!"

He left the room, and while she stood, indecisively wondering whether to follow, she heard his voice raised outside.

"Katie! Katie Ryan, darlin'!" He affected a fake brogue, but behind it, she could hear the tone of pure delight with which he greeted the girl. "Sure, an' ye're the lass I've come here a-searchin' for!"

Tamsen stepped out on the balcony in time to see Dan and Katie enter the next bedroom.

Dan Tallant knew Katie. He had been here before! It was only an accident that he'd found Tamsen herself. For some reason, the thought that he had not been seeking her rankled.

Dan and Katie! Two of a kind!

A hand touched her arm as she descended the stairs. Tamsen turned to look into the hot eyes of Pete Martinez. His mouth curved in a humorless smile as he said, "So our little Poppy *does* go upstairs!"

Tamsen blushed, but said, coolly, "It was a personal matter. We had something to discuss. We went there for —privacy."

The man nodded. "I like privacy. I can understand that, sí. We will have our little talk in privacy, one night, sí? And you do like your work, no?"

She left him standing there and went down to face the knowing expressions of more than a hundred men.

The next day was Sunday. At church services, the bulky Major Arbuthnot pushed into the McLeod sisters' pew. Of late, he had taken to seating himself beside Em, holding her hymn book for her, adding his loud, flat voice to the singing.

During a hymn, a latecomer entered the church, and Tamsen would have kept her eyes on her book, had it not been for Em. Her sister gave a sudden gasp, her hand closing over Tamsen's.

"Look!" she whispered. "Oh, Tamsen! Look who's here!"

Tamsen didn't need to turn to know who the intruder was. Dan Tallant, in his faded trail clothes, had taken a seat at the rear of the church.

After services, Em rushed to greet him, despite Tamsen's staying hand. "If it weren't for you, we wouldn't be here," she said, softly. "You have no idea how we appreciated the loan of your horses!"

"Anything to oblige a lady." He bowed to Tamsen, sardonically. And when Em and Arabella pressed him

106

to accompany them home for dinner, though Tamsen pointed out that they already had one guest, Major Arbuthnot, Tallant accepted.

It was a miserable afternoon. The blustery Major, sensing he had competition, kept up a constant flow of pompous conversation. Dan, in contrast, said very little. He lounged easily, completely relaxed, feigning attention to the Major's words.

He's laughing at the man, Tamsen thought, fuming, It isn't fair! Just because the Major isn't the masculine type! As Dan Tallant is, her traitorous mind continued, lean and good-looking. . . .

"More tea, Major Arbuthnot?" Tamsen managed to interrupt her thoughts and the officer's spate of words with the question. Then she turned to Tallant.

"How long do you intend to remain in Magoffinville?" she asked, politely.

He grinned at her, stretching out his long legs as though he planned to remain right in this spot forever. "Until I've got what I came for," he said.

Tamsen managed, somehow, not to spill hot tea in the Major's immaculate lap.

When the gentlemen took their leave at last, Em and Arabella pressured Tallant to return. His answer was directed straight at Tamsen.

"You haven't seen the last of me," he promised. "Not yet."

Chapter 10

Em flipped a dustcloth across the top of the old table Tamsen had found somewhere. Not that it mattered. The thing was covered with mars and stains, and circles of white had permanently marked the finish. Frowning a little, Em studied the table, thinking as she had so often before, that it must have been used in a saloon to have been damaged in this manner.

Stains were preferable to dust, she supposed. Tamsen had also purchased window glass, which Dusty had installed rather haphazardly, but the dust seemed to seep perpetually around the panes, to shale from the walls, to rise from the cracked adobe floor.

Em couldn't help thinking of home—of the parlor, always shining, of the kitchen with a pump installed right by the big metal sink.

But it did no good to think back. This was their life now, and one must make the best of it. The best, to Em, would be to win the battle against dust.

Feeling hot and sticky, she hastily rolled her sleeves down and tidied her hair at the sound of approaching horses' hooves. She wondered who it could be. It was a Sunday. There was a traveling evangelist in town, and he was holding almost continuous meetings. Today the ladies were serving a lunch between the morning service and an afternoon prayer meeting.

Em had begged off, pleading illness. She felt smothered by the Major's constant attentions, gallant though he was. It would be so pleasant to have a Sunday afternoon without tension. It was clear that the Major and Dan Tallant did not like each other, and Tamsen had seemed on the ragged edge when they arrived after church each Sabbath day to pay their respects.

The sound of hoofbeats stopped before her door. Em pulled off her apron and answered the commanding knock. Perhaps Dan Tallant, she thought. It would be nice to have a conversation with him, uninterrupted.

But it was Major Arbuthnot who greeted her with a smile. "Dear lady!" He bent above her extended hand. Reluctantly, she asked him in, his bulk seeming to fill the shabby room.

"I hope you do not think it unseemly for me to appear here when you're alone," he blustered. "I spoke to your sister, and she assured me that it would be quite all right. After all, I am of a respectable age—a widower. And you are a well-bred young lady. Our relationship has been of the purest . . ."

Then, shut up! Em thought frantically, her cheeks pink. She was angry. Angry at the man for his presumption in coming here when she was alone, angry at Tamsen for encouraging his attentions.

"Do come in," she said, flustered. "I was just making myself a cup of tea."

"A panacea for all ailments," he said, judiciously, "as well as filling a social need. How pleasant it is to chat over a cup—especially in the presence of a gracious lady. To be able to come forth with one's innermost feelings—"

Em fought the desire to shock him with a rude word, or to giggle.

"Please sit down," she said demurely. Pouring hot water from the kettle at the stove, she filled the teapot and set out cups.

He leaned forward, knees spread to allow room for his paunch, gripping the cup she handed him as if it were a lifeline. "It's so good to be here without that chap Tallant," he said, explosively. "I can't imagine what you people see in the man. He's obviously a low type."

"He's been very kind to us. We would have been stranded on the trail had it not been for his assistance,"

Em rebuked the Major, and he was crestfallen, but only for a moment.

"It's just that he seems to have no restraint in the presence of ladies," he explained. "Last Sunday afternoon, for instance. Bringing that notorious Franklin woman into the conversation! Your sister went white! It was certainly not a topic for a social gathering."

Em, too, had noted Tamsen's reaction. "I'm sure he meant no harm," she murmured.

"Deliberate or not, it was an insult to the flower of womanhood, which is what I regard you and your sisters to be. You deserve a better life than this, Miss Emmeline. Your graces would suit a Colonel's home! And, may I say, that is a rank I am soon to attain. A man of my position needs a wife of breeding and charm—"

He set down his cup and leaned toward her, his round, blue eyes pleading. "I'm asking you to consider what I'm saying, Miss Emmeline. I am somewhat older than you, it is true, yet I can offer you a better life. I am a man of high moral character, honesty, integrity—"

Oh, Lord, Em thought numbly. This is a proposal of marriage, and I cannot—cannot!

"And as far as your sisters are concerned, I will offer them a good home. Protect them, physically and financially. Miss Tamsen need no longer work at menial employment. And for young Arabella, perhaps a good school in the east—"

An answer to a prayer, Em thought. He is a good man, lacking in humor, perhaps, but sincere. He would keep to his part of the bargain, but could she?

At her hesitation, he lunged to his feet, coming toward her. His scent of horses, of leather, and of masculinity made her a little faint. The step she took backwards was involuntary. How could she marry him, if she could not bear his touch?

"Please," she said, "I am flattered by your proposal, but I must refuse. It is too soon—"

"Then I will hope."

"No," Em said, "you don't understand—"

"But I do! I have perhaps been premature in pressing

110

my suit. In the military life, being around men"—His chest swelled—"one tends to forget the delicate sensibilities of young girls such as you. I shall try to contain my ardor and progress more slowly. I plead your forgiveness. And now I must go. Next Sunday?"

When the door closed behind him, Em sank into a chair. What a great, bumbling idiot the man was! No, she was the idiot. For she had just thrown away a good life, not only for herself, but for Tamsen and Arab. These last weeks had been wearing on Tamsen. Anyone could see that! And Arab needed an education, as well as a fatherly man's guiding hand. Yet she had refused all that.

Of course, he had not taken her answer as final. There would be another opportunity. But in her heart she knew that no matter how many times he asked, her answer would be the same.

Tamsen and Arab returned from the prayer meeting, both in high spirits. Both kept up a constant chatter. Tamsen described the evangelist as a very good man. He, Reverend Smythe, and his wife were on their way to San Francisco, when they finished two weeks of services here. There they planned to establish a girl's school, teaching ladylike accomplishments along with religion. Such a fine man! Full of inspiration!

"I thought," said Arab, wickedly, "he was full of nonsense."

Later, as they were doing up the dishes, Tamsen questioned Em. "You didn't say anything about your day. I thought perhaps you'd had company."

"I did," Em told her shortly.

Tamsen worked in silence for a moment, drying a cup too carefully, placing it on a shelf. "Do—do you have anything you want to tell me? I had a notion he was going to ask—"

"He did."

Tamsen whirled. The expression on Em's face told her what she wanted to know. She burst into tears.

Tears of happiness, she had assured Em. But as she went mechanically through her songs the next night, she knew that she'd lied. She'd been at her wits' end, lately, with Pete Martinez's eyes following her every movement. In order to keep her job, she was going to have to meet his demands, and soon. The money she'd been taking home wasn't quite meeting the family's needs. And Arab was up to something. She wasn't sure what, but the girl had seemed different lately. She was growing up. Yesterday, Arab had let slip that Dan Tallant had been dropping by occasionally in her absence—to visit Em.

Dan Tallant, who was upstairs now with Katie.

Tamsen left the floor to be confronted by the cantina owner.

Holding her eyes with his own, he said, "Didn't do so good tonight. Got any problems?"

She shook her head.

"Girl in here a while ago. Spanish dancer. Lots of fire. Said she needed a job pretty bad. Willing to go upstairs." He smiled, that cold smile with no humor behind it that chilled her blood. "Told her I had a girl. You got any problems, you talk to me, sí?"

"I will," she whispered. "Yes, thank you. I will."

When he had gone, she slipped into Nell's small room. The big woman looked at her, wordlessly, and waved her to a chair. Leaning back, Nell took a black cheroot from her desk and spent some time lighting it. Then she fixed her small black eyes on Tamsen.

"Pete Martinez?"

Tamsen nodded.

"Sonavabitch!"

"I—I agree," Tamsen said, twisting her hands in her lap. "I—don't know what to do."

"If you was a smart girl, you'd go upstairs. Don't cost nothin'. But you ain't smart."

"I guess I'm not." Tamsen's eyes welled with tears. "I don't know what to do. I have to keep this job. I have two sisters. If I didn't have an income, we'd starve—"

"Oh, hell," Nell growled, her own eyes suspiciously wet, "don't blubber on me! Did the best I could. Martinez won this joint offa me a couple years back. He's a tinhorn gambler, with nothin' betwixt his gawdamn ears. If I hadn't stayed on to run things, he'd be flat-assed busted! I told him if you went, I went, too. Didn't make no difference! He's a bull-headed bastard, mean as they come—"

The meaning of the woman's words penetrated Tamsen's mind. Nell had tried to help her. Jeopardized her own position in order to do so.

"Oh, Nell," she wailed, rounding the desk, throwing her arms around the woman's neck. "Oh, Nell!"

"Hell, honey," Nell said, blinking her eyes rapidly and patting Tamsen clumsily on the back, "I ain't done a gawdamn thing. You still gotcher problem. Now, quit blubberin' down my neck. We'll think of something!"

Chapter 11

Arabella was irritated. Today, David was waiting for her just over the hill, but Tamsen had returned from work cross and restless. Normally, Tamsen breakfasted, then took her place in the one bed they owned, still warm from Arab's and Em's bodies. But this morning, she had paced the floor, worrying at everything, finally exploding when Arabella innocently remarked at a spot high on her cheek that looked suspiciously like rouge.

"It's dye," Tamsen snapped. "From the trim on a dress I was stitching. And if you have nothing better to do than gawk at *me*, why don't you help Em with the dishes?"

Now, at last, Tamsen was abed and—Arab hoped—sleeping. Hanging the dishtowel on a line that ran from the house to the shed, Arab checked the kitchen window with a wary eye, then began to run.

Once out of sight, her footsteps slowed as she saw David waiting in the distance. Of late, he had become more difficult to manage, importunate in his demands. And he had altered his goals to suit hers, in a desperate attempt to win her over.

There was gold in California, just lying there for the taking. He'd heard the tales of its plentitude from men who had stopped by his father's ranch on their way west. With gold, one might provide lovely gowns and a castle to live in for the girl he loved. He intended to run away from home, taking Arab with him, and make their fortune.

When they were together, it sounded reasonable. They would sit for hours, spinning dreams of the riches

114

they would find and how they would spend it. It was only at home, at night, lying wakeful beside the sleeping Em, that Arab began to doubt.

Could they find their fortune? Did she love David enough to go with him? She did not know. At first, it had only been fun to flirt, to know she had a power over the sixteen-year-old son of the area's prominent rancher. But the magic of the desert spring had touched them both. Things were beginning to get a bit out of control, and Arab didn't know how to extricate herself—or whether she wanted to.

Hot, sticky, and a little cross, Arab walked toward the place where David waited. He held out his arms to her, but she did not go into them. Instead, she took his hand, tugging a little to indicate she wished to walk.

"I was afraid you wouldn't come. Oh, Arab, you're so beautiful."

"Well, *some* of us have work to do," she said crossly. "And I'm not beautiful!" She looked down at her gown, still damp from spilled dishwater. "You're just saying that." But his flattering words had reached her. She widened green eyes at him and fluttered her lashes.

"You know I mean it," he said, putting his arms around her. As she drew away, smiling up at him, he reached out to finger a red-gold curl. "You have the prettiest hair," he said, reverently. And as she glowed, he said, "We had a little bull calf, born last week, with hair almost the same color."

Arab froze. In that instant, instead of a handsome lover, she saw a callow youth, his shirt sweat-stained, his face wreathed in a rather foolish grin. The David of her dreams was courtly, bearing gifts, murmuring gentlemanly compliments.

Bull calf, indeed!

"I have to go home," she said, sullenly. As he put out a hand to detain her, his face puzzled, she whirled and began to run. He followed after.

"Arab, what's the matter? Did I say something wrong? Honey—"

He almost caught her, and she veered, running

115

through a rock strewn area, hearing him swear as he stumbled. Then she, too, caught her toe on a rock and went down. Clambering up, she stopped, unable to move, her eyes fixed on the horror that lay coiled before her.

"Don't move, Arab," David's voice sounded behind her. "For God's sake, don't move!"

She remained immobile, staring in blind, hypnotic fear at the creature with its flat, vicious head, its slitted eyes, its flickering tongue.

And then a rock descended on its head and the rest of the body writhed and lashed in death throes. Arab screamed as the slimy thing whipped across her hand.

David scooped her up and carried her to a grassy area where he set her down gently.

"David," she whimpered, "oh, David!"

He knelt beside her, holding the shuddering body, telling her that it was over now, she was safe, that he would take care of her.

As the shuddering subsided, a new emotion took its place. David had become a heroic figure. He had saved her life at the risk of his own. She turned to him, passionately, drawing him down to her. "I belong to you, David—"

Their innocent affair had broken its bonds, moving from kissing to frantic exploration. Dazed with the depth of their feelings, drunk with the sun and the warm, whispering grass, the two forgot their surroundings. In all the world, they were in love and alone. . . .

At the house, Em sighed in exasperation. Arab was to have filled the water pail, and she was gone. Em needed the water now, if she were to dampen down the adobe floors to keep down the dust, peel and wash potatoes for their evening meal. Taking up the pail, she went outside to the well and lowered the bucket, teeth on edge at the creaking of the windlass. Where could Arabella *be*?

She swept the horizon with a worried glance. A cloud of dust announced an approaching carriage.

Oh, no! she thought. Someone coming here! And just

116

when Tamsen had finally gotten to sleep. Em was so worried about her sister. Her own cough was much improved. Perhaps they could change places for a while; she, too was adept with a needle.

Frowning into the sun, Em saw the carriage stop out on the road and wondered why. But no matter, it might give her time to pick up a little in the house. She spilled the water from the bucket into her pail and hurried into the adobe.

A shouting melee erupted when the carriage stopped before the house. Em heard the deep angry tones of a man, the shriller notes of a woman, and above it all, Arabella's voice shrieked with outraged fury. She rushed to the door, opening it on an impossible scene. Arab struggled in the arms of a man. A woman was helping him drag the girl toward the house.

"Reverend Smythe!" Em recognized the irate gentleman. "Mrs. Smythe! Arab! What in the world?"

"We were coming to call," said the choleric evangelist, "and we found this young girl together with a man! They were," his voice lowered to a scandalized whisper, "indulging in fornication."

"We were not!" Arab shrilled. "We were only kissing! And it's none of his business!"

"The Lord's business is always mine!" the Reverend snapped. " *'Submit yourselves therefore unto God. Resist the devil and he will flee from you. James 4:7'.* And the devil did flee, did he not? Leaving you to face God's wrath, alone!"

David had fled. Arab was terrified, angry—and heartsick. Why hadn't he stayed? Stood up to these people, told them that they were going to be married? Instead, he had left her to be bullied, preached at, dragged home like a naughty child! Eyes blazing, cheeks tearstained and smudged, she jerked away from Reverend Smythe's grasp as he shoved her into the doorway.

"Leave me alone!"

"Oh, Arab!" Em was stricken. "Arab, how *could* you!"

"I didn't!" Arabella said sullenly.

117

"Then we are to doubt a minister's word?" Tamsen spoke from the doorway, her face white. "I'm afraid your appearance is against you!"

Arabella looked down. Her clothing was disarranged. She put a hand to her hair, which was tumbled and contained bits of dried weeds. "There was a snake," she began.

"And he told you to eat the apple, I suppose." Tamsen's voice was cold with rage. "Who was the man?"

Arabella's mouth closed tight. Nobody believed her, anyway. Let them think what they would! If she told them it was David, they'd probably try to make him marry her. And she had no intention of being forced into something like that! Especially since he'd run away. And nothing had happened. It might have, she thought, a little guiltily, but it didn't!

Banished to the other room to set herself to rights, Arabella listened to them murmuring about her and simmered with a righteous anger.

Em had dissolved into tears. Reverend Smythe set about comforting her as Tamsen prepared tea to restore their spirits. *Do not be overcome by evil,*" he said gently, " '*but overcome evil with good. Corinthians 10:13'.*"

"It's the creed we live by," his wife said. "There's so much evil in this world, waiting for girls who are young and unprotected. That's why we're beginning our school. To guide the feet of young ladies in the paths of right-eousness. In San Francisco, we hope to—"

"I wish to God it were here," Tamsen burst out. "Oh, Reverend Smythe, what can we do? She's not a bad girl! Truly, she isn't! But I'm so afraid!"

" '*As far as the east is from the west, so far does he remove our transgressions from us. Psalms 103:12'*," the minister said, reflectively. "There is always an answer to be found in God's word. I believe I have a solution for you."

They listened to his words, Tamsen with reluctant hope, Em with a growing unease. Then the minister rose, beckoning to his wife.

118

"We must leave them alone in their trouble. Come, Fanny." To Tamsen he said: "Talk to the girl. If she does not see the light, then we will be happy to take her and enroll her as the first pupil in our school for young ladies. Unfortunately, you must decide in haste. Our wagon leaves on the morrow with a westbound train."

"How much," Tamsen asked, "did you say it would take for her expenses?"

After they had gone, Em looked at Tamsen as if she were a stranger. "You can't be considering this," she said. "You wouldn't send Arab with those people!"

"The man's a minister. And I don't know what to do, Em! We don't seem to be able to handle her."

Em's eyes filled with tears, and Tamsen left her to go to Arabella. The girl was curled on her bed, face to the wall. Arab refused to meet her sister's eyes. Her fear had left her. Now she was angry. Why didn't anybody believe her? Part of what that man said had been lies!

"Who were you with, Arab? You've got to tell me. Just his name, that's all."

Arabella remained stubbornly silent as Tamsen hammered at her with the same question. And at last she snapped, "Maybe I don't know his name. Maybe he's just one of many. Maybe I do this all the time."

Tamsen raised one hand, then dropped it. She had never slapped her sister, but her palm itched to do it now. Turning to Em, who stood pale and oddly shrunken in the doorway, Tamsen said, "Sort out her things. We'll pack them in the morning."

There still remained the matter of money. Expenses for the journey. School fees. And the only avenue of help was Nell. Tamsen already owed Nell a great deal, which she'd been paying off a little at a time. Now she must ask for more. But when she explained her problem, Nell counted out the money, without comment.

Tamsen drove Arabella to the spot where the small wagon train was gathered the next morning. Em remained at home, weak from crying. Arab had shed no tears. Tamsen might have relented if she had. Stony-faced, Arab had kissed Em goodbye and accompanied Tamsen without comment.

She sat stiffly on the seat of the buggy, not answering as Tamsen tried to justify sending her along with Reverend and Mrs. Smythe. "I don't want you to go," Tamsen said earnestly. "But it's best for you. Unless you want to tell us the truth and promise it won't happen again."

Arab was silent.

When they reached the wagon area, Tamsen felt a qualm at the sight of billowing canvas. She thought of the tales that sifted back about the dangers of the trail, the heat of the desert this train would cross. And the train was so small, only ten wagons. If the minister would only wait for one of greater size. If only Arabella would break her silence, turn to her as she would have in the old days! Throw her arms about her with tearful promises that she would behave!

She wouldn't be able to believe her, Tamsen thought wearily. But neither would she be able to send her away.

She stopped a man and asked for directions. He pointed to the Smythe wagon, and they drove on. Then everything became a blur to Tamsen. Arabella, her face still expressionless, was handed down and taken to the wagon by the minister's wife. Tamsen counted the money into Reverend Smythe's hand.

"It's all there. And at the beginning of next year, I'll send more. Write to me as soon as you get to San Francisco. Tell me how she's getting along; that you arrived safely."

He patted her shoulder consolingly. " *'The Name of the Lord is a strong tower; the righteous man runs into it and is safe. Proverbs 18:10'*," the minister said. "Have no fear. I will watch over her as if she were my own."

There was nothing to do but return home, alone. The memory of Arab's white face burned in her mind. She had done the right thing. Arab had been slipping from control for a long time. And if the child discovered Tamsen's occupation, then there would be no control at all. Yet, why this struggle with her conscience?

At home, Em was also having an attack of conscience. If she had married Major Arbuthnot, pretended to return his affections, this might not have happened. But because she'd thought, selfishly, only of her own wants and needs, Arab was traveling west in the company of strangers. The decision to send the girl away was wrong. Wrong! Dusty thought so, too. He'd stated his beliefs and retired to the shed with his bottle.

Em went through the motions of straightening the house. Everywhere there was some reminder of Arabella. A bit of green ribbon on the floor. A pillow that was sodden from her tears in the night.

Please, God! Let Tamsen have a change of heart and bring Arab home.

Em's heart sank when her sister appeared alone, her eyes welling with fresh tears that she blinked away. Tonight it was Tamsen who needed Em.

Tamsen sank into a chair and burst into frenzied weeping. "Tell me I did the right thing, Em," she pleaded. "It seems so awful! Tell me it was right!"

Em sank to her knees, thinking how small Tamsen was, so small and so young to carry the burdens she'd carried for so long. Putting her fair cheek against Tamsen's tear-wet face, she said, "I don't know. I just don't know. But at least you had the courage to do something. Oh, Tam, I'm such a coward!"

The two sisters clung, weeping, together.

Much later, Tamsen rode into Magoffinville alone. Dusty had imbibed too freely and had to be left behind. It was just as well, for Tamsen now had a new worry. Em could not be left by herself at night. Suppose the Indians reappeared, or some strange drifter? And Em had always been afraid of the dark. Tamsen could understand that, tonight especially. The stammering yelping of coyotes, a flight of bats, the sudden swoop of a great horned owl, made her nervous and jumpy. Yet this evening was no different than any other. Dusty was only a small, whisky-sodden body, but he had been companionship. He had been *there*.

She would have to hire someone to stay with Em.

And she would have to find a way to pay Nell back. She drove the night sounds from her mind as she turned to calculating ways in which she might economize. There would be Arab's school fees to pay next year, too.

At the cantina, she turned her horse over to the young Mexican lad who would rub him down and feed him.

What would happen, she wondered, as she changed into the poppy-colored gown that was her trademark, if she lost her job? Somehow, she envied the girls who added to their income by going upstairs.

Chapter 12

Tamsen was always in the back of Dan Tallant's mind, though he refused to admit it. Instead, he wondered at his restlessness, at the fact that he'd changed from the man who'd always enjoyed a little innocent hell-raising. So when the family of Miguel Chavez urged him to go along to a wedding celebration one evening, with many sly comments coupling his name with Maria's, he declined.

It was because of Maria, he told himself. The girl, ripe for love, was ready to fall into his arms—with her family's approval. Dan was beginning to feel crowded. Maria's charms were compelling. At the celebration, where tequila and cerveza would flow freely, he was afraid he might succumb to those charms. It would be years before he could think of taking a wife, and Maria was *only* for marrying.

Dan begged off from attending the wedding, pleading business.

He did have business, but it had to wait until later when he would be just another man in a crowded cantina, going upstairs with Katie Ryan.

He thought of visiting Em while he waited. But since Tamsen sent Arab away with that preacher, Em hadn't been herself. She'd been sorrowful, unreachable. Even his promise to look for Arab when he got to San Francisco didn't seem to cheer her up. Dan Tallant had a healthy male fear of a woman's tears.

Stupid business, that, sending so young a girl away with strangers. He hadn't been able to figure it out. Probably it was all Tamsen's idea. If the girl stayed

123

around, she would eventually have found out about Tamsen's secret life and there would have been the devil to pay.

Em, on the other hand, wasn't likely to find out anything she didn't want to know. Where Tamsen was concerned, she was deaf, dumb, and blind!

His thoughts had gone back to Tamsen again! Irritated at himself, he closed his mind to her as he wandered around the dusty streets of Magoffinville. Then he discovered his feet had led him toward the cantina. He might as well go in. There was always a poker game or two that started early.

Inside, he looked for Katie. She had not yet come down. But a poker game was in progress, and he was surprised to see Tamsen seated in the midst of the regular players. Since she was in on the game, he'd sit this one out. He settled back at a table in a dimly lit corner of the bar to watch the gamblers.

Though he did not admit to it, he was really watching Tamsen.

Despite her air of confidence, almost arrogance, Tamsen was playing more than a card game, and Tallant could tell it. There was something about her that reminded him of a frightened animal at bay. A hint of desperation.

And no wonder. He looked at the pile of chips before the girl. Realizing its value, he let out a low, soundless whistle. It represented a huge amount of money. Through Em, he'd learned that the family was in rather dire straits. His eyes moved to Nell, who was sitting at the table, but not in on the game. She had a worried expression. Tallant wondered whether Tamsen was playing with borrowed money.

The notion persisted as he saw Tamsen rake in a pot, meeting Nell's eyes triumphantly. On the next hand, she bet a little wildly, but won again. The way she sat, a little hunched forward, her shoulders taut, told him that she was going for broke.

Tallant was not the only observer. Martinez, standing at the bar, had his somber gaze fixed on Tamsen. Dan

124

studied the man's face. Normally, the cantina owner abstained during business hours, but tonight it was obvious that he'd been drinking. Dan knew Martinez was a bad actor, sober, and he could be dangerous in his present condition.

As he watched, Martinez stiffened his shoulders and moved toward the poker table, his lurching gait under tight control. He sat down. "Deal me in," he said, "and up the ante." He spun a blue chip into the center of the table, and a lanky cowhand rose.

"Too rich for my blood," the cowboy said, good-naturedly. He went to the bar.

For a moment, Tamsen seemed to cringe. Then, raising her head, she said, "I'm in."

"Stud?"

"Stud."

A third player dealt. Face down, for Tamsen, for Martinez, himself. A deuce for Tamsen, king to Martinez, a ten to himself. A four for Tamsen, but the wrong color. Still, a possible straight. Eight to Martinez, and nothing showing. Jack to himself. And as the dealing progressed, Tamsen bet steadily. Nell's face was purple with repressed advice.

The last card dealt, Martinez showed a high card, nothing more. The dealer had folded. Tamsen flung blue chips recklessly into the middle of the table. Martinez called with an ace high, and Tamsen, trembling and triumphant, turned over her bottom card revealing another deuce. The winning pair.

Nell sank back with a huge sigh that nearly blew the cards from the table. "I'll be a ring-tailed cross-eyed son of a bitch," she boomed. "That either took guts or no brains, I dunno which!"

Tamsen raked in her chips.

But Tamsen's luck had ended. She lost the next pot, bet too cautiously on the following one, lost another . . . another. The third player dropped out as Martinez continued to up the ante, to raise on each bet. Tamsen's control had snapped. She took a small pot, annoyed at herself for her lack of confidence, and lost a stack of chips on the next round. She had to recoup, and she began betting wildly.

Dan, who had moved closer to the game, felt like dragging her from the table and shaking some sense into her. He could see that Nell, too, was concerned for the girl. The big woman's face was apoplectic.

Tamsen's blue chips were gone. There were only three remaining, two whites and one red. The girl looked as if she might faint.

"That's it," she said, her voice trembling. "I'm wiped out. No use in going on. It was a good game—"

Martinez's face split in a mirthless smile. "I don't like to quit while I'm ahead," he said. He pushed all his chips into the middle of the table. "One hand. What I've got against what you've got."

Tamsen looked at him, uncomprehending, and then at her remaining chips. "You mean—?"

He laughed and nodded toward the chips. "You can throw those in, too, if you want. Me, I'm betting this—against *you*."

Behind him, Dan Tallant made an angry sound deep in his throat, then checked the fist that had clenched. This was none of his affair! But Tamsen heard him. She looked over the cantina owner's head into Tallant's cold, disapproving eyes, observed his contempt, and set her jaw.

"What you're putting up isn't enough," she told Martinez. "If you want to play for high stakes, let's make them *high*!"

His eyes narrowed, glinting wickedly. "And what do you think I should put up on my side?"

"The cantina," Tamsen said, levelly. "That might make the game worthwhile."

Her request staggered Martinez. It had been an incredible windfall winning the cantina from that fat old fool, Nell, a couple of years ago. He had become a respectable business man, no longer an aimless drifter. He would be stupid to risk what he had in hand for the favors of this black-haired little *puta*. Yet, was there a risk? She was a novice. He had already proved he hadn't lost his old skills. Though he'd sworn off gambling since winning the cantina, the disease still burned like a fever in his blood.

"*Hola*," he shouted, "all of you! Gather round. You are going to see a *game*!" Then, turning to Tamsen, he said, "One hand? Winner takes what we agreed upon? Stud?"

"Yes," she said faintly. "Stud."

Nell got up, nearly overturning the table as her big bulk struggled from her chair. "You wait," she said flatly, tramping heavily toward the back room.

She returned with a fresh deck of cards. "Too much at stake," she said, her painted face grim. "A helluva lot. And you're a gawdamned cardsharp, Pete. The little lady gets the benefit of a fresh deck. And I deal."

The cantina owner's protests were lost in the hubbub of men's voices. The customers gathered around the table, engaged in conjecture, making side bets. At last he shrugged his assent. This night would be talked about for a long while. It would be good for business.

"Awright," Nell said, "I deal 'em as they come. Here's yer high card down, an t' hell with the deuces!"

Tamsen lifted her card and looked at it. A queen. Then she gripped the edge of the table with trembling hands. Dear God, she had to win! She dared not lose! She kept her head down, unable to meet Dan Tallant's scornful eyes.

"Trey to you," Nell said, "an' a ace to Pete. Lady to you, an' nothing showin'!"

Tamsen stared at the queen she'd been dealt, trying to hide the dawning hope in her eyes. A pair of queens, one hidden! She had a chance.

Her next card was a ten; Martinez drew a king. An eight for her, then another king for the man.

Two kings, both showing. She had lost. It was impossible for the last card—

"Here's the clincher," Nell said. "This here's what's gonna tell the tale."

Tamsen drew a ragged breath at the last card she was dealt. Seeing the five that Martinez drew, her eyes filled with tears. The cantina owner smirked as he displayed his hand. "Pair of queens showing," he said to Tamsen. "Pair of kings here. Can you beat that?"

The room was hushed, then the watchers expelled their breath in a concerted sigh as Tamsen turned over her last card.

A third queen.

There was pandemonium. Tamsen was lifted from her chair, whirled from one man to another, while the room echoed with shouts of admiration and congratulations. Pete Martinez tried to shout above the noise, to make himself heard.

"I got cheated," he yelled. "That fat old bitch stacked the deck! She ain't gonna get away with it!"

Except for a few hard looks that promised violence should he continue, no one paid any attention to the man. Finally, dispossessed of his shreds of respectability, Martinez slunk out into the night.

Later, as Tallant went upstairs with Katie, he paused to look down on the scene. The girl had got what she wanted, he thought, morosely. She was right where she wanted to be, queen of the cantina. Well, what the hell!

Turning to Katie, he swept her into the curve of his arm, hugging her until she squealed with the effort to breathe. "Katie, darlin'," he said, "you're a real lady. You know that?"

"Never wanted to be," grinned Katie, "but if it makes you act like that, I'll do my damnedest!"

Tamsen, who caught the exchange, felt an odd sense of loss. But her depression didn't last long.

That night, as she started home, still giddy with success, her head was filled with plans for building up the business. Things had fallen off lately, due to the gold rush farther west. The Silver Dollar up the street had closed; the Corrida was failing. But she would try to attract their remaining customers. Nude paintings behind the bar, renew the cantina's facade—

With a start, she realized she was alone in the predawn desert. Dusty was sleeping off a drunk in his shed at the adobe. Her horse shied at a shadow. She pulled him to a halt as he fought the reins. From somewhere behind her, she heard the sound of a horse's hooves. It stopped, and she put it down to imagination. Again!

Pete Martinez, she thought, terrified. Had the man, bent on vengeance, followed her? She'd forgotten him in the merriment of the evening.

Bending low over her horse's neck, she urged the animal to greater speed, slowing only when she reached the little adobe house. There she slipped from her saddle, her heart beating like a hammer, to listen again.

Nothing. Whoever had followed her was gone. The first gray light of dawn showed in the sky. She leaned against the animal, all of her strength leaving her along with the euphoria induced by her triumph of the night.

What if she had lost? Oh, God, what if she had lost!

In that same gray light, Dan Tallant was riding back toward town. He was angry at Tamsen. He had seen Tamsen leave the cantina alone and had followed at a distance. Pete Martinez might have seized the opportunity to get revenge, yet the girl had gone home by herself. The little fool!

Dan cursed the impulse that had induced him to follow her this night. What she did about her problems was not his affair. Still, he just might pay a call on Pete Martinez. Convince him that it would be healthy if he sought a change of scene. . . .

Chapter 13

Tamsen's first act, before retiring that morning, was to dispatch a now sober Dusty to Magoffinville's Mexican sector. He was to find a good capable woman to stay with Em. The little man was sorely troubled, wondering how the new help would be paid, yet not daring to question Tamsen in front of Em.

As soon as he got into town, he heard the story of the poker game. He returned, beaming, bringing a Mexican woman with him. "This is Carmela," he said, and the woman bobbed her head and smiled. "She only speaks Spanish."

She would not be much company for Em, Tamsen thought. But at least there would be no possibility of her disclosing Tamsen's identity at the cantina. It was just as well.

Dusty, however, was unable to contain his curiosity. His wispy hair stood on end, his mustache bristling. He could hardly wait until evening to hear the details of the previous night's game.

Tamsen described the game as they rode to the cantina, later. Dusty's watery blue eyes were teary with pride. "By Jove," he said, reverently, "I knew it! That's Nell for you! Stacking the deck for a friend!"

Tamsen reined in. "She didn't! It was played out fairly!"

Dusty chuckled. "You don't know Nell! She is a wizard with a deck! Do you think she would have allowed that Martinez chap to cheat you? That would not have been honest!"

At the cantina they found Nell, who handed Tamsen

the keys, wordlessly, and indicated the cleared desk in the back room.

"Tell me what the hell you want me to do," the woman grumbled. "I useta tend bar. Guess I can go back to the gawdamn job."

"I want you to keep on doing what you're doing," Tamsen said. "Nell—I need you."

The big woman flushed with pleasure, and Dusty beamed. Their expressions turned to concern, however, when Tamsen told them how she'd been followed home in those early hours. How she suspected Pete Martinez to be the culprit, angered, seeking revenge.

"He'd better keep his hands off my women," Dusty said, bristling. "Or he will have to answer to me, by Jove!"

Smiling to herself, Tamsen went to dress for the evening. Her feeling of euphoria returned as she remembered that this cantina was hers—all hers!

The evening crowd was swelled by the curious, who had heard of the previous night's happenings. All of them, former customers, new ones, drawn from surrounding bars, were loud in their praises for the girl who had put Pete Martinez down. In the course of conversation, Tamsen learned that Martinez had packed his things and left town early that morning.

She moved from person to person, accepting congratulations from each, light-headed with the knowledge that now all would go well for the McLeods. There would be money for Arab's education. She would buy Em the home she deserved. Now there was nothing to fear.

Beyond the shoulder of a well-wisher, she caught sight of Nell. The thing Dusty had said, about Nell stacking the deck, was fixed in her mind. It wasn't true, she thought. She didn't want it to be true. Yet Nell had stood by her, and she deserved some reward. The cash receipts, tonight, should more than pay her debt.

Escaping the crush of people in the cantina, Tamsen took Nell into the office, pressing money into her pudgy hands. Nell drew back in alarm.

131

"Hell," she boomed. "What's all this? I ain't done nothin' t' earn it. You trying to go busted in one night?"

"There'll be more where that came from. Lots more." Tamsen was sincere in her promise. For she meant to make the cantina pay. The upstairs rooms would be refurbished. She would buy paint, material for new gowns for the girls. She would have the finest place in all of Texas.

Nell, however, looked doubtful. "Better hang onto this dough, honey. I got all I need. Nothin' to blow it on."

Tamsen kissed the painted cheek. "New gowns, maybe," she suggested. "Make yourself beautiful for Dusty."

Nell's expression was wounded. "You don't think I look good enough? Allus figgered I was the best-dressed woman in Magoffinville. Hell, if you don't think I'm tony enough, well, you're the boss—"

"You are," Tamsen lied, trying to ignore the cerise gown the large woman was poured into. The darts beneath the bulging bosom had given way, and the side seams strained perilously. "I thought every woman liked new clothes."

"Well, speak for yerself," Nell growled. "Yer th' one that needs somethin' flashy. Gonna run this joint, you gotta look like somethin' th' cat didn't drag in."

"Oh, I'm going to, Nell," Tamsen laughed. "You just watch me! I'm going to!"

Going home in the gray dawn, Tamsen was surprised to find the ride had been so brief. All the way, she'd dreamed of beautiful dresses, silks, satins, velvets. She knew exactly how many gowns she wanted, the colors she would choose, and the way she would have them made.

When the adobe appeared before her, ugly, drab in the first light, she was conscience-stricken. She hadn't thought once of Em. There she must take things slowly. Find some way to explain the new riches that would be pouring in. Then there would be a house for Em

132

and new clothing. But first the cantina must be refurbished.

During the day, Tamsen did not get much rest. Her explanation to Em was that she'd been put in charge over a group of apprentice seamstresses—as a sort of supervisor—for the next week or two. Tamsen had to leave for the cantina in the early afternoon in order to get things done. Em had been appalled that Tamsen was expected to work so many hours, but the excuse also provided a way to explain the additional funds that would funnel into the McLeod household.

How she would manage to keep her secret from Em now, Tamsen didn't know. But she would take it one day at a time.

At her desk, she made lists. Dusty was dispatched to El Paso del Norte to find pictures for the cantina's shabby walls. He brought back a selection of too-pink, cherubic-looking nudes that Tamsen found rather repelling. But she had to admit that hung on the newly painted walls of the cantina, they seemed appropriate.

Katie and Maggie were delegated to purchase materials for curtains and for gowns. For several weeks, one of the upstairs rooms was closed to business. An exhausted Tamsen presided over it as the girls, rebellious at the loss of their sleeping hours, stitched away.

The draperies were hung in the cantina's main room, hiding the windows that were warped and crooked. A green taffeta dress was completed for Katie, complementing her Irish coloring. A tangerine for Carmen. Blue for Maggie. It was decided they would all appear in new gowns on the same night.

The girls fretted, for after their gowns were finished, Tamsen kept fussing over her own, shutting herself in the sewing room alone, delaying the big night. Katie voiced the opinion that Tamsen was going to try to outshine them. Guesses were made as to color and style, and just why she was spending so much time in there.

When Tamsen appeared, the girls were startled. Her gown was black velvet, unadorned. Over her arm, she carried a similar one, cut from the same bolt, for Nell.

Nell surveyed her dress, gargantuan in proportions, with a mixture of teary gratitude and some distrust. "Hell," she said finally, "you want me to look like a gawdamn crow?" Then, after a covert look at Tamsen's svelte appearance, she added, reluctantly, what was from her a compliment.

"Yer th' only girl I ever seen," she grumped, "that made black look flashy."

Trying on her own dress, she succumbed to Dusty's sheer admiration. "Jove," he said, feelingly, "you are a vision of loveliness."

Nell felt like a queen the night they all appeared in their new gowns. She had added a few pounds of jangling jewelry, but the effect was still impressive.

Tamsen's dress, cut low to reveal bared shoulders and half her rounded breasts, was set off by a necklace with a red stone that an admirer had given her. She knew she looked her best, but she was timorous. Would the rich gowns, a trifle more discreet in length, put off the clientele? They had seemed to like the gaudy, flamboyant atmosphere.

She need not have worried. Katie was swept upstairs in a trice. Nell nodded to Tamsen as Carmen followed. And awkward, flat-footed Maggie showed signs of being wooed—and won.

The place seemed quieter, with its new paint, the soft shaded lamps set on the scarred old tables; the men were more gentlemanly, better behaved.

Tamsen waited in the back room until the place began to fill. Then, moving out into the room, the full skirt of her gown sweeping like a train, the front artfully slit so that she need not show her legs unless she wished, she went to the center of the floor. She whispered to the man who played the guitar, but he shook his head at her request.

"It's all right," she said. "I do not need the music. Just a chord, to quiet them."

The music had its effect. All eyes turned to the figure in the dim room, a jewel blazing against her breast, dark hair falling to her waist. Hands clasped to her bosom, face raised, an oval of purity, she sang a song her father had sung to her as a child.

"*Black is the color of my true love's hair*," the husky voice rang out, pure and true. "*Her lips are something rosy fair*." The words broke a little, stirring her listeners with old forgotten emotions, mingled with newer ones of yearning and desire. "*The prettiest eyes and the daintiest hands. I love—the grass whereon she stands—*"

The old ballad touched the audience as the girl sang on. At its finish, someone broke the hush that followed with a snuffling sound. Tamsen posed, for a moment, her face upraised, knowing full well the image she created, glorying in it.

Dan Tallant, nursing a drink at a corner table, found himself the target of most uncomfortable sensations. Tamsen's song had touched something inside him. His eyes had misted. He blinked angrily, his hand tightening on his glass as he remembered the girl at her cookfire. He shifted uneasily as he sought to get his feelings under control.

Tamsen saw his face and knew that she'd moved him with her ballad. Eyes dancing with mischief, she launched into a new and naughty song. The applause that followed was loud and long.

In the course of it, Dan stood with his eyes fixed on Tamsen. Her heart thudded under his gaze. He looked as if he were considering approaching her, perhaps to drag her off the floor. He wouldn't dare! Her mouth was dry with fear and anticipation as she returned his steady scrutiny.

Then he turned, abruptly, to look toward the stairs. Katie was coming down, having finished with her first customer. Tallant walked to meet the girl and whispered something that made her look toward Tamsen and giggle. Then they went back up the stairs, together.

Tamsen's lips tightened. She'd managed to rid the cantina of some of its sordid atmosphere. Maybe she could stop that sort of thing and still attract a clientele.

She said as much to Nell, later, and the large woman

shook with laughter. Pushing Tamsen to a blurred mirror, she jeered, good-naturedly, "Look at you! You think yer so gawdamn much better than them girls? You just put a higher price on yerself, thass all! Men's men, an' women's women. Allus will be. So if I was you, I'd forget that kind of crap."

It didn't help when Dusty said, a little later, "You really give the place class, you know. Like Nell used to do."

She pushed their words from her mind. She had tasted the heady wine of beautiful things, of power. Her thoughts ranged far and wide, building air castles that would have put Arabella's to shame.

Day was already gilding the hills surrounding Magoffinville when Tamsen reached home. She found Em pacing restlessly about the little house.

Em was in a quandary. The evening before, Major Arbuthnot had come to call, in Tamsen's absence. Once more he had pressed his suit. Once more, she had refused. But after he had gone, she had not liked herself. If she had accepted him, earlier, Arabella would not be gone from them. Now it was too late. But she could not remain as she was, a drone, useless, dependent upon Tamsen's income. She had almost accepted him. And perhaps, one day, she would, having no other choice. Today, she intended to ride into Magoffinville, to find work of some kind.

Tamsen startled her by bursting into tears at her announcement. "You can't! It would spoil everything! Oh, Em! I'm doing so well! You're taking care of the house, making it nice to come home to! Please! For my sake!"

Em found herself reluctantly agreeing. What was it in Tamsen that made it impossible to cross her? Or was it something in Em, herself? Again, she thought as she had so many times before, I am a coward.

Oblivious to Carmela, Em's Mexican companion, who ate silently, Tamsen kept up a flow of excited conversation at the table. "We're going to have a big

136

house, Em! I'll be able to manage it before long. And then, we'll go get Arabella—and bring her home."

Now it was Em's turn to blink back tears. She'd been so worried about the girl! And last night, finally falling asleep after the Major left, she'd had an awful dream in which Arab was calling for help.

Chapter 14

Em's fears had some basis in fact.

During the ride when Tamsen had taken her to the minister and his wife, Arab had remained stony-faced and quiet. Yet inside herself, she had been in turmoil. She had wanted to cry out to Tamsen, tell her she was sorry. To beg her to turn around and take her home.

But apologies had always come hard to Arabella. And she didn't really believe that she would be sent away. Tamsen was only pretending this, to frighten her into telling that it was David she'd been seen with. David, who had betrayed her by running off.

Arab didn't intend to say his name ever again!

When they reached the preacher's wagon, Tamsen would relent. Arabella settled back to wait. She found it hard to swallow as they neared the area. Horses and oxen were hitched, the train ready to move. The scents and sounds brought back memories of their beginning journey. When they were all happy together.

Wasn't Tamsen going to say, "Arab, I'll give you one more chance?"

Arab's hands, hidden by the folds of her skirt, gripped the seat of the buggy. Her knuckles were white as Tamsen stopped to ask directions to the Smythe wagon. The man she questioned pointed, shouting above the sounds of wagons being readied for departure.

"Won't have much time to visit. We're moving out."

"My sister is accompanying the Smythes," Tamsen explained.

The gentleman looked at Arab, speculatively, and she

138

flushed, wondering if the Reverend had mentioned her escapade. It would be just like him to preach a sermon on her misdeeds!

Well, Tamsen had proved her point. Now they could go home.

But when the buggy moved, it was in the direction of the Smythe vehicle. With a stunned look at the sister who had betrayed her, Arab sat dazed, a smothering feeling in her chest, still unable to comprehend that she was truly being sent away.

Reverend Smythe, who was making some last-minute adjustments to his harness, left his team and came toward them in long strides. "God has led you to this decision," he said piously. Then, turning, "Fanny, the young lady is here. Make her welcome while I discuss terms with her sister."

He set Arab's things, hastily packed in the morning, on the ground, then extended a helping hand to the girl, who obeyed numbly. Then his wife led Arab to the wagon and ushered her inside.

It was still not real. This could not be happening. Arabella turned for one last bewildered look. Money was changing hands. Tamsen had no money. Was the preacher paying to take her? But he was not going to do it! In a minute, Tamsen would come, put her arms around her, and say, "I've changed my mind. We're going home."

Then Tamsen was gone. Arab watched the retreating buggy, her eyes huge as she realized that it had happened. She had been given into a stranger's hands.

Within an hour, the wagon train creaked out. Arab lay on a small, improvised pallet at the rear of the wagon, too confused to cry. The sounds were so familiar —the flapping of canvas, the rumbling of wheels, bringing back memories of those earlier days. Now she was alone. And it was all her fault. If only she could have been good, like Em. If only Papa were still alive. Papa! She put a fist to her mouth to shut off an involuntary keening sound.

The wagons jolted to a stop at the end of an interminable day. Arabella found herself being shaken, none too gently.

"You have duties, girl," the Reverend Smythe said, "the work of the Lord. It will fall to you to prepare the cookfire and the meal. The devil finds work for idle hands."

Arab knelt by the fire, chopping dead wood for kindling, mashing a thumb, getting splinters in her palms. As she did, she recalled how Tamsen had done this chore after leaving St. Louis, while she, Arab, blithely slipped off to flirt and to play. Her face grew hot at the thought.

"And is this your daughter?" Arab looked up to see the two men standing over her. Reverend Smythe had been asked the question by the wagon master, a kindly, fatherly-appearing man. Arab tried to smile.

"My ward," the minister said, pompously. "Poor creature. She was given into my care in Magoffinville, since her family could not control her. The devil enters into her from time to time. She is subject to fits, when he endeavors to speak through her lips. No," he raised a hand as the discomfited man took a backward step, "she is not dangerous. It is only that she makes lewd accusations, turning on her benefactors with obscene allegations."

Arabella was too stunned at his words to speak. The two men walked away, and she rose to her feet, staring after them. Reverend Smythe had lied! Why? Unless he had drawn some mistaken conclusion from his conversation with Tamsen. True, she had talked back to her sister, *sassing*, according to Tam. But the devil? Fits? Her face flamed. What must the wagon master think of her!

When darkness fell, hands blistered from woodcutting, one arm bearing a burn from a steaming kettle, Arab returned to her pallet. She was so exhausted she thought she would fall right to sleep. But from the adjoining bed, separated from hers only by a tarpaulin curtain, came the sounds of lovemaking; grunting

140

sounds that did not seem to fit the character of the man who had kept her on her knees in prayer for nearly an hour following the meal, nor the character of his shrill-tongued, pious wife.

Arab put her hands over her ears. Was that what marriage was like? It bore no resemblance to the emotions she'd felt on those sun-warmed enchanted days with David.

Tears slid down the girl's pale cheeks. Arab cried, for the first and the last time.

That had been weeks ago. Numbly, she had endured the days, seeing curious eyes turned toward her as she tended fires, cooked meals, knowing what the minds behind those eyes were thinking. This girl was devil-possessed, had fits of a kind. Reverend Smythe had done his work well.

After the evening meal, there would be the prayers, long and interminable, while the Reverend chastised her for thoughts she did not have. Then he would touch her —he'd begun this lately—his eyes sliding over her in a slimy sort of possessiveness that she'd found hard to believe, but had tried to ignore.

She could ignore it no longer, for today, Mrs. Smythe had instructed her in her new duties. She was to submit herself to the preacher in all things, since he was a servant to the Lord. It was God's will.

Arabella did not understand her meaning at first, then her horror slowly grew. The woman was suggesting that Arab share his bed! And she was serious. The woman's eyes had a fanatic look in them as she talked on, depicting a kind of religion that was warped and perverted in practice and intent.

I have to get away, Arab thought, in desperation. But in order to do so, she needed water, food, a horse. Surely, someone would help her!

Arabella found her chance later, when the minister and his wife went to another wagon to pray over a sick woman. She had ten minutes free from their guardianship. Not much time, but it would have to do.

The fire was burning, the kettle on. Arabella rose,

casting a hunted look around, then, gathering her skirts, ran toward the wagon master's fire. He had been told lies, as had the rest of the train, but at least, he had a kindly, sensible appearance.

Rounding the leader's wagon, Arab saw the man, his wife and children, busy at their preparations for the night. Even at a distance, she could see an odd expression cover his face as he caught sight of her. He came toward her and stood still, barring her way, as if he were protecting his family. His attitude halted her for a moment, then she blurted, desperately, "Please, you've got to help me!"

The rest of the story poured from her lips; how Reverend Smythe and his wife were evil people; that her sister had given her into their hands because she had made a mistake. And now they wanted her to do something wicked. "They want me," she faltered before the disbelief in the wagon master's eyes, "to—to sleep with him, as his wife does."

The man's face was a study of anger and withdrawal. Arab shrank before his look. His voice when he spoke was placating, the tone one would use with a small child —or one who is mentally disturbed.

"Reverend Smythe is a good man," he assured her. "He has discussed your problems with me, and I understand. Now, let's go back to your wagon, quietly. I'll send someone for him. It will be all right—"

She backed away from him, but he caught her wrists. "Run, Samuel," he called to one of his sons, "get Reverend Smythe! Quick! He's in the Johnstone wagon. Tell him his ward is having one of her spells and I need him."

The minister appeared, muttering prayers for assistance at the sight of the struggling girl. Together, the two men overpowered her and dragged her back to the Smythe wagon. There, the preacher, fumbling behind the pallet that served as Arab's bed, drew forth an odd contraption; a cuff, fastened to a chain. Arabella, frightened into immobility, was still in the wagon

142

master's arms as Reverend Smythe attached the cuff to her ankle.

"I don't like to use this means of quieting the girl," her guardian said, "but sometimes it is necessary. My thanks to you, sir, on behalf of this poor wretch. Now, there is nothing we can do for her but to pray—"

Left alone, Arabella tried frantically to remove the cuff. It was of no use. The chain was fastened to an iron ring in the wagon-bed. It, too, was unbreachable. She sat there forlornly, wishing she'd not gone for aid. It would have been better to run off into the desert to die.

She could smell the food from outside, hear it being dished up. Evidently, this night, she was to do without.

At last, exhausted, she fell asleep. She wakened to the sound of heavy breathing, to the feel of fumbling hands.

Reverend Smythe! What was he doing?

With a stout shove, born of her startled awakening, she managed to push him from her. Rolling to the side, she scrambled to her feet, backing as far as the leg-chain would allow her.

"Arabella McLeod, you must submit to the will of God," the man panted. "Become as a handmaiden to His servant."

"You're no servant of God," she shouted, her fear overcome by her fury, the language of the docks coming back to her, "you filthy-minded old bastard!"

His hand caught her across the cheek. "The Lord chastiseth those whom He loveth," he mumbled, taking her by the shoulders, his fingers tightening, bruising her tender flesh. "I will teach you—"

"You will teach me nothing!" she hissed. "Take your hands off me!"

"You belong to me," he mocked. "I can do what I will with you. Didn't you know you were sold into my keeping?"

Arab shut her eyes as she recalled the money she had seen changing hands. It was impossible! Tamsen was her sister! She loved her! She would not—

143

"Tamsen would *not!*" she said, in a small frightened voice. "She didn't know how wicked you were, or she would never have sent me with you."

"*I'm* wicked?" He laughed, an oily, whinnying sound. "*I'm* wicked! A minister is privy to a great deal of information. Suppose I tell you what your sister is! What she does for a living!"

In a low, relentless voice that hammered at Arabella's ears, he began to talk, to tell the tale of Tamsen's double life as Poppy Franklin, notorious entertainer in a cantina on the seamy side of Magoffinville. He described the way she displayed her body, publicly, singing bawdy songs unfit for decent ears. He told of the rooms upstairs, describing what took place there. Sex, he said. Fornication. Perversion.

That, he finished, was what her sister was. And she'd been happy to have Arabella removed from the scene so that her identity might remain undiscovered.

He paused, and Arabella leaned weakly against the frame and canvas behind her. It was true! His horrifying tale was true! She thought of Tamsen's night work, her return with paint on one cheek, the way she and Em had been kept from Magoffinville, except for church.

"No," she whispered in an agonized tone, "oh, no!"

"It is true," the man swore. "The Gospel truth. I could not save your sister. She is too far gone, drowning in sin! But it has been revealed to me that I must instruct you in the ways of love—"

His hands were on her. Now her anger was gone and she knew only fear. "Please," she pleaded, "oh, please, don't!"

Then she heard someone screaming, and did not recognize the screams as her own.

The wagon master, too, heard the sounds. High thin wails of anguish and hysteria. They made him most uncomfortable. He had daughters of his own. He felt a little guilty. Perhaps he could have handled her differently, kept her from becoming so upset. It had not been a good idea, catching hold of her wrists like that, returning her to the wagon by force. And he could not get

144

the idea of that leg-chain out of his mind. Yet the Reverend Smythe knew what was best for the child. It was clear she was in good hands, and perhaps she would be improved upon the morrow.

When he saw her at the breakfast cookfire, his heart went out to her in pity. She looked worn, bedraggled; the red-gold hair looked drab and faded; her eyes were swollen and dead-looking, but she was rational.

"I see your ward is better this morning, Reverend," he said politely.

"She is, indeed," the minister smiled. "Though I fear we disturbed everyone's rest in the process. We wrestled with the devil all night."

Arabella laughed, a harsh, ugly laugh that startled the wagon master. It was the last sound she was to make on their interminable journey, day—or night.

Chapter 15

The church service was well under way when Dan Tallant slipped into a rear seat. Never a church-going type, he had started coming to services to goad Tamsen, and his attendance had dropped off after a while, but today he had a reason.

He had just received the instructions for which he'd been waiting. He would not be going west, as he had planned, but east to deliver his packet of papers himself. Then, and then only, would he return to California.

He would be unable to seek out Arabella for a while. Somehow he must explain the situation to Em before he left.

He sat back, closing his mind to the minister's exhortations as he surveyed the sisters, who were unaware of his presence. Major Arbuthnot, as usual, sat by Em. Dan wondered how she stood the pompous old devil. He knew that Tamsen encouraged the relationship, so it would probably end in a most unsuitable match for poor Em.

It might not be the worst thing that could happen, he admitted to himself, uncomfortably. The man was a fool, but he could provide for Em, perhaps even take her away from here so that she'd never uncover Tamsen's deception. As for Tamsen, she was well off. Tallant could leave Magoffinville with the assurance that the sisters would have enough money, at least.

Except for Arab. Lately the girl had occupied his mind to a great extent. He was unable to rid himself of his doubts about Smythe. If he had only been sent back

146

to California! But there was no point in considering that now. His work came first.

The service droned to a finish, and Tallant waited until the sisters came down the aisle between the rows of chairs that served as pews in the empty warehouse. Major Arbuthnot followed. Tallant bowed to them.

"I wanted to see you once more," Dan said. "I'm leaving in two days, bound for the East Coast—"

Em's face showed her disappointment. Tamsen's was harder to read. Probably tickled to death to be rid of him, he thought.

"We'll miss you," Tamsen lied. "We'd love to have you visit us this afternoon, but the Major must return to the garrison. And I know you have things to do—"

He acknowledged her snub with a mocking smile, a trace of admiration in the gaze that followed them to their buggy. How lovely they looked. Both young women wore new gowns and bonnets, Tamsen having taken off her mourning for good. The scene lacked only Arabella's shining curls.

Dan turned at the touch of a gloved hand on his arm. Mrs. Tuttle stood beside him, proffering an invitation to return next Sabbath day. In the process of excusing himself, he heard Em's scream.

Whirling, his eyes took in the scene a short distance down the dusty street. A man, reeling about drunkenly, had seized the bridle of Tamsen's horse. She stood lashing at him with her whip. Before Dan could move, the man caught Tamsen's arm and dragged her from the vehicle into the street.

Dan began to run.

Tamsen rose to face her attacker, her face milk-white. For she recognized him, as he had recognized her. Buck Farnum, the trigger-happy youth whom she had humiliated at gunpoint in the cantina. He was bearded now, his eyes bloodshot, and he was drunk, but she knew him the moment he had uttered that drunken shout and reached for the bridle. She cursed her decision to attend church, to put off her mourning.

147

Casting a glance at Em, who was half-fainting in the buggy, Tamsen knew she must bluff it out.

"How dare you?" she cried angrily. "What manner of man are you, sir? Accosting two helpless women on their way from religious services! If I were not a lady—"

"Lady, hell!" He looked at the gathering crowd and snickered. "You know who this is? This here's Poppy Franklin! From the cantina down on the river!"

"He's drunk and lying," Tamsen said, weakly. "I never saw this man in my life!"

"Well, I've seen a lot of you!" The man's voice was menacing. Dan Tallant, pushing through the crowd of horrified onlookers, was too late to keep him from grabbing Tamsen. He saw the man reach out and grab her dress, ripping it from one shoulder. Next Farnum pulled the struggling Tamsen into his arms, pressing his bearded lips to hers.

There was a small, sharp explosion, and Farnum staggered backward, his expression open-mouthed in foolish surprise as he sank to the ground. Tamsen was revealed, her hair tumbled, one shoulder bared, a small, deadly pistol in her hand.

I shot him, she thought. Turning, she saw the shocked faces that stared at her. At a time like this, a lady would faint, she thought, practically.

So she did.

Dan Tallant caught her as she fell and carried her to the shelter of a doorway. "You're not fooling me one bit," he whispered in her ear. "Maybe you can pull it off this time. But think of the harm you can do to Em!"

With the church members as witnesses, Tamsen had the law's sympathy. What kind of town was Magoffinville, when a lady had to carry a gun to protect herself in broad daylight. Major Arbuthnot blustered about martial law. Several citizens hinted at a vigilante committee. The wounded Farnum was whisked off to jail to prevent the lynching someone suggested.

A short time later, having refused the escort of half the male church members, Tamsen and Em made their way home. Em, shocked by the incident, was very quiet.

"Do you think the man will live?" she finally whispered.

"I suppose so."

"He thought you were someone else, didn't he? What was that name he called you? Poppy, something? A cantina girl? Do you know her, Tamsen? How could he have made such a mistake?"

Tamsen turned on her, her face angry. "For God's sake, Em, stop questioning me! How do I know what was in the man's mind? He was drunk!"

"I'm sorry, Tam. It was thoughtless of me. I know how you must feel."

There were more questions Em wished to ask, but they must wait. Why was Tamsen carrying a gun? And where had she gotten it? There were so many things lately that did not make sense.

Em leaned back with a sigh. Her head was aching so terribly. She put a hand to her forehead. It was hot, and her fingers were like ice.

Tamsen looked at her contritely. "I didn't mean to yell at you, Em. It was just that—it was a horrible experience. I'd rather not think about it, if you don't mind."

Dan Tallant, too, preferred not to think about the episode, but it was still with him the next evening. He had retired to the shed behind the casa for a bath. Soaping his lean body in the tub provided for the occasion, he thought of what a luxury it was, and how such facilities would be denied him once he hit the trail again. He tried to think of a way to break the news of his leaving to the Chavez family, especially to Maria.

But his eyes kept straying to his guns. The leather belt that held the holsters was slung over the back of a crudely fashioned, gaudily painted Mexican chair.

If he had reached the man who was molesting Tamsen a split second earlier, he would have killed him! God knows what that would have done to his carefully constructed cover. He would have killed him, and for what? A woman who was only getting what she'd asked for!

Frowning, he towelled himself dry and drew on his trousers. As he fastened them, he heard a noise and turned his head.

Maria!

How long had she been standing there? He reached hastily for his shirt and pulled it over his tanned chest. Maria knew he was bathing. She'd heated the water before going to a neighboring casa. What did she want? Her liquid dark eyes were filled with terror.

He went to her, lifting the softly rounded chin. "What is it, little one? Come, *pobrecita*—tell me."

Her words spilled out like water from a pail, some in English, some in her native tongue. The man who had been shot, yesterday, by a señorita—he and his friends were bad men, *bandidos*. They were staying in a little house belonging to the parents of her friend, Dolores. And they were going to avenge the wounded man, to find the Señorita Frank-leen, to do terrible things—!

Tallant swore. He pulled on his boots, than fastened the gunbelt about his hips.

"How did you find this out?" he snapped.

"They were drunk," she blushed. "We—we leesten."

He brushed past her and was gone.

His anger at Tamsen built as he rode toward the cantina. He was also angry at himself. He was not Tamsen McLeod's keeper. Why did he allow himself to be dragged into her affairs? A girl with her proclivities for causing trouble. That's all he needed now—more trouble!

Reaching the cantina, he swung from his horse and tossed its reins across the hitching post. He burst through the door, quickly surveying the dim room. Tamsen was not in sight. He went to Maggie.

"She's not in," the girl said, sullenly. He could tell that she was lying, and it fanned his anger. Then, across the room, he caught sight of Katie.

Katie gave him the information he needed. Tamsen was holed up with Nell in the back room. She would not appear tonight. The word of Farnum's friends' threats had reached the cantina before their arrival. Yes, the

150

men had been here, but they'd been told that Tamsen was not there. They had left, muttering drunken threats about what they would do when they found her.

"Well, she *won't* be in, now," Dan growled. "She's going home. I'm seeing to it that she gets there! Then somebody ought to do some talking to the law!"

Katie put her freckled hand on his arm. "Dan, you can't get mixed up with anything. Not now—"

"Oh, hell," he groaned. "I'm up to my ears in her problems already!"

He stamped back to the room at the rear and shoved the door open to find Nell and Tamsen hovering in a dimly lit corner. "You'd better get your other clothes on," he said to Tamsen in an ugly tone, "I'm taking you home!"

"Maybe I don't want to go!" Her face was closed and stubborn.

"I don't give a damn whether you do or not!" he shouted. "I don't give a damn what you do! But Em's out there, alone! How long do you think it will take them to find where you live? Maybe the solid citizens of this place are deaf, dumb, and blind, but that doesn't mean that others don't have ears and eyes! I'll tell you how long it would take me. About five minutes. Farnum's friends are looking for you. Suppose they go there and find Em by herself?"

"Em's not alone. Carmela's with her—"

"Then there are two women alone." Tallant looked at Dusty, asleep on the cot. "And there's your protection. Are you coming, or not?"

"You'd better go," Nell interposed. "An' I guess I oughta call the law."

"Don't," Tamsen said. "I'll go. But don't talk to the sheriff."

"No," Dan said, his tone soft but dangerous, "don't do that. Let innocent people stick their necks out to protect you. Let somebody get hurt or killed. But protect your good name. We mustn't let anybody find out what Tamsen McLeod really is."

As Tamsen, face stiff with anger, went to change,

151

Nell studied the tall man. She liked what she saw, she decided. Hell, if she was just a few years younger—! She liked the steadiness of his eyes, the hard clean lines of his body. No wonder Katie was sweet on him. Nell figured his own wants were set in another direction, even if he was too gawdamn dumb to know it himself. Well, maybe she could help it along a little.

"Don't be too tough on the kid," she said, suddenly, surprising him. "It ain't like you think. She's a damn good girl, bright, ambitious, do most anything to work her way up—"

"Exactly what I do think," Dan said shortly, moving to intercept Tamsen on her return. He would bring the horses into the courtyard. There was a little gate in the back. They would circle the cantina, then ride hard out to the adobe.

"A lot of man," Nell said, admiringly, as the two left the room. "A lot of man!"

"Hummm?" Dusty muttered, stirring on the cot where he lay.

"You too, Shorty," Nell grinned.

For the first part of their journey, Tamsen and Tallant rode in silence. Tamsen was wary of Dan's intentions. She jumped a little when he spoke.

"It's going to storm," he said quietly.

Dark clouds were scudding across the night sky before them, and an occasional flash of lightning zigzagged to the top of Mount Franklin, but it was all far away. The atmosphere surrounding them was sultry, still.

"I don't think so," she announced, wondering why she felt compelled to disagree with anything Tallant said. And no sooner were the words out of her mouth than the wind came, bearing a cloud of dust on its wings. A tumbleweed bundled across Tamsen's path, sending her horse dancing sideways. Dan pulled his animal close to hers and placed a calming hand on the bridle.

"We'd better make a run for it," he shouted above the screaming wind.

Tamsen bent forward, urging her horse to greater speed, her dark hair whipping about her shoulders. On the wind came the rain and the rumble of thunder. The horses slipped in the sodden grass and their riders got soaked to the skin.

Then, in a temporary let-up of the sheeting rain, Tamsen saw the light that Em placed in the window of the small adobe every night.

Sitting straight on her saddle, Tamsen laughed triumphantly. "You see! Everything's all right. You can head back to town. We don't need you at all!"

Dan looked at the girl, at her rain-wet hair, at her clothing plastered against the small body, revealing every curve, and felt a tremor of need. He grinned at himself. If he knew what was good for him, he'd turn back and leave her to go on alone. He studied the faint glow in the distance, reflecting on the sense of danger that had brought him here. Perhaps it had only been a hunch.

"I'll go on with you. Check things out." His voice was quiet but firm.

"Suit yourself." Tamsen shrugged her wet shoulders and urged her horse ahead. She dismounted beside the shed, and as she rounded the house, she saw a faint shaft of light from a slightly opened door.

Her breath caught in her throat. "Dan," she said, unsteadily, "Dan—!"

Dan Tallant rushed around her. The door was blocked by something soft and yielding. There was a moaning sound. "Ah, Dios!" It was Carmela! Someone had been here!

Somehow, Dan managed to open the door and scooped up the Mexican woman in his arms. Her head fell limply, bruised, battered, her long dark hair matted with blood.

Tamsen pressed past him, running toward the other room, crying her sister's name. She stopped short at the sight that met her eyes and began to scream.

153

Chapter 16

Earlier that evening, after Tamsen had left for work in Dusty's company, Em had been unable to relax. Carmela insisted on doing the dishes, and Em wasn't able to forget her nagging worries in housework. Since the shooting, yesterday, she had been depressed, left with a feeling of gnawing emptiness. The thought that Tamsen had been keeping secrets from her, and that those secrets had something to do with the man who accosted them, had intensified.

Walking out into the early evening air, she felt oppressed by the hot stillness that surrounded her. She realized, with surprise, that it was fall. Mid-November, almost Thanksgiving. The weather felt strange, the distant hills dusty-appearing, the surrounding vegetation limp. And there was an odd smell to the air that presaged a change.

Emmeline McLeod experienced a sudden surge of homesickness. At home, by this date, there would be snow. She closed her eyes, imagining the flakes falling, mounding in the bare arms of birch and maple, nesting in the evergreens. Clean and pure.

At last she turned her reluctant steps toward the house. Carmela was at the well drawing a bucket of water. The squat woman pointed at the sky and grinned, waving her arm vigorously. She, too, sensed the weather change.

Such a nice woman, Em thought. If only they shared a common language. So far, they had only managed a few words and gestures. If she could just talk to someone about her concerns, about Tamsen and Arabella!

Tamsen was so difficult these days. Last week she'd been starry-eyed and dreamy, but since yesterday she'd been close-mouthed and evasive.

Sighing, Em went into the house. She and Carmela sat in companionable silence for a while, each doing a little mending. Then, lulled by the quiet, Em rose sleepily to go to her bed in the back room.

She was still awake when she heard the front door open with a crash. She sat up, frowning. Tamsen? Then she heard the sound of male voices. Heart thudding in her chest, she stole to the door. In the light of the lamp she'd left burning for Tamsen she saw Carmela cowering before two strange men who had forced their way in. Unable to move, Em stared in horrified fascination.

One of them was Mexican. Hardly more than a boy, with a lean, almost esthetic face. He grasped Carmela's hair, turning her face to the light. "Diablo! We have made the mistake! Thees ees not the señorita!" He looked to the older man in intoxicated bewilderment.

"Hell, she's a woman, ain't she?" the other jeered. "Listen, you! We're huntin' the Franklin girl. Poppy Franklin, savvy? You tell us where she is and you won't get hurt!"

Franklin! The name rang through Em's shocked mind. That was what the Farnum man had called Tamsen yesterday. Em flinched as the older man slapped Carmela. When Carmela did not volunteer information, he struck her again.

Em's eyes went to Papa's rifle. It was out of reach, on the opposite wall. Would Carmela think of it if she could distract them? She couldn't let them hurt the woman any more!

"Stop that!" Her voice rang like a bell. The man stayed his hand, turning to peer at her through drink-blurred eyes.

"Well," he said. "Well!"

"This is private property," Em said, fighting to maintain her surface calm. "You gentlemen are intruding. You have no business here!"

The big blond man looked her up and down. She was conscious that she was in her nightdress, high-necked and demure though it was; that her feet were bare, her hair hanging loose to her waist. The man who eyed her was not as drunk as he had appeared to be. He knew exactly what he had come for. It showed in his cold gray eyes.

"Miss Franklin?"

"There is no Miss Franklin here. You are in error."

He looked around the room in an exaggerated mocking way. "We was told the lady lived here. So you must be her. Mebbe we better introduce ourselves proper-like. Me, I'm Cassidy. This here's Montoya. We're buddies of Buck Farnum. You heared of him?"

Em's gasping intake of breath gave her away. Cassidy's face hardened as he walked toward her with an indolent grace that made her think of a stalking animal. She backed away from him, feeling the impact of his menacing presence. Her knees were undependable. Behind him, the other man voiced a protest in Spanish. Cassidy barked back at him.

"Hell," he said, "you tend to the greaser! She's your kind. You'll getcher turn!"

He closed the door behind him, advancing toward Em, his pale hard face expressionless, pitiless, a cold, brutal machine.

"Please," Em whispered. "Please go. You've made a mistake. My name isn't Franklin. It's McLeod—"

His lips parted in a mirthless grin. "McLeod-Franklin. I was told in town. I was told what you done to Farnum. Names don't make no difference in what I'm going to do to you!"

His flat eyes did not change as he moved toward her, uttering obscenities in a cold, whispering voice. His hands closed on her shoulders, bruising them. She screamed as he pressed her backward, brutally, with his iron-hard arms.

She sank her teeth into his hand, and he struck her—again and again. She felt the weight of his body as he pressed against her, forcing himself upon her.

156

Soon there was another face above her, another, though less brutal, violation of her body. Unable to face the nightmare that was rape, she sought unconsciousness. When the men had gone, she stared into the darkness with blank, unseeing eyes.

Tamsen found her, half on the bed, her features set in horror at the things she had endured.

Weeping, Tamsen covered her sister's bruised and bleeding body with a sheet, and took Em's slender hand in her own. There was a pulse—

"The Mexican woman will be all right," Dan Tallant said, appearing in the doorway. "She's conscious. What about Em?"

"I don't know," Tamsen said. "I don't know!"

Tallant was beside her, his face rigid with anger as he studied Em's condition. Lifting her limp hand, he let it fall. "She's in shock. I'll kill the rotten bastards!" His fists clenched at his sides. "I'll go after them before they get away. I know where to find them. Will you be all right? Can you handle this?"

Tamsen's fury matched his own. "I'm going with you!"

Dan Tallant turned on her, a vein in his forehead pulsing. "You damned little fool!" he snapped. "Don't you think of anything except how you feel? These women here have been through hell! They'll need a lot of comfort and understanding! That may not be in your line of work, but you might try it, this once!"

Glaring at her, he stamped out of the door and slammed it behind him. In a few moments, she heard his horse gallop away into the night.

In the hours that followed, she washed Em's wounds, covered her icy body with blankets, and surrounded her with warm, towel-wrapped stones to take away the chill. Carmela, despite her abrasions, was in better shape. Her reaction to the attack was anger. She lay heavily on her cot, spitting Spanish words which could be nothing but curses.

She would be all right. But Em? Tamsen didn't know. It was nearly dawn when Em turned her poor bruised eyes toward Tamsen. "They thought I was you," she whispered thickly through split lips. "I didn't tell them —I didn't tell them—"

At last Em slept. Tamsen left her, sick with her new knowledge. This had not been a chance attack, embarked upon because Em was convenient and at hand. Em had taken Tamsen's punishment for her.

Dan Tallant was fighting her battles for her, too. She wandered to the window and looked out into the night. The temper of the rain had changed. It was a steady drizzle, now, streaking the pane like tears. Yet before her, she could see the pattern of her actions that had brought them to this pass. And she did not like what she saw.

Turning to the stove, she built up the fire and made a pot of coffee which she set to keep warm at the back of the stove.

Em slept. Carmela slept. There was no sound except that of the dripping rain.

That same rain fell on Dan Tallant as he rode, full tilt, toward Magoffinville, his dark hair plastered against his brown forehead, his shirt molded to his rippling muscles like a second skin. He slipped off his gunbelt and stashed it beneath the poncho he hadn't taken time to put on. It was important that it be kept dry.

He knew where he was going, and he knew what he intended to do. The thought of Em, and what had been done to her, burned in his brain. He shut it out, concentrating on his present mission. Squinting against the rain, his eyes were flat and cold, a killer's eyes, as he galloped toward town.

Reaching the adobe, where Maria's friend Dolores lived, Tallant tethered his horse in a dripping clump of willows to one side. Then, slipping his gunbelt over his hips, he followed the wall that formed a sort of compound. Here, a warped, once-blue door, set between two prison-like windows, led directly into the smaller house where the two men were staying. A glow of lamplight indicated someone was within.

Tallant adjusted his guns, getting the feel of them. He pounded on the door.

Inside, the man called Cassidy sat alone at a rough-hewn table, dealing cards. Peering at the cards with bloodshot eyes, he scooped them up to deal again. Damn that Mex! He'd sent him out for a bottle an hour ago, and he wasn't back yet. Cassidy needed a touch of the hair of the dog that bit him.

Maybe he'd just leave the kid behind when he took off in the morning. He'd got the idea Montoya was squeamish about this night's work. Cassidy grinned at the memory of what he'd done to the girl. This was one case when revenge was sure sweet!

God, his head was pounding! He pushed back his lank, blond hair. And then the knock sounded at the door.

"Get the hell in here," he roared. "It's about time—!" He half rose, than sank into his chair, slowly, carefully, at the sight of the man who confronted him.

A man soaked to the skin. A man with guns low on his hips and death in his eyes. Who the hell?

"Look, friend, you're in the wrong place—"

There was no answer, just that cold, dreadful scrutiny that made chills go through Cassidy's spine. He shriveled inside. He had seen that look before. This man meant to kill him. One betraying twitch as he reached for his gun, and he was a dead man.

A rattle at the door intruded into the silence. Montoya! Despite himself, Cassidy's eyes flickered in that direction. Then his hand moved downward.

It was too late. Tallant's gun fired, and Cassidy fell forward, face down among the cards. Then Dan whirled toward the door to see the Mexican boy, white-faced, pistol in his hand. Tallant fired as he threw himself sideways, feeling the hammer blow of the slug that entered his shoulder.

It was done.

Leaving two dead men behind him, Tallant returned to his horse. Taking hold of its bridle, he half-walked, half-dragged himself to the Chavez house.

159

First, he went to the shed where he washed the wound. It was clean. The bullet had passed through the upper part of his torso, missing vital organs and bone. He bandaged his wound as well as he could with one hand, using the towel with which he'd dried after his bath earlier. Then he emptied the bloodied water and burned his stained shirt in the small cast-iron stove used for heating bath water.

There must be nothing to tie the Chavez family to the deaths of two men in the area. The law would call it murder. The law wouldn't have seen what they'd done to Em.

Slipping into the darkened house, he donned another shirt and gathered up his few possessions. At last he was in his saddle, the precious packet in his saddlebags, his bedroll strapped on behind.

He would not be able to return here. The family that feasted his coming would be left to mourn his manner of going. He wished he could wake them, explain . . .

He would look in once more on Em and Carmela—both victims of Tamsen's foolish behavior.

He put his hand to his shoulder. It throbbed with the horse's gait. His shirt was already wet with rain, but now it felt different, with a slight stickiness. The wound was bleeding once more. He began to curse under his breath.

Whether he was cursing Tamsen or his wound, he did not know.

Arriving at the adobe, he swung from his saddle. The door opened as he reached it. Tamsen stood there waiting for him, lamp in hand. The room behind her was warm. There was a scent of fresh-brewed coffee. Like a homecoming. His lip curled. She had set the scene beautifully. No one would guess this had been a scene of rape and violence a few short hours before.

Ducking his head at the low door, he stepped inside and cast a quick glance toward the Mexican woman's cot. It had been moved from the kitchen, evidently into Em's room.

"Carmela's all right," Tamsen said hastily, seeing the direction of his gaze. "And Em's better. She spoke to me." She lowered her face, guiltily, as she recalled Em's words.

"Good. Everything's taken care of. Those men won't bother anyone again. I would suggest you try to keep out of trouble. I'm leaving Magoffinville, and I won't be returning."

Tamsen stared at him. His face was inscrutable—and cruel. Her breath drew in raggedly as she divined his meaning. Her hand went to her mouth as she saw the telltale stain on his shirt.

"You're *hurt!*"

"A scratch." He drew back as she put a hand to his arm, trying to draw him to a chair. "I've got to go. If anyone tracks me here—"

"Then I'll tell them what you did," she retorted. "You went after those men because they're renegades! Because of what they did to Em and Carmela! They needed killing! There's not a decent man in town who'd blame you!"

"And not a decent man who'd marry your sister after this, either," he growled. "That Major you've been trying to fix her up with would take off like a scared rabbit! Do you want her name ruined, too? Would that make you feel more respectable?"

"I—I didn't think," she whispered.

"You seldom do. You do what Tamsen wants, and to hell with the consequences."

Tamsen's mouth tightened. Still, she must fix his shoulder. She wouldn't let anyone ride out into the rain in his condition. In spite of his hatefulness, she did owe this man an awful lot.

"Sit down!" she said, shortly. To her surprise, he obeyed. Her brows knitted. He was on the verge of chills. There was a bottle in the cupboard, one she'd filched from Dusty in hopes of keeping him sober for a time. She fetched it and he tipped it up, alternating it with sips of the hot coffee she'd provided. He was silent, and she was conscious of his eyes on her as she unbuttoned his shirt, drawing it back to reveal the clumsily bandaged wound.

161

Her fingers trembled on his smooth brown skin as she carefully cut the bandage away. She sensed he knew the effect his body had on her, and she hated him for it.

A pad of cloth had been set in place to cover the injury, front and back. It was held by another strip that kept it in place, passing over his shoulder and under his arm. Removing it, she looked at it in distaste. Dan grinned, guessing her thoughts.

Towels in less-than-prosperous Mexican families consisted of pieces of worn, discarded clothing. This, still retaining a bit of coarse lace at one edge, had clearly been a woman's petticoat.

"*Katie's*, I suppose?" Despite herself, Tamsen's fingers became a little rougher, pressing harder than was necessary as she cleansed the wound.

"No," he drawled, his eyes mocking her. "On the contrary. I believe it belonged to Maria. I lived at her place. A very nice young lady."

Damn him! As if it made any difference to her! She pressed the new bandage home with a vigor that made him flinch. "There you are. All done. You can take the bottle with you."

He rose, the events of the night still fresh in his mind, a little weak from loss of blood. The liquor coursed through his veins along with his anger.

This woman had been at fault for everything that had happened! To Em, to the Mexican woman. Tamsen was, in a way, responsible for the deaths of two men. Because of her, he was being forced to flee Magoffinville instead of leaving in an inconspicuous manner. Because of her, he would never be able to return. And she had dared to hand him a bottle and show him the door! Tamsen McLeod, who was nothing but a cantina girl, who had bet her body to win what she wanted!

Before his dark, impenetrable look, Tamsen faltered. "Thank you," she said stiffly. "I feel we owe you—"

"You damn well do," he said hoarsely. "You damn well do! And I intend to collect my debts before I go."

Reaching out, he took the lamp from her nerveless

162

hand and extinguished it. Then his arms were around her, his mouth on hers as she tried to turn away. Pulling away from him, she banged into a chair and knocked it over. Despite her fear, she thought suddenly of the women in the other room. She must not scream—

She fought silently as his hands sought her body, tearing at her clothing, the only sound the sobbing breath she could not control. She felt herself forced down to the floor, heard him swear at recalcitrant buttons, heard her dress ripping.

Then there was the touch of warm flesh against her own, the weight of his hard body, insistent, brutal, demanding.

The shock of it dazed her. For a moment, she lay limp and still. But as she felt a drawing away, her arms went up to hold him, through none of her own volition, but something to do with her flesh which had betrayed her. She felt a wild, throbbing sensation she had never felt before. And her voice sounded far away.

"Dan," she whispered, "Oh, Dan— Please—!"

Then she felt his weight again. This time, with a difference, this time with tenderness. He said her name, and it sounded like a moan. She felt an obscure delight as if in some way she was the conqueror, he the conquered. But the idea lingered only for a brief space. Then there was no time for thinking, only for feeling, as she met his desire with her own.

In spite of his passion, Tallant made a startling discovery. "Tamsen," he said, "my God, I didn't know—"

But Tamsen was storm-tossed in a sea of emotion, where breakers crashed against the shores of love. And this was no time to pause to discuss the situation.

"Don't talk, Dan," she wept. "Just love me—love me!"

He did.

Afterward, their passions spent, Dan Tallant lay with Tamsen's head pillowed against his good shoulder. He had not intended to do what he had done. It had been the result of his anger, the long terrible night, the

163

liquor. Not that he wasn't glad it had happened. But Tamsen was a virgin. He'd been the first. He figured she wouldn't take this sort of thing lightly.

Neither had he, for that matter. He felt his masculinity being aroused again at the thought and resolutely pulled away from Tamsen's clinging arms. If ever a girl made him feel like hanging around, this one did. But he'd avoided being trapped by females for years, and it was no time to let one hook him now. He had a job to do.

He looked toward the window. It was nearly full light. He reached for his trousers and pulled them on, buckling his belt, sliding the holsters into place over his lean hips.

"Where are you going?" Tamsen's voice was small. He looked down at her where she lay in a flurry of skirts, her face still stained with tears, mouth swollen with kisses.

"Heading east," he said, a little shortly. "I told you." What, he wondered, to say to her? Thank you? As he searched for words, Tamsen sat up, her eyes glinting.

"Is that all any of this meant to you?" she asked, "You—you attacked me! And now you're going to ride off, just like that?"

"I don't think it was all my doing," he reminded her. "If I remember right, you not only asked, you begged—"

Tamsen turned crimson. She must have been out of her mind! "I was only paying a debt," she said, icily. "Or do you consider it paid? If so, there needn't be any further discussion. You can be on your way."

His own anger flared as he moved toward the door. "You can write it off. Though for twelve horses—and two men—it was hardly worth it!"

He slammed the door behind him.

Tamsen rose to her feet, painfully. Trying to pull her torn clothing together, she straightened her skirt. Her expression was stormy as she reflected on what an idiot she'd been. For a while, she'd thought Dan Tallant loved her.

Now he was gone, and so was her virtue. She looked

down at her tattered gown. She had to keep what had happened here from Em. Em had enough to bear.

Wrapping a blanket around her shoulders, she went in to look at her sister. Em and Carmela still slept, though Em was moaning and tossing. The nightmare still held her in its grip. Tamsen drew the covers over Em's bruised shoulders. This was a night they both would remember.

Tamsen put her hand to her mouth to stifle a ripple of hysteria, then dropped to her knees beside Em's bed, her face awash with tears.

Tallant, riding east, had managed to overcome his anger. He was thinking of his surprise at Tamsen's answering fire, the discovery that, for her, he'd been the first. The knowledge gave him an odd feeling, a mingling of embarrassment and pleasure.

Tamsen! A virgin! Son of a gun! He found himself grinning as he rode toward his new destination. God, how he wished he could go back!

Chapter 17

The deaths of Cassidy and Montoya didn't cause much stir in Magoffinville. When it was discovered that they both had criminal records, the law-abiding citizens of the town dismissed the whole affair as a falling-out among thieves. Their killer, a man named Tallant, had been a quiet-appearing man, frequently seen about the local cantinas. He was traced to the casa of a Mexican family, where he apparently resided when in town. The Mexicans closed ranks. They knew nothing about the man, where he came from, or what he was doing here. *Nada!*

It was decided that Tallant was a hired gun, possibly come to seek vengeance for a rival gang of outlaws. He would be arrested when he returned, if he returned.

The case was closed. Within weeks, it was as if the incident had never happened.

Though the town forgot Dan Tallant, Tamsen could not. For a while, because of her concern for her sister, she was able to put him to the back of her mind. Em, after her first coherent words, had lapsed into a kind of delirium. Carmela had quit, announcing through Dusty that she was returning to El Paso del Norte, across the river into Mexico, where a decent religious woman would be safe from *bandidos*.

For several days, Tamsen did not leave Em's side. Tamsen bathed Em's burning forehead with cool cloths and coaxed her to swallow sips of cold drinks. Even when the fever subsided, Em lay in a comatose state for a while, seeming not to care whether she lived or died.

It wasn't until Em began to recover that Tamsen had

time to dwell on her own feelings. Her emotions veered from gratitude to Tallant for his rescue of Em to sheer hatred for the way he had treated her afterward. The blood surged in her veins at the memory of that night. Passion and humiliation were mixed in her thoughts about Tallant. On the surface, her puritanical side won and she convinced herself that Tallant had used her badly. But when she dreamed of that night, and she did dream of it often, she always awoke with a warm afterglow.

One afternoon Tamsen heard the sound of carriage wheels in the distance. Em had recovered enough for Tamsen to be able to leave her side, but she was still not well enough to enable Tamsen to go back to the cantina.

Up to this time, Major Arbuthnot had been the only visitor to the adobe. He came one day insisting on seeing Em, but was immediately put off when Tamsen told him that Em might have something contagious. Promising to send the army surgeon to have a look at Em, the Major backed away hastily from the door. Tamsen prevented him from sending the surgeon by insisting that it might be a shock to her sister's genteel nature to be examined by a man.

Now, fearing that perhaps the Major had sent the surgeon after all, Tamsen jumped up as the carriage stopped. She answered the knock at the door, heart beating in trepidation. The pounding was accompanied by a lusty shout.

"Gawdammit, open up! I ain't gonna stand around all day!"

Nell!

Flinging the door wide, Tamsen collapsed in Nell's arms. "Oh, hell," the woman grumbled, straightening an improbable plumed hat that Tamsen's embrace had knocked awry. Behind her, Katie grinned impishly.

"Come in," Tamsen said, "Oh, come in!" Nell had made an attempt to look respectable, instead, she looked like a funeral hearse, plumes waving, black velvet waist cinched to billow above and below.

Nell waddled to a chair, sinking into it with a groan.

167

"Katie," she ordered, "take off my gawdamn shoes! My feet are killin' me!"

As the Irish girl knelt to do her bidding, Nell fixed a beady eye on Tamsen. "Things is goin' t' hell in a bushel basket at the cantina," she said, sourly. "Dusty told me what happened to yer sis. Figgered maybe I'd better pay me a soshul call—find out what the hell's goin' on."

"I haven't been able to leave," Tamsen said. "Em—"

"Would like to meet your friends," said a composed voice from the bedroom doorway. Tamsen gasped at the sight of Em on her feet. The girl had somehow managed to rise and to slip a robe over her high-necked gown. Her swollen face was rainbow-hued with bruises.

Nell twisted her head to see the speaker. "Well," she said, cheerfully, "Dusty didn't stretch the truth none. You sure are one helluva mess!"

Emmeline ignored Tamsen's insistence that she return to bed. Moving into the room, she chided Tamsen gently for her lack of hospitality, suggesting that she make a pot of tea. As Tamsen quickly set about her task, Em sat down, to talk to Nell and Katie, carrying on a conversation as if she'd known them forever. She did not even flinch when Nell laced her comments with her usual spicy obscenities.

Em poured the tea, and Nell, taking her cup, extended a pudgy finger, gleefully. "Lookut me," she chortled, "I'm a gawdamn lady! Allus knowed I was!"

Finally, Nell got to the reason for the visit. Katie, here, wanted to take a little vacation. She figured she could stay with Em, since business was going to hell without Tamsen's presence, anyway. Then there was this old man—didn't have the brains of an ant, but he could shoot the balls off a buzzard at a hundred yards. Nell had staked him a couple of times and he owed her a pile. He would alternate with Dusty in the shed—

Tamsen was beginning to fume. Nell knew she had kept her occupation from her sisters and now she was taking every opportunity to spell it all out for Em. This visit had been deliberate. If only Em hadn't chosen this time to recover her senses!

168

Tamsen was appalled at her own thoughts. Of course she wanted Em well! Hadn't she nearly gone out of her own mind with worry? But now the cat was out of the bag. There would have to be explanations. And she had no intentions of letting a prostitute serve Em as a companion. The old man, Clem Tulliver, a lanky no-good from the southeast, was all right. A worthless old coot, but harmless. He would do. But not Katie! It was bad enough having Katie in the same room with her ladylike sister. And Nell! Nell, with her rough talk—

Tamsen had the grace to blush as Nell heaved herself to her feet. She loved Nell! The woman had been good to her, yet she felt so torn in her loyalties.

"You think it over," she said brusquely. "We gotta shove off. Ain't been out in the daylight in so long, my gawdamn brains are fried." She looked Em over, approvingly. "Glad to meet you, girl. And thanks fer the hospitality. I had one hell of a nice time."

Katie helped Nell into the carriage, and they were gone. Tamsen turned from the door, an apology on her lips, but something in Em's face stopped her.

"I liked your friends, Tamsen," Em said, honestly, "and I think it's time we had a talk. You are Poppy Franklin, aren't you?"

Tamsen burst into tears. Falling to her knees, she put her head in Em's lap. Em's fingers smoothed Tamsen's dark hair as she wept out her story, telling how she could find no work when they came to Magoffinville. How Dusty had taken her to Nell, and she had begun to sing at the cantina. She had won the place in a card game, she admitted, painfully, not mentioning the stakes, and was now trying to make it into a more respectable place. But she hadn't wanted Em or Arabella to know about it, ever.

Em sighed. So that was why Tamsen had seized on the chance to send Arab away. She was getting the answers to so many questions, all except one!

Putting her hands to both sides of Tamsen's face, she made the girl look at her. "Do you *like* your work?"

She asked softly. Tamsen's flush answered for her, and Em began to laugh.

"Then why apologize?" she wanted to know.

Tamsen stared at her incredulously. Then, "Em! Oh, Em!" She threw her arms about this sister she would never understand, both of them laughing and crying at the same time.

Later that night Em put forth her last and final question. "Those men," she said. "From what I gathered, they will not bother us any more. They—they're dead, aren't they?"

"Yes," Tamsen said in a small voice.

"Who killed them? Oh, Tamsen—not *you*!" Em closed her eyes as she recalled the man Tamsen had shot that Sunday morning.

"Dan Tallant." Just the two words. Tamsen's voice was flat, her mouth a thin line.

"And he's already gone? Back east?" The high collar on Em's gown felt suddenly too tight. She found it difficult to swallow as she read her answer in Tamsen's eyes.

"He won't be back," Tamsen said, still in that same, dead tone.

"I'm sorry." Em spoke with an effort. "I would have liked to see him, to thank him for everything he's done on our behalf. The horses—and now this—"

"He's been paid," Tamsen said, rudely. "Dan Tallant isn't a man who does something for nothing!"

Em studied her curiously. Here was another enigma. Wisely, she refrained from questioning Tamsen further.

Tamsen returned to work, reluctantly allowing Katie to stay with Em for a week. It was a week that Em enjoyed. Katie was bright, perky, someone to talk to. And it was clear that Katie Ryan had no aversion to mentioning Dan Tallant's name. She seemed to interject it into their conversation at every opportunity, and Em was amused at what it implied.

"I've found out something about Katie," she told Tamsen. "Do you know the girl's in love with Dan?

Her whole appearance changes when she mentions his name. I wonder if he knows."

Tamsen wanted to retort that he should know, that he'd certainly had every opportunity to find out, in those rooms over the cantina! But she held her tongue. Em had no idea what went on upstairs. She visualized the place as something along the order of the St. Louis hotel. And when she had asked Tamsen to show her a sample of the entertaining she did, Tamsen had clasped her hands at her breast and sung, "*Black is the color of my true love's hair . . .*"

Em's eyes filled with tears. "Papa would be proud of you," she said.

So Em knew some of the story, but not all. Still, knowing she had her sister's approval, that Dan Tallant was out of the way and there were no present dangers changed her life. Tamsen threw herself into her work with a new abandon that brought the customers in droves. Men vied for her favors, more gifts joining the red pendant that had been her first. She had no compunction about accepting those gifts, even knowing what they expected in return. She laughed and flirted, but she made no promises. In desperation, they would finally go upstairs with Carmen, Maggie, the newly returned Katie.

As time passed and Em's bruises faded, the girl's tender soul began to heal over, though the wound remained deep inside to manifest itself in occasional nightmares. Within a month, she was able to return to church. The last remaining mark that marred one cheek was easily explained away. In her illness, Em had fallen.

Their appearance aroused the sympathy of the congregation. It was their first Sunday at church since the shooting incident. Em's illness had been attributed to the shock of being accosted as they were, and the shooting incident that followed it, a story spread by the attentive Major. The girls were smothered with kindness and beset with invitations. When they took their leave, Major Arbuthnot went home with them, pleased to be able to return to his social Sunday afternoons.

One night, after Tamsen had gone, the Major appeared at the door with an ornate box of candy. Brought from the East, it was rather stale and the box bore signs of the travels it had endured, but it was a sign of his intentions. Though his behavior was most correct, it was evident to a horrified Em that the man had settled in to court her once more.

Night after night, he called. Em sat quietly, closing her ears to his pompous compliments, stitching at an embroidered needle-case she was making as a Christmas gift for Tamsen. She had no idea what a picture she presented to the lonely man as she sat, a symbol of sweet domesticity, the lamp light making a halo of her fair hair as she sewed away.

As Christmas approached, Em felt a touch of the excitement she'd known as a young girl. Early one morning she and Tamsen found a stunted juniper, hacked it off clumsily, and dragged it into the house. Using scissors and gloves, they cut cactus apples, singed them over a fire on a fork to remove their stickery thorns, and strung them as ornaments for their tree. Popcorn and bows of material left from dressmaking finished their decoration.

The tree was quite different from those at home, but it was a tree. They both made new gowns for church on Christmas morning. It would all have been perfect had Arabella been there. Em forced the thought from her mind.

"I feel pretty foolish," she said to Tamsen with a laugh. "I've been so excited over this Christmas! I was actually sick this morning!"

She discovered she was to be sick the next morning—and the next. A strange, queasy feeling that left her dizzy for a time. She said nothing to Tamsen. It would be all right once the holiday was over and gone.

But Christmas morning, fighting back a feeling of nausea during their gift exchange, she knew she'd never be able to dress and ride to the church. "You'll have to go without me," she told Tamsen. "I don't feel well."

Tamsen insisted on remaining with her, but Em

wouldn't hear of it. After she had gone, Emmeline McLeod sat staring at the little tree with its drying, drooping branches. "God help me," she whispered.

For when Tamsen returned, she would have to tell her a truth that had been dawning upon her slowly. A truth that would have to be faced, here and now.

For the nightmare that had begun in mid-November was still with her. It was bearing fruit.

Thank God Arabella wasn't here!

Chapter 18

Christmas Day in Magoffinville and Christmas in San Francisco were quite different. In Magoffinville, the cantinas were closed for the day, a gesture to the stable population of the town. Family men, such as Cal Tuttle, spent the morning in church, or at home with their wives and children. The soldiers at the garrison spent their hours writing letters, after an army-issue holiday meal. The loners, cowhands, and ex-soldiers from the Mexican War either slept off their Christmas Eve celebration or crossed into El Paso del Norte in search of excitement they would not find. The good and faithful Mexican Catholics crowded into the missions. This was a day of worship.

In San Francisco, the holiday was celebrated in the sprawling new city's unique way. The brilliant winter sun shone down on laughing, fur-draped women, shambling miners, pockets filled with gold and stomachs with good whisky; on merchants pursuing business as usual; on soldiers, sailors, entrepreneurs.

The streets were, as usual at this time of year, a sea of noise and mud.

The mud did not deter the driver of a closed coach that drew up near the corner of Clay and Kearney. He drew as near to the covered wagon, where a public Christmas service was being held, as the crowd would allow.

The occupant of the coach, acclaimed as one of the most beautiful women in the world, opened the curtain of her conveyance a slit, to survey the scene for herself.

Most of the people who surrounded the wagon were

174

of the rougher element, she decided. They came here because they had nothing better to do than to harrass and torment the missionary group that would perform.

So much the better. She would be able to learn if what she'd heard were true. If it were not, then at least she would have had an adventure. She smiled as she read the sign that graced the corner of the two streets.

> "This street is impassable:
> Not even jackassable."

How typical of this roaring city, this melting pot which had accepted her to its heart. Marie Dolores Eliza Rosanna Gilbert, far better known by another name, had a sense of humor. The street is jackassable, she thought as the vagrant preacher appeared and began to spout platitudes. For there is a jackass if I ever saw one! Trained in the arts of elocution and of holding an audience as she was, Lola Montez regarded the preacher's attempts at spellbinding his audience as pathetic. Apparently, his listeners were of the same opinion. They began to jeer. A small mud clod flew through the air to strike the man's cheek, making it altogether a sordid scene.

There's nothing here for me, the famous beauty thought. She leaned forward a little to tap for the driver's attention, then stopped. For the preacher was speaking in a quite different tone.

"I know what you want," he called in a cheerful voice of camaraderie. "And I don't blame you. I'll bring her on! The little lady who sings like an angel!"

Crawling into the wagon, he returned, leading a young girl by the hand. The girl stared back at the audience, dull-eyed, her lanky frame swallowed up in a too-large dark dress. Lola Montez uttered a little murmur of distaste and reached to summon her driver once more.

Then the girl began to sing.

The pure notes soared to the sky. A Christmas hymn, sung by an angel—yet with an undertone of sensuality that pulled the crowd to her like a wave! She sang another song, and another. La Montez turned her attention from the singer to the crowd, watching for audience reaction.

My God, she thought, she's got them in the palm of her hand! She was sure of it when the preacher began passing a plate through the throng. He had to return to empty it before he could get through the whole crowd.

Lola Montez rapped on the window, authoritatively, calling to her driver. "Get that man," she said, excitedly, "and bring him to me! I don't care if you have to drag him! Tell him—tell him I have a profitable proposition to put to him. Here, give him my card."

The Reverend Smythe looked at the card in bewilderment, and then at the closed coach. *Lola Montez*, the card read. He knew the name. He had referred to the so-called Spanish dancer a number of times in his sermons, calling her Jezebel and the Whore of Babylon, referring to her theatrical career as sinful, saying that she was doomed to hellfire.

What could such a woman want of him? The surprise he registered upon seeing her card changed to a look of sly speculation.

Her driver had mentioned a proposition. A profitable one.

He hurried to the coach and spoke with the woman for a few minutes. Then he returned to the wagon and came back, leading the weary-looking, shabby girl. Money changed hands, an amount beyond Reverend Smythe's wildest dreams. He handed Arabella into the coach.

Arabella sat, apathetic, as the driver whipped up his team. She had been sold again, that was all. Whatever fate held in store for her, it could not be worse than what she had already experienced. She had learned, the hard way, not to speak until she was spoken to. To do as she was told.

Lola Montez, deep in her scented furs, surveyed the child. An astute business woman, as well as an accomplished entertainer, she wondered if she'd done the

176

right thing. The girl seemed hopeless except when she sang. She was a plain little creature in an older woman's dress; her hair hung limp and drab; her eyes were dull.

How old was she? Fifteen? Sixteen? Lola Montez had been only sixteen when she began her career. Yet this girl's face looked as if she had seen all there was to see, known all there was to know. How would she look if she smiled?

Was it possible that the girl was an idiot? Lola Montez fought instinctive recoil. Then she thought, ruefully, of her impulsive action in taking the girl from the only kind of life she'd probably ever known. The preacher was not her father. She learned that from the person who had brought the girl to her attention. Still it was possible she had a fondness for the man, that she resented being taken away.

The woman's heart swelled with pity as she leaned to touch the girl's thin arm. If that were the case, she would return her to the wagon and take the loss.

"Tell me," she said in her softly accented voice, "did you not wish to come with me? Perhaps you preferred to remain with the preacher."

Arabella's head jerked up. "Him! That son of a bitch!" She spat out a string of epithets that would singe a mule-skinner. Then she stopped, horrified, hand to mouth as she looked at the lady who was her new benefactor.

The lady was smiling in delight, and Arabella smiled back.

Chapter 19

Arabella was very much on Tamsen's mind this early day in March. Tamsen had been unable to sleep, so she took a walk near the adobe. The bone-chilling wind had stopped, at last. There was a promise of spring in the air, the turning of another season. It had been summer when Arabella was given into the Reverend Smythe's keeping. Months had come and gone, and there had been no word of the girl.

Though she had said nothing to Em, Tamsen was worried sick over the girl's safety. There were so many dreadful stories sifting back. The tale of the Donner party, of course, was an old one. The trail and methods of traversing it had improved since then. But it was a gruesome story, calculated to drive away sleep.

Sometimes she had visions of Arabella, frozen in the snow, her rosy cheeks pale with frost. And at other times, she was bedeviled by dreams of the train's few wagons, circled in death in the desert, their frames skeletal, slowly being buried in the blowing sand.

She would not think about it! They should be hearing from Reverend Smythe soon. He had promised to write as soon as they reached San Francisco. After all, she would need an address in order to send him additional funds for Arab's care! Besides, it was a lovely day, and spring was burgeoning.

Em was burgeoning, too, Tamsen thought wryly, as she headed back to the adobe. Now, in her fourth month, Em's pregnancy was beginning to show, no matter how tightly she laced herself. And she looked well, perhaps better than she ever had before—unless

178

one saw the haunted eyes. Tamsen's heart bled for her. How dreadful to be carrying a child of rape! Not even to know who its father was. And if the word got out, Em would be ostracized for something that was none of her fault.

If I were carrying Dan Tallant's child, I'd kill myself, she thought, fiercely. Em seemed to be taking it quietly and well, yet who knew how she'd feel later on, after months of self-imposed isolation? These last weeks, she hadn't attended church for fear of exposure. A coverall apron was handy on a hook, should church members visit the girl who, Tamsen hinted, was "ailing."

Even if they managed to get Em through this pregnancy without anyone the wiser, how did one hide a baby?

Then there was the Major. Tamsen's brow wrinkled again. She was angry with Em. Her problem could have been solved so easily. Major Arbuthnot would have been delighted at a hasty marriage. He would have never questioned the fact that the child was his.

Yet Em had held out, stubbornly, saying that it wasn't honest.

Maybe, Tamsen thought, she should try to talk to her once more. She walked back to the house, searching for the right words to prove her point.

Em was still adamant. The notion had been wrong in the beginning. It was even more wrong now. To present a husband with a five-month child would be stretching anyone's faith! It would make a laughing stock of him.

Tamsen shook her head, angrily. "Don't be stupid, Em! That pompous fool would believe anything you told him! He's the most egotistical jackass—"

She stopped short. Until now, she had been the Major's advocate, pointing out his good characteristics. Now she saw him as Em did. A flicker of the old Em appeared as her eyes danced at Tamsen's obvious discomfort.

"Forget it," Tamsen said. "I guess you're right."

But something must be done, and soon. Reluctantly,

she began to think of the conversations she'd had with Katie, lately. The cantina girl, rather spiritless after Dan Tallant's departure, recently had been afire with the idea of going to San Francisco. California was in the process of becoming a state, a wonderful, exciting place. And, Katie had pointed out, Tamsen had those two wagons, the materials, which should surely bring a fortune in mining country. If she could sell the cantina. . . .

Tamsen had shrugged it off. But the thought had tugged at her mind. Tamsen did not want to leave. She liked it here. But there was Em's plight to consider—and Arabella.

That night, Tamsen broached the subject of a move to Nell. The woman looked at her blankly. "Well, hell! Yer doin' awright here, ain'tcha?"

"It's Em," Tamsen confessed. "Nell, she's beginning to show. We've got to do something."

The big woman shrugged. "Don't make no difference. Here or out there, the kid's still a bastard."

Tamsen's anger rose, but she quelled it. Nell was being honest. Yet her words only added fuel to the plan that was building in Tamsen's mind. The attack on Em had been Tamsen's fault, and Em was suffering the consequences. Em should not have to suffer for the rest of her life. Tamsen would claim the child, herself, after it was born, saying that she was a widow. That would leave Em free to marry if she wished.

But to do this, they must make a move—and at the proper time.

"I'm still considering selling out and going," Tamsen said firmly.

"Suit yerself. Allus say, if you got a wild hair, do something about it. But yer makin' a helluva mistake—unless—" Her beady eyes took on a sly look. "Unless you got a reason? You figger that Tallant fella's gone out west?"

"You go to hell!" Tamsen exploded, flouncing from the room.

Nell took out a pack of cards and dealt them in a pattern, grinning to herself.

180

Tamsen returned home after her night's work to find Em in a state. Mrs. Calvin Tuttle had called shortly after Tamsen had gone the previous evening, catching Em at the well. Em was wearing an old frock, its let-out seams plainly visible. The coverall apron was on its hook in the house—out of reach.

"Do you think she noticed?"

Em shivered, recalling how the woman's eyes had widened and filled with malice, how she had cut her stay short and driven off as if she could hardly wait to spread the news.

"I think she did."

The following Sunday, Tamsen attended church. The room seemed filled with a rustling of whispers as she entered. And when she left, she noticed how the women, clustered in little knots, stopped talking as she approached, and looking guilty, began new conversations.

Em had been right, Tamsen thought, tiredly. Mrs. Tuttle had been tongue-wagging, and with results. The only way to stop the gossip was to prove the gossip wrong, and that they could not do.

Climbing into her buggy, Tamsen surveyed the people in their small close-knit groups. Talking about Em! Good decent Em! All of these women who had gone straight from their father's protection to a husband's home. None of them had ever had to fend for themselves, to fight in any fashion to get food for their loved ones. How dare they sit in judgment!

Tamsen cracked her whip against the horse's back and headed home. When she arrived, she went to the shed to shake a recumbent Dusty into life. "Check out the wagons," she snapped. "Get them ready to move. I need twelve good oxen, and a buyer for the cantina! We're going to California."

The next night, Em had a visitor. Her caller, Major Arbuthnot, was red-faced and breathing hard. Clad in her coverall, her disgrace decently hidden, Em invited him in. He seated himself, his round blue eyes rolled upward toward the roof. He seemed so agitated she feared he would have a stroke. Then, suddenly, he was on his knees before her, covering her hands with kisses.

"Dear lady," he said, brokenly, "oh, dear lady! I fear that in calling here at times when you were unchaperoned, I have compromised your position in the community. Rumors have reached my ears! They say that I—that you—that we—!"

He choked, releasing her hand to run a finger around the collar of his uniform as if it were strangling him. "They have dared to question the innocence of our relationship! To sully the name of a woman whose goodness is without doubt!"

"Major Arbuthnot," Em said, alarmed at his color, "please—"

"Yes," he said, panting, "yes. You are quite right. I am forgetting myself." He got to his feet, with considerable exertion, and mopped his brow with a huge handkerchief. Then he drew himself up in a military manner.

"What I have come to say is this," he said. "Since you've arrived at this pass through my thoughtless actions, I am prepared to do the honorable thing."

Despite herself, Em began to giggle. At last, she was laughing uncontrollably, tears streaming from her eyes. The Major stared at her with an expression that went from shock to dismay to anger.

"I see nothing humorous in the situation," he said, stuffily.

"But it is funny," Em gasped. Then, "Please! Just go!"

She closed the door behind the indignant Major and leaned against it, laughter shaking her frail frame until it stilled at last and there were only tears.

As soon as Tamsen was in the door the next morning, Em told her the story of the gentleman's proposal. But instead of seeing the humor of the situation, Tamsen blazed with anger.

"To think that those—those gossips could invent such a situation! To imagine that you would lower yourself to—to a romantic involvement with that horrible,

182

insufferable, self-righteous boor! That you're pregnant because he—!"

Em's eyes sparkled. "You're right, Tamsen! One doesn't have an affair with a man like Major Arbuthnot. He's the type one marries."

Her tirade silenced, Tamsen stared at Em in admiration, then hugged her, laughing.

"I'm sorry, Em! So sorry! Oh, Em, forgive me!"

That night before Tamsen left for work, the two girls sat over coffee at the round, battered table. The barrier of silence that had existed between them seemed to be lifted. Em was able to speak what was in her heart.

"I don't want this baby, Tamsen," she said. "I can't help feeling that way. I keep seeing those men in my mind and wondering which—" She covered her eyes with her hands for a moment as if to shut out the sight. "—which one it was, who is the father of the child. But it's something I can't help! I'm not going to hide any longer. I suppose I'm doomed to be a fallen woman, and I've been thinking. . . ."

Em outlined her plan. It was unnecessary for Tamsen to have a long ride each day. They would move to town, somewhere near the cantina. It didn't matter if the decent women drew back from her on the street. After the baby was born, Em would find a woman to care for it and work at the cantina as Tam did. Who cared about respectability?

You do, Tamsen thought, seeing the new, defensive look in Em's eyes. *You do.* Gently, she told Em of her plan to move on to California, that the wheels were already set in motion. And when Em protested, Tamsen reminded her of Arabella and how they would be able to see their dear little sister once again.

Despite a flurry of activity, months passed before traveling arrangements were completed. It was a long and trying period. Several members of the local congregation called upon Em to verify their suspicions. She calmly served them tea, with no explanations or excuses for her condition. They went away scandalized, with "Did you ever!" or "She's shameless, that's what she is!"

Major Arbuthnot asked for, and received, a transfer, thus setting the blame in many minds. They would never have believed it of such a nice Christian man. Apparently, *that woman* had led him astray.

In the meantime, the wagons were readied for the journey. Dusty found and purchased oxen from a Dutchman who had come overland with supplies to set up a general store. Tamsen set out to sell the cantina.

Until May, she had no prospects. The gold in California had drawn much of the cantina's clientele. Two similar places on the same street had closed. Tamsen, herself, was the drawing card that made her business prosper. No one wanted to gamble.

But surprisingly enough, her best offer finally came from one of her competitors. The man evidently believed that by changing his location, he would improve his reputation and his fortunes. In her desperation, Tamsen let him have the place for half its worth.

"Won't work for that sonofabitch," Nell snorted. "He's a slave-driver. Seen his girls?"

Tamsen had. They were pitiful, used creatures, pale and disease-ridden.

Here was the solution to another problem. Tamsen would miss Nell, and she needed Dusty. If Nell moved, Dusty would, too. "You can come with me," she said, "to California. The girls, too."

Nell banged the table with her open hand. "Hell, yes! Deal me in!"

Katie, Carmen, and Maggie followed Nell's lead. Tamsen's invitation was conditional. She planned to open a respectable business, a sewing shop, where she would design and make gowns for fine ladies. If they accompanied her, they must work out their passage upon arrival, rather than return to their former trade.

The details were worked out by the end of May, but there were further problems. The usual route would take them north to Santa Fe and then on to pick up the California Trail. The most auspicious time to leave was

184

in April, in order to ensure that the pass leading over the mountains and down into Sutter's Fort would be open. The trains, which were already late in leaving, refused to take along a party of women—one of them obviously expecting.

As the days passed, Tamsen grew more worried. She had not expected Em to be so far along in her pregnancy. Perhaps they should winter in Texas and try again in the spring.

Em scoffed at the idea. That would be foolish. The cantina was sold. There would be no income for any of them. Besides, she felt wonderful—and she'd rather die than stay here any longer.

Finally, Dusty found the way. As a new group of billowing canvases congregated in the wagon area outside Magoffinville, he got himself dressed in his ancient best. He went to check out the newly arrived train and returned in elation.

This train wasn't going the long way around. It was going to Santa Fe and heading straight out across Indian country to reach the Mission San Gabriel in Lower California. It would be a hot and dusty trip, but by the time they reached the desert country, it would be fall. They would have to jettison most of their possessions in favor of water barrels—

"What did they say about taking women?" Tamsen demanded.

Dusty flushed. "Jove! I didn't think to ask! They wanted to know how many are in our party, and I told them six adults, in addition to myself. Besides," he brightened, "it's a religious group. There's a priest who heads the train, along with a guide, and five good Catholic families. Also," he grinned, showing the missing teeth beneath his scrubby mustache, "a wagon full of nuns."

"Dusty, you didn't imply that we—"

His evasive eyes told her that he had.

Nell began to wheeze. "Those gawdamn barrels you mentioned," she gasped. "Whadda you want in 'em? Holy water?"

As the wagon train moved out, one day late in July, the Reverend Father Duran, circling the area on his spotted pony, his black cassock flying, gave rein to his horse. The newcomer's wagons were stout, driven by good, healthy oxen. He had noted that with approval, from afar, the wagons having arrived just in time to form. But on the front seat of the one—surely, that was a young girl! She looked small and frail, and her perspiration-soaked gown clung to her body in a most suggestive way.

Riding alongside the wagons, Father Duran noted that Mr. Wotherspoon, the mannerly gentleman to whom he had spoken, was driving the second. That was in order, but he must talk to him tonight. At the rear of the wagon, he saw with consternation that the tailgate was down, and on it were seated three women of dubious-appearing character, swinging their legs in a most provocative way for the benefit of the driver behind.

For an instant, the priest had a wild impulse to stop the train, to discover exactly who these people were and what they were doing here! But the train was already moving, and he should be up front leading it.

Turning his pony, he started forward, to pause again as he spied an elephantine vision in purple silk framed in the circle of canvas at the rear of the first wagon. His ears were shattered by a voice that rose above the noise of the wagon train.

"Git the lead out, Dusty," the woman roared. "What the hell you waitin' for? We're on our way!"

Father Duran made the sign of the Cross and moved quickly to take his place at the head of the train.

Chapter 20

Three weeks out of Magoffinville, Tamsen had begun to regret the decision to move on to California. As the days on the trail dragged by, Em grew pale and tired, and dark hollows appeared beneath her eyes. Maybe they should have stayed and faced the outraged stares, the sniggering gossip. Tamsen didn't know. But they had set out and now they were committed.

Bracing her feet, Tamsen shifted the reins to one hand, raising the other to adjust the bandana that covered her nose and mouth. The dust settled in a gray mask around her eyes, but at least, this way, she was able to breathe.

A passing rider gave her vehicle a quick glance to check that all was in order. He quickly averted his gaze. She didn't blame him. Some holier-than-thou wife had probably given him his orders. She knew what the rest of the train thought of the McLeod outfit. That was why they were eating dust here at the rear.

The good father had sent a messenger for Dusty on their second night out. Since Dusty had been hitting the bottle, Tamsen went in his stead. The priest was clearly embarrassed at what he had to say.

This was a family train. He'd had complaints, and he could afford no disruptions on the trail. He inquired about the relationship of Nell and the girls, asking what they planned to do when they reached the coast. When Tamsen described her idea for a dressmaking establishment, he raised his brows in disbelief. He did not wish to be unkind, but as he had said, there were complaints. He was certain that the other women on her wagons

187

were of good character, but they were in such lively spirits. Perhaps if Tamsen could encourage them to be a bit more discreet. And it might be more comfortable if they brought up the rear of the train. It would be checked, periodically, of course, in case they had trouble.

Tamsen had returned to her wagon, her cheeks blazing with humiliation. It was clear what the man thought they were. And worse, as she approached the one area where no cookfire showed, she saw Nell calling out to a woman bending above a pot.

"Hey, honey, how the hell do you light a fire? The lady-boss is off, sky-hootin' around somewhere, Dusty's too damn drunk, an them other girls don't know how to set anything on fire but a man!"

He didn't misjudge us, Tamsen thought. He sees us as what we are. Perhaps I'm the one who's deluded.

The next morning, Tamsen fell back behind the other wagons. And each day, she'd been dropping farther behind because of the dust. The priest didn't indulge in closing a circle with his train. God would protect them, he said. So Tamsen tried to choose a spot quite distant from the others. If God truly watched over them, a few feet more or less wouldn't make any difference! At least none of their sinful ways would rub off on these good people!

Tamsen flinched as a wheel hit a stone thrown into her path by the wagon ahead. Even with Nell's weight added to that of the water barrels, the vehicle jounced a lot. She was worried about Em.

Em, in the meantime, had cause to worry, herself. The trip had been more grueling than she cared to admit, though yesterday she had seemed to feel much better. Good enough to want to get out into the sunshine, away from the dusty, smothering aura of the wagon. But it was agreed that she would remain out of sight of the other wagons all day and come out only at night until they were safely past Santa Fe. Tamsen feared that the priest might insist that Em remain behind until after her confinement.

So Em kept herself hidden. If it weren't for Nell and her cheery conversation, Em thought she would have gone mad. But today even conversation bothered her. She was trying to will away the pain that had beset her almost all day. An odd pain that seemed to begin lightly, to rise to a swelling crest, then fade again. Which proved she could control it, if she tried.

Another? So soon? This time, a little moan escaped her clenched teeth.

"Huh? Whatcha say?" Nell's flow of comment stopped and she studied the girl's face. "Somethin' wrong? You awright?"

"No, I'm fine." Em's voice ended on a sigh as the pain faded. But the big woman smoothed Em's pale brown hair, perspiration-darkened now, and felt the dampness of Em's forehead.

"Don't tell Tamsen," Em moaned as her body arched again. "We'll be stopping soon. I can wait."

But Nell had already lumbered to her feet. "Get the hell off the trail," she boomed at Tamsen. "We're havin' us a kid." Then, moving to the rear of the wagon, she wigwagged a signal to Dusty that they were planning to stop.

Tamsen drove the oxen into a small clearing and stopped. Heart thundering, she joined Nell, who was standing over the agonized Em.

"What do we do now?" Tamsen asked in a frightened voice.

"Hell, I don't know." Nell scratched her head. "Boil water, I guess."

Tamsen hastened to find wood. She was aided by a fumbling Dusty, frightened out of his senses by the coming event. It developed that Maggie and Katie knew how to handle the details of birth. Both women were the eldest of enormous families, and had had to assist at births many times. Tamsen, silently giving thanks for having had sense enough to bring the girls along, knelt to breathe life into the fire.

Suddenly she was conscious of a tremendous silence. All the excited chatter had died away. Raising her eyes

189

to look across the fire, she saw Nell, her flabby cheeks white and trembling; Carmen and Maggie transfixed beside the wagon wheel; Katie at the opening in the canvas, her face a freckled blur in the dim light. They were staring beyond her. She sensed someone at her shoulder and turned.

"Dusty?"

Her voice caught in her throat. For behind her stood an Indian, his face painted into an evil mask. And behind him stood five—no, six more. Then Dusty appeared around the corner of the wagon, his arms filled with wood. He dropped it with a clatter.

"Mescalero Apaches!" he whispered. "Don't move! I think they're on the warpath. Do you suppose they'll accept gifts—the shovels?"

But as he took a step backward, a lean brown brave, wearing a menacing mask, leaped forward to pinion Dusty's arms and drag him to stand beside Tamsen. Another dragged Nell forward, the big woman's tongue stilled for once.

Then there was a moan from the wagon.

The Indians were immobile for a moment. The one who seemed to be the leader issued a guttural command and one of his men started toward the sound.

Tamsen threw herself in front of him, eyes blazing, her own fear forgotten. "You leave her alone," she shouted. "Leave her alone!" The man brushed her aside and moved toward the wagon. Then he stopped.

All the Indians in fact, were standing still, staring toward the wagon. And there was Em! Deathly pale, head erect, she faced the Indians, while around her throat, she wore the medallion she had been given so long ago.

One of the painted war party gave a shout of recognition. Moving in front of the leader, he began to jabber away in his strange tongue, doing a sort of dance, a weird, capering pantomine as if he were telling a story.

"Jove!" Dusty said, softly, "Jove!" And Tamsen recognized what the man was telling the others.

190

It was the tale of the young Indian who had pursued Arab into the house and had his backside blistered for his reward. "Ai—eee!" the Indian howled, grabbing his posterior. His action brought a spate of laughter from his comrades. Encouraged by his success, the man continued with the parody. He pointed to his head. A feather. Then, with mincing steps, he was a woman walking.

"Boom!" His shout made her jump. He fell to the ground and sat up, ruefully examining the feather.

Tamsen almost laughed, too. He had most successfully described the death of her hat.

Now, it was Em's turn. He walked toward the haggard girl who stood stiffly with pain-blind eyes, holding herself erect through strength of will. He pointed to the medallion, raising his hand as though in benediction as he spoke, then turned to look at his audience.

They stood in stony silence for a moment. Then the leader moved forward, making a similar gesture, speaking the same strange phrases. He was followed by the others, one at a time.

Homage paid, they looked at each other, the stern visages breaking into semblances of smiles. The storyteller, intent on dragging the last vestiges of humor from his tale, clapped his hand to his posterior once more, with an "Ai—eee!"

Finally, still laughing, the group disappeared into the surrounding night.

Em swayed and drifted gracefully to the ground. Katie and Maggie carried her back into the wagon.

Tamsen, tending the fire, helpless in the face of what was happening, thought bitterly of her decisions that had led them to this time, this place. If they had remained in Pennsylvania, Em would have been safe. At home, at least, there had been a featherbed.

She jerked herself back to the present. Em must survive! Perhaps it would be better if the child did not. What chance did it have? Conceived in rape; born with a bawdy old woman and three prostitutes in attendance;

191

looked after by a dance-hall entertainer; with Dusty, a dismal drunken ex-patriate Englishman, playing the part of proxy father.

A moan from the wagon cut through Tamsen like a knife. And despite herself, she moved toward the scene of Em's labor. The lantern inside the wagon threw the figures of Katie and Maggie in silhouette against the canvas. They moved jerkily. What were they doing?

Another moan hastened Tamsen's steps. She climbed inside the wagon, and Katie, pushing back her rusty hair from a white face set in irritation, turned to her.

"I told you to keep away! It's too crowded in here! There's nothing you can do—"

"How—how is she?"

Katie's stony face was answer enough.

Tamsen moved past her, past Maggie who knelt bathing the girl's feverish face. Em tossed in delirium, and Tamsen caught her icy, clutching hand.

"Em," she whispered, "oh, Em! You're going to be all right! Listen to me!"

But Em flailed out, tearing her wrist from Tamsen's comforting fingers. "Arab," she said. "Where's Arab?" Her words were followed by another shuddering moan that racked her fragile body.

Hand to her lips, Tamsen backed away. Katie caught her shoulders, guiding her to the opening in the canvas. "I told you," she said. "You can't help here. We can do all that's needed."

"She doesn't want me," Tamsen said in a dazed voice. "Em doesn't want me."

"Don't be a fool! She doesn't know what she's saying. The baby's coming the wrong way—"

"But Em! Will she—?"

Her question went unanswered. Katie had handed her, gently but firmly, down into the waiting arms of Nell.

"Get her out of here," the Irish girl pleaded. "We've got enough on our hands without having to keep her still, too."

Nell led Tamsen back to the fire. "Yer gonna stay

right here," she said, firmly. "Hell, honey, you gotta learn there's some things you can't ramrod, an' this here's one of 'em. Leave it to them as knows how."

"But Em didn't want me." Tamsen's voice was small, piteous. Nell fought back her sympathy.

"Don't reckon she even knowed you was there. Got her mind on doin' whut she's gotta do. Now, you gonna set there while I hunt up that gawdamn Dusty? Gotta have some firewood—"

"Don't worry, Nell," Tamsen said, forlornly, "I'll stay." The big woman lumbered off, grumbling, into the darkness.

Tamsen stared into the flames. This can't be real, she thought. This can't be happening. The Indians, Em's suffering. It was all dream-like. Yet she could smell the fragrance of wood-smoke in her nostrils. The silence of the night was disturbed as the oxen, grazing nearby, moved restlessly as if they too sensed that something unusual was occurring.

It is true, she thought, dully. It is all really true. A pain-filled cry from the wagon tore through her, and she felt tears on her cheeks.

Because of her, Em had come to this pass. Because of her, Papa lay dead beside the trail to Santa Fe. And Arab was gone. Arab, for whom Em cried out in her pain. Tamsen had never felt so lost, so helpless. She folded her arms across her breast against the chill that shook her body, eyes fixed on the wagon, her ears deaf to all but Em's terrible sobbing cries. She did not see the shadow that moved out of the trees behind her.

"You have trouble, my daughter?"

Tamsen whirled at the voice. Behind her stood the black-clad figure of Father Duran.

"You were not with the train," he explained. "We feared some accident, a broken wheel, perhaps. And there are Indians about. I came back to look for you."

"Father! Oh, Father!" Tamsen launched herself into the priest's arms. "Help me! Help Em! Oh, help me pray!"

She poured out the story of Em and what was happening to her to the startled priest. When she had finished, her eyes went to his face. It was impassive. Well, what should she have expected? They were not of his flock or his faith. She backed away. "I—I'm sorry," she said hopelessly.

But his hands reached out to take hers. She could feel the strength in them as, with a downward pressure, he said, "Kneel, my daughter. Kneel with me."

They knelt before the fire, Tamsen's head bowed, Father Duran's lifted to the star-filled sky. They prayed together and then he offered a long prayer in Latin that Tamsen could not understand. But it was enough to know the intent behind his words. She let them fill her ears, shutting out the whimpering sounds carried on the night wind.

Finally, Carmen brought them news. Tongue-tied by the unexpected sight of a priest, she lowered her eyes and mumbled until Tamsen gripped her arms and shook her. "What did you say?" Tamsen cried, her voice sharp with fear. "Is Em—?"

"A little girl," Carmen said. "Katie says to tell you it's all right—"

Tamsen sank to the ground, burying her face in her hands as she sobbed with relief. And at last, the priest's quiet voice intruded. "May I give the mother and child my blessing?"

"Please," Tamsen choked. "And, Father . . . thank you . . ."

A short while later, Em's baby was laid in Tamsen's arms. A blessed baby. Blessed at the hour of her birth by the good father who returned to the train to declare a rest stop for all the wagons. They would wait a couple of days, until Em had time to recover. Em was sleeping, a sleep of exhaustion. And Tamsen could not believe the small miracle she now held in her arms.

"Don't look like much," Nell observed, looking at the tiny blanket-wrapped form.

"She's beautiful," Katie said, surprisingly. "She's going to look more like Tamsen than Em. See how dark she is?"

"Well, hell, we can't jes' call it she," Nell grumped. "Ain't she gonna have a name?"

"Martha," Tamsen said. "After our mother, her grandmother."

Martha. But there must be a last name. Tamsen stood holding the child long after the others had gone—Katie to sit with Em, the others to their beds. If Em had married George, the baby's name would be Harper. Martha Harper. That had a nice valid sound.

She thought of her plans to pose as a widow, to take the baby as her own. But she, too, would need a new name. She had been Tamsen McLeod. She had been Poppy Franklin. So why not the Widow Harper? She grinned a little, remembering phlegmatic George, so proper and dull.

My daughter, she said to herself, feeling a new and fierce possessiveness as she looked down at the baby. Em would be free of a child she didn't want, free to find a good respectable marriage one day. No matter what her beginnings, little Martha would have all the opportunities Tamsen could give her.

The huge dark eyes in the tiny face opened. They stared at Tamsen, solemnly. Impulsively, Tamsen turned, the infant in her arms, to face toward the West —the West, where a city of gold guarded a gateway to the sea; the West, with its dreams and its promise of riches and respectability.

Book Two

Madam Franklin's Parlor
For Gentlemen

Chapter 1

The trip was a long, hard pull from the time Em's baby was born. The train waited for three days, until Em was able to travel. When they reached Santa Fe, however, the consensus held that the McLeod wagons should remain there and perhaps take the northern route through the pass on the Platte in the spring.

Em steadfastly refused to hear of such an arrangement. She had come this far. She could go on. Despite warnings from local people that the priest's intention to head straight across country was suicidal, the McLeod wagons moved out with the train.

It was a long trek, and a dangerous one. Many times they picked up Indian sign, or saw them in the distance on horseback. Mescaleros; the dreaded Chiricahua, Navajo. Father Duran often dismounted to walk, holding a cross high. The black-robed nuns followed him on foot. Whether this deterred the superstitious tribes, Tamsen did not know. But it was evident that something did. Perhaps the priest was right, and maybe the aura of his goodness served as protection for the train. She had not forgotten the night he prayed for Em.

The days were burning hot, the nights chill. The wagons moved in a cloud of choking dust. Tamsen drove like an automaton, too tired to think of anything but controlling the team of oxen. Inside the wagon, Nell tended Em, washing her feverish brow with the precious rancid water that was running low.

In their other wagon, Dusty occasionally wet his whistle from one of his prodigious supply of bottles. The girls tended the baby. Tamsen thought it best to

199

keep mother and infant separated, out of deference to Em. One of the families on the train had a cow that produced a little milk. Martha was fed by the process of dipping a cloth in the milk which she was then allowed to suckle—in lieu of her mother's breast.

Em did not ask to see the baby, for her physical condition veered between delirium and apathy. Martha learned the feel of maternal love at night when Tamsen, arms aching from the day's drive, held her close with great tenderness.

As they neared San Gabriel, Em's state of health began to improve and tensions lifted as they learned they had little to fear from that point on. Finally the McLeod wagons broke away from the train, with reluctant goodbyes, and moved across the California terrain alone.

They reached Los Angeles, a drowsy village of mud huts surrounded by ranchos. There were no newspapers, public schools, or libraries. The village slept in the sun, far removed from her sister city to the north in both wealth and disposition. There was, however, a harbor, and ships plied back and forth along the coast. Tamsen, who had had enough of journeying by wagon, booked passage for her group and cargo aboard a northbound ship. The journey was expensive, but she was able to recoup her losses by selling her cargo of tools and teams of oxen for double the price to a speculator before the trip was completed.

So she was at ease in mind and heart as their ship sailed into San Francisco harbor. Standing on the deck, her dark hair blowing in the wind, Tamsen saw a forest of masts. And beyond them, a city shining in the sun. The little group stepped onto the docks, dazed by the color and sound of the place; by the sight of strange, foreign faces, the exotic mixture of languages; by the barrels, crates, and bales being lifted from shipboard by windlass; by the crowding merchants bidding as auctioneers shouted out items from ships' cargoes.

From a newcomer's point of view, it looked like a city of promise. And for some, it was.

In that early spring of 1851, San Francisco was a sprawling octopus, reaching tentacles up and down the surrounding hills in the form of mud-slick roads. A monster created of gold, it fed upon the precious materials found farther north in the Sacramento valley, upon the wealth that came from the sea, and lastly, upon itself.

The speculators, entrepreneurs, and manipulators, had begun to exploit the area. San Francisco's government had broken down in the eight months since it had been installed and had been taken over by a lawless element. Many of its officials were straight from Australian penal colonies. Thus a rape of the city had begun, with the "officials" voting themselves huge salaries and dipping into the government till. Criminals at a lower level roamed the streets. There were shootings every night, burglaries, and holdups.

Speculators knew they were into a good thing and were willing to push it to the limit. Scarce commodities, such as tobacco, were sold at an inflated figure of one to four hundred times their price. Property soared out of sight. Lots that once sold for from sixteen to six hundred dollars per lot now cost as much as two thousand dollars per frontage foot. Lumber from the Northwest coast and from Mendocino was priced at as much as four hundred dollars for a thousand board-feet.

San Francisco was a building city for those who could afford to build. And a landlord's market when it came to rental property. A city, drenched in fog, doused in sunshine, perfume, and whisky, and ripe with chicanery. Such was the place that the small group from Magoffinville found at the end of their journey. Its darker aspect was invisible to them as they marveled at the hustle and bustle of it, dreaming of houses, real beds, and stores in which one might shop for any need.

They did not realize that they were as strange a sight as any they surveyed as they traversed the city streets—six women, a baby, and one slightly tipsy gentleman leading a cow.

They were directed to the City Hotel, where Tamsen

had her first inkling of the housing situation in San Francisco. There were no empty rooms. But the clerk gallantly shifted the male tenants of one room into others, already overcrowded, so there would be a place for the ladies. Dusty had to share the shed at the back with the cow. The price the clerk named for his accommodations was exorbitant enough to make Tamsen gasp.

It would only be for a night or two, she told herself. The important thing was to have a place where Em might rest, a base from which to carry out her plans. First, she intended to find Arabella. Then, a place to set up shop.

Neither was to be found.

Early the next morning, Tamsen went to the newspaper office. The editor, in his gartered sleeves and sunshade, told her that he had no knowledge of a school for young ladies such as Tamsen described. Nor of the minister. He directed her to the city offices, where she received short shrift. San Francisco was a place where people went purposely to lose themselves. Some of the city officials could understand that point of view all too well. They did not intend to offer her assistance.

Shaken, Tamsen went at last to the churches. Surely there would be some sort of communication between people of the ministerial profession. There again, she found nothing. One minister vaguely recalled hearing of an itinerant preacher who might have been the man she sought. But he'd heard the man had left town, taking a ship for somewhere. Perhaps if she checked the passenger lists at the shipping offices—

Tamsen hurried to the docks, praying to find a clue to Arab's disappearance. She discovered two of the names she searched for. The Reverend Wilbert Smythe and his wife had taken passage for Hawaii in January of the previous year.

There was no mention of Arabella McLeod.

Grief tightened Tamsen's throat. She feared that her sister was dead. Indians, pneumonia, cholera, injury, all the things that went hand in hand with the long trek to the West ran through her mind. But why had the minister not notified her? How could he have let them go on wondering and hoping?

She must not tell Em what she'd discovered. She would tell her that the minister had decided not to establish his school in San Francisco, but had moved on to select another site. That there were people here to whom he would be sending his forwarding address.

When Em remarked on her taut face and circled eyes, Tamsen merely said that she was tired. It had been a gruelling day, and she was exhausted.

In any case, there was no time to worry or to grieve over Arab's disappearance. The City Hotel was no place for a group of unattached women. Katie, Carmen, and Maggie could not help flaunting their charms, and the men who crowded the hotel were a rough lot, hungry for the companionship the girls had to offer. Em was exhausted, Nell grumpy, Dusty seldom sober. And the cost of their accommodations swiftly depleted Tamsen's funds.

She had to find a home for them all, and a place of business, soon.

Tamsen threw herself whole-heartedly into the project, but she soon came face to face with the reality of life in San Francisco. Her original plan had been to purchase a shop in a good area, to decorate it in a manner to attract respectable trade. But she discovered that buying such an establishment was out of the question. Even rentals represented a sum beyond her wildest dreams.

Little by little, she was forced to discard her requirements for a place of business. A tiny pie-shaped lot had to be forgotten when she learned the cost of building supplies. A fire-gutted structure had possibilities, and she might be able to afford the cost of renovation, but San Francisco had no labor force. All able-bodied men were off making their fortunes in the gold fields.

Each day, Tamsen moved father from the center of

203

respectable shops in her search. And at last, she found something she could afford in an area of casinos and small, shabby bars, near the docks. It was an old fruit-sales-and-storage building, with an open front where the wares had been displayed in bins. Behind the open area was a rambling shed-like space.

The man who owned the place was eager to get to the gold fields. Otherwise, he told Tamsen, he would not be giving her such a bargain. As Tamsen paid him all of the money with which she'd expected to purchase and furnish a shop, receiving only a year's lease in return, she looked around and sighed. The bright sun revealed cracks in the structure; the walls had never been painted, and she wondered if it would be possible to make the place livable. When a large black rat ran across her feet, she began to regret her transaction.

How could she bring Em and the baby to a place like this?

Oddly enough, Em was delighted with the move. The crowded cubbyhole at the hotel had worn on her weakened nerves. During Tamsen's absences, little Martha had needed attention, and Em had drawn close to the baby, feeling the deep stirrings of maternal love.

Now they would have a home.

It was Em who pointed out the possibilities of the storage building. The open front could be enclosed and divided to make a reception and fitting room. The cavernous, echoing shed could be curtained off to make a sewing room and bedrooms.

Too frail to join in the renovation, Em sat in a chair, holding the baby, directing the others at their tasks. Tamsen went at it like a fury, wielding hammer and saw. The girls worked sulkily, but steadily. Dusty lent an occasional hand, but Nell was put out of the running early in the building, with a mashed thumb that she greeted with a string of profanity.

Finally, the restructuring was completed, and Tamsen Harper's Sewing Establishment opened for business. The day her sign was painted and affixed in place was a day of celebration. And then her real worries began. She had purchased fine materials at an exorbitant price, but because of its location, the shop did not attract a monied clientele. The drabs of the waterfront drifted in through curiosity. Fingering the wares, they stayed to buy. And Tamsen underpriced her work.

She had business, but with the price of yard goods, business was about all she was getting. And to make matters worse, the girls and Nell and Dusty, wearied after the long hours spent in renovating the building, were not very enthusiastic about putting in long hours sewing. Nell and Dusty spent the evening hours at a nearby bar, where they felt at home, and the girls scattered to the four winds when night approached.

The sewing establishment had been a mistake, Tamsen thought ruefully as she stitched away one damp, foggy evening. But she would find a way to make it all work out. She had to! Yesterday, she had put in fourteen hours of steady work; today, sixteen. And her orders were still behind. If only she could make more of a profit! If only the fog would dissipate. Her fingers were cold, and her eyes felt strained.

Little Martha whimpered from the cradle Tamsen had found for her. Tamsen dropped her sewing, but before she could rise, Em leaned from her bed. Her gold-brown hair hung about her face as she reached to rock the cradle, crooning softly.

The maternal picture made Tamsen ache inside. Em was getting too attached to the child, and it was not really wise. Tamsen was known as the Widow Harper, and the baby was Martha Harper. At first Em seemed to go along with the idea of Tamsen's adopting the child as her own. Or, at least, she didn't seem to care. Was she having regrets now, Tamsen wondered.

As Tamsen forced a reluctant needle through a thick seam, she was startled by pounding on the shop door.

Jumping at the sound, she pricked her finger. Her eyes met Em's questioning ones, and she tried to hide her apprehension as she put her sewing down. The shop

205

was closed. There was no reason for anyone to come calling at this hour. Crime was rampant here. Only a few days before, two thieves entered the C. J. Jansen store, beat the owner almost to death, and robbed his safe of two thousand dollars. Nell and the girls would have come to the small door at the rear. Perhaps it was a wandering drunk.

Carrying a lamp, Tamsen went through the small, partitioned reception area, to peer cautiously through a crack in the boarded-up front. The lantern that swung outside to illuminate her sign was dim, haloed with the fog that had crept in from the sea, but it served to delineate two figures. The smaller one turned, and the light revealed the dark oval face and braids of an Indian girl. The larger figure was that of a man.

There was something about him that seemed familiar, something in the way he stood. Oh, God, it couldn't be Daniel Tallant!

Numbly, she unbarred the door.

Face to face with the man, she could see that she was mistaken. Something in the way he moved had deceived her. He, like Dan Tallant, was lean, tanned and moved with a pantherish grace as if he were built of coiled springs. But there, except for a frankly virile presence, the resemblance ended. This man's face was made for laughter. Laugh wrinkles surrounded the bold blue eyes that looked at Tamsen in frank admiration. His nose was turned up a little and a few freckles showed beneath the tan. The corners of his mouth lifted in a grin, and she could tell by the flush on his cheekbones that he had been drinking.

"Want you to make a dress for this little gal," he said. "Fix her up like a lady, expense no object."

Tamsen shifted her gaze to the girl. She was clearly one of the tribeless Indians that hung about the fringes of San Francisco scavenging. True, she was dressed in a print frock, much too short for her, rather than in rags or animal pelts like some Tamsen had seen. But the dress had clearly been worn for months. The girl stank of rancid grease. Her bare ankles, below the dress, were caked with mud.

"We—we're closed at this hour," Tamsen said doubtfully.

"Well, hell, open up. Glad to pay you for your trouble." Taking a snap purse from his pocket, he began pouring gold coins into his palm. Tamsen's eyes widened, but she lifted a staying hand.

"No extra charge. Wait until we see what you want."

She led the sullen girl into the fitting room, closing the door firmly in the gentleman's face. The Indian stood silent as Tamsen went about her work. Her measurements were much like Tamsen's own, except for her waist, which was somewhat larger. It would be simple to make the gown.

When they returned to the reception room, Tamsen attempted to get an idea of what kind of gown or material the man desired. He was vague. "Just something with class." Tamsen told him she didn't think fittings would be required and that she could have the dress finished within a week. He tossed a wealth of coins on the counter.

"Be seein' you," he said.

"Wait!" Tamsen called after him, certain that he'd wake in the morning with second thoughts. "I must have your name. And this is far too much money."

"Sam Larabee," he yelled back at her. "And, hell, what's money for?"

Then he was gone.

Tamsen counted out the money he'd given her, then counted it again before she thrust it into her apron pocket. It was more than she'd made in a month. She would keep it separate from her other funds, since he would surely want a refund when he sobered up.

That night she dreamed of Dan Tallant and awakened in an agony of passion, his name on her lips. She sat up, hugging her knees as she stared into the darkness, overcome by a wave of longing and loneliness. She'd thought she'd managed to get Dan out of her life and her mind.

Sam Larabee had brought back those memories, she supposed. She brushed at her forehead, trying to erase Dan Tallant from her thoughts, forcing them toward Sam Larabee and the money he'd left with her tonight. She hoped the purchase was a temporary aberration due to drink, that he would forget all about it by morning, and not come back at all.

Chapter 2

The visit of Sam Larabee seemed to have brought good luck to the sewing establishment, for business began to boom. The next day a young woman who introduced herself as Polly Simpson appeared. Dressed in a sweeping black gown, which flared beneath a tiny waist, wearing a plumed hat and carrying a feathered sunshade, the girl seemed reluctant to state her business.

For a time, she wandered about, looking at materials, touching them to feel their textures. Tamsen watched her, noting her pallor, the ornate hairstyle, her way of walking, and made an assumption. This was a night person. She was sure of it.

Finally, the girl approached her with a defiant little lift of her head. "I know this is a most respectable place," she said, "but I was told you are quite good at design. The truth is, I need some costumes made. Something a little out of the ordinary—"

Tamsen listened and made a hasty sketch of something she had designed for herself at the cantina, a provocative gown with bared shoulders and a long slit up the skirt.

Polly Simpson studied the sketch eagerly. "That's exactly what I want. But we will need ten, to start with. Could you send someone to take our measurements? To do the fittings?"

The address she gave was that of a prominent San Francisco madam.

"It takes one to know one," Nell chortled when she related the story. The remark gave Tamsen pause. The kind of life Polly Simpson represented was behind her.

209

She would stitch the garments. That was her job. But the measuring and fitting—that would be up to Nell and the girls.

Katie and Nell visited the madam's residence that very afternoon. They returned filled with excitement at the wonders they had seen.

"Gawdamndest plushest place I ever been in," Nell said, exuberantly. "They must make a mint. It's one helluva joint."

Katie described the carpets, the mirrors, the hanging chandeliers with prisms, and the pretty girls in lovely gowns.

Tamsen, listening, felt an odd yearning for the old cantina days. She had missed those days, though she would not admit it to herself. They had been filled with excitement and adventure. She missed the feeling of power she'd had, the knowledge that in the eyes of her customers she *was* someone.

She clenched her needle-pricked fingers in her lap. There was no comparison between those times and this. That life was over. It had brought nothing but danger and trouble. Now she was on her way to both respectability and fortune. For she had named a price that was out of all reason for the seductive design. The madam, according to Nell, had accepted it without question, hinting at work in the future.

Em, improved a bit, took on the chore of making the dress Sam Larabee had ordered. She took tiny stitches in soft turquoise velvet, transforming the material into a simple gown with sweeping, classic lines.

"Don't wear yourself out, Em," Tamsen begged. "If you'd seen that girl! She was filthy, and she smelled! I don't think they'll pick the dress up, but if they do, it will be a rag within the week."

"The poor thing may never have had anything nice," Em said, gently. "Please, I want to do it."

Maggie, Carmen, and Katie for the first time evinced an interest in their work. The costume-making was fun. So, in spite of the workload, Tamsen was able to slip away for her daily walk. On the pretext of taking little

210

Martha out for fresh air and sunshine, she walked the streets searching for a laughing girl with red-gold curls. If Arab were alive, she would be here somewhere.

One night, exactly a week after his first visit, Sam Larabee returned with the Indian girl. Throughout the day, Tamsen had convinced herself that she had seen the last of him. But when, late that night, she heard the banging on the door, she knew who was knocking.

Sam Larabee was in the same condition he'd been in previously, his smile-crinkled face just as roguishly charming. But there was still that shock that touched her nerve ends at his appearance, which reminded her of Dan. The Indian, too, looked as she had before, except, if possible, she'd collected a week's more dirt.

Tamsen looked at her in distaste as she went to bring out the lovely gown which Em had spent so many hours making. When she returned with it, the girl looked at it, stolidly, without comment, but the man beamed. "She'll wear it," he said. "Help her get it on."

Tamsen faltered. The notion of the girl donning the gown over all that filth repelled her. Em, appearing in the doorway behind her, spoke.

"The streets are so dusty. Perhaps the young lady might wish to wash up a little first?"

Sam Larabee studied his companion as if he were seeing her for the first time. "She is a mess, ain't she? If you ladies could rig up some kind of a bath, I'd be proud to pay."

"Gladly," Tamsen said, quickly.

Leaving Em to talk to Larabee, Tamsen added wood to the stove and set to heating water. When she had filled the wooden-staved tub behind a curtain in the room she and Em shared, she put out a sizable chunk of homemade soap and a couple of towels. Then she went to fetch the girl.

Em volunteered to show the girl to the bath. As they left, Sam Larabee mentioned that he might like to have a couple more gowns made for the girl. But before Tamsen could discuss material or price, she heard Em's voice raised to a panicky pitch.

211

Running to the bath area, Tamsen found Em backed into a corner. The Indian girl had seized a stick of stove wood, and, holding it over her head like a club, she was threatening Em. The girl's bodice was half undone.

"She won't bathe," Em gasped. "I tried—"

The Indian whirled, but Tamsen was too quick for her. Rushing toward her, she gave a tremendous shove, and the girl, caught off balance, landed in the tub, with a mighty splash. She came out of the water, spitting like a cat, her dress plastered to her body, and ran toward the door.

She ran smack into Sam Larabee, who gripped her clawing wrists. "What the hell's going on in here?" he growled.

"The lady does not like water," Em said.

He spoke a few words in a strange tongue, gave the girl a shake, and she turned, still with a sulky expression, back toward the bath.

"What did you say to her?" Em gasped.

"Told her if she didn't wash up, I'd beat the hell out of her!" The man looked as if he meant it.

An hour later, they led the girl toward where he waited in the reception room. She was bathed, her hair washed and put into a coronet on the top of her head. She looked almost pretty wearing the turquoise velvet gown and a pair of slippers Em had sacrificed. Larabee was elated, though he eyed the dress dubiously. "Sorta plain, ain't it?" he wanted to know.

"It would look better with a necklace of some sort," Em admitted. "Perhaps a single pendant—"

"Hell, I'll buy her one the size of a turkey egg," Sam Larabee announced, recklessly. "Come on, honey, let's go spend some more money."

"The shops are closed now," Tamsen interposed.

"Well, let 'em open up. I can pay 'em for their trouble!"

When Nell came in at a late hour, Tamsen and Em had just turned their attention to the floor. Their whole room seemed awash, and a trail of water led to the front door.

"What the hell's going on?" Nell boomed.

The two girls exchanged smiles. "The roof leaked," Em said, demurely.

Nell looked dubiously at the ceiling. "But I just come in. It ain't rainin'."

"That," said Tamsen, dolefully, "is what makes it so bad."

The big woman stared at them for a moment in confusion, then, "Oh, hell! Yer both a pair of gawdamn loonies!" She marched off to bed, while Em and Tamsen collapsed in helpless laughter.

Later, their chores finished, after an admiring look at little Martha who had slept through the commotion, the girls sat down to have a cup of tea. Em asked, "You're worrying about something, aren't you, Tam?"

"Not really. I was just thinking about that man. Sam Larabee."

"I was, too," Em admitted. "He seems such a nice man. How do you suppose he got mixed up with the likes of that girl?"

"I haven't the slightest idea," Tamsen said. She had been thinking of Larabee's resemblance to Dan.

"Don't be too hard on him," Em said, defending Sam Larabee against the anger in Tamsen's tone. "After all, it isn't up to us to judge his actions. And men are different. I suppose if they find a girl who is willing to— you know—they don't consider it's wrong—"

Before Tamsen's eyes rose a vision of that night in the adobe out of Magoffinville, of the way she'd given herself to Dan Tallant for a brief time, body and soul. "I don't think it was all my doing," he'd said, afterward. "If I remember, you not only asked, you begged—" Then he had ridden away.

"Good night, Em," Tamsen said, shortly. "It's late."

It was a long time before she slept, and when she did, her pillow was wet with tears.

Chapter 3

The next morning, Sam Larabee was waiting in front of the shop when it opened. Clean-shaven, stone sober, he was spruced up like a gentleman. He entered the shop and, making a pretense of looking at the materials displayed, wandered about while Tamsen wondered if he'd remembered what he'd paid for that gown and perhaps wanted his money back.

Finally, he said, "Say, didn't I see a little kid back there last night—in a cradle?"

"You did," Tamsen said, shortly.

"Yours?"

"Yes."

He cleared his throat, his face crestfallen. "Well, I'd be proud to meet your husband, ma'am. Is he around?"

"I'm a widow."

"Yahoo!" He grabbed her hands, whirling her around in a kind of dance. Then, "I mean, I'm sorry, ma'am, about you being a widow, and all," he floundered, "but I'm glad. I made me a killing, and I come to town to shoot my winnings, and there just ain't too many available women around."

"I'm sure the young woman you purchased the gown for was available," Tamsen said, her eyes filled with sparks of anger. How dared he think she'd replace that —that *creature*!

"Oh, no! No!" Sam Larabee put out a helpless hand as if to erase the Indian girl from existence, his eyes widening as he caught Tamsen's inflection. "You've got the wrong idea! She's the squaw of an old guy up at the diggin's. He saved my life once, an' wouldn't take

214

nothin' for it. I found her livin' like trash. White women won't have nothin' to do with her, Indians neither. I bought him a little shack and figgered I'd kinda fix her up to match. He's comin' down this week . . ."

His words trailed off lamely. He looked so confused, so comically embarrassed at her interpretation of his relationship with the Indian girl that Tamsen knew the improbable story was true. Her mouth quirked at the memory of the night before and she began to laugh.

A wave of relief passed over his features, then he started to chuckle. "Didn't know what I was lettin' myself in for," he said. "Whew!" He mopped his brow. "Well, now we got all that straightened out, can I ask you something?"

"Yes, I suppose so."

He stood for a moment, turning his hat in his hands. Then he blurted, "Miz Harper, I'd be proud to escort you to the Jenny Lind theater, tonight. Maybe grab some grub first at one of them new hotels. I ain't much on knowin' what respectable ladies like to do—"

Tamsen's mind whirled. How she'd longed to see some of the glamorous places of this city! But she could not go alone, and she was unable to afford the fantastic prices. Still, a negative answer trembled on her lips until he'd said the word respectable.

"I would be honored. But please don't put yourself to any trouble."

"Hell, you'd be keepin' me outta trouble."

As he strode down the road, Tamsen stood in the doorway, watching. He had Dan Tallant's shoulders, his trim waist. He was so like Dan. She wondered how it would feel to have his arms around her—

She stopped short. A little warning bell in her subconscious sounded, saying, "Go slowly, Tamsen. Go slowly."

The evening was an enchanted dream. In a soft apricot-hued gown, a cream-colored stole about her shoulders, Tamsen swept into a plush hotel on the arm of a handsome, well-tailored man. As they were escorted to their table, she could not help noting the deference

215

with which Sam Larabee was treated. He was clearly not well-educated, but there was an air of distinction about him. He was certainly the best-looking man in the room.

The room glittered with its before-theater crowd. The jewels the ladies wore shimmered, as did the chandeliers, their prisms shimmering from the hundreds of candles they held. The table was covered with snowy linen, real silver, delicate china, and crystal. And soft music played nearby.

Luxury! Pure luxury! Tamsen reveled in it. After Sam had ordered their dinner, he presented her with a small velvet-covered box.

She looked at him, startled. "Go on, open it," he urged.

The silken lining displayed a pendant of delicately carved jade in a strange and intricate pattern. As she gasped in delight he said, "It's a good luck charm, straight from the Orient. I bought it down at the wharf. It just came in today."

She touched the pendant reverently. It had the feel of caramel, but with life pulsing inside the stone. "I can't take a gift such as this," she whispered. "It must have been frightfully expensive."

"Hell," he growled, "that's what I come to town for, to shoot the works. I got a knack of making money, and a knack for losin' it. Made three fortunes and lost 'em all. Then when I hit bottom, I just naturally start right back up again. I like to make it, but I don't like havin' it. Makes me feel tied down."

She studied the pendant, wistfully. How it would complement this gown. If only she could accept it! Seeing her hesitation, he barked. "Put the damn thing on! If you don't, I'll do it for you!"

She lifted the pendant and donned it, the precious jade falling between her breasts, a thing of mystic beauty.

"You're as purty as a nugget in the bottom of the pan," he said, admiringly. His crude compliment aroused Tamsen's sense of humor and she laughed.

Sam, raising his glass in a toast to her, chuckled with her. Her feeling of nervousness faded. This man was nothing like Dan Tallant at all. True, hc was a rascal, but an honest one. She liked him.

Their dinner was served, course after course of rich and excellent dishes. And as they ate, Sam talked. Another way in which he differed from Tallant, Tamsen thought. Dan was close-mouthed, as if he had something to hide. But Larabee was open and garrulous, telling all about his background.

His family were what they called poor white trash in the south, he told her. And they were happy. But it just so happened they were shirttail relations of a plantation owner who died with no other heirs, leaving them the lot. And then things changed. His folks changed, trying to act like something they weren't, now that they'd come into money. And he'd stayed away from them, preferring the company of the field hands.

"My folks was ashamed of me," he said, morosely, turning his glass in his hands. "Did their damnedest to make a gentleman outta me. My best friend was a nigger kid, a little younger'n me. They sold him off. So I skedaddled when I was fifteen." He blinked rapidly at the memory, then grinned.

"So that's why I ain't got any use for money. Made a lot of it in my time, but I'd just as soon get rid of it. Don't want it to make me into somethin' I wouldn't like to be—"

It's like old times in the cantina, Tamsen thought. So many men had told her their life stories, unburdening their troubles to someone who would listen, whose life was separate from their own. They could tell her their problems and walk away feeling better.

The thought of Sam Larabee walking away hurt her, somehow. And that was ridiculous. She did not intend to let herself become involved with him. She jumped a little as a strange voice cut into her musings.

"Sam! Sam Larabee! You old dog, it *is* you!"

She looked up to see a most distinguished-looking gentleman, his tanned face crowned by prematurely white hair, leaning over them. Sam jumped to his feet, pushing back his chair. "Senator! You're a sight for sore eyes, sir!" He clapped the man on the shoulder, vigorously shaking his hand. Then he turned to Tamsen.

"I'd like you to meet Senator Alden, a good friend. Donald, this here's Miz Harper—"

As the introductions were made and acknowledged, Tamsen was thrilled to her toes. Her evening was complete. Eyes full of stars, she thought of actually living like this. In these luxurious surroundings. Hobnobbing with the wealthy and influential. How she wished Em were here!

The two men talked for a moment, discussing upcoming legislation to protect the Indians from exploitation, the recent rise in crime, the plans for forming a vigilante committee. Tamsen hardly heard what they said. It was enough that she was privy to the type of conversation carried on among the elite.

When the Senator had gone, after bowing to Tamsen and again shaking Larabee's hand, Tamsen said, "You didn't tell me you are in politics! That you know people like that!"

Sam Larabee looked uncomfortable. "Hell, honey, I only met him by accident. Met him back East, when I got his stepbrother out of a jam. The kid, Adam Wheeler, his name is, is a little bastard. I shoulda left well enough alone. Nope, I ain't Don Alden's type. A gentleman's like a smoke, no good unless you start with the makin's."

"I know better," she teased. "Look how we're treated in here! They all know you. The waiters—"

"That's because I throw money around," he said, ruefully. "Now the casinos over on Kearney, that's where I'm really known."

With a sinking heart, Tamsen knew he was telling her the truth. She had seen his type before, laughing men who won and lost fortunes at the tables, who went upstairs with the girls, leaving them squealing with delight at the prodigious sums paid for their favors.

Her escort was not a gentleman, and he had no desire to become one.

For that matter, she had been evading questions about her past all evening. She was no lady.

As Sam assisted her from a hired carriage, before the Jenny Lind theater, Tamsen's head was a little fuzzy with wine. Sam carried her across the muddy street and stood her on her feet. Then she heard the music, familiar music blasting from the Eldorado Casino next door. Suddenly, with the crowds milling around them, the sound of harsh male voices as counterpoint to the sound of a tinny piano and the crashing chords of guitars, she felt transported in time.

In a naughty, husky voice she began to hum the words of the song that was being played, her body swaying seductively. Then she saw Sam Larabee's startled eyes and snapped back to her senses. Her face turned pink at what he must think of her. She quickly placed a small hand in the curve of his arm and swept into the theater like a lady born.

Em was waiting up for Tamsen when she returned. Because Tamsen could see the vicarious pleasure her sister took in hearing about her evening, she described it in glowing detail. The carpets, the draperies; silks, satins and velvets; snowy linen, china, and silver. The shimmering candles, chandeliers dripping crystal. And the people. "Tonight, Em, I met a senator!"

The dream was with her as she readied herself for bed; a dream of a glittering oasis in San Francisco's sea of mud, where she moved through a hushed and lovely room like a princess.

But when her head touched the pillow, less beautiful thoughts intruded. The jade pendant, which she had removed before coming in to see Em, now lay hidden beneath her mattress. A lady would not have accepted such a gift from a strange gentleman! Recalling the moment when she had forgotten herself before the casino, she blushed in the dark. It had been the wine, the music! But it had left a question in Sam Larabee's mind.

As he returned her to her door, she had been elated, laughing, and he had taken her two hands in his. She lifted her face, for if he wished to kiss her, it would add a wonderful finish to this marvelous evening. But his brows were knitted, the bold blue eyes a little bewildered, his face somber as he looked down at her.

"I don't feel like I really know you," he said. "Sometimes I think you're the most honest-to-God lady I ever met, then sometimes—" His voice faded off. "Oh, hell," he said with a laugh, "forget it! I had one helluva time tonight. Did you? Let's do it again."

What had he been going to say out there, with the light of the lantern gleaming on his sun-browned face? She had been a cantina entertainer, displaying her charms and much of her body to the eyes of appreciative men. Did it show? Or was it possible a man had a way of telling when a woman had been used? Her face grew hot at the thought.

After a sleepless hour, she did something she had not done in a long time. She slipped from her bed, and on her knees, uttered a prayer of thanks for this glorious night. But on another level, she was praying, "Let me have all this for myself, for Em, for the baby! Wealth, dignity, beauty, respectability. Let me find a way . . ."

But when she drifted off to sleep, the music of the casino sounded in her ears and she was dancing in front of a faceless sea of men.

Sam Larabee, walking off into the night, cursed himself for being seventeen kinds of a fool. He could have kissed the girl. It was plain that she wanted him to. But he knew if he had, he wouldn't have been able to stop at that. All evening, a fire had been building up inside him, and it had scared him a little. He didn't really know how to act around a lady.

Memories of the women whose approval his mother sought entered his thoughts. They were ladies. He recalled their stiff reserve, their rigid morality, their mealy-mouthed manners. Even their daughters, his contemporaries, were exact copies of their elders. Tamsen certainly didn't fit in their category. He thought of the

220

little dance she had done outside the casino, and it sent the blood thundering in his ears.

It was his fault, he thought. The wine. She wasn't accustomed to it. Perhaps all women were the same, beneath their veneer.

No, he stubbornly asserted to himself, this girl was different. She could not have known how tantalizing, how seductive she was with those movements of her body. How, when she'd raised her lips to him, he had wanted to smother her with kisses.

But all that was beside the point. Right now, he wanted a woman. He thought of Polly Simpson, over at Madam Foster's house, and hurried his steps.

Chapter 4

Em sat by little Martha's cradle, rocking it gently with her foot. Tamsen had gone off with Sam Larabee for a drive along the shoreline. Though it had been beautiful earlier in the day, the fog had moved in, blanketing everything with its gray, furry wetness. She could feel it curling through the cracks in the building, dimming the lights. The room felt clammy, despite the fire in the cookstove.

They had been gone for so long! Perhaps they had found a place to wait out the fog and were having a pleasant tea somewhere. She could visualize the two of them, and the romantic picture caught at her heart. Clearly the man was head-over-heels about Tamsen. Em was certain he'd propose. But Tam had shrugged it off, saying he was nice, she liked him, but he was not a gentleman.

Em tried to think of any man she'd met who was a gentleman. The boy who had jilted her was a farmer, his gentility assured by the number of acres he'd owned. She recalled Mama scolding Papa for his sometimes crude behavior. Dan Tallant? Not a gentleman, but a man! Major Arbuthnot? The memory of his pompous manner brought a smile to her lips.

The smile faded as the baby made a strangling sound. Em caught her up, bending her this way and that, helping her to breathe again. Martha regained her breath on a little choking cry.

"Hush," Em said, "it's all right, honey. Mama's here."

Then she jumped a little, looking around guiltily. She

loved these times when Tamsen was gone, when she could sit with the baby and pretend. She'd been too ill to care when Tamsen announced her intention of taking the baby as her own, and now it was too late. She was known as Tamsen's child.

What if Sam Larabee proposed? And what if Tamsen accepted him, despite her statements? What then?

Sighing, Em put the baby down, covered her, and went to look in on Nell. Maggie had been the first to come down with an influenza-like ailment, now it was Nell. Though Maggie had recovered quickly, Nell had a more serious case. Never having been truly ill before, she was a difficult patient.

"Are you feeling better?" Em asked, touching the feverish forehead. She noted that Nell's temperature was down.

"Hell, no," Nell groaned. "I'm gonna die!"

Em looked at the metal pan that served as dinner tray. There had been broth, toast, and tea. It was gone to the last crumb.

"I see you managed your lunch."

"You call that piddlin' slop lunch? It ain't bein' sick that's a-killin' me! I'm starvin' to death! How about a hunk of ham, er some beans?" The woman's jowls quivered pitifully. "An' where's Dusty?"

Dusty, who believed a pint of prevention was worth a pound of cure, had retreated before the illness, holing up in the frame-and-canvas shed that had been erected for his sleeping quarters. At the moment he was sleeping off the results of his own brand of medication.

Em pulled the covers over the mound in the bed, tucking them securely beneath the lowest of Nell's chins. "Maybe later," she said, soothingly. "I'll tell Dusty you're better, and tonight you can eat something more—"

The baby made a choking sound and Em sped back to her own quarters. This time, the small face was almost blue as the baby fought for breath. Though Martha had seemed all right when Tamsen left, Em felt a surge of resentment. If she would only come

223

home! There was a small apothecary shop nearby which was run by an old Chinese gentleman. If she could get some herbs, make a croup kettle as Mama did when Arab was small—

Picking the child up, she jounced her into crying, then walked about the room with her. It was this horrid weather! The fog! And Martha felt hot to the touch. She was burning with fever! The apothecary might close soon! The day was dark with fog, she had no way of telling the time. And croup was worse at night, she knew. She could not wait!

Carrying the baby into Nell's room, she put the child beside the big woman. Nell struggled to a sitting position, her eyes round with consternation.

"What the hell you doin'?"

Em explained that she had an errand, that Nell must watch over Martha until she returned. "If she coughs, pick her up, pat her on the back."

"I can do that," Nell conceded, "but, hell, what if she—"

"It won't hurt you to change her once," Em said with asperity. "She's dry now, and I'll be right back!"

Em hurried to find her cloak, smiling to herself. Nell adored the baby. Em had caught her playing with the child when she thought nobody was looking, making ponderous kitchy-koo sounds. Martha would be well-cared-for in her absence. She was certain of that.

Stepping out into the fog-filled afternoon was like being smothered with a wet blanket. There was enough dampness to make the mud of the street slithery under foot, and Em had to pick her way carefully to avoid falling. Ahead of her, the oil lamps that marked various places of business were dim blobs of light shining through grayness. As she turned up Kearney into the casino district, she could hear the music, the noise of men who mobbed these places on miserable afternoons such as this. The sound seemed eerie, muffled by the fog. An occasional foot-traveler would loom before her, distorted by the mist, pass on silent feet and disappear.

Em had been housebound most of the time since

they'd arrived in San Francisco, and this was new to her. New and frightening. Her heart beat faster. She was breathless when she reached the apothecary, a narrow tunnel of a building where the proprietor had taken advantage of the space between two other structures, by wedging in a roof, adding front and back walls. The building, which was unpainted and weathered, was black with moisture, giving the place a look that was dark and forbidding.

Em forced herself to enter.

Inside, it was rather pleasant, though the room had an alien atmosphere, oddly scented with pungent spices, herbs, and incense. The Chinese man added to the foreign air of the place, in his pajama-like clothes and small round hat atop hair that ended in a queue. But he spoke some English, and he was most polite as Em made her purchases of eucalyptus leaves, camphor bark, and horehound. She felt more secure when she left to retrace her steps toward home.

She was passing the last casino on her route when a door burst open, spilling sound into the night. A figure lurched into the street, mumbling to itself, and Em stopped short. The man was clearly intoxicated. If she stood very still, he might ignore her presence and she could continue on.

It was a vain effort. He shambled toward her, saying, "Lady? Lady?"

She side-stepped; if she could circle him, she would run. But it was too late. A hand clawed at her arm, found a purchase. He shoved his face into hers, revealing a wet, flaccid mouth with snaggle-teeth, his breath sickening with alcohol.

"Let me go," she said quietly. "I'm on the way home. My daughter is sick——"

He howled with drunken laughter, then turned truculent. "Don't give me that stuff, woman. You come lookin' fer me, didn'cha? You was lookin' fer ol Charlie, here." He pulled her to him. She could feel the harsh material of his denim coat against her face as she struggled, calling for help. It was like a nightmare.

225

"Charlie!" A forceful voice sounded from the saloon door, and the man relinquished his grip a little to turn toward the speaker. "Let her go, Charlie!"

"Mind yer own damn business! This yere's my woman. Git one of yer own, dammit!"

The challenger, an enormous man who completely filled the casino doorway, approached. "That's where yer wrong, Charlie. She's my woman, come lookin' fer me. And if you don't git off down the street, I'll kick yer ass from hell to breakfast!"

Mumbling imprecations, the old drunk wandered on. The burly man approached the shivering Em. He was a huge, light-haired fellow, with a blond beard that made him look like a Viking. "I'm sorry he bothered you, ma'am. Ol' Charlie's harmless, but—"

He stopped as the faint glow of light touched Em's upturned white face. His eyes lit with pleasure and disbelief. Then she was snatched into another pair of arms that nearly squeezed the life from her. She was lifted struggling into the air, then lowered to receive a resounding bearded smack upon her cheek.

"Miss Em!" the stranger cried, "Miss Em! Don't you know me? Mike Dunnevant! You tried to bury me onc't! Oh, lordy! I never thought I'd lay eyes on you folks again! Where's them sisters of yers?"

Em welcomed the sight of him, almost babbling in her relief. She explained her errand. The baby was ill, and she must hurry. If he accompanied her, she would fill him in on the details. Tamsen would be so happy to see him!

"Baby? What baby?" he looked at her, uneasily. "One of you girls got married?"

Em caught herself. "Martha is—is Tamsen's," she said, her heart contracting at the lie. "She—she's a widow, now."

"A purty high-steppin' one, I'll bet." He grinned at her, then took her arm. Together they slipped and slithered through the mud toward the shop, where they would await Tamsen's homecoming.

Tamsen, meanwhile, was in a quandary. The pro-

226

posed sightseeing trip had been in the nature of a surprise. Sam Larabee wished to show her his newest acquisition. There was just time to view it as the fog bank moved in from the sea. A trim white sailboat of ocean-going dimensions. Then, as fog blanked out the road as they returned, he stopped the carriage before a small tarp-and-frame structure where a miner's wife sold coffee and little cakes at inflated prices.

The place was almost empty. Sam carried the steaming tin cups to a table in the corner and they sat. "Now," he said evenly, "I want to tell you my plans."

Those plans included Tamsen and little Martha. Sam had made a fortune here. Now he had an itchy foot and wished to move on. He had Honolulu in mind. Maybe even China. So he had purchased a boat, intending to make the cruise alone. He had reckoned without his feelings for Tamsen. He knew he wasn't good husband material, footloose like he was. And he couldn't change. But he'd had this idea.

Tamsen was a widow, with a little kid to raise. If she'd marry him, he'd buy her a house in Honolulu and put enough gold in a Honolulu bank to assure her a comfortable living. Then, if he just took off now and then, it wouldn't matter. The boat trip would serve as their honeymoon.

"Oh, Sam!" Tamsen's eyes misted. "I can't. But, thank you, Sam."

He looked downcast for a moment, then his mouth turned up in that irrepressible grin. "Well, hell, I ain't leavin' 'til the end of May. Lots of time to change yer mind. You be thinkin' on it, y' hear?"

"I will, Sam. I promise."

As they drove home through the fog, Tamsen wished her answer could have been different. She did not love Sam Larabee, but she liked him. To think of living comfortably without having to fight for it every inch of the way was very tempting. But she could not leave Em. Nell, Dusty, the girls all depended on her. None of them would be able to handle a business.

And business was picking up. Every day, the fund in

the cashbox was growing. Next year, she might be able to set up in a more profitable location, buy a beautiful home, be known as the wealthy Widow Harper.

"Somethin' on yer mind?" Sam asked. Tamsen felt guilty. She had forgotten him, forgotten his proposal as she dreamed away. It must have been a terrible struggle for him to consider marriage at all.

"Thinking about you," she smiled. "You're such a very nice man."

As they reached the shop, she kissed him. How good it felt to be held in his arms, to put her face against his chest and hear the beating of his heart. If she only loved him! And if only things were different!

Sam Larabee was also thinking, as much as his thudding pulse would allow him to. He was not a nice man, he decided, ruefully. Because right now, if they weren't standing on a public street, he might not be able to control himself. What was he going to do with this girl? She did not, she could not know what she was doing to him! He had to make her marry him, for her own safety's sake, to protect her from less scrupulous men.

"Remember what I asked you," he said, a little roughly, forcing himself to release the warm curves that burned against his body.

"I will, Sam. And your ship is beautiful. Good night."

She hurried into the house to escape the urge to say yes to him.

The place smelled of eucalyptus and camphor. And from the rooms in the rear came sounds of laughter. It sounded like a party of some kind. Mystified, Tamsen hastened toward the space she shared with Em and the baby.

The room was filled with people. Nell, red-nosed and snuffling, was wrapped in a blanket. Katie, Maggie, and Carmen sat in a row on Tamsen's bed, swinging shapely ankles for the benefit of an enormous, bearded creature who bent over Martha's cradle making ridiculous, cooing noises.

Who in the world?

228

Em looked up. "Tamsen! You're back! We have a surprise. Look who's here."

The burly man came toward her. He was dressed in typical miner's clothing, the mud from his caked boots leaving a mess on the floor. She could have sworn she had never seen him before in her life. Yet there was something familiar about him.

She gasped as he reached brawny arms to lift her off her feet in a bear-hug that left her fighting for breath against the flannel-clad chest.

"Miss Tamsen! Lordy, it's good to see you! Ain't seen you since the night you stole Dan Tallant's horses. Good thing you tied me up like that. When he found out, all hell busted loose. Wouldn't of missed it fer nothin'!"

Mike Dunnevant. She uttered his name with a cry of delight, laughing with him as he mentioned the horse-stealing. Then her merriment faded. Why hadn't the man kept his mouth shut? Behind him, she saw Em, her face a study in shock and bewilderment. Em, who had been told the horses were borrowed and returned.

"Oh, Mike!" Tamsen said, helplessly. He looked at her, puzzled at her tone. "Oh, Mike—it's so good to see you! Now, tell us, what are you doing here? And how did you find us?"

"Already told them," Mike indicated the others a little self-consciously. But at Tamsen's insistent questioning, he retold the tales of where he had been and what he'd done, with a mixture of boyish shyness and braggadocio that was endearing.

Dear Mike! Tamsen thought. It was good to have him here. But what in the world could she say to Em about Tallant's horses? How could she explain?

She need not have been concerned. By the time Mike took his leave to return to the cubbyhole he shared with three other men at the City Hotel, Em had come to a decision. It was clear that there was something mysterious in the way Tamsen had obtained those animals. She'd been concerned at the time. But not concerned enough to question Tamsen in regard to her dealings. She would not question her now.

After all, Dan Tallant was friendly enough on those visits to the adobe outside Magoffinville. He and Tamsen must have reached some sort of agreement, even if she'd done as Mike said.

But stealing the horses! Great brutes of draft animals that they were! And tying up that mountain of a man! How on earth did Tam manage it?

She would not ask. She didn't want to know.

Chapter 5

Mike Dunnevant continued to call. And though Tamsen welcomed his visits as a delightful change from the chatter of the girls, she began to be concerned. Em, too, enjoyed those visits. And Mike was certainly not right for Em. In the end, it was Em who pointed out to her where the big man's real interests lay. His blue gaze rested often on Katie Ryan.

Katie didn't seem to be returning his attentions, however. That was just as well, Tamsen thought. Mike knew Katie only as a seamstress, not as the girl who enjoyed her work at the cantina. Katie had voiced her opinion of the married state quite often, and Tamsen had a notion Mike was the marrying kind. She didn't want to see him hurt.

But it was good to have him visit, and exciting to hear his tales of a river of gold above Sutter's Fort in the area of Sacramento.

Mike had gone to Sutter's Fort after Tallant paid him off in San Francisco. Taking his wages, Mike bought supplies and headed into the hills with a number of other men. Each carried a blanket roll; cached inside it were bacon, flour, coffee. Each had a pick and shovel and a frying pan. There were young men, old men, boys. Some, like Mike, were lucky enough to go on horseback. Others were afoot, carrying their supplies like pack animals.

Some of the seekers found death instead of gold, death through tuberculosis, rheumatism, smallpox, pneumonia, scurvy, and dysentery. They were buried in their soiled blankets.

Some found their fortunes.

Mike Dunnevant accumulated a sizable poke of dust before he returned to San Francisco to live it up while his more ambitious companions remained "wintered in." He figured on heading back into the hills somewhere around the first of May, he told them one evening. This time, he'd make him a stake to start a business with. Maybe even "think on getting married. A man gets tired of hellin' around."

Tamsen saw his eyes move toward Katie. The girl averted her face, sullenly, and Mike's face was a study of hurt and bewilderment. May isn't far off, Tamsen thought. And maybe he'll forget about her while he's gone. Mike deserves someone who really loves him. Still, the life had gone out of that evening. Mike grew quiet and morose. It was only when Sam Larabee arrived, filled with his usual ebullient cheer, that the pleasure returned to the group.

There were many evenings spent in convivial company. Sam and Mike had a sort of contest going, each trying to out-brag or out-lie the other. Some of their tall tales were so ludicrous that the group broke up with side-splitting laughter. And there were musical evenings. Tamsen discovered Larabee could play a guitar and pressed him into bringing it. Mike Dunnevant had a passably good voice, though it shook the rafters of the establishment. And he looked with silent awe at Tamsen one night when she ventured a ballad alone.

"Hey," he marveled, "that was right purty! You sing good enough to get paid fer it!" Then his ears reddened. "Not that I was sayin' you oughtta go on the stage, you bein' a nice girl, and all. But what I meant was you sounded good enough."

As he floundered in his apology, Katie snickered. Tamsen shot her an angry look. One rule of their new life was that the cantina was not to be mentioned.

"Thank you, Mike," Tamsen said.

Mike's compliments were reinforced by Sam Larabee, but despite their pleading, Tamsen would not sing again.

232

That night, after they had gone, she lay awake for a long time. She missed the cantina. It had been a happy time in her life, and she had traded it for this! She admitted to herself, in all honesty, that she would return if she could. Yet she was trapped here, if she were to build a respectable life for Martha and Em.

At last she sat up, pummelling her pillow into a more comfortable state, her mind borrowing a word from Nell. "To hell with respectability!"

"Tam?" Em's soft voice murmured. "Did you say something?"

"Nothing," Tamsen said, forlornly. "Nothing at all."

But she had taken a giant step in admitting this life was not for her. And her unhappiness intensified as the days sped by. Mike would be leaving soon, then Sam. The pleasurable evenings would end with their going. Nell and Dusty would return to their evenings out. The girls would scatter in search of their own interests once more. And she would be left to the long, dull evenings with only Em and the baby for company.

On the last day of the month, the girls held a farewell party for Mike Dunnevant. Tamsen had dipped lavishly into her funds, purchasing eggs—and even raisins for a cake. Em baked it and was pink with pleasure at its success. Sam Larabee furnished fish, fresh-caught from the vessel he'd christened *Tamsen*. He also produced two bottles of wine.

Unlike other nights, when there had been story-telling and merriment, the celebration fell flat. Both men were silent and wore long faces. Mike Dunnevant was understandably moody, since he must part with his friends for a time, but Larabee would be in San Francisco for some weeks. Surely he was not this upset to see Dunnevant go.

Tamsen eyed his brooding face, the laugh wrinkles magically erased. "What is it, Sam? You don't seem to be yourself. Is something wrong?"

He turned his hands palm up, shrugging his shoulders in a gesture of defeat. "It's like I told you about having

233

money. Try to do something good with it, and everything goes to hell."

Prodded, he told his story. It had to do with his old buddy at the mining claim, the one who had the Indian squaw. He'd run into him the other night at the El Dorado. The man was drunk, on a crying jag. He'd come down from the miseries of winter at the mining site, only to find his girl had left him. He heard she was working in a brothel, wearing fancy dresses and real jools—and undermining her health. By God, she took a bath every day!

Tamsen smothered a giggle. But, since Sam's concern was very real, she said, "You did what you thought was right, Sam. Maybe it was for the best."

He would have none of her comforting. "I meddled," he said simply, "when I shoulda left just as well alone. Like I said, money changes people. It's bad luck. Be glad when the damn stuff's all gone."

The next day, Mike left, still without any sign of encouragement from Katie. And Sam Larabee did not show for several days. The only report came from Dusty. Sam was raising hell in every casino in town, spending gold dust like it was water. He'd sat in on every big game—and left every one of them a winner. He couldn't seem to lose. The man had the golden touch, Dusty said, reverently. But he'd be lucky if they didn't find him in an alley some morning, a bullet through his head.

May third was Tamsen's birthday. Sam had not shown up yet. Tamsen was depressed. He had no way of knowing this was a special day. Yet it seemed he might have called by. She hadn't realized how dull it was with nothing but the chatter of women to listen to. That thought pricked at her conscience later in the day when she was presented with small gifts from Em, Nell, Dusty, and the girls. Good, utilitarian gifts, all of them. A pair of gold-handled shears from Germany, a packet of precious needles, an embroidery frame, some silks for fancy work.

The celebration had taken place at the evening meal,

234

since the girls were preparing to go out for the evening. After Dusty milked the cow, he and Nell, too, went out in search of the night life they both missed so grievously. Tamsen and Em retired, though neither could sleep.

Em, especially, was wakeful. As always, Arabella was on her mind. And Tamsen seemed so odd when questioned about Arab. Yes, she was still in touch with the people to whom Reverend Smythe had promised to send his new address. No, there had been no word as yet. Something in her attitude troubled Em. But then, Tamsen was not herself these days. Though she did not complain, she did not seem happy. She wondered if it had anything to do with Sam Larabee. How she'd hoped something would come of that relationship!

She slept at last, fitfully, but was awakened by the clanging sound of a bell, and sat up drowsily. She had dreamed it. That and the sounds of concerted shouting. It was only the wind.

But the red glow in the room! The iron stove often glowed cherry-red, but not at night, with the fires banked. And it was so warm, like the hot dry heat of the desert. . . .

The sound of an explosion shook her fully awake. An explosion followed by the yells of men in panic. The bell again! And the smell of smoke!

Lighting a candle with trembling fingers, Em saw that Tamsen, too, had been awakened. They looked at each other, eyes wide in horrified surmise.

Fire!

Tamsen ran to the front door and threw it open. The sky above San Francisco was a sheet of flame. Some blocks distant, the blaze lit up the night. But between the dress shop and the fire, buildings stood intact, silhouetted against the red heat of the conflagration. Bits of debris soared overhead, borne on the wind like giant birds with flame-tipped wings.

As Tamsen watched, one of the structures which seemed to stand protectively between their street and the blaze exploded outward to the sound of a hoarse outcry from human throats. She could see the tiny black figures of men, like ants, running to and fro in apparent confusion.

Tamsen reentered the shop, hurrying back to where Em waited, pale-faced, wide-eyed, little Martha clasped to her bosom.

"The city's afire. I don't think it will reach here," Tamsen lied, "but we'd better be prepared. Get dressed. Heavy shoes. A warm cloak." They dressed quickly. Thank God they'd left their bathwater in the tub, conserving it to wash in the morning. Tamsen stripped three blankets from their beds. One for herself, one for Em, one for the baby, and put them into the tub to absorb the moisture.

Even as she worked, she could feel the heat intensifying. They would have to run. But where? She started for the door to inspect the fire once more, but before she could reach it, she heard someone pounding.

"Sam!"

She flung herself into his arms, weeping. His shirt was charred, hanging in strips from his body, and his face was soot-blackened, but she'd never seen such a beautiful sight in her life.

"We've got to get you out of here," he rasped. "Head for the wharf! Hurry! Wet some blankets. You have? Good! Now, where are the others?"

He raced back to the bedroom, already dim with smoke, and, wrapping Em and the baby in the damp blankets, led them to the door. Above the noise, they could hear the bawling of the cow tethered in back. Em stopped. "We can't leave her that way! Take Martha. I'll turn her loose."

Sam swore. "I'll do it. Now go on! Run. I'll catch up with you!"

When Sam returned he found only Em standing at the end of the block, holding Martha tightly, bits of burning paper drifting down to smoulder against her soaked draperies. Tamsen was gone. She had forgotten something and gone back to the shop. The shop, where a tongue of flame licked greedily at the roof. The place, once it caught, would go up like tinder.

236

"The damn fool!" Sam exploded. "I'm going after her! Go on, Em. Run for the wharf. You have to, because of the baby! Now, run!"

Then he was gone. Em stood still for a moment, watching the great city in the process of cremation. A scene from hell! The bells, the screaming of horses, people caught in the titanic horror of destruction. Then she turned and began to run.

Tamsen had remembered the cashbox and had gone back into the shop to get it. Choking on the smoke, she felt her way through the dark front rooms to the bedroom she and Em had shared. A bit of the roof had already collapsed. Little Martha's crib was ablaze. Tamsen's own mattress was smouldering. Reaching under the bed, she found what she sought, then stumbled, gasping for breath, to the front door.

"Grab her! She's got something."

Two men, their sooted countenances as frightening as the warpaint of the Indians on the trail, caught at her as she half-fell through the exit. One of them held her as the other tried to wrest the cashbox from her hands. She fought them, screaming, the sound of it lost in the roaring of the fire, the cracking and rending of flaming timbers.

Sam Larabee saw the struggling figures from a block away. Swearing, he drew the pistol he carried in a holster beneath his jacket as he pounded toward them. Before he could reach them, one of the looters had struck Tamsen a hard blow, knocking her back into the doorway of the blazing structure. The other picked up the cashbox she had dropped, and they turned to run.

There was a gunshot, another. And then Sam was scooping Tamsen up, carrying her away from the flames. She looked at him with eyes huge in a soot-stained face.

"You shot them," she said in a small voice.

"Dammit," he began, "if you'd done what I told you to! If you hadn't come back——"

But she was pummelling at his chest with her fists.

237

Startled, he let her go, and she ran to the body of one of the men, frantically trying to push it aside.

He saw what she was after. A corner of her cashbox protruded from beneath the body. Shaking his head grimly, he retrieved it for her. It was still hot to the touch, but Tamsen snatched it from him.

He turned her about, roughly, heading her toward the wharf. "Now, dammit," he shouted, "run!"

This time, Tamsen obeyed. And as she hurried, panting, through the falling ash that sifted around them, she was grateful, at last, for the location of the building she'd rented. Behind her, the city was an inferno. But here, there was an escape route. And Martha and Em were safe.

There was no time for rejoicing. Sam Larabee found a boat tied up at the dock and he helped them to board it. Then he carefully maneuvered it from the wharf, using a pole to keep a distance from the other boats bobbing there. At last, they reached open water.

There, he gave them instructions not to show a light unless it appeared they might be rammed. There would be other small boats leaving the wharf this night. Looters getting away with ill-gotten property. If any attempts were made to board the vessel, they must shoot to kill. He gave Tamsen his gun.

"But where are you going?" Tamsen asked, tremulously. "What are you going to do?"

He didn't answer, but dived into the water. She could see the glisten of his wet hair as he swam back toward the blazing city. All hands were needed to fight the fire.

The baby was crying, unable to understand the frantic haste with which she'd been snatched from her bed and transported to strange surroundings. Her screams rose above the distant clamor. At Tamsen's suggestion, Em took her below. In the cabin, lit only by glowing flames that showed through the tiny window, Em found some tinned milk and made the child comfortable on a bunk. How precious she was. And how much they owed Sam Larabee! Em thanked God, silently, for saving their

238

lives. But now what were they to do? They had lost everything. She wondered what Tamsen was thinking.

Tamsen stood on deck like a figurehead, Sam's pistol in her hand, her mind numb. Except for the contents of the cashbox—a few gold coins, the family Bible, a sprig of dried forsythia, the jade pendant that was supposed to bring good luck—everything else was lost. The shop had burned, and with it the materials to make a fresh start. What would become of them?

Then Em appeared at the top of the steps that led down to the cabin. Her hair was streaked, her face smudged, and her blue eyes filled with worry.

"What about the others?" she asked, her voice frightened, "Do you think they got out safely? Dusty? Nell? The girls?"

Tamsen's eyes echoed the horror in Em's. "I don't know, Em. Oh, God! I don't know!"

She looked toward San Francisco, a raging inferno. It seemed impossible that anyone could escape from such a place alive. And suddenly the enormity of what was happening seemed more than she could bear.

Dusty and Nell, cut off from the dress shop by several blocks of burning buildings, had joined the exodus to the hills. Nell gasped as she tried to heave her huge bulk up the steep inclined streets, with Dusty sometimes shoving from behind. And all around them, the crowd milled. Women shrieked as they became separated from their children in the throng. Horses reared at the noise and the scorching heat. Some people sat down, partway to safety, looking back at what they had lost, too numbed to go on.

Nell slipped and sat in the mud, panting for breath, her heart palpitating. "Oh, hell, Dusty. Go on. I'll ketch up in a minute."

But Dusty would not leave her to be trampled in the hurrying mob. Getting behind her, he heaved and grunted until at last he got her to her feet.

She grinned at him fondly. "Yer a gawdamn hero,"

239

she said. He beamed as she studied the hill before him. "Let's go," she panted. "It's still a hell of a long way up."

Reaching the top, she sat. "Ain't gonna move until the damn thing's out," she said.

At her bidding, Dusty left her sitting there and went searching for their friends. He found Carmen, Maggie, and Katie. Katie's red hair had been singed as short as a boy's. But there was no sign of Tamsen, Em, or the baby.

"Didn't think so," said Nell. "They was caught the other side."

"Jove! Do you think they had a chance?"

Nell's eyes brimmed with tears. "Hell," she said irritably, "how would I know?"

The reunion before the charred remains of the Harper Dressmaking establishment the next day was both a sad and a happy one. Sam Larabee had returned to his small ship with the news that the fire was under control, but that three-fourths of the city had burned. He mentioned that his own wealth was safe, in a bank built to be fireproof. It had not burned. He appeared to be conscience-stricken at the fact.

Tamsen insisted upon an immediate return to her shop, though he advised her against it. Finally, exhausted from the night, he agreed to escort the girls there and then to the bank where the cashbox could be locked up for safekeeping. Looters and ne'er-do-wells still roamed the streets. And even law-abiding people had grown desperate.

Tamsen's hope of being able to salvage anything was a vain one. The building was a pile of charred ashes. Toward the back, the metal bedframes stood, twisted and melted into grotesque shapes.

Em burst into tears, but Tamsen was white-faced and stiff. She could not cry.

Then they saw the little party making its way toward them. Despite Nell's stated intent to remain on the hill, she had been the first to insist on returning. They had crossed the smoking graveyard of a city, stopping only to beat out skirts that caught fire from dying embers.

Nell's voluminous skirts were charred to the knees, revealing enormous bulging limbs above her tiny strapped shoes. Her face was stony, the beady black eyes snapping.

"Heered somebody started this fire a-purpose," she said, angrily. "If they ketch the sonofabitch, I'll kill him myself!"

There was no time for thoughts of vengeance. The first thing was to find a place to live, a roof over their heads. They couldn't remain in the streets. Especially with the baby. In a city of homeless people, there was nowhere to go. Again, it was Sam Larabee who came to their rescue.

Aboard the abandoned ships, there was spare canvas. And perhaps there was wood to be salvaged. Working together, they managed to construct a house of cloth-and-frame by nightfall.

"It ain't much," Sam said, grudgingly, surveying the results of their labors. "But it's a roof. Tamsen, if you'd marry me—"

Tamsen put a finger to his lips. "It'll do fine, Sam. And we owe it all to you. We owe you a lot. And, Sam, I—I like you better than anyone I know."

"Tamsen," he started, but stopped short. Seeing the smudged little face that looked up at him, the long dark hair that had escaped its moorings and was as wild as any gypsy's, he began to laugh. She joined in, sensing the reason for his laughter. His own face was black, accentuating the blueness of his eyes.

"We're a mess," she finally sputtered. "Both of us!"

"But we like each other," he grinned. "And that's all that counts!"

Tamsen thought of that night two weeks later, as she sat at dinner with Sam Larabee. He looked so handsome, his face clean-shaven, dressed like a gentleman. He would be leaving on the morrow, and she would miss him. Dear God, she would miss him!

The waiter tapped at the door of the room they occupied, bringing in the dinner they had ordered. Sam had said money could buy anything, and here was proof.

He must have gone to great expense to manage this place where they could be alone. This was one of the small, private gambling rooms above a casino which had not burned. A bed in a corner, hidden by a priceless lacquered screen, was evidence that someone had been dispossessed for the night. Someone who was perhaps standing in the casino below at this very moment, planning to spend the night on his feet.

For this was a city of disaster; the entire population was trying to crowd itself into one-fourth the space it had occupied. Many, priced out of the luxury of a bed, slept on the ground somewhere; others slept in shifts.

And the food! Tamsen looked at the meal that was brought in at Sam's request, purchased at inflated prices from some enterprising restaurateur. It was plain fare, true. But there was enough to feed everyone at home.

"Tamsen, wake up! Hell, this is my last night here! Fine meal. Purty girl! An' she doesn't even hear me sayin' she looks beautiful tonight!"

Tamsen's head snapped up. She forced herself to smile at his rueful expression.

"I'm sorry." Her fingers toyed with the jade pendant. It went well with the gown she'd borrowed from one of the girls. "I suppose I was thinking about the fire."

He poured a glass of wine for her. "Don't think about the fire. Think about me. How you're going to miss me."

"I am, Sam," she admitted.

He grew sober, his tone no longer teasing. "Then come with me, you and the baby. Never thought I'd take on a kid, but—"

"You forget, Sam. You're the man who doesn't like responsibilities. I think you were relieved when I turned down your proposal."

His eyes darkened. "Well, maybe. But I've thought on it some, since. The offer still goes."

Tamsen bowed her head. What would he think if he knew Martha wasn't hers? Though he was fond of the baby, he was not exactly father material. Would he

242

expand his proposal for settling her and the child in a little house in Honolulu to include Em? It would not be fair to ask him, nor to marry him under false pretenses. He'd been so kind!

Then, too, there were Dusty and Nell, the girls. Even Sam Larabee might balk at a honeymoon for that crowd.

"Let's not be so serious, Sam. Here we are, your last night in San Francisco, with all this," she indicated the table laden with food and wine. "We're worrying about something that's already settled. Let's just have a good time."

And a good time they had. He told funny stories of his boyhood, of the gold fields, and the wine flowed until Tamsen's head was fuzzy with it. She watched him as she listened, her vision a little blurred. Sometimes, his face was his own. Sometimes, that of Dan Tallant.

"Tamsen," he said, finally, "you've told me nothing about yourself. Sometimes I feel like I don't really know you."

"Maybe it's because there's nothing to tell," she said, toying with her glass.

He shook his head. "Sometimes I get the idea you're really two people. I remember that night I took you out to dinner. The first time. Real prim an' proper. Then, out in front of th' theater, you started singin'—"

She stood, smiling. "Like this?" She raised her arms, moving her body seductively, suggestively, singing in her broken, husky little voice that said, *Take me . . . Love me . . .*

Larabee was on his feet, knocking his chair over as he rose. "My God, Tamsen! Stop it! Don't you know what you're doing to me?"

"Yes," she said, slowly, "I suppose I do."

He came toward her, his face white, his eyes questioning, and she met his look squarely. "Tamsen," he choked, "I want you!"

"And I want you, too."

It was true, she thought, as his hands fumbled at the

243

fastenings of her gown. It had been in the back of her mind all evening. She felt an affection for Sam that was not love, but very close to it. She could not bear to have him go away without giving something of herself, keeping something of him.

The borrowed finery fell away, and his arms closed about her, his mouth touching hers. And she could feel the trembling in the lean, hard body—so like Dan's—as he lifted her, carrying her toward the bed in the corner.

Then there was only the feel of his burning flesh against hers, and she was meeting his passion with her own, clawing at his naked shoulders and crying his name.

In the morning, she woke from a heavy, wine-drugged sleep, her head throbbing. She had only the feel of rumpled sheets against her flesh. That, and the pendant. There was no head on the pillow beside her, and she felt an awful sense of loss.

"Sam?"

There was no answer. Maybe he'd gone out to order breakfast before she woke.

Sitting up, she clasped her knees and buried her face against them. There was no point in fooling herself. She knew Sam too well. He had gone, slipping away to spare her—and himself—the agony of goodbyes.

Finally, she rose and dressed herself mechanically. She saw that Sam had placed her slippers in the middle of the table. Lifting them, she found they'd been used to cover a note. It was written in a very literate, beautifully inscribed hand, showing another side of rough-talking Sam Larabee.

"Thank you for last night," it read. *"Now, I'm going to ask you for another favor. I'm leaving three bags of gold."* Tamsen's eyes shifted to the three cloth bags at the end of the table. Dear God! A fortune!

"You know how I feel about money," the note continued, *"and I think you can use it better than I can. Invest it in something, something that will give you a*

future. Then, maybe if I show up broke some day, you can give me a stake."

Tears blurred her eyes until the lines on the paper danced and disappeared. "Sam," she whispered. "Oh, Sam!" Then, wiping at her tears until her vision cleared, she read on.

"I hope you'll find yourself a good man, someday. You're too young and pretty to stay tied to a dead husband. I guess I didn't know how much you loved him until you kept saying his name last night, calling me Dan."

"Dear God," Tamsen whispered, "dear God!" The paper dropped from her nerveless fingers. She had given Sam Larabee her love last night and had taken it away with one word!

She hurried downstairs. Except for a few drunks, sleeping it off here and there, the casino was empty. After she persuaded the sleepy-eyed clerk on duty to put her gold in his safe for the time being, Tamsen stepped out into the gray light of morning.

The hired carriage Sam had employed the night before was still waiting, the driver asleep on the seat. Leaping into the vehicle, Tamsen shook him awake and ordered him to drive to the wharf, and to hurry.

She was too late. His boat was gone.

Tamsen gave fresh directions, turning the carriage toward home. She would tell Em that she and Sam Larabee had spent the night talking, so that she might see him off at dawn.

For a moment, but only for a moment, she put her face in her hands and wept. She cried because Sam was gone, and she would miss him. Because she hadn't loved him enough to accept his proposal, to share his life. She did not weep for having spent the night in Sam Larabee's arms. For that, she was glad! But how could she—how *could* she, in those intimate moments, have called him by Dan Tallant's name!

245

Chapter 6

As the carriage neared the cloth-and-frame structure Tamsen now called home, she dried her eyes and pulled herself together. There would be more explanations than just a night out to give to Em. How was she going to account for the money Larabee had left her?

The money! For the first time, the significance of it, of what she might do with it, came home to her. Now, her spirits began to rise. Sam had left her a fortune to invest. With it, she would be able to set up a good dressmaking establishment, in a nicer part of the city. She would be able to buy a home for Martha and Em. They could live decently.

With a pang, she realized that, for a moment, the thought of the gold had driven Sam Larabee from her mind. But it was his money, and he had been as glad to get rid of it as she was to receive it, hadn't he? It wasn't as though she'd slept with him because of that. She'd given herself to him, truly and honestly.

If only she hadn't called him by Dan's name! But it was over and done. Sam was gone, and she would probably never see him again. The carriage stopped before the ruins of the dressmaking establishment. Holding her skirts away from the blackened timbers, Tamsen rounded it, and entered the little cloth-and-frame at the back of the lot. The shack was filled with the sleeping girls, Em among them. In the crowded room, Tamsen had not been missed in the night.

Gratefully, Tamsen lay down on her pallet, not to sleep, but to dream. To dream of all that money and

246

the comforts it would bring them. Tomorrow she would start looking for a business—and for a home.

In the bright light of day, that dream became a nightmare. For the city of San Francisco, its business district a mass of charred timbers, redolent with offal, teeming with rats, was beginning to rebuild. And the speculators were having a field day. The price of brick and timber soared. Builders could name their own prices for teetery structures erected in haste. There was not enough skilled labor. Workmen, skilled or unskilled, could only work for a certain number of hours in a day.

Existing buildings sold sleeping space at a premium. Tamsen discovered that a fortune would not buy a building that did not exist or build one without a builder who had the time, or purchase materials that were already spoken for.

She would have to wait.

In the meantime, she transferred her gold along to the bank where her cashbox and her jade pendant were in safe keeping, telling Em and the others only that Sam Larabee had left a moderate sum with her for investment.

Em did not question her. Sam Larabee's only fault, Em thought, was the way he threw money around. Now he'd have something set aside for a rainy day. Perhaps that meant he was really serious about Tamsen.

Tamsen chafed at the delay. She was determined not to touch the money Sam had given her for daily expenses. And the contents of the cashbox were running low. She considered selling the jade necklace, but could not bring herself to do it—it had brought her luck. She knew that she must take some kind of action soon. Little Martha was creeping now. The board floors of their cloth-and-frame home were rough and splintery. At night, when the wind came in off the sea, they all shivered in misery. Dusty had no shelter. Fortified with alcohol, he slept in his bedroll, close against one of the tarpaulin outside walls, away from the wind.

So Tamsen walked the streets, day after day, carrying

Martha to give her the sun. But there was nothing to be had in the way of shop or shelter.

Katie brought home Tamsen's first ray of hope. She'd been out, just walking, when she had run into Polly Simpson, of all people. The poor girl was almost in tears. The madam on Stockton Street, from whom Tamsen had obtained so much of their dressmaking business, was talking of selling out and returning to the East. Now Polly would have to make some other arrangement—or settle for cooking and cleaning up after some man.

But Tamsen wasn't listening. Here was a building, already standing, about to be sold! Katie had dropped her bit of gossip just as they sat down to supper, and Tamsen found herself unable to swallow. She stood up. "I'm going out. I don't know when I'll be back. Don't wait up for me, Em." Ignoring Em's protests, she took down her cloak from the peg and, dropping her little gun into its pocket, went out.

Once outside, she began to run, her mind whirring with ideas. She had not seen the house, though she had an idea of its approximate location. It would be a big house of several stories. They could all live on the upper floors and put the lower rooms to use for fitting and sewing. There would even be a nursery for Martha. The girls and Nell had described it as a mansion.

Her heart sank as she approached the area. It was a street of tall frame houses which had once been owned by the important citizens of the area in the city's beginnings. Some had business offices on the lower floors. But those people were gone now, moved on up the hill, away from the criminal element and the fires that plagued San Francisco. Now the buildings were rooming houses. The streets teemed with men, rough and dirty from their day's work.

The house was not difficult to find. It spelled out clearly what it was. Apparently it had been built for a brothel. A sign reading *Madam Foster's Place* creaked before it. The structure of unpainted lumber was gray from several years of wind and fog. It stood tall and gaunt, with small windows. A light in an upstairs room revealed silhouettes—of a man and a girl—against a crookedly hanging shade.

Tamsen watched as a man went up the steps. When he entered, the open door let a blast of dreary, desultory sound into the night.

Pulling her courage together, Tamsen went up to the door. Once inside, she could see why Nell and the girls were impressed. The floor was carpeted, though the carpet was muddy and worn. There was a chandelier, half its candles burning, prisms missing. The long bar in the large room was of fine mahogany, but neither it nor its fixtures had been polished.

The crowd was a seedy-looking one. Tamsen kept her hand on the small gun in her pocket as she explained to the yawning girl who approached her that she wished to see the madam—on business.

Madam Foster was ill, the girl told Tamsen—she would have to check. She disappeared for a moment, then returned to lead Tamsen up the stairs.

The second floor was worse than the first. Several doors stood open, and Tamsen could see that larger rooms had been partitioned off, making cubicles only slightly larger than closets. Though some of them held tarnished, cracked, gilt-framed mirrors, they held little more furnishings than the usual iron beds, pitcher and bowl.

Madam Foster's room on the third floor was a little larger, more tastefully furnished. As she entered the room, it only took one look for Tamsen to see that the gaunt woman in the big bed was terminally ill.

Ill, but ready to talk business. Madam Foster explained that she had been confined to bed for a year, while her establishment went downhill. She was sick of the fogs, the fires, the wind. Admittedly, she was going home to die. But she intended to take enough profit with her to make it worth her while. The price she named staggered Tamsen. It came so close to what

Tamsen had intended to spend overall. And the place was a wreck! It would need a great amount of money to repair and paint and refurbish.

She pointed this out, and the woman shrugged. "Hell, honey, I know it, you know it. But I can turn this joint into a rooming house, just like it is, three-four men to a room, and draw down thousands. By the time it falls down around their ears, I won't give a damn. I want the cash now, while I'm here to spend it."

Tamsen wavered. "Will you give me a week to decide —before you sell to someone else?"

The woman grinned. "Time's what I ain't got much of, honey. I'll give you a coupla days." She coughed into a handkerchief, leaving a pinkish stain, and waved Tamsen out the door.

It won't do, Tamsen told herself as she walked back toward the shack that was home. The neighborhood was not conducive to the respectability a dress shop required. Few decent women would dare this street to have a gown fitted. Yet the house could be fixed up, cleaned, and painted. She began to calculate her funds, then checked herself. She could not move Martha and Em into such surroundings. The place had a bad reputation.

With a start, she realized it was very late. She had spent too much time in conversation, haggling over the price. Em would be worried. She would save time by cutting across the plaza, hazardous though it was. The area was still stacked with bricks and timbers, rubble from the fire.

The moment she entered the square, cutting across the plaza at an angle, her heart began beating a little more rapidly. She cursed herself for her foolhardiness. She should have brought Dusty with her. A woman without a male escort was asking for trouble, day or night, in San Francisco. Especially, on a night like this, with a clear sky and bright moon, there'd be homeless men sleeping here, drunks dragged from the one casino still in operation. Her hand on the gun in her pocket was damp with perspiration as she ran lightly on her toes, hoping to escape an ugly confrontation.

250

Then there was a man before her, a tall man, made of angles. Moonlight glinted on the rifle he pointed at her.

"Who are you?" he asked. "What is your business here?"

Tamsen fought to control the shivering that began at his sudden appearance, the sight of the weapon. "I am Mrs.—Mrs. Harper," she stammered. "I've been to see someone on business. I didn't realize it was so late—"

"Well, Mrs. Harper," the man said, "I suggest you return to your home. I will see you to the street. A decent woman should not be out on a night like this, alone. Especially after what's happened here."

When she saw that he had no intention of harming her, she grew angry at his implication. "Now, I would like to ask a few questions," she snapped. "Who are *you*? What business is it of yours what I'm doing here? And what *has* happened?"

He gestured toward the old adobe building in the plaza, the old army barracks. She followed his moving hand, seeing nothing but the structure itself.

Then she saw the figure, black against the moonlight. The figure of a man, suspended from a crossbeam. As she stared, it moved slowly in a half-arc.

"Oh, *God*!" she whispered. "Who is it? "Why—?"

"Man by the name of Jenkins. Stole a safe from the shipping office. Tried, sentenced, and sentence carried out by the Vigilante Committee, of which I'm one. More'n a thousand people here to watch the proceedings. And there's going to be a lot more of it until we get this town cleaned up! Outlaws, bars, brothels— excuse me, ma'am, for the mention of such things. How come you didn't hear the commotion? You just get to town?"

Tamsen wondered what this man would say if she told him she'd just returned from trying to make a deal to purchase a brothel.

He saw her to the street, left her there, and returned to stand guard over the body with a group of his com-

251

panions. Tamsen walked on alone, shocked at what she had seen, imagining the crowd that had gathered for the hanging. This was a cruel place, this town where fires were set deliberately, where men were murdered in the streets for a few ounces of gold. But to gather in one spot, to watch a man die so horribly, and then to leave him there! It was horror beyond imagining. She knew she would dream of that grotesque suspended shape for many nights to come.

Perhaps they should take the money they had and return to Pennsylvania. But to what? Home was no longer there. She and Em were strangers to the girls they'd been. And somewhere, somehow, she hoped to find word of Arabella. No, it would never do.

Fortunately, Em was either asleep or pretended to be when she got home, because Tamsen had no desire to discuss the thing she had seen. She slid into bed, putting it from her mind. She must concentrate on what was best to do for them all. She must consider Madam Foster's proposition. It would never do for what she had planned, but then, anything was better than nothing at all.

The next afternoon, on the pretext of taking Martha for an airing, she went to the house again. Today, in the bright sunlight, it looked even worse than she'd thought. She stared at it through narrowed eyes, seeking its possibilities. How poorly the place had been managed. If she were to operate a house such as this, she would do it far differently. She'd fix it up, cater to an exclusive clientele. And the girls! Even in their fancy costumes, they looked like what they were. If *she* owned it, they would spruce up or go.

Handled properly, it could work. It would work! This city was full of wealthy men—politicians, ship-owners, merchants, professional men. Even an elite group of foreigners here for adventure. With a proper atmosphere, insistence on proper dress and demeanor, good entertainment—the place could make someone a fortune.

Martha began to whimper a little. Tamsen looked

once more at the structure with a hard, professional eye, and started homeward.

She walked head down, cooing to Martha as she went, but lifted her face as a man passed her. Even then, it took a second for what she had seen to register in her mind. It was not! It could not be! She was mistaken! She whirled to look after him, only to find that he, too, had turned back.

She looked straight into Dan Tallant's startled eyes.

Chapter 7

Dan Tallant had almost passed the woman by, but something, he didn't know what, had made him turn for a second look. For a moment, his brain refused to accept the truth. Because he didn't want to accept it, he told himself, an old guilt stirring within him as he looked at the tired waif in shabby clothing, eyes darkly circled, a heavy child in her arms.

"Tamsen," he said in a hoarse whisper, "Tamsen? Is it you?"

For an instant, it seemed as though her eyes had filled with tears. Then she lifted her head proudly, defiantly, and he was certain it was Tamsen.

"Hello, Dan."

Still thunderstruck, he approached her. She stood her ground as he drew back an edge of the blanket that concealed little Martha's face from the wind. The baby looked up at him with solemn dark eyes from a face that might have been Tamsen's own, then smiled, saying "Ma-ma," her word for everything.

Dan flinched as though he had been struck. "My God," he said, huskily, "my God, Tamsen! I'm sorry! I'm so sorry! I didn't know!"

Tamsen looked at him blankly, searching for his meaning. Why did he appear to be so shattered? Then the truth dawned on her. He thought Martha was theirs, conceived of their lovemaking that night. What a joke! What a monstrous, ridiculous joke! Well, if that was what he wanted to think, let him! She fought back the smile that tugged at her lips and looked at the ground, trying to assume the expression of an unwed mother who has just been found out.

"Believe me," he said again. "I didn't know." There was suffering in his tone, and the sound was music to Tamsen's ears. Martha wasn't his, but she could have been! He must have known it was possible when he walked out on her. It didn't make any difference then. Here she had a perfect method of revenge. She lifted her eyes to his.

"I didn't know how to find you," she said, piteously.

Dan's answer was profane, but it was directed at himself. As he took her arm, she felt a surge of her old passion at his touch, and she shrank away. He mistook her action for fear of him.

"I won't hurt you," he said gently. "I just want to find someplace where we can talk. I want to know how you got here, how you're living." His eyes darkened with horror as he had another thought.

"Tamsen, how long has it been since you've eaten?"

Again, she had to suppress her laughter. The gown she was wearing was straight from a charity barrel, collected by the good people who hadn't suffered from the fire. It was very worn and much too large. Then, too, she had lost weight in her search for a business to buy, and the conditions in the cloth-and-frame structure were not conducive to an elaborate toilette. She must look like a beggar to him! When had she eaten?

"Yesterday at noon," she said in a faint voice. It was true. After her visit to Madam Foster, she'd slept until a little over an hour ago, then snatched a sip of coffee before leaving the shack.

"My God," Dan groaned. "Oh, my God! What have I done to you!"

Taking her arm tenderly, he led her to a restaurant that had recently opened. Despite the most inflated prices in San Francisco, the place managed a booming business. But it was nearly empty at this hour.

Still overcome by the enormity of the joke on Tallant, Tamsen kept her head down as she ordered a meal of the most expensive items on the menu. Though she had a difficult time choking it all down, she managed to eat as though she were starving.

Tallant's eyes were haunted. And they should be, she thought. They should be!

Finished at last, she was ready with her story. Much of it paralleled the truth.

They had left Magoffinville, she said, for the sake of the unborn baby. While a woman could bear the stigma of having a child out of wedlock, it was dreadful for the child. Carefully deleting names, Tamsen told the whole tale; how there was an Indian attack the very night the baby was born; how, because of ill health—she didn't say whose—they'd come by boat the last part of the way; how she'd been cheated of her true profit on the farming equipment she'd brought all the way from Pennsylvania.

"I opened a sewing shop here," she said, lashes lowered to hide the laughter in her eyes, "and it was burned out in the fire. Since, we've been living in a cloth-and-frame shack."

Dan's face was white. "You mean my—the baby's been living in a tent?"

"She's only had croup once," Tamsen said, hoping he'd mistake the quivering of her lips for some more tragic emotion.

Tallant put his hands flat on the table. "That settles it! How much do you think it would take to get you back to Pennsylvania, to find a decent house, to raise the child?"

In other words, Tamsen thought, how much does it take to rid himself of us? To get us off his conscience? Her mouth set tightly as she said, "I don't know."

"Don't hold back, Tamsen! This is no time to be stiff-necked. How much do you need?"

Need? Now that was quite different. She needed all she could get. And this was quite an offer, coming from a man who probably wouldn't have a dime in his pocket after this meal was paid for. She might as well make it good. Her lips curved in a malicious little smile as she spoke.

"Fifty thousand dollars."

His face hardening, he stared at her for a moment, seeing the triumphant expression in her eyes. "It's blackmail, isn't it?" he asked. "You have no intention of forgiving me, do you?"

She was silent, and he sighed. The money would be no problem. Several years of back pay rested in the bank, along with a considerable inheritance. It was the fact that this—this gold-digger was using him that hurt. Still, the child was his responsibility.

"I made the offer," he said, "and I won't back down on it. You'll find the amount you asked for deposited to your account in the morning. Now, may I ask which bank?"

Their business concluded, he left her without a backward glance. Later when his anger had cooled to the point that he could think coherently, he remembered that he had not thought to inquire about Em. And there was Arabella. He wondered, uneasily, if the girl had been found, and under what conditions they were truly living.

Maybe that fifty thousand would take them all home. If so, it would be doing some good, after all.

As for Tamsen, it was too painful to think about her. She had come a long way from the innocent young lady on the trail. First the horses, then the cantina. And now, taking a man for all she could get.

But there was the baby. Reluctantly, he had to admit he'd contributed to what Tamsen had become.

Tamsen had remained at the table as he walked away. She was stunned, unable to believe that Dan Tallant had that kind of money. He didn't even blink an eye when she mentioned that impossible sum! It had only been part of the joke on him! She'd merely picked that figure out of the air to taunt him.

Perhaps he was lying about depositing the money in her account. But he seemed sincere. Maybe he'd found a gold mine! Or struck it lucky at the tables.

257

She couldn't take his money! Martha wasn't his. She'd be taking it under false pretenses.

Of course, he had made love to her, then gone off and left her. What if she'd become pregnant? It could have happened. She could have found herself bearing a child without a name.

She would take the money—if it was there! But she had no notion of using it to return to the East. She would add the money to what she had and invest it in her business. Someday she would be able to throw it in his face, with interest, and laugh at him for being such a fool.

The next morning, Tamsen presented herself at the bank. The clerk who waited upon her checked a page of figures as he studied her, curiously. "Yes, Mr. Tallant has been in." And, "Yes, the transaction has been completed."

Tamsen left the bank on shaky, uncertain legs. But she didn't go home. She went straight to the house of Madam Foster. For last night she'd had a dream. In that dream, the house on Stockton had been refurbished, but not as a dressmaking establishment.

She saw herself standing at the top of the curving stairs, dressed elegantly in velvet, the jewel Sam Larabee had given her at her throat. At the bottom of the stairs a sea of faces looked up admiringly. They were the faces of men, and they were all paying customers.

Tamsen would manage the place as it had never been managed before. It would be luxurious, opulent, geared to attract a wealthier class of clientele.

Nell was the first she told. The big woman's face brightened. That was the kind of life she could understand.

"But gawdamn," she boomed, "what you gonna tell Em? She don't go fer that kinda stuff."

"I don't know," Tamsen confessed. "I've been trying to think of some excuse. After all," she lied, "it's not my money. It's Sam's."

"She won't buy that, neither," Nell said glumly. "Em don't look at things normal, like we do." She pondered

258

for a moment, then said, "Hell, it's easy. We got us some kinda hotel. We live there. You come over an' work nights on the desk. You said you an' Em was gonna live someplace else, didn'cha? It'll work fine."

So that was the way it was left. Em was told of the purchase and left behind to care for Martha while the others set to work at redecorating the building. Tamsen haunted the docks, picking up painted silks to paper the walls, precious china, glassware, silver, vases.

There would be no breakage in Madam Franklin's Parlor for Gentlemen!

Between her shopping forays, when ships came in from far places, Tamsen looked for a home. She intended to resume her double life of Magoffinville. She would be the madam of the most elite brothel in town. Her life outside would be of the utmost respectability.

When a home did not materialize, Tamsen began to get panicky. She could not take Em to the house on Stockton Street, and she could not leave her in the cloth-and-frame shack they shared now—not through the winter, when the wind sometimes blew cold off a gray sea. And not at night, when there were worse things than pneumonia abroad. If only she knew someone who might help her—someone of importance.

As she worried, little Martha turned loose of a chair she was holding and staggered a few toddling steps toward Em, to bury her face in her skirt, saying "Ma-ma."

Tamsen's heart constricted with an emotion she could not define. She had been gone so much. Too busy throughout the day. Once they were settled, things would change. She would need only be gone at night, and the days could be spent with Martha.

Tamsen continued to brood about finding someone influential who could help her in her search for a house. Then she remembered the man she had met when she went to dinner with Sam. Senator Don Alden.

Early next morning, Tamsen set off for the Senator's offices. She had dressed most carefully, in a sedate black faille that billowed into ruffles from its cinched-in waist. At the hem, the ruffles were lifted at one side, pinned in place with a black velvet bow, revealing a hint of crisp white petticoats. Her hat, too, was sedate. Black with plumes, but tilted at a slightly provocative angle that was most becoming.

She knew exactly how she looked. She had dressed to fit the picture of an attractive young widow, well-to-do, but most helpless in business matters.

The distinguished gentleman she had met in the hotel was in his shirtsleeves. He lifted the prematurely white head, his blue eyes narrowing in surprise, then stood, struggling into his coat.

"Forgive me," Senator Alden said. "I do not often have ladies as visitors in this office. Now, what can I do for you?" There was no recognition in his face as he looked at her, expectantly.

"You probably do not recall," Tamsen said, her expression demure, "but we've met. We were introduced by Mr. Larabee one evening at dinner—"

He brightened. "Of course! Now I recall. You wore a beautiful gown. It was—"

"Most unsuitable for a widow, in mourning." Her voice was a chastened whisper. "But Mr. Larabee suggested that it might help take my mind off my problems." The eyes she lifted to Senator Alden's were bright with unshed tears. His face reflected pity.

"I sympathize with you in your bereavement. Though it comes to us all. I recently lost my stepmother, a fine woman—"

"I'm so sorry!"

"Well," he said, "what's past cannot be helped. We must attend to the business of living. Now, what is the reason for your call?"

She told him. Her husband had died of pneumonia on the trail. Here, she touched her eyes delicately with a handkerchief. He had left her a widow, with a child and a delicate ailing sister. She had attempted to open a respectable business in San Francisco, but had lost her building in the fire. Though she had money—her husband had left her well-to-do—she, her sister, and

260

her baby were homeless. At present, they were reduced to living in a tent.

Perhaps the Senator might have some idea where they could obtain suitable living quarters in a respectable area.

"I'm very sorry," the Senator said regretfully. "I might have been able to help you before the fire, but as it is, there are so many homeless people everywhere."

The dark eyes confronting him filled again, this time with disappointment. He felt vaguely uncomfortable, as if he were in some way at fault for her plight. He was even more discomfited when the girl choked back a sob.

"See here," he said in alarm, "give me a moment. I'll think of something—"

It didn't take too much thought. There was only one possibility. His own home. Since his stepmother had died, Senator Alden had been rattling around in the big house on the hill, lonely despite the cook and Lin, his Chinese man. He'd been a little guilty about living in such comfort when, all around him, people were homeless. He'd written his young stepbrother, Adam, asking him to join him, but there had been no response. The rooms behind the office, here, would be quite suitable for a single man—

So, why not?

"I think," he said, "I can offer you exactly the kind of place you have in mind."

When Tamsen left, hardly able to maintain her dignity in the face of her exuberance, Donald Alden followed her to the door and watched after her. The suddenness of his decision to let his home had surprised him. Yet it would work well all around. The rental he'd suggested was very low, unheard-of in San Francisco, but he was sure that the furnishings, his stepmother's fine things, would be cared for. One did not often meet a woman of such gentility in San Francisco.

As he watched Tamsen round a corner, the wind lifted a ruffle to reveal a shapely ankle. "Where in the

261

hell," he asked himself, "did a lady like that meet Sam Larabee?"

Tamsen, too, was thinking of Sam Larabee. His gold had gone to purchase Madam Foster's establishment. Now, his friendship with the Senator had found a lovely house for herself, Em, and the baby. Dan Tallant, unknowing, would be paying the rental on that home.

She wondered what he'd think when he discovered she hadn't left for Pennsylvania, what he'd do when he learned about her new business—which he surely would.

Not that it made any difference, she smiled to herself. She had never said that she would return to Pennsylvania. He had merely taken it for granted. There was no contract, verbal or otherwise. There was nothing he could do.

Chapter 8

Dan Tallant was in no position to hear of Tamsen's new enterprise. He had a set of written orders, requesting him to travel, incognito, with the monthly mail service between San Francisco and Salt Lake and to submit a full report on the hazards of the journey. The person who signed those orders would not consider one small dark-eyed girl justification for shirking one's duties.

Tallant presented himself to Major George Chorpenning, recipient of the mail contract, and hired on as an armed guard. A letter of recommendation he carried made his employment almost mandatory.

Joining the small group carrying the consignment, Dan boarded a river steamer which carried the mail as far as Sacramento, a city growing out of the mud around the American River.

At Sacramento, the mail was transferred to muleback. From there it went to Placerville, the last stop before challenging the peaks of the Sierra Nevada. Throughout the trip, Tallant took notes, wrote obscure figures on pieces of paper, drew maps, all of which he stored in a waterproof packet beneath his flannel shirt.

One of the other guards called Dan's mysterious activities to Major Chorpenning's attention. "Don't seem right," he said, "the way that feller writes down things. Me, I cain't hardly sign my name. Ol' Zeb there jest makes his mark. Nuther thing, too. While we're drinkin', he's thinkin'. Feller like him bears watchin'."

263

George Chorpenning agreed and began to keep Tallant under strict surveillance. It was clear the man had his mind on something. Chorpenning had received the contract as the low man among thirty-seven bidders. Tallant could have been sent by one of his competitors, to achieve revenge. Or he could have mail theft in mind.

Still there was his letter of recommendation, though with the fellow's talent with the pen, it might have been forged. It was a nervous journey for Major Chorpenning, with a guard who stayed sober, didn't head for the nearest bordello at Sacramento, Placerville, or Salt Lake, took notes, drew maps, and had something on his mind.

It was a nervous journey for Tallant, too. For the first time, he found himself unable to play his part. It was of the utmost importance that he not stand out among the others, that he be just a man, a hired gun. It was almost impossible. His own problems were weighing on him too heavily.

He was not just Dan Tallant any more. He was a family man. A father! The memory of the child with Tamsen's face was a picture his conscience would not erase. True, the baby was an accident, the by-blow of a situation that set emotions out of control. But he was responsible. He should have seen Tamsen and the baby on a boat headed around the Horn before he left. But there had not been time. Tamsen was not to be trusted. He knew that from experience. But his little daughter—how strange that sounded in his mind—was going to have every opportunity to grow into a decent human being. When he got back, he would make certain they had gone back East.

At the first stop, in Sacramento, he went to a bar with his companions. There, a girl named Callie looked at him, obviously liking what she saw. A hard-muscled, wide-shouldered, dark, lean-hipped man. Threading her way through the thronging customers, she slipped in beside him at the bar, insinuating her body against his.

Dan Tallant jerked at the feel of her warm flesh. Looking down at the top of her silky black hair, he spilled his drink. *Tamsen! Here?*

When she raised her face, pretty, but hardened from her years of plying a rough trade, Dan came to his senses. Turning on his heel, he forced his way through the milling crowd until he reached the door leading outside. There he took a deep breath of the clean, unsullied air. He had acted like a fool, practically running from the girl as he did. He should go back in and take advantage of what she had to offer. But he couldn't.

The incident only deepened his determination to seek Tamsen out immediately upon his return and make sure she and the baby had departed San Francisco. But his return was to be delayed. The man he was to meet in Salt Lake City did not arrive before George Chorpenning began his return trip. Tallant was forced to wait for the next consignment of mail, delivered by Chorpenning's partner, Absalom Woodward, before he saw San Francisco again.

Thus Tamsen's fears of meeting Dan on the street, of having him discover what she was doing, were unfounded. She assumed that he had gone back East when she didn't see him again. And if her conscience pricked at the thought of the money she had taken from him, she managed to quell it in the hustle and bustle of redoing the Foster house.

She had managed to assemble a work crew with Dusty's help. Dusty hung around the gaming tables in the casinos, bringing home miners who had lost their fortunes, and needed a stake to make another one, and alcoholics who needed the price of a bottle. Tamsen had a hard and fast rule. At the end of a productive day, there would be generous wages and a bottle waiting for each man. There would be no drinking while at work. With this carrot dangled before them, the workers were eager to sign on, though the work crews fluctuated. Once a miner had earned the price of a pack animal, a shovel, some grub, he would leave for more lucrative fields, or a drinker a few dollars and he would find some easier way to obtain the liquor his system required. Still, there were plenty of others to take their places.

Tamsen watched with impatience and delight as her dream took shape.

The partitions that separated the upstairs rooms into tiny cubicles were knocked out, leaving five good-sized rooms on each of the two upper floors. These she had papered with exotic hand-painted silks from the Orient. Glass in the gold-framed mirrors was replaced; the iron bedsteads were gilded. Oriental carpets covered the bare plank floors. Window shades were banished and heavy velvet draperies with valances that matched the luxurious spreads covering the beds hung in their places.

Downstairs, the ancient chandelier had been replaced. Above the new one was an eight-foot round mirror. When the faded dirty carpet was removed, Tamsen discovered the floor to be of a most beautiful parquet. Polished and scattered with Oriental rugs, it achieved the effect of opulence she was striving for. The mahogany bar, gleaming now, proved to be the gem she had thought it to be.

In a very short time, Tamsen was able to wander through the lower rooms, viewing them with satisfaction. The larger room, except for the bar, might have been a queen's drawing room, glittering candles reflected in the mirror above. Small gilt chairs sat around the walls; furnishings were of the Biedermeier style. The room to one side was the gaming room, with plush dark-red walls, framed hunting prints and leather-upholstered chairs—a man's room completely.

Behind it, there was a private dining room. Here, too, a mirror reflected the lights of a chandelier. The tables would be covered in the finest damask.

Tamsen returned to the large room and stood fingering the keys of a grand piano. It was all she had dreamed. Tomorrow, Dusty, Nell, and the girls would move into the third-floor rooms. She and Em would transfer their belongings to their own new home. And Madam Franklin's Parlor for Gentlemen would open at the end of the week.

"It's one helluva joint," Nell observed, passing through.

"It is, isn't it?" Tamsen said, softly. "It *is*!"

When it was time to return to the cloth-and-frame home for the last time, Tamsen suggested the others go on ahead. Standing across the street as she had on the first night she'd come here, the night she'd been so bitterly disappointed, she studied the place. The roof, with its hand-hewn shingles, had darkened to a charcoal; the remainder of the house had been painted white. Pink shutters flanked the small windows and small wrought-iron balconies added an elegant touch. The front door was of heavy polished oak, which helped to give the place a substantial look.

Now all they had to do was attract the right sort of customer. Already, the word was being spread that Mrs. Franklin's would be a different sort of place. Coats and ties would be required. There were house rules. There would be no brawling, no public drunkenness. It would be a quiet place where a man could come for a social conversation, good entertainment, a drink—and a girl, if he wished. A place of dignity, of elegance.

Tamsen grinned as she thought of what those first nights would be. Some old customers would show up at first through curiosity. But they would not remain long —not at her prices. It might take time to reach the clientele she desired, but she would wait.

In the meantime, she had employed two stout young men to stand at the door. Both were from good families back East and had lost their shirts at the gaming tables in the casinos. Neither had a desire to do manual labor. They would help keep the clientele restricted to gentlemen. The job was tailor-made for them.

Still smiling, Tamsen walked toward home, cutting

267

across the plaza without a look toward the adobe where Jenkins had hung.

The next morning, Tamsen and Em went off to meet Donald Alden at his house, which they were now to occupy. Em, a little nervous at meeting a Senator, had dressed in her best. Tamsen studied her approvingly. She wore a powder-blue gown, a white fichu filling the V at the neckline. Her long, bell-shaped sleeves had a detachable undersleeve, gathered into a band at the wrist. A small poke bonnet of the same blue was set to the back of her head, framing soft brown hair, worn madonna-like over the ears and gathered into a chignon at the back.

"You look beautiful, Em!" Tamsen whispered. With a small pang, she realized how housebound Em had been. It need be that way no longer. Now Em could be launched into a society worthy of her.

Tamsen wore the same widow's garb in which she'd first approached the Senator. She insisted on carrying Martha who was fussing because of the long ruffled dress she had been made to wear.

Senator Alden, meanwhile, was preparing to relinquish his home and he was having problems. He had decided to take his Chinese man to his new quarters behind his offices, and to leave Birdie Faraday, his cook, with the house. Mrs. Faraday, a little white-haired woman with corkscrew curls, was not happy.

"I cooked for your stepmama for twenty-five years, young man," she said, spiritedly, "and we got along fine. She didn't interfere in my kitchen. And here's one of the family renting me out like an old mule! She'd turn over in her grave—"

"That's enough, Birdie. We've been over all that. I explained there's no place for you where I'm going." The Senator was tired. "Besides, it's only temporary, I'm sure, and," he had an inspiration, "you'll be able to keep an eye on my stepmother's things. After all, these people are strangers."

It worked. He could see the fierce protectiveness in

Birdie's face, and he gave a sigh of relief. Birdie and his Chinese man were constantly at war, with Mrs. Faraday referring to Lin as "that heathen Chinee." It would be good to live in a place unoccupied by women.

When the women arrived, Lin answered the door, ushering Tamsen, Em, and the baby into the parlor. Tamsen came first, carrying the baby. Em followed. The Senator stood almost speechless, staring at Em. A vision in blue against the warm plum furnishings of the parlor, she reminded him of his girl-wife, dead long ago. Yet there was something more about her, a gentle tranquillity, a flower-like sweetness that caught at his heart as she raised her blue eyes shyly to his.

In that moment, Senator Donald Alden lost his heart. Mrs. Faraday, watching, sniffed. It was just like she thought. Young master Donald had been taken in by a pretty face.

Em, in turn, felt a start of surprise. She had expected to see an elderly gentleman, perhaps an older version of Major Arbuthnot. This lean, hard man with keen blue eyes did not fit her idea of a professional politician. The white hair was deceptive, she decided. He could not possibly be over forty. The way he looked at her . . . Perhaps her scrutiny of him was apparent. Blushing, she lowered her gaze.

Before handing over the keys, Senator Alden took them on a tour of the house. Upstairs, Tamsen chose a bedroom done in red and white. For some reason, the Senator was obscurely gratified. Miss Emmeline would have his stepmother's room, a room done in pastels, with crisp white curtains at the windows. A room that suited her.

He was leaving almost everything behind—furnishings, linens. He was certain they'd find a use for them, since they'd lost their own possessions in the fire. When they descended to the kitchen, he explained about Mrs. Faraday, asking if they minded if she stayed on. Tamsen was delighted, but Em frowned.

"I was so looking forward to working about a kitchen," she said, a little disappointed. Then her face brightened. "But perhaps we can work together. I'm sure Mrs. Faraday wouldn't mind a little help."

Birdie Faraday, arms akimbo, curls fairly standing on end at the thought of an intrusion into her domain, said nothing. Senator Alden thought it an appropriate time to make a hasty exit.

As Em walked with him to the door, she raised troubled blue eyes to say, "I feel so guilty! As if we're putting you out of your own home. You will come to dinner, I hope?"

"I would appreciate an invitation." He bowed, gallantly.

He walked from the house, his lips pursed in a soundless whistle, some very unpolitical thoughts in his mind. For in his imagination, he could see Emmeline in that bedroom upstairs. She would be wearing a flowing gown, a gauzy thing that left her slim white shoulders bare. And that mass of soft hair would be down.

He imagined himself calling to her from the doorway. She would turn, face shining in welcome, slender body limned against the light behind her, arms outstretched. He would go to her and lift her in his arms—

Good God, he thought, with a rueful chuckle. What's wrong with me! He was acting like a love-struck boy, and he thought he'd left that sort of thing behind. After all, the lady had offered him nothing but an invitation to dinner, an invitation he knew he would accept with celerity when—and if—it came. And here he was already dreaming of getting her into bed!

He'd have to get out more. He'd been away from the company of women far too long.

At the same time, some distance away, an armed guard with a mail train was considering a similar cure for the same ailment. For Dan Tallant, lying in his bedroll at the foot of the Sierras the previous night, had dreamed of Tamsen. She was lying beside him, warm and willing. Even now, he felt the curves of her body pressed against his. The dream had been real and vivid, so vivid he feared it showed in his face.

There was only one sure cure for what ailed him. Another woman. And he just might start looking for one when he reached San Francisco and had made sure that Tamsen had truly gone.

Chapter 9

The opening of Madam Franklin's Parlor for Gentlemen was a smashing success. As Tamsen had predicted, the curious, the clods in their ill-fitting coats, ties constricting adam's apples, were soon weeded out. They found an atmosphere that awed them and made them uncomfortable. When they discovered the cost of both whisky and women, they beat a retreat to the bordellos in Portsmouth Square.

"It was like a goddam teaparty," one complained to a compatriot. "I'll take the cribs, anytime!"

Tamsen had purposely waited upstairs, sending the girls down one at a time. At last, Nell came to report. "A buncha swells come in," she said, "just like you wanted. The girls is all upstairs. Carmen's been twice. Coupla fellers from the East. Said it was a real Western experience."

Tamsen breathed a sigh of relief. The other girls had taken to their new gowns, adopting the manners she'd insisted upon, all except Maggie, who had been relegated to the kitchen. Carmen had been a doubtful experiment. Sent to a dentist to have her missing front tooth replaced, she returned with one of solid gold, made from a nugget. While her flashing smile was not too unattractive with her dark skin and crimson gown, it had not been exactly the image Tamsen wished to present. Nevertheless, it seemed to be working.

"Thanks." Tamsen smiled at Nell. "I will be down in a few minutes. And, by the way, you look very nice."

"I better," Nell scowled in her dowager's black, her paint toned down to Tamsen's specifications. "I still think I shoulda got gussied up." As she turned to go, she said as an afterthought, "You look purty good, yerself, honey."

I hope so, Tamsen thought. Oh, I hope so! She smoothed the flame-colored gown that bared her shoulders, clung close to her bosom, and accentuated her waist. It was snug over the hips, terminating in a mass of chiffon ruffles looped up with ribbons to disclose her ankles and daring new French-heeled slippers said to be the latest rage in Europe. With it, she wore her jade pendant for luck.

I'll need it, she thought, trembling a little. I'll need it. For she felt as she had that first night at the cantina. A young girl from a Pennsylvania farm who had no business being here. Again, she had to be a success. So much depended upon it.

She went to the stairs and down, pausing at the landing. The crowd below was not large. Perhaps twenty or thirty men. But she heard the sharp intake of breath as several of them saw her and began nudging others to draw their attention.

With her heart hammering, Tamsen moved like a queen as she descended the stairs. She signaled the piano player who had been playing soft chords, and he began the song they'd rehearsed.

She clasped her hands to her bosom and raised her face. Her hair hung down her back, smooth and unadorned. And her husky voice picked up the melody.

"Black is the color of my true love's hair . . ."

When she finished the song, the room was deathly quiet for a moment. Then there was a concert of applause. She moved across the floor, her hand offered to each in turn.

"I'm Madam Franklin. So glad you're here."

As her hand was kissed and bowed over, Tamsen felt a sense of triumph, discovering here someone in a government position, there a merchant. This man a lawyer, that man an official in the shipping offices. They were gentlemen, important men. And Madam Franklin's

273

Parlor had something to offer them that they were unable to get elsewhere.

Tamsen sat in one of the gilt chairs, surrounded by a throng of admiring men, and did not sing again that night. Instead, she watched as the other girls walked about, singly and in pairs. Once more, she had guessed correctly—dressing them in gowns that suggested but did not reveal their charms worked as she had hoped it would. Katie and Polly Simpson, a holdover from the Mrs. Foster days, also entertained. Though their singing and dancing was naughty, each song, each movement selected for its effect on masculine emotions, it was done in a cheerful, almost wholesome, manner.

Men preferred mystery, Tamsen thought with amusement. Their imaginations were titillated by seeing part of the product, rather than the whole. Each of them, she was certain, was considering the possibility and the cost of getting Madam Franklin up those stairs.

Tamsen was wined and toasted. When the glittering room began to spin a little, she excused herself. Some of those who had been hoping to have her all evening would go upstairs with one of the other girls. Some would leave. Others would remain, eyes on the stairs, waiting for her to return. They would be disappointed, and they would come back tomorrow night. The word would spread. They would bring their friends.

Her prophecy proved to be correct. By the end of the following week, her place was crowded with moneyed gentlemen. Dusty, who moved among them unobtrusively in impeccable evening garb, told her that she'd earned the reputation of being untouchable. Some of the men had made rather large wagers as to who would bed Madam Franklin first. Gifts began pouring in, and she recognized them as part of their campaign. The jade necklace was put into a drawer and forgotten. Now, when she descended the stairs, she rivaled the glitter of the room.

She felt the surge of power that had first struck her at the cantina. And she was happier than she had ever been in her life.

"Gotta hand it to you, honey," Nell grunted. "Wouldn't of give this place a hoot in hell, as far as amountin' to somethin'. But you done it!"

Dusty, who counted the gold coins, weighed in the dust, and tabulated each day's receipts, was certain the success of the parlor was due to Nell's ample charms.

Em, in the meantime, was in a state of excitement unusual for one of her tranquil nature. For Senator Donald Alden was invited for Sunday dinner. The day was chosen because Tamsen did not have to control the desk at the hotel on that night. Tamsen explained that it would be wise not to mention her occupation to the Senator. He was an old-fashioned man in many ways and would not approve of a woman working. She did not wish him to think they were in need of charity. He'd done so much.

Em explained the situation to Mrs. Faraday, who clamped her jaw virtuously, and said, "I don't gossip, ma'am." Though, secretly, she resolved to find where Tamsen worked at her first opportunity. She liked Tamsen. The girl had a little spice to her, not like her milk-faced sister. Em was a pretty thing, Birdie had to admit, and maybe she didn't give her her due. But she wouldn't keep out of her kitchen.

It was worse on that weekend. On Saturday, Em made a cake and a pie. Secretly, Birdie hoped the cake would fall, the piecrust turn out tough. But, when the cake was high, light as a feather, and the pie lifted from the oven gold and flaky, Birdie had to content herself with a few dire remarks.

"Used all the eggs in that cake. May not be able to get any more. And you had a heavy hand with the lard in your pie!"

The climax came when Em, who insisted on cooking the roast, took it out long before it was done.

"It smells good," Birdie admitted, "but nobody's going to eat raw meat."

"It isn't raw," Em laughed. "It's rare. And that's the way most gentlemen like it."

"Not Donald Alden! He's been eating my cooking most of his life, and he's never complained yet."

Em ignored her, and Birdie subsided, thinking gleefully to herself that all she had to do was wait and see. When she took Master Donald's plate off the table, still full, the girl would know she'd made a mistake.

Her hopes were dashed when Alden ate every bite he was served. She had no way of knowing that he was hardly aware he was eating. His eyes were on Em the entire evening.

Tamsen was in a state of pure bliss, her Parlor for Gentlemen completely forgotten. She had at last reached the goal she wanted. Respectability! A small dinner served well, a guest of importance. She looked with approval at the silver spread in shining array beside the serving plates, the crystal. It was a far cry from the tin cups and eating pans of the trail! And she had achieved it all. The fact that it actually belonged to the Senator made no difference. With the golden flood pouring in at her establishment, she could replace it all.

The truly important thing was that this was a polite atmosphere, a handsome man, genteel conversation. She looked at the Senator, mulling over what she'd learned about him. A longtime widower, he would be a good catch for any woman. She had no need for a man in her life, but there was no harm in keeping him interested. She sought for tidbits of intellectual conversation she'd overheard at her place of business.

"I understand we're still having problems along the Texas border, Senator Alden. I thought the Mexican War settled all that. But there seems to be some dispute. Have you heard anything about that?"

The Senator turned to her, his face alive with interest. "Indeed I have. The treaty did not provide a positive demarcation from the area known as Magoffinville, now Franklin, to the Pacific." He took a paper and pencil from his pocket, sketching a map.

So Magoffinville was now Franklin. Tamsen suppressed a giggle, wondering if the place was renamed for the mountain that rose above it or a certain cantina girl who had set the town on its ear. To cover her amusement, she said, "But the area is so Godforsaken. I can't imagine why our government would want it. Nothing but cowboys, ruffians, cactus, and mesquite—"

The Senator was looking at her oddly. "Then you've been there?"

"No—o," she stammered. "My—my husband once visited the area."

Em stared down at her plate.

"There is more to it than just the area," Senator Alden continued. "There are some who believe it to be a site for a transcontinental railroad, linking the East with the West."

"Trains? Replacing the wagons?" Tamsen leaned forward. "How wonderful! But I cannot believe it!"

"It will be a while," Senator Alden admitted, "but it is coming. I recall what Zach Taylor said . . ." He launched into a story that left Tamsen gasping. He'd known Taylor, Fillmore, too. He mentioned James Gadsden, a dear friend, a railroad president from South Carolina. Gadsden was being considered as a minister to Mexico, and he was greatly in favor of the transcontinental route. Next year might tell the story.

The girls were enthralled, Em envisioning the end to the miseries of the trail, Tamsen thinking of how her business would expand.

Birdie Faraday brought dessert, and the Senator helped himself liberally to the pie. "I've never tasted better," he said. Birdie's face flamed and she looked at Em accusingly. Em sat quietly, letting the credit for the piemaking go. It had been a mistake invading the fiery little woman's kitchen. They would probably never be friends.

After the meal, the Senator turned gallantly to Em. "I like to walk a bit, after I've dined so well," he said. "Would you think me rude if I suggested a stroll? In your company, of course?" His eyes moved to Tamsen. "And will you excuse us, dear lady?"

Before Tamsen realized that she had been excluded, they were out of the house and she was alone. She felt

277

an instant's pique, then her eyes lit with laughter. Son of a gun! The senator was interested in Em! The queen of Madam Franklin's Parlor had been ignored, cast aside in favor of her quiet older sister.

She was glad, for Em's sake. Her business was her life, now, it and little Martha. Em and the baby were growing too close of late. If Em could marry someone like Senator Alden and move into a good social circle, it would be better for them all. Then Tamsen's brows drew together in a worried frown. If only Em had a little gumption! If she'd only try to attract a man! There were little tricks she could teach her. But she wouldn't use them. Not Em. Right now, she was probably engaging in stilted, polite conversation, with nothing except entertaining a guest on her mind.

Tamsen was wrong. Em was as nervous as a girl on her first date, all shivery inside at being alone with such an attractive man.

"This is a beautiful night," he said.

And it was. It had been cool for some days, a fresh scent blowing in from the sea. The moon was a silver disk in a sky sprinkled with stars. Em felt almost choked at the loveliness of it. Senator Alden offered his arm. She could feel the long, hard muscles that rippled beneath his coat. With a weak, heady sensation, Em wondered what it would be like to be enfolded in those arms, to put her head against his shoulder, to feel loved and protected.

That shivery feeling again. And this time, he sensed it. The white head, silvery with moonlight, inclined toward her. "Are you chilled?" She shook her head, numbly.

He didn't seem to notice her silence as they walked together. He spoke of his love for the state of California, touching lightly on his political career. He mentioned his plans to retire from politics, when his present plans for the country reached fruition; of the house he intended to build on a bluff, overlooking the sea. Then he halted suddenly, turning her to face him. She looked

278

up into his compelling eyes, feeling her heart beating much too fast.

"You haven't told me anything about yourself," he said quietly. "I've been monopolizing the conversation far too long. I want to hear about you."

His words struck her like a blow, shocking her back into sanity. She was not a young girl, out with her beau. She was a woman who had borne a child, who was living a lie. That the child had been conceived through none of her doing did not count—the woman was always at fault.

"I think we should return to the house," she said faintly. "Tamsen will be wondering where we are."

Graciously, he bowed assent. Now it was she who hurried and he who took long steps to keep up with her.

When the Senator took his leave, Tamsen proffered an invitation to dinner the following Sunday. He bowed his acceptance. "With your permission, I'd like to bring a friend. A young shipping executive of my acquaintance. I think you would enjoy meeting him, Mrs. Harper."

Tamsen's eyes danced. Not only was she being shunted gracefully aside, but company was being provided for her. When the Senator had gone, Tamsen turned to her sister. "I think you've got yourself a beau," she teased.

To Tamsen's surprise, Em burst into tears and fled to her room.

Tamsen followed, to find the frail girl weeping on her bed. She sat down beside her, smoothing the soft brown hair.

"Em, what is it? Tell me."

Presently the smothered sobs died down, and Em turned to Tamsen, her face weary and hopeless. Senator Alden was interested in her, and she liked him, too. But now his visits must be discouraged. She dared not be alone with him again.

Tamsen's anger flared. "Em, he didn't! He didn't try to—"

"He didn't do anything," Em cried. "He was a gentleman! Tamsen, it's me! I can't let him keep seeing me, thinking I'm something I'm not. If he knew the truth, he'd hate me! If he knew what happened in Magoffinville—"

"Em, you listen to me! You didn't do anything wrong! It was done to you. It's a pretty stupid world when a woman is blamed for something she can't help. It's over and done now. What difference does it make? There's no reason for him to know!"

"It would be a lie," Em said, sickly. "I should have claimed Martha as mine in the first place. If I'd had any sense, any courage, I would have. If I hadn't been so ill—" She turned her face away, and Tamsen felt a pang of fear.

"But what's done is done," she whispered. "Believe me, Em, it's best this way. And if you just say nothing, that's not lying. Maybe nothing will come of this—just a few pleasant hours, a chance to meet exciting people. But if it does, he will never know."

"I would know."

"Oh, Em!" Tamsen put her arms about her sister in exasperated affection. "You're still you! You've got to pretend it never happened. Forget it."

"I'll try. Oh, Tam, I wish I could be like you! Able to put things out of my mind and go on living! I'll try."

Tamsen held her, rocking her like a child, as she thought how mistaken Em was about her. For Tamsen had been unable to forget the feel of Dan Tallant's arms, the fire of his lean brown body against hers, the sweetness of surrender. How could she expect Em to erase a night of horror from her mind, when she, herself, still clung to those moments of rapture?

Chapter 10

A gift arrived for Em within that week. A simple single strand of small matched pearls. A family heirloom, Senator Alden wrote. He would be pleased if Em would wear them.

"I can't accept this," Em said. "It's far too expensive!"

"I don't see why not." Tamsen thought of the jewels that rested in her safe, gifts meant to purchase something from her. "He said it would please him. He might be hurt if they were returned."

"Do you really think so?" Em clasped them about her throat, her eyes shining. There was true happiness on her face, Tamsen realized. Perhaps Em had been able to come to terms with the past.

Tamsen thought of her sister often during that week, envying her a little. What would it be like to be loved, to be given gifts because the giver wanted her to have them, not because there was something he wished to gain?

Ironically, as Em's happiness grew, Tamsen was beset with problems. The old cookstove in the shed kitchen behind the dining room burned through and had to be replaced. The cook, a cranky Chinese, quit, leaving the kitchen to the not-so-tender mercy of Maggie. As Tamsen moved through the parlor, enchanting one man, then another, she wondered if they guessed at what cost the Parlor's respectable facade was preserved. And she wondered what it would be like to look into eyes that reflected love, rather than a lascivious desire to get Madam Franklin into bed.

Nell apprised her of possible trouble.

"That young Wally Knight—you know, that little snot-nose that brags about his rich folks and how he run off? Well, him an' that Frenchie are gonna mix over you. There's gonna be trouble."

"I'll take care of it," Tamsen said.

As she entered the parlor, peopled by only a dozen or so regulars, since it was early, she heard the sound of loud voices raised in argument. Deftly, she moved between the two men, linking arms with each, smiling up at them.

"Now, who's going to buy me a drink?"

"I am," Wally shouted, glaring at the other.

"Then you can buy my second one," Tamsen laughed up at Pierre Lebeau. "Now, let's sit down and be friends."

Dusty brought their drinks as Tamsen talked to them. There must be no quarreling here. Those who did not obey her rules would be asked to leave and would not be admitted again. And she would miss both of them—terribly.

She returned to her room, sure that she had handled it well, but Nell shook her head. "Them two's like a coupla roosters after one hen. They're gonna make us trouble. Oughta boot their butts out before it comes."

Tamsen laughed at Nell's dire warning and forgot the incident in the further excitement of the evening. A party of visiting politicians from Washington had entered her establishment. As she appeared before them in her newest gown to sing her one song of the evening, she knew she had her audience in the palm of her hand.

And afterward she moved among them, being introduced to well-known names, feeling their hands linger over-long on hers. One gentleman whispered a proposition that included a home in Georgetown and a considerable monetary settlement to live on, if she would consider his white-haired, rather paunchy self.

When Tamsen left the parlor, Nell followed her and whispered, "There's one feller, the local one, what brung 'em. Guess they ast 'im to, 'cause he ain't no man fer the

282

girls. Settin' out there stiff as a gawdamn poker, red in the face, skeert as hell."

Tamsen looked out into the entry hall and saw a young man seated on a straight-backed chair. Nell's description of the man was quite correct. He certainly looked miserable. She approached him.

"I'm Madam Franklin," she said, extending a hand.

The man jumped as if he'd been shot, his eyes rolling a little wildly. "I'm—how do you do?" he said stiffly. His own hands remained clenched in his lap.

"I don't believe I've seen you before," she said. "You are—"

"I'm an aide to—I'm an aide," he said. Then, rather pompously, "I do not frequent this type of place. I was told to see that the gentlemen from Washington were entertained, and they insisted on coming here."

"I see." The man was funny, but she did feel sorry for him in his predicament. He'd apparently been sitting stiffly on the small gilt chair for hours. "Would you care to join me in my office? Perhaps some tea and refreshment?"

Again his eyes rolled, his nostrils flaring like those of a frightened horse. Instinctively, his hand went to his coat, as if to ascertain that it was completely buttoned. "Thank you," he said, haughtily, "but no. I'll wait."

Tamsen returned to Nell and collapsed with laughter. "He thought," she said, weeping tears of honest mirth, "that I was after his virtue! Who is he, do you know?"

"Beats me," said Nell, cheerfully. "He sure as hell don't belong here, though."

"No," Tamsen giggled, "he sure doesn't."

The week drew to a close without further incident. On Sunday morning, the candles guttering out in the chandeliers, the music ended, the glittering night over, Tamsen, Nell, and Dusty counted the receipts.

"You're gonna be richer'n hell," Nell growled. Tamsen smiled wearily. Her efforts were well worth it. Their cash income had doubled. The word was getting around in the right places. Now she could go home.

283

Em had taken little Martha and gone to church. That should be my job, Tamsen thought. If only she weren't so tired. She lay down to rest.

When she woke, it was to find Birdie Faraday going through her wardrobe. She had taken out a gown of crimson velvet and was holding it against herself, looking into the mirror.

As Tamsen sat up and looked at her, the woman flushed. "Thought I'd help you pick out something to wear tonight," she said, guiltily.

"I'm afraid that wouldn't do," Tamsen said. "Perhaps the black."

"Black!" The woman spat the word out. "Black's for when you're old. For when you've got a husband. You want a man to look at you, you wear some color."

Tamsen smiled to herself. Birdie had evidently concocted a campaign of her own. She would help Tamsen catch Donald Alden. In return, she would get a kitchen all to herself.

Tamsen dressed with Birdie's help. The expression of admiration on the woman's face was almost enough to waft away Tamsen's feeling of fatigue. But after the housekeeper had gone, she sat on the edge of her bed, wondering how she could manage to get through the evening. The problems of her double life were wearing on her. Perhaps, she thought, she should take some of the advice she'd given Em. Find some nice gentleman with marriage in mind.

Walking restlessly to the window, she saw a carriage arrive, and two men alight. The guests were here. Sighing, she prepared to go down to meet them.

When Cleve Sommers first saw her, descending the stairs in her crimson gown, her dark hair piled high in an ebon cloud, a wide grin covered his face. He had been dreading this evening, feeling that the Senator was taking advantage of his friendship by dragging him along. But no longer. In a city where women were a rare commodity, where his friends had picked up with dregs they would have had nothing to do with back home, he had found a jewel.

284

Tamsen, in turn, looked down at him and liked what she saw. A clean-cut man with steady gray eyes beneath a shock of sandy hair, his gray suit impeccably cut. A gentleman.

"I'm so glad you could come," Tamsen said, acknowledging the Senator's introduction.

"The pleasure is mine," Sommers answered gallantly, bowing over her hand. But his eyes said more. And Tamsen recalled her thoughts of a short time before. A nice gentleman, with marriage in mind.

It had been only a fleeting notion, she told herself. She was quite happy with her life as it was. Though she deliberately set out to charm the newcomer, she excused her actions by convincing herself that she did it for the sake of Em and the Senator. Yet it was a heady feeling to be admired for being herself, rather than Poppy Franklin.

For his part, Cleve Sommers had already made up his mind. And he had always prided himself on that mind, considering it to be quick-thinking and efficient. The girl was beautiful, and she was a lady. She would be an asset to him, socially and in his business. They looked well together. He had noticed that in the hall mirror.

He offered his arm to her as they went in to dinner.

The meal was gracious, candle-lit. And Mrs. Faraday had outdone herself. While they ate, Tamsen drifted into a dream in which this was her own home, the handsome gentleman seated across from her was her husband, Em and Alden were their guests. The discussion, low-keyed, on politics and finance, was music to her ears. She jumped a little when Cleve Sommers addressed her.

"Deep thoughts, Mrs. Harper? You seem so far away."

Tamsen blushed. "No thoughts at all, Mr. Sommers. I'm sorry. Were you addressing me?"

"The Senator and I were plotting," he smiled. "Trying to find a way to avail ourselves of your charming company and to repay your hospitality as well. Perhaps a dinner at a restaurant during the week?"

285

Tamsen flinched a little, looking at Em. Em was silent, her eyes on her plate, remembering that Tamsen's job was not to be mentioned. For the first time, Tamsen realized how her Parlor could cut into her private life. For the first time, she resented it.

"I have a little girl," she said. "I feel my evenings must be spent at home. I'm certain the Senator has told you I'm a widow."

Birdie, serving the dessert, awarded her a surprising wink. Was it possible that she knew something? Tamsen was uneasy throughout the remainder of the meal.

As they finished eating and sat chatting over their afterdinner coffee, there was a knock at the door. Tamsen, waving Em to her seat, rose to answer it.

A boy of approximately her own age stood staring at her in surprise. Then his dimples flashed and blue eyes glinted with mischief.

"Don didn't tell me," he said, teasingly. "If he had, I might have been here sooner."

The Senator appeared beside her. "Adam!" he said. "Adam! Tamsen, Em, this is that young scapegrace I've been telling you about! My stepbrother, Adam Wheeler!"

As the young man came into the room, smiling, exuding charm, Tamsen recalled Sam Larabee's words. *He's a little bastard. I should have let well enough alone.*

Bastard or not, he had certainly upset a peaceful evening. Cleve Sommers had seemed most unhappy at the interruption. Donald Alden explained his change of living quarters, then turned to Em. "I must see the boy home," he said. "Forgive me for cutting such a pleasant evening short. But Adam has traveled a long way—"

"It's perfectly all right," Em answered. "I understand."

But Tamsen felt cheated somehow. What if she never saw Cleve Sommers again?

She need not have worried. That gentleman, considered one of the most astute in the shipping business, had already reached his decision. The lady-like impression Tamsen made on first sight had been sustained

286

through the evening. And vice presidencies were usually reserved for family men. On the way home, he plotted his campaign for wooing her.

Only the color of her gown had been a mistake. When they were married, he would insist on a shade that was more genteel. Should they have three children, he wondered. After an acceptable interval, of course. Or maybe four?

Chapter 11

Em, for her dinner out with the Senator, had chosen a new gown of a moiré faille that changed color in the light, picking up the blue of her eyes, the color of the ribbon at her throat, occasionally showing a pink tint that flattered her skin. As Tamsen had suggested, she put the past from her mind. Breathless with excitement, she looked forward to the evening ahead.

Her happiness did not prevent her from tangling with the obstinate Birdie Faraday. Guilty at leaving the child, Em pressed minute instructions upon that good lady. The baby was to be covered warmly. She had a slight cough—

"Goose grease," said Mrs. Faraday, "and a warm flannel."

"I don't hold with that," said Em. "Instead—"

"Maybe her mother ought to give the orders," the woman said.

Em was silenced. She had no answer for this. But Tamsen, who was preparing to leave for work, said, "Oh, for heaven's sake, Em! Forget about the baby this once. Birdie knows what to do."

The woman beamed.

Tamsen took a look at Em and cooed with admiration. "You're beautiful. I've never seen you look so well."

That was what Senator Alden thought as he watched Em descend the stairs. He was enchanted at her loveliness. It was a long time since he'd taken a pretty woman to dinner. He was going to enjoy walking into a restaurant with this sweet creature on his arm.

The restaurant was new, built upon the ashes of an old, less pretentious building. The red-flocked paper on the walls was echoed in the deep rich tones of the carpet. The waiters wore full formal attire. Em had not been taken out to dine since St. Louis. She looked at the handsome man across from her and thought, *I'm so happy, I could die!* This would be an evening to remember.

The Senator was a gracious and thoughtful companion, ordering fine wines and translating the menu, printed in French. On the surface, he seemed calm and collected. But beneath the well-tailored jacket he wore, his heart was racing madly. I feel like a love-struck boy, he thought, amused at his reaction to the girl. But how beautiful she was—

As the evening progressed, they slipped into a more informal basis. She was to be Emmeline, he, Donald. Em tried his name, blushing. It sounded so *right*.

When their meal ended, it was Em who suggested walking for a while. Though she had only sipped at the wine, it had left her feeling a bit light-headed. Once outside, it was nice to have a strong, protective arm to lean on. She'd not been on the streets of San Francisco at night. Nor much in the daytime, for that matter. All purchases were made, all errands taken care of by first the girls, now Tamsen or Mrs. Faraday.

As they walked quietly, talking, they passed a theater. Em hoped sometime to see a Shakespearean drama, she told Donald Alden. He flushed a little, saying that he'd obtain tickets when the next troupe of actors appeared, but that the show now playing was not one she would want to see. Studying the billboards, she saw the reason for his embarrassment. For the present show starred the notorious Lola Montez. Birdie Faraday had mentioned her, saying she heard the woman rode a horse onto the stage almost naked. Em, too, turned pink, and started to look away.

Then a picture in the lower corner of the billboard caught her eye. Crudely painted, with a minimum of clothing, calculated to draw masculine attention, was a girl whose face was very familiar.

It was not! It couldn't be! And the name—!

Em closed her eyes as nausea swept over her, nausea mingled with hope and dread.

"Are you all right?" Donald Alden was looking at her in concern. "Emmeline!" He was certain she was going to faint. She was as white as paper.

Em's hand dug into his sleeve as she stiffened, turning to him, her blue eyes filled with a desperate pleading.

"I want to go into the theater, Donald. Don't ask any questions, please. I have to!"

He studied her in bewilderment. "Are you sure, my dear? This is no place for a lady. I've been told it's a most shocking performance. Perhaps another time—"

But her eyes were squeezed shut in a kind of agony. "Please, Donald! *Please!*"

He went to the little window that opened on the street, leaving her standing like a statue. He returned with the news that all seats were sold out. The eyes she turned on him were blank with shock. He felt she hadn't heard.

He approached two men who were entering the theater and bought their tickets for an incredible sum. He returned to escort Em into the building, cursing himself for being a fool. What was wrong, he could not guess. He had been carried along with the urgency of her plea.

He hoped for Em's sake that the performance wouldn't be too risqué as he seated himself, grimly, beside her, conscious of the male eyes upon the only woman in the place.

Two gentlemen, rather pudgy individuals in checked coats and vests, wearing round-topped stiff felt hats, dragged chairs before the curtain, seated themselves, and took up their violins. In rather reedy voices, they began an olio of bawdy tunes. Donald Alden eyed Em, warily. She did not flinch at the words. He had an idea that the sound flowed around her, unnoticed.

The rowdy audience was not appreciative of the

music, either. They had come to see Lola Montez. The catcalls and ribaldries drowned out the singers, and presently the manager came to the stage. Miss Montez preferred to come on last, he told them. In the meantime, he would appreciate their patience with the other performers. With their kind permission, he would now present that lady's protégé, an act he believed they would find to their liking.

As he spoke, several attendants extinguished most of the lamps in the room. A shadow-lantern at the rear focused a spotlight on the closed curtain. Heavy velvet curtains parted, revealing other curtains of silk pongee. These, when opened, revealed another of transparent gauze. And behind that gauze a silhouette.

Em sat up straight, holding her breath. Donald Alden could feel her tension.

As the silken gauze shimmered away, the light played upon the figure of a young girl. She stood in a garden behind a small concealing fence, leaning upon the gate. The illumination touched her hair, turning it into a halo of red-gold.

Em caught her breath, and Donald Alden reached for her hand, feeling the bite of her nails as she gripped his, leaning forward.

The girl, ringlets falling to uncovered shoulders, began a song, a melody of purity and innocence, about a love in which that innocence was lost.

As the song trilled to its ending, there was a clash of cymbals and the girl threw open the gate, and stepped out into the changing light, which was now a pulsing, throbbing red. The music grew raucous and the girl, her skimpy skirts revealed, whirled and twisted, thrust her hips sideways, forward, kicking her net-stockinged legs high as she danced.

The audience was on its feet, whistling, stamping, roaring its approval. "Goddam," one man swore above the noise, "I never saw nuthin' like that!" Another screamed an invitation to meet him after the show.

Alden looked worriedly at Em. "Wouldn't you like to leave now?"

But Em's eyes were still on the dancer as she bowed, blowing kisses to the shouting men. Then, with a graceful pirouette, she was gone.

"Yes," said Em, shivering a little, her mouth blue, "I want to go backstage."

Resigned, he led her to the dressing room area and bribed a man who stood watch at the doors to let them in. There, he stood rather embarrassed as a troupe of half-nude dancing girls pushed past him on their way to the stage.

Em pushed open the designated door.

She found herself in a small cubicle. A dressing table to one side was strewn with powder and pots of face paint. A screen stood in one corner, and a naked female arm was tossing garments over the top of it, oblivious to a man who occupied a chair in the room.

As Em stood, hesitant, the dancer emerged from behind the screen, dressed only in her corset and long lace-trimmed drawers. "Hank," she said, "will you—?"

She stopped, her eyes widening in shock.

"My God! *Em!*"

"Arab!" Em moved toward the girl, her arms outstretched. Then they were both laughing and crying at the same time, in each other's arms. It was a long time before either could come to her senses. Then Arabella shouted at the astounded man.

"Hank, get the hell out. Can't you tell when you're not wanted?"

"My manager," she explained to Em, blushing. But Em's mind was not on proprieties. She had found her little sister at last, though there was nothing of the child in this tall, fair-skinned girl with her confident bearing.

"We've been looking for you everywhere," Em said, with a quivering smile as she mopped at her tearstained face. "We've been so worried!"

"We?" A hard smile curved the girl's lips, a smile that Em was too overcome to notice.

"When we got here, we found the Reverend Smythe had moved on," Em said. "He was supposed to send his

292

new address, but he never did. We thought you were with him. We never dreamed——" Her eyes blinked as she thought of the disparity between what she'd thought Arab to be doing, and this! Arabella must have run away from the good man and his wife, have fallen on bad times—been desperate enough to be forced into such an occupation! But she could not know until she had the whole story.

"But we've found you now. I want you to come home with me. We live in Senator Alden's house on the hill. We'll all be together again, the three of us. Tamsen will be so happy!"

"Tamsen!" The girl's voice turned ugly. She spat out the name in a way that made Em flinch. "Do you know what she is, Em? Do you know what she did to me?"

Some time later, Em left Arabella's dressing room, her mind reeling with horror at the tale the girl had related to her. How much more dreadful than her own experience Arab's had been. What a thing for a child to endure! It was not surprising that she felt such bitterness toward Tamsen, though Em had tried to explain. It was true Tamsen had worked in a cantina, but it had been for them. As for selling her to the minister, that was out of the question!

But the hatred that had been festering inside Arab was not so easily dismissed. Em could not prove Tamsen's good intent. And Arabella did not intend to see her sister.

As Em left, Arab caught her hands. "Don't tell her I'm here," she pleaded. "Please, Em. We're sailing for Spain, tomorrow. Don't tell her until I'm gone. Don't tell anyone." When Em hesitated, she said, "You owe me that much!"

That was true, Em thought tiredly. She should have listened to her own misgivings, put her foot down, have had the courage of her own convictions when Tamsen sent Arab away.

Guiltily, Em promised.

Senator Alden was still waiting, his mind spinning with all kinds of wild conjectures. What kind of hold did that woman in there have over his delicate, precious Emmeline? Several times, he'd almost come to the point of storming the room and taking Emmeline out of there. When they were married, he wouldn't stand for—

When they were married! The thought loomed large in his mind. He would ask her, and soon.

The woman who came out of the dressing room to join him, at last, was far different than his vivacious companion of earlier. Em looked tired to death, her eyes haunted. It was plain she had been crying. Again protective instincts swelled in his breast. At the moment, the most important thing was to get her out of here. The noise from the theater suggested that Lola Montez had gone into her infamous act! When it ended, they might have to fight their way free.

With a firm hand, the Senator guided Em to an outside door.

He did not speak, nor did she, until they were in a carriage and on their way up the clay street that led to home.

"Now," he said, "what is it? I know it is none of my affair, but I feel—"

"Please," she whispered. "I know this has been a strange evening, but I'm not at liberty to talk about it. I—I thought the girl was someone I knew well, some years ago."

"And you were wrong?"

She didn't answer. Obviously, that was not the case. If the girl had been a stranger, Em would not have remained in the room so long. She would not have emerged looking as if she'd taken a blow she could not bear.

Perhaps a girlhood chum gone wrong, he guessed. And Em, with her angelic character, was shocked. He had hoped he would be able to distract her from her concerns, show her that he needed her love and attention. But this was not the time.

Leaving her at her door, he said, "I'm sorry this was not a happy evening for you."

She looked up at him, startled. "Oh, but it was. It was happy—and sad, too."

Alden left Em with a gentle pressure of his hand on hers, and she went into the house, closing the door behind her, leaning against it. And again the tears began to fall.

Arabella was found, but tomorrow she was leaving for Spain. Who knew when Em would ever see her again?

The next afternoon, Em insisted that Tamsen go with her to the docks in the carriage. Tamsen, half-irritated, half-amused, went along with her sister's request. When they reached the area, Tamsen sat in puzzled silence, while Em sat beside her, twisting her hands in her lap. And at last, Em said softly, "There it goes."

Tamsen followed her gaze to a ship, a steamship with auxiliary sails. The canvas was up, now, swelling in the wind as the vessel tacked and turned out to sea.

"The ship? You brought me down here to see *this*? Em, I've seen ships before!"

"But this one is different." Em's eyes had a faraway look. "This one's going to Spain."

"Indeed," Tamsen teased, "and how would you know *that*?"

"I know someone aboard her." Em's voice was a whisper.

"And who would that be?"

Em turned toward Tamsen, searching her face for her reaction as she said, "Arabella."

Arabella!

Tamsen was shaken to her shoes. Her first thought was that Em's mind had come unhinged. But in the steady gaze that met her own, she saw it wasn't true.

"You've seen her?" When Em remained silent, she said, "Why didn't you tell me! Oh, Em!"

"She didn't want to see you," Em said, flatly. "She didn't want you to know until she was gone."

When Em finished telling about seeing Arab, and

relating the story of the things the girl had endured at Reverend Smythe's hands, Tamsen was too stunned to cry.

While Tamsen and Em watched the ship that carried their sister disappear over the horizon, another chance meeting was taking place. Katie Ryan, hurrying back from a shopping expedition to Madam Franklin's where she occupied an upstairs room, caught Dan Tallant's eye.

For a moment, he was puzzled. Her hair, badly singed in the fire, was cropped almost like a boy's. But there was no mistaking that honest Irish face, those sparkling eyes.

"Katie," he shouted. "Katie!"

The girl whirled, her face alight with excitement and welcome. "Dan! Oh, Dan!" She ran toward him and he swept her up in a bear-hug. "Lordy," she said happily, "I never thought I'd see you again."

He drew her into a nearby casino and ordered drinks for them both, taking a table in a corner.

"Now," he said, "tell me about you. How did you get here?"

She sketched the story briefly, noting that he began to scowl when she told how they'd all traveled together, she, Nell and Dusty, the girls, Em, and Tamsen.

"Then you were there when Tamsen's baby was born?"

Her head jerked up. So he knew about the child. But . . . *Tamsen*'s? She had sworn with the others to keep Em's secret, but she had never had secrets from Dan. She smiled a little crookedly. Let him think it was Tamsen's! For her money, she'd bet he'd had an interest in the girl.

"Yes," she said, "I was there."

His face reddened, and he set his drink down. "Strong stuff," he explained. Then, "Who is the father? Do you know?"

"Haven't the slightest idea," Katie said, briskly. "Listen, Dan. I've got to get over to the house. And say,

I've been keeping my ears open. Still want the same kinda deal?"

Dan nodded and she grinned, impishly. "Then we better just see each other in a *professional* capacity, huh? And, honey, this place is made-to-order for what you want."

"A new place? Where is it?"

"On Stockton Street. Madam Franklin's Parlor for Gentlemen. You can't miss it." She kissed her fingers to him and was gone.

Madam Franklin!

Dan Tallant sat in silence for a moment, digesting her information. Then he began to swear.

Chapter 12

Tamsen's spirits were low as she went to her establishment that night. For the first time, there seemed to be an intangible wall between herself and Em. Em had not blamed her for Arab's terrible adventures, but she had felt some censure there. Or was it, she wondered, because she blamed herself. Sick inside, she desperately needed comfort. She went to Nell.

Nell swore when she heard the story of Reverend Smythe. "The son of a bitch," she said, her face a furious red. "The dirty son of a bitch! I hope he roasts in hell!"

"I hope so, too," Tamsen said. Then, "Nell, I thought I was doing the right thing. She was involved with some boy—"

Nell scowled at her. "Did you, now? Lissen, honey, don't you know how it is when kids is young? They mighta wound up havin' t' git hitched, but what the hell! Wasn't you ever in love? Ain't you got no romance in yer soul?"

Despite her worries, Tamsen almost laughed at Nell's righteous indignation. For a picture appeared in her mind of Nell and Dusty, engaged in a romantic interlude. "I suppose not," she managed to say with a straight face.

"Then don't go talkin' down them what does," Nell said, angrily. "Arabella an' her feller mighta made a purty good team. And sending her off with a man like that was gawdamn stupid."

"He was a minister," Tamsen defended herself.

"He was a man, weren't he?"

Nell busied herself with checking the accounts, a signal that the conversation was over, but Tamsen would not let it go.

"I was wrong," she said, hotly, "I know that now! But I was only trying to keep Arab from getting into trouble! She—she's always been headed for it. There's something inside her! I was scared—" She broke off at the expression in Nell's eyes.

"Skeert of what? Skeert of somethin' inside her? Or somethin' in *yerself*?"

Unable to answer, Tamsen hurried to dress. Tonight she had a new gown of gold cloth that clung to her body all the way to the floor. The shoulders were bared, except for a floating chiffon over-dress through which the metallic material shimmered. The costume was both discreet and revealing. She felt its impact upon her audience as she descended the stairs.

She began an old ballad, its simple words highlighted by her sensuous movements.

"Light, light, my little Scotchee, and stay all night with me. I have a bed of the ve-ry, ve-ry best, I'll give it up to thee. I'll give it up to thee . . ."

She sang on, telling the tale of the man who could not stay, since he had another girl a-waiting; how the singer of the song had stabbed him to the heart, and how, with the aid of her little lady miss, he had been thrown into a new-dug well. In the end the girl pleaded with her little bird, offering it a cage of the very very best, only to be told it could not light upon her knee for fear of being served *"like you sarved your little Scotchee, your little Scotchee."*

As she bowed to the applause, Tamsen did not see the somber-faced man by the door. Dan Tallant stood thinking that the song was a most appropriate one. That any man who came into contact with this girl should watch his heart, his back, and his bank account.

Tamsen moved through the room, greeting old customers, welcoming new ones. As she passed Tallant, he gripped her arm.

She tried to jerk herself free, but he held tightly,

pleased to see a touch of fear in those huge dark eyes.

"Let me go," she hissed, finally. "All I have to do is call the man on the door. He'll throw you out on your ear!"

"And make a scene?" Dan smiled at her, his face hard. "We don't want to do that, do we? Not in Madam Franklin's Parlor for *Gentlemen*."

"You're not a gentleman," she said furiously. "You don't belong here." She turned her head to call.

"I wouldn't," he said mildly. "If you do, I'll raise enough hell to put this place on the map. And I might just tell everyone that you bought this business with my money."

"But I didn't," she said, in helpless anger. "I used—" She stopped and he began to propel her toward the stairs.

"In that case, maybe we'd better have a little talk. I'd like to know what the fifty thousand I gave you *did* go for."

She followed him up the steps. For a moment she felt that she was reliving the scene in the Elkhorn Bar, when she'd tried to buy his horses. But she had the top hand now. One scream, and she could bring the house down on him. If he wanted to talk, he'd have the opportunity, for all the good it would do him.

She intended to speak with him in her office, but he pulled her inside the first open door.

"All right now," he growled, "let's have it! I gave you the money to go East, and you know it! Now I come back to find you running a—," he looked around, "a plush whorehouse. I feel like beating the hell out of you! You need it!"

"I wouldn't try it." She backed from him, her eyes narrowed.

"I suppose you're still carrying your gun," he taunted.

"I don't need to, here. This is a respectable place."

He cursed and looked at her with loathing. "And where's the baby? In one of these nice respectable rooms?"

"No, she isn't. She's well cared for."

"Then where is she?"

"I don't have to tell you."

"No, you don't. I'll find her, and I'll take her away from you—legally, if I have to!"

"You can't," she said triumphantly. "No court would take a little girl from her mother."

"Mother! Look at you!" He reached out, grasping the tissue-thin material of her gown, ripping it from her shoulders. Another hand went to her hair, pulling it down. It fell across her face as she tried to fight away from him, but then he had both shoulders in his grasp, turning her, propelling her toward a mirror.

"Look in there," he commanded. "Tell me what you see!"

She saw a hard-eyed, spitting mad, half-clad girl—who might have belonged to the profession. Whirling, she clawed at him. He snatched her wrists, his eyes boring into hers. She felt the anger go out of her, replaced by something else, a trembling in her knees.

"Don't you touch me," she whispered through dry lips. "Don't you dare—"

"Honey," he said insolently, "you don't need to worry. Touching you is the one thing I don't want to do!"

Shoving her from him, he walked out, leaving the door open.

She must not be seen like this! She crept toward the doorway, putting her hand to the knob—and then she heard Dan Tallant's shout. "Katie! Katie, honey! I was looking for you! Come on, let's find ourselves an empty room!"

Tamsen's heart pounded with fear. Katie, she recalled, had been in close contact with Dan Tallant at the cantina in Magoffinville. Suppose she let slip that the baby was not Tamsen's, but Em's?

There was nothing she could do about it, short of following them into the room they'd entered. Her face grew hot at the thought of them together.

When the coast was clear, she hurried to her own room to change and re-do her hair. This time, she put on a simple dark gown with a white frill at the throat. Let Dan Tallant dispute her character in that!

Before she finished dressing, she heard Nell's heavy feet tramping along the hall. The door opened. "Things are goin' t' hell in a bushel basket downstairs," Nell said, irascibly. "Them two young cocks, Knight and Lebeau, are at it again. Not only that, it's makin' up t' storm outside and customers talkin' about headin' fer home afore they git wet. If you wanna keep 'em around, you better getcher butt on down there."

Sighing, Tamsen complied. She separated the two young men with a few choice words, a promise of a song—and a promise of something more intimate in the smile she gave to each. They were beginning to weary her. She might just take Nell's advice and have them barred from the Parlor. She did not like Wally Knight— he had pudgy hands that roved. And she suspected the stake he'd come west with was rapidly evaporating.

Pierre Lebeau was something else. His dark eyes worshipping, he declared his love for her at every opportunity. Even going so far as to threaten suicide, if his affections were not returned.

Tamsen moved into the center of the room to sing.

Upstairs, Dan Tallant closed the door against the sound that rose from below. "I've got some questions," he said, "and I'd like some straight answers."

Katie had already begun to unbutton his shirt, yearning to lay her cheek against his smooth brown skin. She looked up at him, puzzled.

"Aw-w, Dan, can't it wait? It's been so long—"

"I'm not in the mood for games tonight," he said, shortly. "Some other time. Now, tell me, where did Tamsen get the money to go into this business?"

Tamsen again! "She got it off a man," Katie said, sulkily. "Sam Larabee. Supposed to be an investment for him, but I witnessed the deed. Didn't say Larabee anywhere on it, as far as I could tell."

"Then how did she get the money?"

Katie's lip curled derisively. "The usual way, I suppose. Some of us are luckier than others, I guess."

Dan's eyes softened as he looked down at the pixie face of the girl who had been a partner for so many years. True, she was a whore, but she was honest about it.

"And what about her child? Does she keep it here? In this place?"

Katie's eyes widened in mock surprise. "Oh, my, no! Miss ritch-bitch keeps her sister and the baby far away from here, so they won't be contaminated. They live in a big house on Nob Hill."

Thank God for small favors, Tallant thought, as he recalled the child's innocent face, Em's flower-like goodness. "She must have taken this Larabee for a cleaning," he said, "to run this—" he indicated the rich surroundings, "and to live in such style." Certainly the money she'd taken from him wouldn't stretch such a long way. Not in San Francisco.

"Oh, no. She got her home from another man. But she's only renting it. Senator Alden moved out of the house and she's getting it almost rent-free, according to Nell."

"Alden? Donald Alden? I can't believe it!" Senator Alden was as straight as any man Dan knew, not the type to get mixed up with a money-hungry little bitch.

"If you can't believe it, you can go and see." Katie said, sounding hurt.

"I suppose I do believe it," he said. "I guess anything's possible when that girl makes up her mind she wants something. Well, Katie, thanks. I'll be seeing you—"

"Dan!" Her voice was heart-broken. "Dan! What is it with you? We used to be such good friends. But things started to be different in Magoffinville. And they're worse now. Do you realize you haven't—"

"I'm sorry, Katie," his voice was gentle. "You know, you're too good for this business you're in."

"That's an old line, Dan." Her words trembled on the edge of tears. "But I am in this business. I chose it.

303

Does that make a difference to you? Would you like me better if I quit? Is that what's wrong between us? You didn't use' to mind."

"Maybe," he said, "I just decided you're too good for me, no matter what profession you're in. You'll have to be patient with me, Katie. I'm sorry."

Her bright head lifted in a gesture of defiant pride. "Sure," she said, flashing her gamin grin. "Now, about the other things. I think I can round up some things you need to know. If *that* deal still goes."

"It still goes." He drew a packet of papers from inside his shirt. "Here's what we're working on now."

Her burnished head moved close to his dark one as she studied the maps and figures he showed her. Uttering a crow of delight, she asked, "Do you really think it can be done?"

"Yes," he said, "I think it can—and will."

As they pored over the papers, Tamsen's song, downstairs, was drowned out by a roll of thunder, a spatter of rain borne on a shrieking wind.

"God pity the poor men who must go to sea on a night like this!" A grizzled sea captain laughed, raising his glass in a toast. He could not know how his words tore at Tamsen's heart. For out there on the turbulent ocean, somewhere, was Arabella.

In the hours of early dawn, Tamsen found Katie helping Maggie at her work of replacing the bed linen for the coming night.

"I want to talk to you," she said.

Katie followed Tamsen to an empty room. Tamsen closed the door.

"Dan Tallant was with you tonight," Tamsen said.

"Yes, he was." The girl's face was defiant, unreadable. Tamsen sighed.

"I'm not telling you who you can or can't see, Katie. I want to make sure you remember your promise to me. Martha's my child, not Em's. Did you mention it to him?"

"We didn't gossip," the girl said in a silky voice. "We had better things to do."

The two women stared at each other with hatred in their eyes. "I'd like to strangle her," Tamsen thought.

And Katie was smiling inside with a purring satisfaction. Dan Tallant wasn't one to saddle himself with a woman who had a child. And there were things Katie could do for him that Tamsen could not do.

Chapter 13

Dan Tallant did not appear at the Parlor the following night. Instead, he paid a visit to Em, laden with gifts for a baby.

Mrs. Faraday let him in, looked him over, and smiled in approval as she went to fetch Em. "There's a real good-looking man downstairs, wanting to see you," she said.

Em went to the head of the stairs and looked down. Then, gathering her skirts in one hand, she fairly flew down the stairs.

"Dan Tallant! Where did you come from? It's so good to see you!"

He tossed the packages to the table and took both her hands in his. How sweet this woman was! So unlike Tamsen! Laughing, he tried to answer the questions she fired at him all at once. Yes, he had just returned. He would be here for a while. And he'd run into Katie, who'd given him the address.

"And you knew about the baby." Em's eyes looked at the things he'd dropped on the table and returned to his, wondering what Katie had told him. Shame stirred inside her as she recalled that he had been there on that awful night. He knew what had been done to her and had sought out those men and killed them.

"Dan," she said, stopping at the hard look on his face. "I—"

"Katie told me Tamsen was a widow and that she had a little girl," he said, impersonally. "I was walking through a store and saw these things—" He indicated the stack. "I figured I'd come bearing gifts. Where is the kid?"

Em felt torn. She had always sensed an attraction between this man and her sister, and she was tempted to blurt out the true story of Martha's parentage. Yet she had promised Tamsen. "She's asleep, right now," she said. "Would—would you like to see her?"

As they mounted the stairs, Em said, "Tamsen will be so sorry to have missed you. She works at night, you know, operating a small hotel, an investment made by a friend who's away just now."

Tallant studied her. She was telling the truth. She didn't know. "I might be tempted to change my place of residence. What type of place is it?"

Em blushed. "I haven't been there. That sounds odd, doesn't it? But it seems I'm always so busy with the baby. Tamsen sleeps days. I seldom go out, unless Senator Alden—" She blushed again in pretty confusion.

So that's the way the land lies, Tallant thought, relieved that it was Em, not Tamsen, Alden favored.

The baby, a toddler now, lay sleeping in her small white-canopied bed. Long black lashes fanned against her dark little face, above cheeks stained with wild rose; silky dark hair contrasted with her pillow.

"She looks like Tamsen," Em said. Raising her gaze to Dan's, she was surprised at his look of yearning, of loneliness. He bent to touch a chubby, star-shaped little hand, almost with reverence, and she wondered at him. What was there in this man's background that made him react to the sight of a child so strongly? There was so much about him she did not really know.

She thought about it long after he had gone.

Tamsen, too, was surprised by an unexpected guest that night. Moving into the thronged room, following her song, she came face to face with the dancing eyes of Adam Wheeler, Senator Alden's young stepbrother. For a moment, she stood frozen. Then she extended her hand.

"So glad to have you here," she murmured, mechanically. "I hope you are enjoying yourself?"

307

"My evening has been most enjoyable." Wheeler laughed. "This is quite a place you have."

"Thank you." She moved on, her brain spinning frantically. The young man was more than a little drunk. Perhaps he did not recognize her as the woman he'd met in his most respectable brother's home. She should not have been surprised at seeing him. After all, from what she'd heard about him, this was the type of place he would frequent. Yet what could she do? Even if he had not guessed her identity tonight, he would put two and two together sooner or later and go to his brother with his information.

Money? He didn't seem to be afflicted with scruples. She would talk to him, face the issue, and see if she could buy his silence.

But when she went to look for him again, he had gone upstairs with Katie. Busy with the clientele, she did not see him leave. And the next night, he was not present.

Senator Alden and Cleve Sommers were expected for dinner on Sunday. Tamsen faced the occasion with trepidation. She would know by the Senator's face if the boy had told him.

She searched among her gowns for one that would complement the jade pendant. She would wear it today, for luck. What would such a revelation do to the relationship between Donald Alden and Em?

The Senator, however, was as bemused as ever. Em, too, seemed to be transported into a kind of dreamy delight. And meeting Cleve Sommer's steady gray eyes, Tamsen thought she knew something of how they felt. For the first time since she'd opened the Parlor, she'd had questions shivering inside her. Was it worth all the hiding? What would happen if a good, decent man—a man like Cleve Sommers—became interested in her?

The afternoon was crisp, but sunny. As soon as the dinner ended, Senator Alden suggested a drive. He had come in his carriage because there was a place he particularly wanted to show Em.

Though Tamsen and Cleve Sommers were included

308

in the invitation, it was apparent they were not being urged to come. Tamsen saw an answering amusement in Cleve Sommer's eyes.

"If Mrs. Harper doesn't mind," he said, "you can count me out. I vastly prefer it here before the fire, and with such pleasant company." He bowed to Tamsen, gallantly, and her eyes sparkled.

"I believe I, too, would prefer to remain at home," she said, demurely.

When the others had gone, she and Cleve Sommers took their coffee in the parlor, before a fire that was unnecessary, but cheery and homelike in its effect. The hours passed, enchanted ones, as he talked of his work and his ambitions. One day, Tamsen thought, he would be a very important man. And some of his greatness would lie in having an ambitious and helpful woman at his side.

"I beg your pardon, Mr. Sommers," she said, realizing he had posed a question requiring an answer. "What did you say?"

"I asked if you'd be kind enough to call me Cleve," he said softly. "I would appreciate being on a first-name basis."

"Of course—Cleve."

"Thank you—Tamsen."

They both began laughing at the absurd formality, and he reached to touch her hand. She caught her breath and met his gray eyes. "Tamsen," he began, unsteadily.

An unfortunate knock at the door interrupted him.

Tamsen pulled herself back into the present. Recalling that Birdie Faraday was upstairs with the baby, she excused herself and answered the door.

Adam Wheeler.

"Well," he drawled, "aren't you going to ask me in?"

"Of course," she said, stammering a little.

He walked past her and into the parlor, greeting Cleve Sommers. "Hope I'm not intruding," he grinned, "but I thought Donald would be here. He said he had an invitation to dinner."

309

Tamsen explained that he and Em had gone for a drive, and young Adam settled himself comfortably before the fire. "I'll wait," he said, "and drive home with him. If you don't mind."

Tamsen did mind. And when she went into the kitchen to get a cup for him, Wheeler followed. "I had a cousin once," he said at her shoulder. She backed away a little at the scent of liquor on his breath. "This cousin and I were forever into hot water, but we had a good thing going. We always said," he paused and looked at her with narrowed, dancing eyes, "*if you don't tell on me, I won't tell on you.*"

Tamsen suppressed a sigh of relief. Carefully, very carefully, she set a cup into a saucer. Then she turned to face Adam. "A wise statement, I should say." But inside, her heart was singing. Her secret was safe.

Meanwhile, Donald and Em had driven out of the city. The Senator's team, a spanking pair of matched bays, was guided into a road, little more than a cart track, that ran along the edge of the sea. Halting the animals, Donald Alden got out and walked around to assist Em to the ground. Then he led her forward to look at the view.

They stood on a high, salt-grass bluff, the vegetation wheat-colored, now in the wintertime. But the sun was warm despite the wind off the water. Beneath them was a long stretch of sandy beach. The ocean stretched into the distance, blending with the blue of the sky. Nearer, in the hollows of sea-caverns formed by rocks just off-shore, the waters deepened to shades of cobalt, laced with white froth as the waves rolled lazily inward.

"How beautiful," Em said, tears starring her eyes. "This must be the most beautiful place in the world. Look!" She pointed toward a white-winged gull that swooped seaward, pivoting on one wing.

But the Senator was not looking at the view. He could see nothing but the girl at his side. "I'm glad you like it here," he said, "because this is my property. This is where I will build my home one day. That's why I

310

wanted you to see it. Your opinion is very important to me, Emmeline."

She had turned to him, hearing the strange timbre in his tone. Now she shrank before what she saw in his eyes. "Donald," she whispered, "please! Please don't—"

"Don't ask you to marry me?" He caught at her hands. They were like ice as he imprisoned them in his own. "Em!"

She jumped a little at the sound of her name on his lips. "Yes, I said Em!" he said huskily. "I'm sick and tired of all this false formality! Of beating about the bush! I love you! With a love that's real and honest. I want to marry you, Em!"

"No," she whispered. "Please—"

He looked stricken. "Then I'm entitled to know the reason for your answer. I have thought you might return my affection. I'm not a poor man, nor one without influence. I have tried to be honorable—"

"But I am not," Em said in a dead voice. "Please, Donald, let me go."

"I will not," he said firmly, "until you favor me with some explanation of that last remark. And there's nothing you can say that could change my opinion of you. You are the loveliest, sweetest—"

He halted as she began to cry, tears streaking down her white face. "Em," he said helplessly, "don't—don't do that!" He put a tentative hand on her shoulder and she buried her face against his chest.

"There," he whispered, his lips touching her hair, "there! It can't be that bad."

"But it is," she said, drearily. "It is."

Her eyes hidden, she told him her story, sparing nothing; of Tamsen's occupation in Magoffinville, the shooting, the night she was violated. Then about the birth of the baby, and how the child he'd thought to be Tamsen's was really hers.

She felt him stiffen as her story progressed. And at last she raised her face to his in a hopeless gesture. His eyes were as cold as winter, chilling her. Dear God, what was he thinking!

311

"Those men," he said. "What happened to them. Did they go scot-free?"

"They're dead," Em said, adding murder to her list of failings. "A . . . friend of ours shot them that same night."

"That was wrong, you know." She bent her head before the steely sound of his voice.

"Shooting was too easy! Too quick!" He was raging, now. "They should have been beaten to a bloody pulp! Hanged slowly! I would have been glad to handle it, either way. Good God! Putting their filthy hands on you! If I'd been there—"

His anger left him, slowly, and his fists unclenched at his sides. "Em! My poor sweet Em! It's over and done. Something to be forgotten. I love you. I want you to be my wife. Will you marry me?"

Disbelieving, she looked at him, looked at the prematurely white hair shining like silver, the blue honest eyes in his tanned face. A handsome, gentle, distinguished man. Yet moments ago, his features had borne the look of a man who could kill, should he need to. He would love her, protect her all her life.

"There is still Martha," she said in a small voice.

"Who will be my daughter. You love her, don't you, in spite of her beginnings? Then why can't I love her? Since she's a part of you?"

"Oh, Donald!" She was in his arms again, weeping, this time for joy. The arms that surrounded her felt as she'd dreamed they would. She could feel his strong heart beating beneath his coat. Its tempo matched her own. Over his shoulders, she could see the rippling of the sun on blue waters, the blurred image of a gull in a gliding turn. Then there was only the feeling of his firm mouth on her own.

They returned to the house on the hill, to discover a disconsolate Cleve Sommers lounging in a chair. Across from him, Tamsen yawned as Adam Wheeler spun impossible yarns about his adventures. Tamsen sat up straight as the glowing couple entered, seeing something new in Em's eyes.

312

"Adam!" the Senator exclaimed. "I'm glad you're here. Em, our families are present, yours and mine. This is as good a time as any to make our announcement, don't you think?" He put an arm around the blushing girl.

"Since we're all gathered here together," he smiled down at Em, his eyes warm with love, "Em and I have something to tell you. We are going to be married."

When he finished, Tamsen was the first on her feet. "Em," she said, half-laughing, half-crying with joy, "this is the best news I've ever heard! I'm so glad for you! I've wished—I've hoped—!"

"And I'm wishing the same thing for you," Em whispered. "Oh, Tam!"

Adam shook his brother's hand in congratulation and called for champagne. They spent the remainder of the evening toasting the happy couple.

Cleve Sommers took his leave first. Tamsen, a bit giddy with champagne, saw him to the door. He held her hand a little over-long as he whispered an invitation for dinner the next evening. After a moment's pause, she accepted. It would mean going late to her own establishment, but surely it wouldn't matter, just once.

He looked as if he wished to say more, but the Senator's stepbrother chose that moment to appear in the hallway.

Adam Wheeler joined them, asking Cleve to drop him off at the rooms he shared with the Senator behind his offices. And for the first time, Tamsen thought about the practical aspects of the situation. Where would she live, once Em and Donald Alden were married, she wondered.

She returned to the parlor where the couple sat, lost in a dream of each other.

"The wedding?" she asked. "When do you plan on—?"

"We thought Christmas," Em said. "We haven't had much time to plan. Donald has to go to Placerville on business. We'll go there on our honeymoon, then return here until our new home is built."

313

"Here? Then I'll start looking for a place for myself and Martha now—"

"Oh, no!" Em's eyes were evasive. "You'll always have a home with us, Tamsen."

"And I intend to adopt Martha as my own." The Senator's gaze was steady.

Tamsen reeled a little, catching the back of a chair for support. "What did you say?" she asked, her mouth suddenly dry.

"He knows," Em said. "Tamsen, I've told him everything. And he doesn't mind. Everything's going to be wonderful!"

"Yes," Tamsen whispered. "Wonderful."

Leaving Em and Donald alone, she went upstairs, but not to her own room. She went to the nursery. There she knelt for a long time beside the baby's bed. It was right that the two start their marriage without a shadow between them, right that Martha should have a mother and father, too. But she felt the terrible ache, the wrench at her heart, that she had experienced at her father's death.

Could the glamour of her new life, the feeling of power she experienced, the flow of gold into her coffers make up for a baby?

The prospect of loneliness was still in her mind the next night when she had dinner with Cleve Sommers. Though he was most correct in his behavior, circumspect in his speech, she could read his face. He was going to propose marriage. Tonight was just a prelude. And what was she going to say?

His hand touched hers as it lay on the white damask of the table, and she felt the emotion pulsing through it. This man would be gentle, tender in his lovemaking. A gentleman. He could never take a woman as Dan Tallant did.

At the thought of Dan, she felt a surge of passion that must have shown in her eyes, for Cleve Sommers looked startled. Blushing, she looked down at her plate.

Cleve studied her. Blushes were becoming to a

314

woman, especially to Tamsen's dark face. Yet for a moment, he thought he'd seen a look of wanton hunger, inappropriate in a lady. He could have been mistaken, and a little fire might not be amiss.

It was late when he returned her to her home. His mouth was cool in the chaste kiss he daringly pressed against her cheek. How Tamsen wished he would catch her into his arms, hold her. Then she would know!

Know what? How she hated her traitorous body and its needs. Even more, she hated Dan Tallant for first arousing them.

She went into the house, still shivering, waiting until he was out of sight. It was nearly midnight. She was late for work. He had suggested a drive another evening this week, but she had put him off until the coming Sunday. That way, she would not neglect her work, and she could sort out her thoughts. This strange urgent feeling she had might be only a reaction to the romance between Donald Alden and Em.

Tamsen did not want to saddle a horse or take the carriage. She would walk to the Parlor, and let the chill night wind cool her hot face as she tried to put erotic thoughts from her mind.

Reaching the street the Parlor was on, she began to run, a kind of premonition drawing her to the place. The door was open, and there was a sound of milling men. Trouble! As she reached the walk, she was almost lost in the exodus. Something had happened and the respectable men were fleeing so as not to be caught up in it.

When she managed to enter, finally, she found fewer than a half-dozen men left. A man lay on the floor. Another stood over him with a gun. Tamsen's startled eyes went to Nell.

"That gawdamn Wally Knight," the woman roared. "He jes' shot Lebeau!"

Tamsen went forward, leaning her head against Knight's arm, looking up at him adoringly. "You did it for me, didn't you?" she whispered. As he turned to her,

315

she struck his wrist with a quick motion. The gun went flying across the room and was picked up by one of the guards at the door.

Then Tamsen dropped to her knees beside the fallen Lebeau. Pulling the bloodstained clothing away from his slender brown body, she gave a sigh of relief. The bullet had passed high on his chest, above his collarbone. He would live.

She stood up, wiping her crimsoned fingers on her skirt. "Take him upstairs," she said, "and put him to bed. Dusty, you go for Doctor Dimmick. He's a customer here, and will keep his mouth shut. As for him," she turned to Wally Knight, "get him out of here. He is never to be allowed here again. This is a respectable place!"

One of the guards grabbed Knight and took him out to the alley, where he emphasized Tamsen's command with a few well-placed punches.

Dan Tallant leaned in a shadowed corner, lazily nursing a drink. The lamplight played on his mocking features as he spoke to the men around him.

"You heard what the lady said," he told the room at large, "and I agree. It wouldn't do to give a brothel a bad name."

She gave him a look of pure hatred and followed the men carrying the unconscious Lebeau upstairs.

Chapter 14

The week that followed was filled with problems both at home and at work. Em, secure in the knowledge that she would be living in the house as wife and mistress for some time, indulged herself in an orgy of housewifery that did not set well with Birdie Faraday.

Birdie had been in command of Senator Alden's home for many years. His stepmother had been an invalid who took little note of her activities. Now, Birdie found herself in the position of having to take orders from someone else. She didn't like it at all.

"That kitchen isn't big enough for two women," she told Tamsen. "I can't see why Master Donald didn't marry a woman who knows her place. I'm quitting!"

Tamsen soothed her, telling how important she was to them, begging her to wait until after the wedding. Finally Birdie conceded ungraciously. "Until after the wedding, then, but no longer. She don't want me around."

Tamsen had to concede the truth of that statement. Em was the domestic type. She would want to cook and clean for her new husband, as a gift of love. Tamsen, too, would be in the way. She would move into the Parlor with Nell and the others, even though such a move seemed a break with all that was clean and decent. To live at the Parlor would be to be a part of it.

Reading her mind, Birdie said, "Why can't I go and work for you?"

Tamsen was shocked silent for a moment, then remembered Birdie thought she operated a hotel. "We have someone to cook," she said uncomfortably. "I'm—

I'm sorry. And you wouldn't like the job, I'm sure." It sounded feeble. She had a feeling the woman was not convinced.

One evening Tamsen visited Pierre Lebeau. Despite herself, she found she was developing a fondness for the boy, though he still persisted in making foolish protestations of love.

"I think you're getting well," she'd laughed at him. "But if you're so lonely, I'll send you some company. Polly? Katie? Aimee?"

He'd shrugged off her suggestion, wincing with pain from his healing shoulder. Polly liked Wally Knight, and so she was mad at Lebeau. Katie preferred Wheeler, or the Tallant man. And Aimee was a tramp. Only Tamsen would do.

"Then I guess you're going to have to stay lonely," she said with a smile. Still, it was good to see his eyes brighten when she came in, good to be needed.

Sunday arrived, and with it, the carriage drive with Cleve Sommers. Instead of leaving the crowded areas, he guided his team to the docks.

The day was a cold, wet one, and Tamsen tried to be appreciative of the things he pointed out. He listed his company's holdings, named a few of the ships that sailed under its auspices. He explained the company's plans for expansion until Tamsen touched a hand to her lips to hide a yawn.

"I'm boring you with all this," he said, contritely. "Though I do have a reason for wanting to show it to you. I wanted to show you my offices, too, but I find I failed to bring a key, and there's no one else there on a Sunday."

"I found it all quite interesting," Tamsen lied.

He smiled. "Then we'll drive into the hills someplace, where we can find a better view."

He turned the carriage and drove sedately, speaking of the weather, his work. The vehicle, drawn by a pair of matched grays, was warm and comfortable against the misty rain that fell ceaselessly outside. Tamsen was

318

lulled by the sound of his voice and the restfulness of the atmosphere.

It's almost like being married, she thought. Mr. and Mrs. Cleve Sommers, out for a Sunday drive. A roast in the oven at home. The maid seeing to the children. She thought of little Martha with a dull ache. Martha, who would be lost to her. And suddenly, a home and children seemed to be most desirable.

She looked at Cleve with a sudden rush of affection. She didn't love him, but surely that would come. Her hand went out, tentatively, to touch his, then she caught herself in time. Cleve intended to propose, she was certain of it. But he was a man who did things in his own time, in his own way.

They reached a spot high in the hills, and he pulled up the horses where there was a view of the bay with its masts and funnels, a dim scene, almost obscured by the grayness of the day. Cleve looked disappointed. "I wanted you to see how it looked from here," he said. "But even I can't tell which ships belong to our line."

Tamsen suppressed a giggle. Mr. Cleve-all-business-Sommers, she thought. And then he surprised her.

Turning to her with a kind of fierceness, he said, "It's a golden city! A place where a man can make a fortune and a name for himself! And I'm going to make Sommers the most important name in town! Tamsen," his gray eyes were shining, his sandy hair tumbled boyishly with the damp, "I want you to share this with me."

She looked at him, uncomprehending. Was this the proposal she'd expected? "I—I don't understand."

"I want you to share it with me," he repeated with a touch of impatience. "I want you to marry me. I—I'm very fond of you. You're the kind of woman I've always dreamed of."

"Cleve," she gasped, "I—I don't know what to say."

"Say you'll be my wife. I'm a forthright man, Tamsen, a businessman. I've never learned how to play games. I've told you of my present position, explained my expectations. Perhaps I seem less than romantic,

319

but I wanted to show you what you could expect. I will be kind, considerate—"

"I—I think the way you proposed is—very sweet," Tamsen said, her mouth trembling. It had been. Her experiences had been with men who grabbed, men who pawed, who thought they'd purchased her favors and acted accordingly. And he was offering her more than jewels, more than gold. He was offering her a secure marriage, a home, such as Em would have with Donald Alden.

But he'd said he was fond of her. He didn't mention love. And he'd made no move to kiss her.

In answer to her unspoken thought, Cleve leaned forward and placed a chaste kiss on her lips. Instantly, she reacted, putting her arms about him, pressing her body to his.

He stiffened and drew away. He looked shocked, almost prudish. Tamsen's ardor dissolved in a wave of humiliation. He was a gentleman, and she had behaved in an unseemly manner. What would he think of her?

"Good heavens," he said weakly. "I suppose I had forgotten you were a widow, that you have known a man. Here I've been holding back, fearing I'd offend your sensibilities! Oh, Tamsen—"

He pulled her against him once more and she could feel his body quivering with emotion as he sought her mouth in a far more ardent embrace. But she felt no response; the moment had been lost. He tried to awaken a passion to match his own, but his fumbling hands made her think of Will Franklin, her beau back in Pennsylvania.

Sensing her withdrawal, he grew embarrassed. "I don't know what got into me," he confessed. "I completely forgot myself. You see now how I feel about you, Tamsen. We must be married, and soon."

"I have to have time," she whispered.

"Naturally." He nodded his approval. "Very wise of you. As for myself, I never sign a contract without sleeping on it. And this is a most important contract, you must agree. A lifetime."

320

"Yes," she said, "it is."

That thought was uppermost in her mind as they drove home. A lifetime. Cleve had reverted back to his businesslike self, except that now, the talk was about, When we are married . . . Our home . . . When we have children. He seemed to have taken her answer for granted. Did she really have a choice? How could she weigh an important position in society against a life as madam of a brothel?

And, unlike Em, she could never confess her past life to her future husband; it would never be understood.

If only she had felt some stirring at his embrace!

He attempted to kiss her once more at her door, but she backed away. "I'll give you my answer tomorrow, Cleve," she said. "At four."

How she wished she could talk to Em! But Em was so in love that she thought everyone else should feel as she did. Her advice would be without value.

Tamsen did not sleep that night.

Apparently Cleve Sommers didn't, either. When he came to the house the next afternoon, he was far from being his spruce, imperturbable self. His hair was rumpled, his eyes darkly circled as though he'd been wakeful until the very small hours.

Earlier in the day, Tamsen had mentioned her plans for moving out when Em married. And she was certain she saw a flicker of relief in her sister's eyes. "You don't need to—," Em began. Tamsen, however, was adamant. The session ended with Tamsen's promise to remain with little Martha until Em and the Senator returned from their honeymoon.

Everything had changed, Tamsen thought. Em was more decisive, sure of herself, now that she had her love.

She, Tamsen, could have one, too. She looked at Cleve with a trace of pity. He clearly was a man, and a man who'd spent the night in need of a woman. His gray eyes said he needed her, he loved her. She thought of Madam Foster, old and dying, with nothing . . . no one . . .

Cleve came toward her, his hands twisting at his sides, as if he could hardly contain himself. Then he just stood, silent, his face alight with hope.

"I've decided the answer is yes," Tamsen said, on impulse. Then, for no reason at all, she was crying. His arms were around her, and it was good just to put her head against his chest. It was only for a moment. She felt his body begin to tremble, his hands tighten at her waist, and knew his control was gone. She backed from him.

"We won't tell anyone else for a few days," she said, quietly. "We don't want to take away from the attention Em and her wedding plans deserve—"

"Tamsen—," he began.

But she fended off his advance, "It has to be this way. Promise me!"

He did, reluctantly, then pressed her to go to dinner, to the theater, for a carriage ride, anywhere. She refused, telling him she needed to be alone.

He left, knowing that if she had not held back, he would not have behaved like a gentleman. Yet she had aroused him to such an extent that he determined to have a woman. Until the wedding day, he had to find some other way to subdue his passions. He wondered if there were a place in San Francisco that was dignified, safe and discreet.

He would ask young Adam Wheeler.

That night Tamsen, dressing for her act, remained in her room a long time. She had made an instant decision agreeing to marrying Cleve Sommers. But it was the right one to make, and she knew it. Still, her head ached, terribly, as she thought of the future. First, she must make plans for the Parlor. Perhaps Nell could operate it, and Katie could be taught to stand in for herself. The money could be deposited in a secret account, should she ever wish to be free—

That thought horrified her. It was no attitude to take into marriage. She could not imagine such a situation existing between the Senator and Em!

Then there were Cleve's friends and business acquaintances. Surely some among them would recognize her. She shrugged off the notion. Adam Wheeler had taught her a lesson. "I won't tell if you don't—"

Hurrying down the hall, the skirt of her elegant gown lifted in one hand, Tamsen turned at the stairwell to look down. And she looked straight into the eyes of a man she knew. A man who was climbing the stairs with Katie Ryan.

Cleve!

The expression of horror in his gray eyes was terrible to see. "Good God!" he jerked out. "You!"

"Cleve—"

He stared at her extended hand as if it were a snake, then turned and plunged down the steps. Heads turned to watch his precipitous flight into the night, then back toward Tamsen, whose face flamed.

Deliberately, she made herself walk down the steps, moving into the room to stand beside the piano. What am I doing here? she wondered. I should go after him. But she saw Katie still standing on the stairs and her chin lifted, paraphrasing an old English tune as she sang.

"I had a true love but he left me. Oh, oh, oh, oh. And I now am bro-ken-hearted. Oh, oh, oh, oh."

Then, changing her voice, she gave a sly answer to the tragic girl she'd been before.

"Well, if he's gone, I wouldn't mind him, Fol de rol de hay ding do, You'll soon find one that'll prove much kin-der, Fol de rol de hey ding day!"

A titter ran through the room as all eyes turned to Katie, who apparently had been deserted by the man who was to pay for her favors. It was Katie's turn to redden. She didn't understand exactly what had happened, but she knew that the sight of Tamsen had caused the man to leave. And Tamsen had made a laughingstock of her before the eyes of the clientele. Katie spotted Dan Tallant in the crowd below.

She descended, took his arm, and led him toward the stairs, turning to sing the last words of the verse toward Tamsen.

"What care I for rings or money,

Fol de rol de hey ding di do,
I'm for the man who calls me honey,
Fol de rol de hey ding day."

Tamsen joined in the laughing applause for the song that made up in vigor for what it lacked in melody. But inwardly, she hated the red-haired girl who had answered the song so saucily with one of her own, turning the joke against Tamsen. Katie waved from the stairs, then she and Dan went on up together.

Later that night, Tamsen climbed those same stairs to change her clothes before she went home. She had finally come to some understanding of Cleve Sommers's actions. It was clear, this afternoon, that he had wanted her. He had probably come here to find release. In male circles, such an action would be encouraged, not frowned upon. She knew that she would never see Cleve again, that the proposal he'd made was dismissed the moment he saw her in this place.

Why?

Why was there one standard for men, another for women? After consideration, she might have been able to forgive him. He would never forgive her.

It was not fair.

Passing Lebeau's door, she hesitated, then set her hand to the knob. She was on the outside of Em's life now, and she had lost Cleve forever. She desperately needed reassurance—

But Pierre Lebeau was not alone. Cradled against his uninjured shoulder was Aimee—Aimee, whom he'd once referred to as a little tramp—both of them blissfully lost in sleep.

Tamsen closed the door quietly, leaving them alone.

The next day, she learned that Cleve Sommers had left town, sailing on the first one of his ships that left port.

Chapter 15

In the days that followed, Tamsen numbed her feelings about Cleve's desertion through work. There was Em's wedding to arrange. Em, herself, had become a bright-faced stranger, a whirlwind of activity at one moment, bemused with love at the next. Then there was Birdie Faraday to contend with. The woman refused to acknowledge the upcoming nuptials. It was as though, if she ignored the preparations, the affair would not take place.

At work, a weary Tamsen had to listen to Nell's dire predictions about the failing attendance at the Parlor. Many of the sober citizens who had been frightened off the night of the shooting did not return, and they had spread the tale by word of mouth.

"The gawdamn story didn't get in the paper," Nell growled, "but it might as well have! Then there's you—"

Tamsen raised her eyebrows, questioningly.

"Yer heart ain't in it no more. You go through the motions like you don't give a damn. Hell, Tamsen, folks gits hitched ever' day! You got you a business to run. And lately everthing's been goin' t' hell. It's them gawdamn girls!"

Tamsen listened to Nell's list of complaints. Polly had been sulking ever since Wally Knight had been evicted from the premises. Katie made her preferences for Dan Tallant and Adam Wheeler clear, going upstairs with either, leaving bigshots to cool their heels. Aimee spent most of her time with that Frenchie feller. Thank God, Carmen wasn't too pertickler. But one purty *chola* couldn't handle all the trade.

"What would you suggest I do?"

"If it was me, I'd give 'em all a boot in the butt," Nell raged. "They're gittin' too big fer their britches. Tie a can t' their tails! If you don't wanna do that, let's git us some new girls in. Give 'em a little competition. Hell, they think they got this place sewed up. Think they can pick an' choose! They—"

"I think you have a good idea there," Tamsen interrupted. "Do you have anyone in mind?"

"There's two girls down to the Bella Union. They work the tables, but I figger they do somethin' else on the side. An', hell, they'd prob'ly give their eyeteeth to do it respectable-like. Sue, she's yaller-headed, built like me." Nell looked down complacently at her own bulk. "An' Belinda, she's a black gal, and a good-looker."

Tamsen's heart sank. "Nell, I don't think—"

"They's some men likes 'em exotic," Nell said, stubbornly. "Go take a look at them. An' I figger we ought to get us one of them *celestial females*." At Tamsen's bewildered expression, Nell laughed. "A hell of a madam you are! Them's those Chinee gals, brung in on boats and sold. Them kind don't give you no trouble."

Though doubtful of Nell's wisdom in the matter, Tamsen made her way to the Bella Union. Her sense of guilt at neglecting the business forced her to at least consider the big woman's ideas. To her surprise, she found Nell had looked these girls over with a judicious eye. The girl who was supposedly built like Nell had a lush, overblown figure and bedroom eyes, but hardly Nell's proportions. She would definitely appeal to the clientele.

The other girl was the color of coffee-with-cream, with slender graceful limbs. She had a slow, soft, New Orleans accent. The two of them complemented each other, and both could dance and sing. Tamsen employed them and left, shaking her head at Nell's sagacity. Because Nell had been right so far, Tamsen decided that she would go down to the docks the next time a ship from the Orient arrived.

326

It was not too long in coming. Dusty, who had been sent to inquire about such an arrival, woke Tamsen at noon the following day with the report that the worn and buffeted sails of a ship from the Orient had been sighted. She was waiting when the captain set foot on shore. Stating her business crisply, Tamsen said she wanted first pick of the girls he'd brought from China. And that she'd pay well.

The captain had exactly what she was looking for, he informed her, grinning as he looked her figure over, assessing its potential. Nervously Tamsen boarded the ship with him to inspect his human wares.

The girls were packed in the hold like sardines. Tamsen's heart sank at sight of them. Of course, they had been at sea for many weeks. That would account for their unkempt appearance and the odor that pervaded the crowded area. But most of them were hard-faced, afflicted with Asiatic scrofula—or even worse diseases.

These would be what Nell referred to as "boat-girls," girls from the seaboard towns, already used and misused by white sailors. One screamed something, tauntingly, at Tamsen, and the captain struck her across the mouth. Sickened, Tamsen insisted on returning to the deck, where she breathed in great gulps of clean sea air.

"I'm sorry," she said. "There is no one here that I would consider. I have a very high-class business—"

The man leered at her, calculating something in the back of his eyes. "How much you pay?" he asked. "Maybe I've better thing that you don't see yet."

"Price is no object. It depends upon the girl's quality."

He grinned, laying a finger beside his nose. "I got. I show."

He led her to the door of a cabin which, when opened, proved to be little larger than a closet. A small figure, dressed in a soiled but rich-looking cheong-sam, cowered away from them. The captain took one slender bare arm, roughly, and dragged her into the light.

"This Ming Yee," he said. "Special order for big

327

Chinese merchant. You pay more? She virgin. Make good Daughter of Joy."

Tamsen studied the girl. What had appeared to be a waif was an exquisite, miniature woman. Woman? She was hardly more than a child, Tamsen was certain, but her femininity was apparent. Dark, frightened eyes glowed in an ivory-tinted face. She was no common boat-girl. Her fine-boned body showed breeding.

Tamsen gasped as the meaning of the girl's presence here penetrated her mind. Nell had said that many young girls were kidnapped in China by agents of San Francisco dealers. This must be such a girl—

Sick inside, Tamsen thought of Arabella.

"I'll take her," she said. "How much?"

The captain was wily. The merchant in Chinatown had offered two thousand dollars. He would more than double it to allow room for bargaining. "Four thousand five hundred," he said.

"I'll take her."

He could not believe his ears. Those in the hold would be sold for from two to five hundred dollars. True, this one was an exceptional creature, but untried. Unless she learned to ply her trade properly, she would be of little use. He'd considered breaking her in, himself, but the merchant had specifically demanded a virgin. This Madam Franklin was either a novice—or a fool.

He took her money hastily. Then he handed her a form which read, "*For the consideration of four thousand, five hundred dollars, I, Ming Yee Song, promise to prostitute my body for the term of ten years. If, in that time, I am sick one day, two weeks shall be added to my time, and if for more than one day, my terms of prostitution shall continue an additional month. But if I run away, or escape from the custody of my keeper, then I am to be held as a slave for life.*"

It was signed in delicate Chinese characters, apparently the girl's name.

Tamsen felt cold as she read the contract. By this

328

token, the girl was a slave for life. Her anger showed in her eyes as she looked at the captain.

"Is good paper," he said, virtuously. "Is usual contract, good for California law. All paper read like this one. No problem."

"Get her things," Tamsen said, icily, "if she has anything of her own. And please inform her she is to come with me."

Once in the carriage, with the girl beside her, Tamsen had second thoughts. What was she to do with her? Katie, Carmen, the others, they had chosen their profession. But, if the captain were to be believed, this child was still innocent. Untouched. She looked at the girl. She could not just toss her to the wolves. And she was too delicate, too refined for making beds and cleaning floors. Perhaps Em might find a place for her in her own household, after her marriage. Right now, however, Birdie Faraday would probably consider that the last straw.

Yet now she was responsible for the girl, who had nothing but the ragged costume she wore—and a strange stringed instrument unlike anything Tamsen had ever seen. Impulsively, Tamsen leaned over and touched the strings. They emitted an odd, lovely sound. The girl's face did not change, but she looked at Tamsen, a question in her eyes.

Tamsen pointed to her own mouth, making a humming sound, then to the girl's. She drew her fingers across the strings of the instrument once more, then placed the girl's hand upon it.

Ming Yee's small perfect features lit with understanding. Caressing the strings, she brought forth strange wonderful notes. Above those notes, her voice sounded like a tiny silver bell. Strange words, strange music. But somehow captivating. Tamsen considered as she listened. It might be worth a try.

Several nights later, Ming Yee, her slim body sheathed in a straight Chinese gown of gold cloth slit to the knee, made her first appearance in Madam Frank-

329

lin's Parlor. As foreign as her songs and mannerisms were, it was clear she made a tremendous impact on the men present.

Tamsen, circulating after the song, added to Ming Yee's legend. No, this girl did not go upstairs. She was an entertainer, the daughter of a Mandarin, imported at great expense. Furthermore, she had never known a man. Such a tiny helpless creature was someone to be protected, not used.

By appealing to each man as though he alone were responsible for taking care of Ming Yee, Tamsen cleverly assured the girl's future as the untouched darling of the establishment. "As long," Tamsen smiled to herself, "as that's what she wants to be."

After Ming Yee's song, Sue, the blond girl from the Bella Union, and dark and sultry Belinda danced and sang.

There was a rush from the gentlemen who wished to go upstairs. Polly, Katie, Carmen, and Aimee eyed the new girls' success with envy and began to advertise their own charms.

It worked; Tamsen breathed a sigh of relief. God bless Nell! With everything running smoothly at the Parlor once more, Tamsen would be able to devote more time to preparing for Em's wedding.

As Tamsen left the house for work in the early dusk one evening, she was deep in thought considering what would be best to do. Em had pleaded with her to stay, to make her home with her and the Senator, and Tamsen was torn. She and Em were on an easier basis, now. Arabella's appearance, which had erected a wall between them, seemed to have been forgotten in Em's new joy. Yet, Tamsen knew her presence might have an inhibiting affect on the romantic pair. And there would be her work at night to explain. She had an idea the Senator was not as gullible as Em.

Suddenly, she became aware of the fact that she was being followed. It was only a feeling, an odd sensation that prickled the hair at the nape of her neck. Though it was not yet fully dark, the people she passed were only gray shapes that loomed and were gone. There were footsteps that slowed when she slowed, stopped when she paused, sped up when she hurried a little.

Rounding a corner, she ducked into a doorway, then stepped out to intercept the slight figure that followed on her heels.

"Birdie Faraday! Are you spying on me?"

The small woman drew herself up, bristling. "Can't I take a walk, if I want to? It's my night off. I can do what I please! That Em's rearranging my kitchen. I don't have to stay and watch, do I?"

Though Birdie's voice was cross, there was a pathetic note in it. Tamsen pitied her. The kitchen had been hers all these years.

"It just frightened me when I saw you," Tamsen said. "A lone woman shouldn't be out at this hour, especially not in this neighborhood, with all these men—"

"You don't think they'd pay any attention to an old woman like me?"

Tamsen stifled a giggle. There had been a rather hopeful sound in the question. "You're not old, Birdie. You're a very attractive woman. It's just that this is not a respectable area."

"Then what are you doing here?"

"I—I have some business to attend to," Tamsen temporized. "Now, you head on back that way. I'll watch until you're out of sight."

Disconsolately, Birdie turned, then turned back once more. "You haven't changed your mind about getting me a job at your hotel?"

"No, Birdie. I haven't. It's not the right kind of place for you."

At the finality of Tamsen's words, Birdie sniffed and began to retrace her steps. Tamsen, as she'd promised, watched until she could no longer see the stiff little back. Then she continued on her own way, wondering why the woman had followed her. Birdie was an intelligent woman. Tamsen had an idea she'd never swallowed the hotel alibi and that she was determined to catch her out.

Why?

Did she intend to use her information to try to break up the Senator's marriage to Em? That was quite possible. Tamsen would have to take greater care from now on, at least until the wedding was over.

As she walked on, that strange sensation of being followed moved into her consciousness again. She turned quickly, but saw nothing. Had Birdie trailed her once more? Was she hiding back there somewhere?

No, this feeling was different. She sensed some evil behind her in the darkness, something malign following her.

Preposterous! She forced herself to walk slowly until she neared Madam Franklin's Parlor for Gentlemen. Then she began to run.

Chapter 16

The day of Em's wedding, Christmas Day, dawned bright and clear. The California sun chose to favor San Francisco with weather fit for a bride. The house was decorated for the holidays. A tall spruce stood in one corner of the parlor with tinsel and shimmering candles that gave the room a soft glow.

In the center of the room, a small bower of white latticework rising into an arch had been erected. It was decked with interwoven pine boughs, white tissue bells tied with satin ribbon, and flanked by pots of enormous live poinsettia plants.

In the kitchen, Birdie muttered and clucked over trays of small sandwiches and her own incomparable canapés. All this trouble to go to for a wedding she didn't approve of anyway.

Upstairs in Em's room, Tamsen helped her sister to dress in her bridal gown and then stood back to look at her. The dress was perfect for Em. Made of heavy white watermarked moiré, the off-shoulder neck-line was detailed with tiny tucks caught into a band of satin. The tight basque bodice, which was boned to minimize Em's already tiny waist, ended in a sharp V at the front. But it was Em, herself, glowing like a candle with inner happiness, that gave the dress its real beauty.

"You look lovely," Tamsen said. "Now, turn around."

Em turned. Behind her, the sweeping skirt, scalloped, piped with satin, flowed smoothly. She wore an exquisite bridal veil of rose-point lace in the new fashion, as one would wear a shawl or stole, draped over her head.

"I feel lovely," Em said.

Tamsen had to acknowledge that this new Em was a stranger. She seemed to stand taller, to move with confidence. Her eyes were bright, her normally pale skin touched with a natural color. She was no longer the quiet girl from Pennsylvania. She had been changing ever since she met Donald Alden.

"Well," Em asked, "will I do? What do you think?"

"I think you're probably the most beautiful bride in the world," Tamsen said, soberly.

"That's because I'm the happiest bride. Oh, Tamsen, I wish you were getting married, too. I thought, for sure, that you and Cleve—"

Tamsen flushed. "For heaven's sake, Em! Forget about matchmaking, at least for today."

"I'm sorry, Tam. It's just that I'm so happy, I want the same thing for you."

"There's only one Donald Alden." Tamsen forced a laugh. "And you got him."

The sound of carriage wheels cut into her conversation, and Em felt suddenly nervous and frightened. "The guests! They're arriving. Oh, Tamsen, I'm scared!" Her eyes filled with tears, and Tamsen soothed her.

"I think all brides feel that way. Try to relax until Birdie comes to tell us they're ready."

The girls stood at the window, peeping from behind the curtains, as guests descended from their carriages. At last, there were no more arrivals. Time stretched interminably, and there was no sign of the groom.

"Something's happened to him," Em said finally. "An accident with his carriage, or something! Oh, Tam!" Her lovely color had faded, and she looked drawn and worried.

"He'll be here," Tamsen said. The Senator didn't seem the type, but if he left Em waiting at the altar, he would answer to her!

"There he is!" Em cried at last. "Look."

The Senator had arrived, alone and on horseback.

334

Perhaps Em had been right in assuming he'd had an accident. As he strode into the house, Tamsen could see that he seemed upset.

Birdie brought the news of what had happened. Adam Wheeler, that rascal, who was to serve as his brother's best man, had disappeared, and Master Donald had been looking all over for him. His aide was still searching. But Donald said the scamp wasn't going to spoil his wedding. Mr. Charles Crocker would serve in Adam's place. They were to come to the head of the stairs, now. The pianist was about to begin.

The color had flooded back into Em's cheeks by the time they heard the first strains of music. First, Tamsen walked slowly down the steps. She had chosen a gown of muted green, so as not to outshine the bride, and wore a circlet of holly on her dark hair. In her arms, she carried a sheaf of late-blooming roses, red to match the holly berries, cut from their own garden.

The guests were seated and waiting. She heard a low murmur of approval as she moved into her place. Then all necks were craned as a flicker of white appeared on the broad stairs.

A slipper, a gliding train of scalloped skirt, and then—Em.

She stood poised there for a moment. This time there was no whisper of sound, only a reverent hush. Delicate, fragile, with a halo of gold-brown hair, Emmeline McLeod was not a human creature, but a vision from a dream—an angel, lacking only wings. She glided down the stairs as lightly as a spirit.

All eyes were upon Em as she moved to stand beside the groom.

"We are gathered here together," the minister began. Finally, he was saying, "I now pronounce you man and wife." And Emmeline McLeod was Mrs. Donald Alden.

Following the ceremony, Tamsen went about her duties as hostess. There would be a small reception for now. The larger one, for those who had not attended the ceremony, would be held later in the day at one of San Francisco's largest hotels. As Tamsen moved among the guests, she was thankful that what she'd feared most had not occurred. There was no one here who knew her as Poppy Franklin. Here, she was just the sister of the bride.

She recognized the names of some of the guests, but only because she'd heard them mentioned by the Senator. Charles Crocker, Collis P. Huntington, Mark Hopkins, Leland Stanford—all of them were considered very important people.

Alden was talking to Charles Crocker, in fact, when Tamsen noticed that he'd been so surrounded by well-wishers he hadn't had a chance to get near the punch-bowl. She took him a cold drink.

He took it absently and continued to thank Crocker for standing in for his stepbrother. "He'll get here before we leave for the hotel," Alden said, his face set. "I sent my aide, Henry Sloan, to round him up. If Adam doesn't show, I'll break every bone in his body! A day like this—!"

"Sloan," Crocker interrupted. "Wasn't he the fellow who used to work for Sheldon Harwell? A rather stiff-necked sort of fellow?"

Alden laughed, flushing a little. "That's the one. I guess old Sheldon's sinful ways got to him. It appears he considers my entourage something less than exciting. He begged me to take him on. I must say, I didn't feel exactly complimented."

"Not a likable man, but he is fanatically loyal, I understand."

"Fanatic's the word," Alden said ruefully. Then, "Why, Tamsen, I didn't see you there. I've been wanting to tell you what a lovely maid of honor you are."

"You didn't even see me," Tamsen teased. "You didn't see anybody but Em!"

Alden grinned. "Guilty," he said.

"Excuse me," she said, "I see someone with an empty glass," and hurried back to her duties.

The group assembled for the wedding was small, but still a great many for the limited space. Talk flowed freely, and Tamsen's head began to ache from the

336

noise. She barely heard the banging at the door above the gabble of the crowd.

She hurried to answer it. Her greeting was swallowed as her heart rose in her throat, for one of the gentlemen at the door was an inebriated Adam, the other could be no other than the Henry Sloan she'd heard mentioned. And Tamsen knew him.

Sloan was the young man of impeccable character who had accompanied the Washington visitors to her establishment. The young man who had considered her invitation to take tea a proposition.

Sloan's face was afire with embarrassment at the sight of her. Only Adam Wheeler's loudness, his insistence that he kiss the bride, broke the silence. Somehow, Tamsen managed to usher them into the reception. Despite the fact that his brother was drunk, Senator Alden's face wore an expression of relief. Adam, after all, was the only relative he had. And it was right that he should be here.

Tamsen was stunned. She wanted only to escape. Sloan was not like the others. Fanatically loyal, Mr. Crocker had said. This time, it wouldn't be a case of "I won't tell if you don't." For Henry Sloan had only brought guests to her parlor; he hadn't come there on his own. He would tell, she thought frantically. Dear God! What should she do? Could she appeal to his sympathy? One look at his rigid features told her that would do no good.

"Tamsen," Em called, "get your wrap. We're ready to leave for the reception at the hotel."

Tamsen went to her. "I have a headache," she said weakly, "and I think I should stay with Martha——"

Em looked at her as if she'd just confessed to murder. "My stars," she gasped, "I never heard of such a thing! How could I go through this without you? Bathe your forehead with cologne. We'll wait. And you know Birdie will be here with the baby!"

There was nothing for it but to go. Nothing must mar this day for the bride. Tamsen hurried upstairs, grateful for a moment's respite, and bathed her temples.

Then she noticed that her gown was stained with something she had spilled while serving the guests. She had to change.

Deliberately, she chose her simplest gown. An off-white brocade that was almost virginal, with its high collar and clean lines. She had worn it only once, and Nell had commented, "You look like a gawdamn saint, which you ain't."

She had an idea it would not impress the loyal Henry Sloan.

It was a relief to discover that Sloan would not be crammed into the bridal carriage, but would follow in another. Perhaps, in the crowded ballroom, she would not see him again. It was a comforting thought. But that hope was soon crushed.

Forced into the receiving line, she was to meet more than one pair of amazed eyes, more than one dropped jaw. One elderly gentleman, at sight of her, grew so apoplectic that his wife led him back to their carriage.

Tamsen felt hot, as if all eyes were upon her, as if tongues were wagging throughout the ballroom, saying, "Mrs. Alden's sister, do you know who she really is?"

Henry Sloan had stationed himself where he could keep an eye on her. Tamsen wondered, furiously, if he thought she might steal the hotel silver.

It was some time before she could excuse herself for a moment. Then, taking the opportunity to escape, she ran through a rear door, down the hall, into the lobby and out through the front, bumping into a late arrival as she fled.

Two strong hands gripped her arms. Gasping, she stared at the man who held her. Dan! Dan Tallant! For a moment, she had not recognized him in his tailcoat, silk-and-beaver hat and ruffled shirtfront. He was gloved and carried a walking stick tucked beneath his arm. When he spoke, however, he was unmistakably Dan.

"Just where the hell do you think you're going?"

"Home," she flung at him, "if it's any business of yours!"

338

"Running out on Em?"

Tamsen's expression was answer enough.

"By God, you are," he said, his face stern. "I've had you figured for a lot of things, but I never thought you'd be a quitter. What do you think it'll do to Em when she finds you're gone?"

"What do you think it will do if I stay?" Tamsen gritted. "There's a room full of men in there who know who I am, and just what kind of business I run!"

"Ashamed of it?" Tallant's eyebrows quirked.

"You know I'm not! But what if someone goes to Em with the story—today of all days!"

"Seems to me you should have thought of that a little earlier," he said, dryly. "But for now—you're going back in there." His hand closed about her elbow and she tried to pull away.

"I'm not, I tell you! I'm not!"

"Dammit, Tamsen," he exploded. "Do you think anybody's going to brag about any association with your place? We're going to walk in there and give that bunch of hypocrites something to think about! Let them sweat for a while!"

She stared at him for a minute, then smiled. He had a point. None of those good gentlemen would turn to their wives and say, "Dear, this is the madam of the brothel I patronize."

Only Sloan was a matter of concern. But it was possible that he'd be too embarrassed to admit that he'd entered the Parlor's doors.

Tamsen took Dan's proffered arm and went back with him into the room where the reception was being held.

"Show me someone you recognize," Dan whispered. Tamsen indicated an elderly, corpulent man standing with his equally corpulent wife.

"Come on," Dan said, a note of deviltry in his voice. They approached the couple.

"Mr.—Menchen, isn't it? I'd like to present the bride's sister, Mrs. Harper. And is this your charming wife? Mrs. Menchen, I'd like you to meet—"

He was interrupted by the gentleman, who had gone first red, then white, and now indulged in a violent fit of coughing. His wife looked concerned.

Dan made excuses, and he and Tamsen moved on. "See," his amused whisper reached her ear, "it's easy, once you jump in."

Surprisingly, Tamsen began to enjoy herself. Introduced to a Mr. and Mrs. Phillips, Tamsen saw a look of total fear in the man's eyes. It was almost funny. Joe Phillips was one of the establishment's habitual visitors, very catholic in his tastes, having gone upstairs with any girl who was available.

"How do you do?" she said, demurely, to his wife. Then, to him, "I'm sure we've met before. Something about you is so familiar."

"I—I'm afraid I haven't had the pleasure—"

"Oh," she whispered, taking advantage of the fact that his wife's attention had been diverted, "But I'm sure you have!"

Dan Tallant overheard. His wide shoulders shook with amusement. No matter what she was, the girl had guts. She was nervous, though. He could feel the tremors that pulsed through her hand on his arm.

Tamsen felt those tremors, too. They were not due to nerves, but to his touch. She pulled her hand free and swept ahead of him, deliberately seeking out men who had been among the establishment's clientele. She dropped a sly word here, an insinuating remark to the men as she ingratiated herself to their often dowdy wives.

"You know, George," said one dowager, "she's a sweet little thing. Perhaps we should have her to dinner one night."

"Heaven forbid," her husband said.

The woman looked at him, puzzled. "What did you say?"

"She's a nice kid," he said hastily. "A nice kid."

Em watched as Tamsen cut a swath through the room. "Look at Tamsen," she said to her new husband. "She's having such a good time!"

340

There were refreshments. There was dancing. Tamsen did not lack for partners. Those men present who had not met her in a business capacity were enchanted by the small, innocent-appearing girl. She fended them off. "I'm a widow," she explained. "I'm only out of mourning for the wedding—for my sister's sake. You do understand."

The others who sought her out were usually dispatched by their wives. "Dance with that nice little Harper woman." Or their prime purpose was to discover whether Tamsen might let something slip about their extramarital activities. She remained non-committal.

It was bad for business, she knew. Many of these men would not return. Perhaps they would walk the straight and narrow for the rest of their lives, in fear of being exposed. Well, let them worry. It seemed small punishment for men who cheated on their wives!

Soon it was time for the bridal party to go. Em blushed beneath congratulatory kisses. Tamsen, one of the last to approach, kissed her sister and her new brother-in-law, then kissed the cheek of the next in line, the Senator's aide, Henry Sloan.

The man almost fell over backward in his haste to get away, but she smiled in satisfaction. Poor man! He'd probably be scrubbing away at that cheek all night to avoid contamination.

"Try a little whisky," she whispered to him. "It is an antiseptic."

Em and Donald Alden climbed into their beribboned carriage for the drive to a steamer that would carry them to Sacramento. Tamsen stood staring after them, long after they were out of sight. Then Dan Tallant jostled her arm.

"It's time to take you home."

At her door, she turned. "I suppose I should thank you," she said, haltingly. "I really am glad I went. You were right."

"And you had one helluva good time, didn't you?"

341

She tried to maintain a straight face, but her dimple flashed. "I suppose so," she confessed.

"I did, too," he said, unexpectedly. "Every time you stuck your chin up in the air and deflated one of those old windbags, I was proud. I said, 'That's the mother of my child!'"

Tamsen froze at his words. And before she could put out a hand to fend him off, he had kissed her, soundly. And, just as quickly, he was gone.

She stood for a moment, dazed, the feel of his mouth still burning against her own, his words a fire in her mind. "The mother of my child—"

Martha was soon to be adopted by the Aldens. What would Dan Tallant think then?

She moved into the house, to stand in the parlor before the wilting bower. Her glittering triumph of the evening was over. Now she felt unutterably lonely. Fumbling listlessly at the buttons on her gown, she thought of how lovely Em had been. She was glad she'd stayed for the reception, though her presence had not quite been enough to perfect the scene.

The last words Em had said, as she kissed her goodbye, were "Oh, Tamsen, if Arab could have been here —it would have been so wonderful—"

Chapter 17

At that moment, in far away Spain Arabella thought fleetingly of her sisters. The tour of Lola Montez's troupe, making a quick sweep across Spain, was proving very successful. In the course of the tour, they had appeared before Queen Isabella II, and the Queen's approval made them the darlings of the Continent. Now, at her expressed desire, they had accompanied the Queen to her favorite hideaway in Sevilla.

Today, the troupe had been called to attend the Queen in her garden. Isabella's gaze had fallen first on Arab, a nymph-like creature in a gown of changeable green set off by jewels that matched her eyes. The dissolute woman whispered a few words to a courtier who conveyed her message to the daydreaming Arabella in stumbling English.

Her Majesty wished the red-haired lady to dance for her. Something naughty, no?

Standing in the open space before the Queen, Arab curtseyed, a lady of breeding. Then, in a trice, she became a street girl, with skirts lifted to reveal flashing limbs beneath her petticoats, body weaving sensuously in invitation, her red mouth like a passionate flower, opened to receive a lover's kiss. It was a dance of seduction. When it was finished, Arabella held her skirt as the street girls did for coins. The audience filled it with a shower of gold.

Arab joined the other members of the troupe on the fringes of the gaily colored group who hovered about the Queen chattering like birds. The other dancers met her with silence, not a whisper of congratulation. And she realized that they were jealous of her. She tossed her head a little guiltily. It was not her fault she had been singled out!

But the afternoon dragged on interminably. There was much conversation going on, and all of it in a foreign tongue. She eyed the gardens in the distance, wondering if it were possible to escape from the company. A man was standing before Isabella, haranguing her, and the Queen was spitting back at him in Spanish. Arab knew who he was. Lola had pointed him out to her. He was General Narváez, leader of the Conservative Party, who disapproved of the Queen's behavior and her despotic ways.

Arabella smiled to herself. There was one gentleman who had not become an admirer! She wondered if her dancing were the topic of his angry speech. At least, he had distracted everyone's attention.

Behind her, the green fingers of a willow drooped to the ground. A step backward, another, and she was concealed in the foliage. She emerged on the other side, her eyes dancing in mischievous delight. For a moment, she stood still, her green gown blending with the tree behind her, savoring the blue sky with its fluffy lamb-like clouds, the garden paths before her.

She chose a path and wandered along it toward the tinkling of a distant fountain. Behind her there was music now, a soft strumming of guitars.

She slipped into a girlhood dream. She was not Arabella McLeod. She was an enchanted princess, and this was her kingdom. Somewhere, a prince was waiting. Her skirts, swaying, touched the petals of winter-blooming flowers that lined the path, stirring a fragrance that scented the air about her. A peacock strutted across her path, his feathers fanned into a jewelled arch. Two stone lovers embraced above a small waterfall cascading into an azure pool where bright birds dipped their beaks and spread their glistening feathers.

It was a magical world.

So magical, that when she reached a turn in the path and a tall young man, dressed in a crimson uniform, stepped from the shrubbery, Arab was certain she was dreaming. The gentleman spoke, a liquid flow of pure Castilian. She stood uncertainly, uncomprehending.

He smiled. "English?" he asked.

Arabella's face shone with delight. "American. I am Arabella McLeod."

"The little singer. I must confess I was startled when I saw you. Surely, I told myself, this is not a girl, but a vision. Diana, perhaps. A goddess wandering in the gardens." His dark eyes were intent on her, and she felt a warm glow within. "I have not heard you sing, but I have heard of your charms. But—let me introduce myself." He bowed. "I am Juan Narváez, nephew to General Narváez. At your service, milady."

Nephew to the General who disapproved so of the Montez troupe. He probably had heard of her, she thought, wryly. "I—I am surprised," she said, searching for a topic of conversation, "that you speak English so well. Very few people in Spain do."

He laughed. "Ah, that!" Then he went on to explain that his uncle was attempting to influence the Crown toward a more equitable form of government through a Cortes, the Spanish equivalent of the Parliament of Britain. To this end, Juan had been sent to England for his schooling. There he had studied the language and parliamentary procedures in order to be of use in the movement.

Arabella scarcely heard what he was saying. She was too bemused by the sound of his soft voice, his eyes that caressed her lips, her hair, her bared shoulders.

Suddenly, he asked, "But I have spoken of myself too much. What are you doing alone in the garden?"

Blushing, Arabella confessed that she had run away from the group gathered before the Queen, escaping through the branches of the trailing willow.

"If I had seen you then," Juan Narváez said, looking at the slim figure of the green-clad girl, "I would have thought you a tree-nymph. I would have fallen to my knees to kiss the hem of your gown—"

He paused, and for an instant, it was as if the world paused with him, as if that moment would stand alone forever in time; a sky forever blue, the scent of flowers —two people like the stone lovers at the pool. Arabella knew he shared her feeling. There was a kind of dawning wonder in his face, and for a moment they swayed toward each other, drawn by some magnetic force.

A peacock's shrill cry shattered the illusion, and Arab drew back, breathlessly.

"I suppose I should return to the others," she said, stumbling a little as she turned toward a path.

He caught her arm, supporting her. His fingers were hot on her flesh. He, too, sounded breathless as he said, "But it is not this way. I think perhaps you are lost?"

She smiled at him. "Yes," she admitted, "I am."

"Then allow me to be of service." He bowed and offered his arm. As they strolled slowly across the gardens, passing the lovers entwined above the pool, following the sound of distant music, Arabella thought, dizzily, that it was the happiest moment of her life.

"You have seen Seville?" he asked, after a long silence.

Arabella had not.

"It is a most interesting place, the chief city of Andalusia, of all southern Spain, in fact. There are many little crooked streets and enclosed squares. I would like to show it to you; the Alcazar Palace, the Torre del Oro, the tower of the Church of San Marcos, which was once a Moorish minaret—"

I am dreaming, Arab thought. This is a fairy tale!

"Seville has a romantic history," he said, softly. "It was taken by Julius Caesar in 45 B.C. There are still Roman ruins to be seen. Then the Moors, Syrian Arabs from Emesa . . ."

He talked on. The sound of his voice penetrated the bright bubble of happiness surrounding Arabella, but his words had no meaning to her. It was enough that he was there, that her hand was cradled in his arm, that they were alone.

346

She did not wish to return to the spot where the Queen held court.

Her reentry into the circle was not as inconspicuous as her departure had been. The Queen, enthroned regally in the midst of the group, raised angry eyes that changed to a look of surprise, then of amusement. She turned to gaze at the bleak face of General Narváez beside her, then hid a smile with a flutter of her jewelled fan.

Juan Narváez escorted Arabella to her place with the rest of the troupe, the General's eyes boring into his back.

Lola Montez, also, wore a look of disapproval. "Her Majesty asked that you perform again," she said, icily. "Where have you been?"

Juan Narváez excused himself in a whisper. Then he approached the royal lady herself. With a deep bow, he made an appeal to the Queen.

Isabella tapped him gently with her fan, answering something that brought smiles to the faces of the listeners and a choleric flush to that of the General. He scowled as his nephew returned to Arabella's side and, offering his hand, raised her to her feet.

"I told her that you became quite faint from the excitement of performing in her royal presence and had wandered away to regain your composure. She has given me permission to return you to your chamber." His eyes sparkled as he led her toward the glittering palace with its round towers.

"That was most kind of her," Arab whispered.

"Kind? Isabella is not kind, make no mistake!" He laughed. "It is the uncle, you see. The General is most upset at my choice of companions, therefore the Queen is amused."

"I thank you for explaining my absence, but I don't want you to get into trouble on my account."

His teeth flashed white in his dark face. "If this is trouble, I shall seek more of it. I have an affection for my uncle, but he is an old-fashioned man. He does not know an entertainer can be a lady."

347

"And can they?" Arab asked.

"A short while ago," he said, pausing, raising her hand to his lips, "I met one in a garden. And I knew immediately that she was a lady. The loveliest lady I have ever seen."

They looked into each other's eyes and felt, as they had in the garden, the sense of a moment frozen in eternity. Then, they caught hands and began to run, each conscious only of the other's grace and beauty.

Reaching the castle-like structure, they brushed past startled servants blindly, seeing only each other. And at last, mounting the carpeted stair that led to a far wing, they stood before the door to Arab's chamber. Arab thought, numbly, what if he says goodbye? I may never see him again—

But he had pushed the door open and followed her in. As she tried to think of a way to express her feelings, he looked at her steadily, a question in his eyes.

"Yes," she whispered. "Oh—yes!"

He closed the door, shooting the black iron bolt that locked it.

Much later, hair tumbling about her shoulders, Arabella propped herself with an elbow on her pillow and looked down at the sleeping Juan. He does look like a prince, she thought again. Even without his uniform. In fact, her lips curved, impishly, he looked better without it. She'd tell him when he woke.

As for now, it was enough to think of the thing that had happened between them. A thing of passion and fire, and of beauty. There had been other men, but she had not known love before.

Ah, Juan! She looked at him with adoration, her green eyes soft with the depth of her emotion.

Then there was a rap at the door.

She drew her breath in with a quick sound, then held it, hoping that whoever it was would just go away.

"Arab?" called Lola Montez. "Arabella? Let me in."

"Please," she made her voice sound weak, drowsy, "I'm in bed. I don't feel well. Can't it wait, whatever you want?"

There was a silence, and Arab sensed a listening ear against the wood of the door. Finally, her mentor said, "All right. We'll talk in the morning. I just wanted to warn you not to—to get involved. We'll be moving on soon."

Not *we*, Arab thought. For tomorrow, Juan was taking her to his own home, in Màlaga. That had been decided as they made love through the long sweet hours. The troupe would go on alone, and she would remain in Spain with Juan.

"Little liar." His whisper made her jump. She turned to see him facing her, the long lines of his trim, muscular body dark against the silken sheet. She blushed.

"I suppose I am," she admitted. "But I didn't want to be disturbed. I'll tell her the truth before we go." Then, as he lazily pulled her down to him, his lips seeking hers, she said, "I'll never lie to you, Juan. You know you're not the first—but you're the only man I've truly loved and wanted."

"And you are my one and only love," he said, his eyes dark with sincerity. "Arabella, I have a theory. Everything in our lives, in yours and mine, has led us to this moment, to each other. If this is so, neither of us has anything to regret."

Arabella's cheek was wet as she placed it against his. For what he said was true. She had endured some terrible experiences, but they had led to this. For a love such as she experienced now, she would relive it all over again.

"Those are tears of happiness?" he asked.

"They are, my love."

Gently, he began to caress her once more, and soon the dim room was illuminated with the glow of love.

349

Chapter 18

Tamsen, placing a rose from her maid of honor's bouquet in the Bible, had come across the sprig of dried forsythia from the Pennsylvania farm.

It brought back a vision of a small Arab, playing hide-and-seek, a grubby, elfin face peering big-eyed through the yellow blooms, eyes that danced with mischief. Tamsen and Em would pretend to be unable to find her, while Papa watched from the porch, pipe in hand.

A wave of homesickness swept over Tamsen. Papa was dead, the girls gone their separate way. Would things have been different if they'd stayed in the place that had been home?

Sighing, Tamsen replaced the withered sprig and closed the book. Why did she keep recalling her own arguments that had led the family to move? Would she always feel this hurting twist of guilt?

Yet even that guilt feeling was preferable to the other thoughts occupying her mind. Somehow, she'd had an intuition that Dan Tallant would return. She found herself listening for his knock at the door, watching for him at the parlor, heart in mouth as she saw a tall figure on the street that invariably proved to be someone else.

If he came at all, she thought, it would not be because of her. It would be because he'd heard of Alden's plans to adopt the baby Dan considered his own. She had no idea how he would take the news, and it troubled her.

350

I don't care, she thought, packing the things she would move to the Parlor when the honeymooners returned. Her emotions seemed so battered lately that she just felt numb. Martha was toddling now, and Tamsen grabbed her up a dozen times a day, hugging the chubby little body, trying to hide her own tears.

Days she spent with the little girl, nights at her place of business, except for one, which Birdie Faraday claimed adamantly as her own. "Thursday is my night out," the woman had declared, arms crossed, "always has been, always will be."

Tamsen frowned. It wouldn't be good for business to be absent the same night each week. The customers who came to see her might fail to show. "Tuesday, this week," she said in a firm voice, "then Thursday the next."

Birdie agreed, reluctantly, and Tamsen laughed. "You don't fool me one bit, Birdie! You like to argue."

The little woman replied with a sly, mischievous grin.

When Tamsen returned to the Parlor on Wednesday evening, rested somewhat after her night at home, she had that eerie feeling of being followed once again. She forgot about it when Nell met her with news of trouble brewing.

Polly and Sue had indulged in a hair-pulling bout. "That yaller-headed one got her face messed up," Nell said, gloomily. "Nothin' but catfights since we brought the new girls in. Oughta throw th' whole damn bunch out and start over."

"I'll talk to Polly," Tamsen said, wearily.

Polly was hard-eyed and defiant. The new girls cut into her business. They put on airs, since they had a starring act. She didn't like that Chink girl, trying to steal the show. She used to sing and dance when Madam Foster ran the joint.

"But she doesn't run it now," Tamsen said, "and we have a different type of clientele. Your act doesn't suit the atmosphere I'm trying to create."

"Too cheap for you, huh?" the girl sneered.

351

"If you want to put it that way, yes." The two women glared at each other. Tamsen didn't like the threat she saw in Polly's eyes.

"I'm leaving the choice up to you," Tamsen said, levelly. "Either cooperate or I'll see that you leave the premises."

"Like Wally Knight? You'll have me taken out in the alley, beaten to a pulp?"

Tamsen fought for control. "I know how you felt about the man. But he shot someone, Polly. I can't have that here. Now, I've told you what I expect from you. As I said, you have a choice."

The girl shrugged. "I'll stay. But it won't be for long, you can count on that!"

Tamsen busied herself with some papers. "That's entirely up to you. I hope you have another position in mind. I'll be happy to give you a reference."

"I don't need a reference," Polly said, insolently. "When I leave here, it'll be in style. Let's just say I plan on coming into some money."

"While you're here," Tamsen said, shortly, "just behave yourself. That's all."

Polly left, and Nell stuck her head in the door. She looked at Tamsen, small and forlorn behind the big desk, and thought, as she had so many times before, that it was a damn shame a kid like that had to be mixed up in this tough business.

"Got some more bad news," she boomed. "Didn't wanna throw the whole mess in yer lap to once."

Tamsen stiffened her spine, and listened as Nell continued.

"You heared of George Hecker?"

Tamsen hadn't.

It appeared he was the head of a citizen's committee. Last night, he had called at the Parlor and had a talk with Nell. When he learned that she wasn't the owner, he said he'd come back to speak with Madam Franklin herself. He was going to try to close the place down.

"What can he do? We're not illegal!"

"He kin cause us all kinds of trouble," Nell admitted.

"Keep a lookout so our customers will be skeert they'll be found out. Give the place a bad name. Sanctimonious son of a bitch!"

"I'll talk to him," Tamsen sighed.

"Told him you was gone fer a couple of weeks," Nell winked. "Gives us time to figger somethin' out. Mebbe if you'd threaten to git that brother-in-law of yers on his tail. Use yer influence—"

"I can't do that," Tamsen said, dully.

"Then yer a damn fool!" Nell lumbered toward the door, turning to make one last remark. "Say, I didn't tell you. We got ourselves a new cook, startin' a week from Monday. Sets Maggie free fer upstairs, in case Polly quits on us."

Tamsen rubbed her aching forehead. "Thanks," she smiled, tiredly. "I think that's a good idea."

No one would have guessed at her fatigue an hour later when she appeared before the crowd downstairs to sing a song that nearly brought the house down with prolonged applause. Nor was there any hint of exhaustion in the flirtatious manner in which she approached her guests, greeting them one by one. She was still the reigning queen of San Francisco.

It was only later, when she opened the office door to find massive Nell and diminutive Dusty gazing soulfully into each other's eyes, that she drearily recognized her heavy feeling as loneliness. Everybody has somebody, but me, she sighed.

That night, Katie went upstairs with Adam Wheeler. And Polly was requested by several gentlemen, but was not to be found. Perhaps she had already decided to quit. *Let* her, Tamsen thought angrily. We'd be better off without her.

All in all, it was a successful evening, financially. Nell said as much as they counted the take. "We're doin' purty damn good. Now, if that gawdamn Heckerfeller don't throw a monkey wrench in th' works!"

"He won't," Tamsen told her. "I'll think of something."

On her way home, Tamsen sensed once more that

353

someone was dogging her footsteps. She was sure that the sounds behind her were made by a man's boots. It could be one of the winos who hung out on the street, watching for a woman to come along, but why had he never tried to catch up to her?

Tomorrow she would take the carriage. She would miss those walks through the night that seemed to clear her head, and it was a bother to hitch the horse for such a short distance. But her nerves would not take much more, despite the little gun she carried in the pocket of her cloak.

At home she slept for a few brief hours, willing herself to wake early. She could not miss these few short days with Martha. She found the little girl playing on the floor under Birdie's watchful eye and knelt beside her, hugging her to her heart. Birdie put out Tamsen's breakfast and while Tamsen ate, Martha sat in a chair munching toast.

The older woman kept up a constant clatter of pots and pans. Finally, she said, "Say, I forgot. There was someone here asking for you last night."

Tamsen's heart turned over. Dan Tallant? No, Birdie knew him, and he knew where to find her at night. "Who was it, do you know?"

The housekeeper shook her white curls vigorously. "Some woman. Didn't leave a name. Just asked when you'd be here for sure. Told her it'd be next Thursday, when I got my *rightful* night out again."

"What did she look like?"

Birdie shrugged. "Couldn't tell. It was dark and all."

Tamsen was perplexed. Who would call on Widow Harper? At night, alone?

She put it from her mind as she went through the long days ahead. When Thursday came at last, she had completely forgotten the incident.

She was glad when Birdie Faraday left to go out, though she hinted it might not be too wise this night. The fog had rolled in, cloaking the city in a mantle of gray. Tamsen didn't like to think of the woman on

354

streets that were dark enough to conceal a lurking character with robbery in mind.

The older woman did not appreciate her interference. Brandishing her black silk umbrella, Birdie said, "Wasn't going to tell you until your sis got back, but I'm quitting. I got myself another place. And they're trying me out, to see how I do. And what I do with my nights off is none of your business."

Tamsen took the woman's hand, impulsively. "I'm so sorry, Mrs. Faraday! I know that Em will be, too."

"Humph! That's a damn lie, and you know it!"

"Mrs. Faraday!" Tamsen stared at her, open-mouthed. The woman had the grace to blush.

"Well, it's true," Birdie defended. "You know that woman can't wait to get back in my kitchen! And after all these years, I'm not about to take second place, not in my own house!"

Tamsen had to concede that Birdie Faraday had established a sort of squatter's rights here. It was her own house, if one considered tenure.

"Just be careful," Tamsen said, smiling to cover her pity. "Don't catch cold. And—good luck."

Tamsen watched as the tiny figure jammed her hat straight on her head and walked out into the fog. Sighing, Tamsen returned to the baby. Tonight she must not think of anyone's troubles, her own or Mrs. Faraday's. This must be a happy time to remember.

She sat on the floor and played with Martha until the child's silky lashes began to droop. Then she carried her into her room. After Tamsen slipped the long flannel nightdress over Martha's head she thought how much Martha looked like a very small angel.

Tamsen picked Martha up, but she could not bear to put her to bed—not just yet. Instead, she sat in the nursery rocker, holding the warm little body close, singing lullaby after lullaby, until long after the baby was asleep.

Finally, lifting her tenderly, Tamsen carried the little girl to her bed. She drew the coverlet beneath her chin and stooped to kiss the small face. As she lit the night light for the child, she heard a crash downstairs.

For a moment, she froze. Then, with a wave of relief, she decided it must be Birdie Faraday, returning. Leaving the small child-proof lantern burning across the room, Tamsen lit a lamp for herself and went downstairs.

She had extinguished all the lamps before she went upstairs, thinking not to come down again. It was pitch-black as she descended the stairs, her lamp an oasis in the darkness.

At the foot of the stairs, she paused, troubled. Birdie knew where the lamps and candles were kept, yet there was not a sound.

"Birdie?" Her voice was hesitant, small. She called again. "Birdie!"

There was no answer. Tamsen sensed a presence, the malevolent thing that had followed her through the streets. There was someone in the house! Someone who did not belong!

As she turned to run up the stairs, her heart beating in her throat, her only thought was to reach the nursery, to barricade herself and Martha in the room. Then a dim, shadowy figure appeared on the periphery of her vision.

Something crashed against her temple, and all went dark.

She awoke to gray morning. The horrified eyes of Birdie Faraday loomed over her. Gentle hands applied a wet cloth to her blood-soaked hair.

"I shouldn't have left you," the woman was babbling. "I knew I shouldn't have left you! You must have fallen—"

Tamsen sat up, almost crying with the pain that lanced through her head. Her sight was blurred, and she blinked to clear it. With a shaking finger, she pointed to a heavy candlestick on the floor beside her. The base of it was bloodied.

"Someone," she moaned, thickly, "someone—" Then her eyes filled with terror. "Oh, God! Martha—"

Birdie Faraday left her to rush up the stairs. Tamsen gritted her teeth and, pulling herself up by means of the railing, followed. The door to the nursery was open. She could see the older woman standing there frozen, a piece of paper clutched in her fingers.

The small canopied bed was empty. Little Martha was gone.

Tamsen felt darkness closing over her once more. She fought it away. This was no time for fainting or hysteria. Taking the note from the old woman in trembling fingers, Tamsen carried it to the window.

"Keep your mouth shut," the paper read, *"or we kill the kid. Leave one hundred thousand dollars under the hanging beam of the adobe in the Plaza. Monday, midnight."* In another hand, someone had written, *"Or else."*

Tamsen felt a wave of nausea. The money would be there. No matter how much they'd requested, she would have to raise the money somehow. But would the ransom ensure the baby's safety?

Oh, God! Em would be home tomorrow! A happy Em, returning to her baby, left in Tamsen's care!

Who could have done this? Someone who knew of the Senator's affluence? The paper was folded—

"Birdie?"

The woman turned a white, agonized face toward her. She was still shocked into silence.

"Was there an envelope?"

The woman stepped aside, picking up the torn envelope she had dropped to the floor. Still speechless, she handed it to Tamsen.

The envelope had been ripped open, torn across the middle in Birdie's frantic haste, but the name written upon it was still legible.

It was addressed to *Madam Franklin.*

Chapter 19

An hour later, Tamsen sat at the kitchen table, the note before her. Birdie Faraday, once over her first shock, had gone into hysterics. "The poor little mite," she'd wept, "oh, the poor little mite!" She had been all for going to the police for help, but Tamsen restrained her by reading her the note once more.

"I guess you're right," the woman had said. "But what are we going to do?"

"I don't know," Tamsen said, honestly. "I have to think."

To quiet her nerves, Birdie had set to work. First Tamsen's head had to be bandaged properly. Then she made her strong coffee, lots of it, laced with brandy.

Tamsen forced herself to study the situation as calmly as possible. The note was directed to her. Therefore, it had to be someone who thought the child was her own. And, it was not addressed to the Widow Harper, but to Madam Franklin. Most of those who frequented the Parlor did not know of her double life, or about the child.

She thought of the footsteps she'd heard behind her on so many nights as she'd walked home; of the sense of evil she'd felt then, just as she had last night. The footsteps were heavy. The intruder was probably a man. Dan Tallant? He had threatened to get custody of the baby. But Dan would not have struck her down. No, it was not Dan.

Then, who else? Certainly not Dusty. Sam Larabee knew about Martha, but he was gone. Not Mike Dunnevant. He had gone to the gold fields and still had not returned.

Her mind turned to the girls. Was it possible one of them might have entered into this, with a male accomplice? Katie hated her—she knew that—but Katie wouldn't do such a thing. Carmen, Aimee? They were not the type. The new girls knew nothing of Martha's birth, nor were they aware of the location of Tamsen's present residence. Polly?

A woman had come here, on that Wednesday night a week ago, asking to see Tamsen. And Birdie Faraday told her she'd only catch Tamsen home on Thursdays. That night, Polly was missing for a while. And that was the day Tamsen had fought with her.

She closed her eyes, recalling the girl's words. *"When I leave here, I plan on leaving in style. Let's just say I plan on coming into some money."*

Polly, who'd hated her since Wally Knight had been barred from the establishment. Polly, with her jealousies, her anger at having her strip tease act removed from the entertainment.

"Birdie," Tamsen said, grimly, "take a look at the writing on this note. The first part. Was that written by a man or a woman?"

Birdie adjusted her glasses. "A man, I'd say," she said, squinting.

"A man with some education, wouldn't you think?"

"I'd say so."

"And what about this?" She covered the rest of the sheet with her hand, leaving the words *Or else* standing alone. The letters were childishly formed, rather laboriously written, but unmistakably feminine.

"A woman?"

"I think so, too. And I think I know who!" Tamsen rose, her face set in cold anger. "Birdie, I'm going to be gone for a while. Make Martha's bed up, and have it ready for her. I'll be bringing her home with me. Are you afraid to be here alone?"

"No. Tamsen," the woman's voice trembled, "you

don't think it's young Adam? He's always been a rascal—"

Adam Wheeler? That was a thought. But intuition insisted she was on the right track. She was going to the Parlor. There was something she wanted to check.

Madam Franklin's Parlor for Gentlemen was locked up tightly; it was a house that slept all day and only came alive at night. Tamsen had only the ransom note in her hand. She had forgotten her key. She banged on the door with her gloved fist, raising no one. Then she picked up a stone and flailed at the wood with that, denting the heavy oak.

Nell finally appeared, still in her face paint, her small eyes glazed with sleep, wearing a dressing gown of bright pink. It looked like a tent trimmed with florid ostrich feathers. Her drowsy expression changed to one of anger.

"What the hell," she sputtered, "whyncha use yer key! Us decent folks is tryin' t' git some sleep!" Then the small eyes widened. "Migawd, girl! What th' hell happened to you? You look like you tried ter fight off a bear with a stick!"

"I'm all right," Tamsen said, impatiently. "I want to look at the records, Nell! Hurry!" She rushed into the office, Nell following. She watched as Tamsen rifled through papers, drawing out the girls' signed chits. Finding Polly's, she matched the girl's signature against the two words on the ransom note.

There was ice in the dark eyes she raised to Nell's. "Get Polly," she said, in a flat, ugly voice.

"But, hell—," the startled woman began.

"No buts about it," Tamsen demanded. "Go get Polly!"

"Polly's here. Who wants me?" The girl stood in the doorway, dressed for the street, in a pale yellow gown.

"I thought you was in bed," Nell blurted. "Where the hell you been?"

"For a walk, if it is any of your business," the girl said, contemptuously. "I'm on my own time. And there's

360

no law against it. Is that what this commotion's about?" Her eyes met Tamsen's and slid guiltily away.

Tamsen noticed a silky black hair on the bosom of the auburn beauty's gown.

"Nell," Tamsen said, "leave us alone. And shut the door after you."

Nell swallowed her protest. She could not argue with what she saw in Tamsen's face. She would find out what was going on, in time. She waddled to the door, closing it on the tail of her dressing gown, leaving a few ostrich feathers behind.

"Now," Tamsen said, "where is the baby?"

Polly's expression was both sly and defensive. "I don't know what you're talking about."

"Yes, you do." Tamsen walked toward her; grasping a handful of the girl's thick hair in one hand, she turned Polly's face to hers.

"You do know," Tamsen gritted, "and you're going to tell me!" She gave an added yank on Polly's hair, for emphasis.

Polly's reaction was sudden and unexpected. She struck Tamsen an open-handed slap, then came at her with clawing nails, pushing her back against the desk. Her fingers closed around Tamsen's throat, and Tamsen, fighting for her life against the larger girl, gave her a mighty shove.

Polly went backward and, catching a heel in the thick carpet, crashed into the wall. She slid slowly down it, semiconscious, as Tamsen stood above her gasping for breath.

Such was the scene that greeted Nell as she opened the door. The other girls crowded in behind her.

"Migawd," Nell said in awe, "you whupped hell outten her!"

There was no time for explanations. Tamsen reached for a pitcher of water and poured it over Polly. The girl came to, sputtering.

"Now," Tamsen panted, "where's the baby? You'd better start talking."

Polly, breathing raggedly, answered at last. The baby was safe. She was locked in a shack in Sydneytown, an area that was a collection of dives, dance halls, and cribs on the waterfront. She described its location.

"You left that baby *alone*?"

"She'll be all right," Polly said, sullenly. Katie, in the doorway, saw a sudden flicker of her eyes that Tamsen missed.

"I'm going after her," Tamsen said, shaking with rage. "And if she's hurt in any way, I'm coming back! You just remember that!"

Tamsen brushed past the women at the door and was gone. Katie picked up the paper that Tamsen had dropped. It was the ransom note. She read it aloud, and the other girls cried out in horror. "Gawdamn!" Nell boomed.

Then Katie went to the fallen Polly and, giving her a shake, said, "You lied, didn't you? There's somebody else there, isn't there? You sent Tamsen into a trap!"

There was an ominous murmur as the others crowded in. Nell's ham-like fists were doubled. "Move over, Katie. I'll take keer of th' little bitch, myself!"

Polly, paralyzed with terror, spilled the whole story. Wally Knight was in on the deal. He was with the child at the shack in Sydneytown.

Nell was horrified. Wally Knight was trigger-happy, dangerous. This was a job for a man. Fleetingly, she thought of Dusty. He had the guts, but he wasn't too good with a gun. Little bastard might shoot hisself! Her mind went back to Magoffinville, to the story Tamsen had told her of the night Em was attacked.

"Katie," she said, "do you know where to find that Tallant feller?"

Katie's face wore an anguished look, but she slipped into a cloak and sped out into the day.

Tamsen, meanwhile, was walking the long distance to Sydneytown, cursing herself for not having brought her carriage. She did not know what she looked like, the bandage torn from her temple, her face bruised and bleeding, one sleeve half-torn from her shoulder. She could only think of little Martha, in a filthy shack somewhere, frightened, perhaps hurt.

Curious passersby turned to look at Tamsen. One man stepped before her, his tone compassionate as he said, "What's wrong, ma'am? Can I help you?"

She looked at him blankly, until, embarrassed, he moved out of her way. Then she hurried on.

The shack Polly had described was little more than a shed. Dance halls flanked it; a row of cribs stood across the street. The place at this hour seemed uninhabited. Tamsen ran to the small structure and pushed at the door. Martha was locked in, Polly had said. Why hadn't she thought to search Polly for a key?

The door had to be broken down and she needed help. Looking frantically about her, she saw only one man, a gray-bearded wino, his matchstick limbs propped into position against a wall, his eyes rolling blearily to show their whites. He would be of no assistance.

She put her ear to the door. Was that Martha's cry? Or had she imagined it?

She must find a way to get inside!

The shack was windowless in front. But perhaps, at the back . . . ! Squeezing her way between the buildings in an area little more than a foot wide, a place that smelled of urine and excrement, she rounded the shack. She found a small, glassless window, one shutter gone, the other hanging from a single hinge. It was a high window, above her reach.

Looking around, she spied a wooden keg behind the dance hall next door. She picked her way through rubble of broken glass to reach it. The keg was empty. Tipping it onto its side, she rolled it back to the shack and set it on end. At last, she managed to climb onto the empty keg. Her face was level with the window.

It was dark inside. Her eyes, blinded by the brilliant California sun, had difficulty adjusting. "Martha," she called, "Martha, honey?"

There was an answering whimper that pierced her heart. Recklessly, she heaved her small body over the sill. The baby's cry had come from across the room, and

363

there had been a dim shape below the window, a cot, perhaps, that would break her fall.

She did not expect the half-naked man who waited for her on that rumpled bed; the hands that caught at her, taking the force of her weight, then drew her close in a strangling hug that nearly broke her ribs.

"Looks like you figured this one out," Wally Knight said, in a triumphant, gloating voice. "It's just as well. You and I have a score to settle. We'll just have to send a little note to your sister. If the Senator wants his sister-in-law and her kid back, he'll have to pay through the nose!"

Tamsen struggled for a moment, then lay still, sick at the sour sweat and liquor smell of the room. Why had she been so stupid? Polly had let her come here, knowing that Knight was waiting. Why had she come without her gun? Not that it would have done much good. His arms held her like iron bands.

"Wally," she whispered, "let me go. Let me take Martha with me. You'll get your money. I give you my word."

"Your word," he scoffed. "Remember how you sweet-talked me the night I shot Lebeau? Word, hell! Now, let me give you my word, honey! I swore to get even with you that night, and I'm going to do it. You want to know what I'm going to do?"

The baby screamed as if she sensed Tamsen's danger. Knight paused and, throwing Tamsen against the wall, got up.

"First," he growled, "I'm going to shut that kid's big mouth. I want to enjoy this without any distractions."

He started toward a corner. Tamsen, her eyes adjusted now, could see the child cowering on the other side of the room.

She pushed her restraining skirts away and leaped to her feet. "No," she called. "No! Please, I'll do anything!" As Knight snatched at the baby's arm, Tamsen screamed.

"I don't think I'd do that, Knight," came a voice from the window behind her. "Not unless you want a bullet through your head. Now, back up, slowly. Back to the wall. Put your hands above your head."

Tamsen gasped as Dan Tallant eased his lean figure through the window, dropping lightly as a cat, gun still pointed at Knight. The kidnapper began protesting that Tamsen was here of her own accord, that she'd brought the baby with her. Dan shut him up with a look and eased toward the door. He shot the bolt, letting in a shaft of sunlight, along with Katie Ryan.

"Take Tamsen and the baby home, Katie," he said, in a level voice. "There's something I have to do."

Once the women were safely in the carriage, Tallant turned to the blubbering Knight, his voice dark with loathing.

"Start walking," he said.

At pistol point, he directed Knight toward the docks. There he spoke with a man he knew for a few minutes. That gentleman agreed to row him out to a ship lying offshore—for a price.

Forced into the little boat, Knight began to beg and to plead, certain that once on the water, he would be killed and dumped over the side. The owner of the small craft had a distaste for crybabies, as well as a sense of humor.

"Hell," he said with a grin. "This here's jes' a little fishin' trip. Hey, Tallant, we fergot th' bait!" Shipping the oars for a moment, he eyed Wally Knight wickedly, then took a knife from his pocket and ran the blade along a calloused finger. "Maybe we can think of sump'n to use," he said. "Sump'n fat 'n' greasy."

By the time they reached the ship, the prisoner was a shivering wreck. Prodded up the rope ladder, Knight saw faces lining the rail above and began to regain his courage. By the time he was pushed into the captain's cabin, he was vociferous in his complaints.

"Heard you are headed for Australia," Dan told the captain, tersely. The man nodded. "Heard you needed a crew, and weren't too particular how you got it."

The captain studied Tallant's face. "Right."

"Then here's a man—I *think*." Dan shoved Wally

forward. The young man's fleshy features were a greenish hue. "If he isn't, he should be by the time you return."

"I won't be shanghaied," Knight blustered. "This is illegal! My father is an important man! I'll have the law on you!"

"If he gives you too much trouble," Dan sighed, "dump him over the side. Who knows, his folks might be grateful."

Chapter 20

Katie was mightily relieved to find Birdie Faraday at the Alden mansion. The sprightly little woman, eyes shining with relief, snatched up Martha and said to Tamsen, "You sit down, young lady. I'm going to feed and bathe this one and put her to bed. Then I'll be back to tend to you."

Tamsen sank into a chair; the strength that had kept her upright during the ordeal was gone. She felt limp and drained, conscious of all her hurts. Katie looked down at her, stifling her pity. Tamsen had a knack for getting herself into trouble. Why was it always Dan who had to pick up her chips. If anything had gone wrong today, he might have been killed.

"I'm going now," she said, a little defiantly. "You don't need me."

Tamsen raised her head wearily. "Thank you for what you did."

"I don't need your thanks," Katie snapped. "I did it for the kid and for Em."

"Whatever your reasons, they were appreciated," Tamsen said. "And if you ever need help, if there's anything I can do in return—"

"I always manage to take care of myself," Katie said, and stormed out.

Birdie Faraday appeared, beaming, soon after Katie left. "Baby's fed and down. Sleeping like a little lamb. You wouldn't know anything ever happened. Now it's your turn, missy."

She bathed Tamsen's cuts and scratches, exclaiming over the extent of her injuries. "That blow on the head

367

was pretty bad. You're going to have a black eye, girl! And those scratches! How'd you get them?"

"I—I had to persuade someone to tell me where Martha was."

"Must have been powerful persuading." The woman clucked. "Like to see what the other party looks like!"

Tamsen looked at herself in the mirror. She gasped. One whole side of her face was swollen, a greenish color. By tomorrow, it would be black and blue. And those marks from Polly's pointed nails! They would be impossible to hide.

"Birdie," she whispered, "what am I going to tell Em? I don't want to spoil her homecoming—"

"Wouldn't tell her anything." The woman's voice was emphatic.

"But look at me!"

Birdie smiled. "That horse you were thinking on buying. I told you he was a wild one. I could tell by the way he rolled his eye. A wicked critter. But you wouldn't listen to me, oh, no! You had to try him out yourself!"

"Birdie!" Tamsen looked at her in admiring wonder.

Birdie clasped her heart. "It was awful, seeing you dragged down the road like that. My, I almost had an attack. And that animal rearing, trying to trample you! Why, if I hadn't grabbed his bridle—"

"Wait a minute," Tamsen laughed. "Don't get *too* carried away."

Tamsen hugged the older woman. She prayed that things would work out for Birdie at her new job. She was going to miss this spunky little creature.

At last, Tamsen undressed and slipped in between the clean fresh sheets with which Birdie had made her bed. They were cool against her fevered body. She would not go to the Parlor tonight. Katie would tell Nell what had happened, so that Nell would not expect her.

Tamsen wondered what Polly did after she left. Probably packed her things and got out in a hurry! And Wally Knight! She shuddered, wondering whether Dan had killed the man.

If it hadn't been for Dan's intervention, little Martha

368

might have been seriously harmed. She wished she could see him to thank him.

Her wish was granted as she made it. Birdie Faraday appeared in the doorway of her bedroom, face alight, white curls bristling. "Company," she said.

She pushed Tallant into the room, gave a conspiratorial smile, and closed the door behind him.

Tamsen and Dan stared at each other. He saw a tiny figure with silken hair spread against a white pillow. The dark oval face was bruised, and there was a patch of bandage on the forehead.

"I—Birdie took me in to see Martha," he said. "She seems to be fine."

Tamsen nodded, her dark eyes huge in her small face. "She wasn't hurt." A pause, and then, "Wally Knight—you didn't . . . ?"

He grinned. "That gentleman's taking a sea voyage—for his health. I don't think you'll be seeing him again." He approached the bed. One delicate hand lay atop the coverlet. It seemed right to take it in his own.

"Tamsen," he asked, huskily, "are you all right?"

She burst into tears.

He sank down on the bed beside her, gathering the trembling body into his arms. "Don't, sweetheart," he said, "oh, sweetheart, don't! The baby's safe, now, it's all right. I won't let anything happen to either of you."

She raised her tear-filled eyes to his, her guilt at the way she had deceived him more than she could bear. He couldn't go on thinking Martha was his. She would have to tell him.

"Dan—"

"Sh-h-h." He placed his mouth against hers, shutting off her confession. It began as a gentle kiss, protective, consoling, but blazed into something far different as a fire sparked between them.

"My God," he whispered, "Tamsen!"

Her arms went up to him, drawing him down again. They came together with a passion that engulfed them both.

Tamsen woke in the gray light of morning, turning

her face toward the one on the other pillow, wanting to make certain that last night was not a dream. Throughout the dark hours, they had come together often, first in passion, then in tenderness. She put out a finger to trace the lines of his mouth as he slept. Why had she never seen it as it was, gentle, sweet—?

A knock sounded at the door and Tamsen sat upright. Birdie Faraday! She had forgotten her! Birdie had ushered Dan Tallant in, last night, but not out! Perhaps she thought he had left on his own.

"Yes, Birdie?" Her voice had a tremor in it.

"Thought maybe I ought to call you. About time for the steamer to be coming in. Em and Master Donald will be home soon."

Tamsen drew in her breath. "I—I'm dressing," she said. "I'll be down in a few minutes."

"You feel all right? Sure you don't need some help?"

"I'm fine. Perhaps you'd fix me a bite of breakfast. I'll eat with you, in the kitchen." That should work. While Birdie prepared breakfast, she would ask Dan to slip out the front way.

"Tell her not to hurry," the man beside her whispered, lazily. "Come here."

But Tamsen was out of bed and slipping into a robe. "I want to see to Martha." She fled to the baby's room.

Dan followed, buckling his belt as he entered the nursery. His face, as he bent over the sleeping child, was warm with love and awe. "She is beautiful, isn't she?" His hand went to touch the chubby fingers.

This charade could not go on.

"Dan, you must leave. Try to slip out without Birdie seeing you. I'll see you at the Parlor, later. I'm moving over there today."

His head jerked up. "I don't understand."

"This is Em's home. I don't belong here. The baby—"

"The baby's not going to live in a brothel!" His eyes were like flint. "Not my kid! Not even if I have to marry you."

370

Have to marry her? Then those sweet words of love in the night had all been lies?

The look on her face brought Dan up short. "I put that badly," he admitted. "It is inconvenient for me to get married at this time, but——"

"You don't *have* to marry me," Tamsen said. "I'm not in the habit of marrying every man I spend the night with! You've forgotten my profession."

"Tamsen, I don't give a damn about your past! It's the future that concerns me! Look at what happened yesterday!"

She scowled at him. "You're blaming me?"

"I'm blaming the kind of life you lead, the things you get yourself mixed up in. You've brought nothing but trouble to your whole family!"

Martha whimpered and Tamsen gave Dan a withering look. "You're shouting!"

"I'm not doing any damn such thing! It's you!" But he drew her away from the nursery and back into the bedroom.

"Now, let's talk this over, calmly and rationally. I am going to try to make some living arrangements for you two. I'll be back in a couple of hours." He started toward the door and her voice stopped him.

"Dan! Martha isn't going with me. Senator Alden is starting adoption proceedings on his return."

He stopped, looking at her with an incredulity that changed to anger. "What kind of a woman are you? You'd give your baby away?"

"She's not mine to give. She's Em's."

His face was almost comical. "You mean—she's not mine? I—didn't—?"

"You *didn't*."

"I don't understand," he said, confused. "You said she was yours—ours——"

"I said nothing," Tamsen informed him. "It was *you* who said it."

"My God," he whispered, understanding dawning at last in his eyes. "You! You liar! You cheating little

371

tramp! I ought to wring your neck! You used that money—!"

She backed before the loathing in his face. "I needed it for the baby," she said, defensively.

"You needed it for your fancy whorehouse! For your fine house on Nob Hill! You even lie to yourself, don't you!"

"You'll get your money back," she flung at him.

"Money!" He was furious. "I don't want the damn money! It's a small enough price to pay for a lesson! I hate to think what a fool you made of me. A damn stupid fool! Here, I've been acting like a loving father, and you've been laughing up your sleeve! Now I know enough to stick to the *honest* ones, like Katie!"

"Then go to Katie," she shrieked, "and leave me alone! You—you!"

The anger hardened in his face. "I will," he said shortly. "At least, with Katie, I know where I stand!" He started toward the door.

"Dan, wait!"

He turned to face her furious gaze. "I meant it, Dan, about the money, I mean. It's in the safe at the parlor. If you'll come by tonight, I'll see that you get it. Then I don't want to see you there again. Is that clear?"

"I don't want your damned money! And you can't keep me away. Not as long as I obey your rules. It's a place of business, isn't it? Or—are you just trying to keep me away from Katie?"

Leaving Tamsen sputtering with anger, Dan went out, slamming the door behind him.

He was almost blind with fury. Tamsen had made a fool of him. And he'd made a fool of himself. If it weren't for his mission here, he would leave San Francisco. Then he would never have to see that girl again.

But he had to go back to the Parlor. It was part of his job. He and Katie were on to something. He had established an identity as a speculator in mining supplies—buying up equipment from an outfit that had gone broke, selling to someone who needed those items —at the Parlor. The place attracted some of the people he wished to keep under surveillance, and he'd passed the word that he would always be available there. It would not do to let Tamsen drive him away.

Damn her, he thought, viciously. Damn her! But he could not drive the memory of the night away from his mind, the way her small body had felt curled close to his, the thoughts he'd had of the future.

He fueled his anger by thinking of little Martha. He'd come to love the baby, thinking of her as his own. Now, he must think of the little girl as Em's— Em's and Alden's.

He tasted salt upon his lips and brushed at his wet cheek. Damn it, he'd gotten something in his eye.

After his departure, Tamsen forced herself to dress. She ached all over. Yesterday's bruises had not been helped by the night with Dan. She hated him, she thought, as she went to the nursery. Hated him!

She woke the baby and dressed her in a pretty gown for Em's homecoming. As she did so, she thought about the night before and how, for a brief while, she had dared to hope that she, too, might have a life like Em's.

She suppressed a harsh laugh at how she'd deluded herself into thinking her feelings for Dan were love. It certainly took on a different aspect in the light of morning.

Love was something she didn't need. All women were brought up, as she had been, to believe that marriage was the final goal. They settled into dull and unexciting lives. And where did their husbands go? To Madam Franklin's Parlor, that's where! How many other women had businesses that paid as well as hers? How utterly stupid to settle for the sometime attentions of one man when one could have the adoration of many. Tamsen forced a smile that hurt her bruised face. Then she scurried about, picking up the few articles of her own that still remained. Most of them had already been sent to the Parlor.

The room cleared of her belongings, Tamsen went back to Martha's room. She hovered over her crib in an

373

agony of love and longing, not wanting to say goodbye.

Then she heard someone come in the door down-stairs, and Em and Donald Alden were home.

Tamsen started down the stairs, pausing as she heard Em's happy voice, Alden's answering rumble, and then Birdie Faraday.

"Tamsen's fine," Birdie was saying, "except she got hurt. It was that horse she insisted on buying. I told her he was a wild one! Could tell by the way he rolled his eye. But, no, she wouldn't listen to me!"

Dear Birdie, Tamsen thought, she was going to miss her, too.

Holding the rail for support, Tamsen went down the stairs.

Chapter 21

Em had enjoyed the last leg of her honeymoon. As
the steamer headed down the quiet river with its towering trees and tule jungle, she kept saying to herself, "I'm
going home." The sun had shone on them during the
earlier part of the journey, and she spent most of the
time on deck, clinging to her husband's arm. He was
very much a man, she thought, looking up at him. The
thought brought a pink tint to her cheeks.

Such a sweet and gentle lady, Donald thought. Yet,
in the act of love, her enthusiasm had equalled his own.
He was both surprised and elated at her ardor. It was a
good thing he trusted and believed in her—knowing
what he now knew about her sister.

As the steamer neared San Francisco, Em's eager-
ness to arrive was dampened. It would mean the end
of something for her, the end of a time when she had
Donald to herself, when she was the most important
thing in the world in his eyes. Now he would have to
return to his responsibilities, she to hers. Things would
not change between them as far as their love was concerned, but life would be different.

The fog that enveloped them as they reached their
destination was not unpleasant. It seemed to wrap
around the two of them like a warm blanket, insulating
them from everyone else.

Henry Sloan's voice broke in on their reverie. The
boat was anchored and the plank put out for landing.
If they would wait here, he would return with a carriage,
he told them.

"I don't like that man," Em whispered when he had

gone. "He's always so disapproving. He makes me feel uncomfortable."

"I know what you mean," Alden acknowledged. "But having him along freed me from a lot of business."

"And I'm glad. But he's so—so prissy. He acts as if we're living in sin!"

The Senator whooped with delight at his bride's remark. "Well, poor fellow, I imagine being along on our honeymoon made him miserable. Don't you think?"

"I suppose so," Em admitted. They had been unable to conceal the way they felt about each other from any of the passengers.

Henry Sloan returned with the carriage and seemed happy to learn that Senator Alden planned to drive on home with Em and that he was dismissed for the day. Sloan disappeared into the fog, but not from Em's thoughts.

"Another thing about that man," she said, frowning a little. "He acted so strangely when I mentioned Tamsen. Donald—you didn't—you wouldn't mention anything about Magoffinville to him—the cantina—"

"Em! You know better than that!" He sounded angry.

"I'm sorry. I do know better, Donald. I was just wondering why—?"

"You're not supposed to think about anything but me," Alden teased. "Sloan's just my aide. He's most unimportant in our lives. If you want me to, I'll get rid of him. But I'm not going to have you thinking about him. I'm the jealous type."

Em laughed and leaned her head against his shoulder. As if anyone could be jealous of Henry Sloan!

The carriage turned up the hill, and Em's heart began to beat a little faster. Stopping before the house, Alden lifted his bride from the carriage and carried her up the steps. Before he could knock at the door, Mrs. Faraday opened it. He set the laughing Em on her feet.

"Hello, Birdie," he said, "how are you?"

"And Martha and Tamsen," Em added, breathlessly.

"We're all just fine, me and Martha. Tamsen's fine,

376

except she got hurt. It was a horse she was thinking on buying—"

The rest of her words were lost on Em as she looked up the stairs to see Tamsen standing there. "Oh, no," she gasped. "Oh, Tamsen! Your poor face!" She ran up the stairs to clasp her sister in her arms.

Birdie was still telling her story to Donald Alden. "It was awful," she gasped, "seeing her dragged down the road like that. My, I almost had an attack—"

The senator's cool blue eyes met Tamsen's over the woman's head, and she could tell that he did not believe a word of what Mrs. Faraday was saying. He knew! Henry Sloan had told him of her establishment, just as she'd known he would.

When Tamsen told Em that she had moved her things to the hotel and, in fact, was on the point of departure, herself, Em was shattered. "At least stay a few more days, until you're all well," she begged.

But Tamsen was adamant. Tearfully, Em watched her sister go. Then it dawned on her that her husband had not added his pleas to hers. "Donald," she said, bewildered, "why didn't you stop her? She's in no condition—"

"We have to live our own lives," he said softly. "Your place is here with me. And Tamsen had chosen her own. Don't you think she has that right?"

"I suppose so." But her answer was hesitant. He gathered her into his arms, wondering what she'd think if she knew that her sister ran one of the most famous houses in San Francisco—and, worse, that she had tried to seduce poor Henry Sloan.

As he and Em began taking their baggage up to their bedroom, Alden continued to think about Henry Sloan. Henry was going to be a problem. He had been very upset at the Senator's reaction to the gossip about Tamsen. He had obviously expected Alden to explode with righteous anger.

Sloan had even muttered something about the seriousness of the situation in regard to the Senator's office and promised to "take care of everything."

377

Alden told him in a few well-chosen words that it was a family affair and none of his business. Nevertheless, he didn't trust Sloan to let matters rest.

The Senator was right in his assumption that Henry had no intention of staying out of the Tamsen affair. In fact, Sloan went to Madam Franklin's Parlor that very evening and asked to see Tamsen.

Tamsen was sitting in the third-floor apartment that she had converted for her use—and hating every minute of it. Until her bruised face healed, she had to remain upstairs, hidden away like a wounded animal. Tamsen longed to go downstairs, to sing, to receive the adulation of the men below. But now, even that was denied her.

So when Nell knocked at the door and asked if she was decent, Tamsen was almost relieved to have any interruption to her boredom and misery.

"Feller downstairs wants to see you. Won't take no fer an answer."

"George Hecker? The man who wants to close us down?" Tamsen was shaken. She had not given the problem enough thought.

"Nope. That stiff-necked fancy-pants that brought them Washington fellers in. Got the hell skeert outten him ever' time one of the girls got close—"

Henry Sloan.

Tamsen had an overpowering sense of foreboding. "Send him up," she sighed.

Henry Sloan was shown in. He looked shocked to see Tamsen's battered features, but tried not to stare. At first, he left the door open a crack, then straightening his shoulders, he closed it with an effort. What he had to say was for Tamsen's ears alone.

"Forgive me for intruding," he said. "I trust you are not busy." The implications of what he'd said turned his ears red. "I mean, I—"

"I'm not busy," Tamsen cut in. "Now what exactly did you want?"

"This is not easy to say." He fiddled with his hat. "So I'll try to make it as brief as possible. You are very fond of your sister, I am sure." He waited for her nod.

378

"And of your brother-in-law, of course." Again a pause. "There is also the child. I'm certain your feelings toward her—"

"Oh, stop it!" Tamsen exploded. "For heaven's sake! State your business!"

He cleared his throat. "Senator Alden is an important man. Your establishment here—forgive me—is a notorious one. Your presence at the wedding reception was—shall we say, ill-advised, most embarrassing. Your choice of profession is most unfortunate for the Senator's reputation. It would be well to avoid association with the Senator and his lady—"

"In other words, I am not to see them again. Is that what you're saying?" Tamsen's eyes were sparked with fury. He backed before her anger.

"I'm only requesting that you use discretion," he said, sounding a little hurt.

"Who sent you here? Senator Alden? Em?"

"Please," he said, "let's not dwell on personalities. Let's say I'm trying to speak for all concerned."

He reached behind him, scrabbling for the doorknob hoping to make a hurried exit. Fists clenched, Tamsen followed him into the hall. But the hall was not empty. Dan Tallant and Katie Ryan were just coming out of a room. Tamsen stopped short at the sight of them.

Then, with a flash of impulse, she flung her arms about the startled Sloan's neck, pressing her mouth against his. He reeled in shock, putting his arms around her as he strove for balance.

"It was wonderful, Henry," she breathed, just loud enough for it to carry. "And to think, you chose *me*, for your very first time. Please come again—often."

Then she stepped back into her room, closing the door against him. She began to laugh, but her laughter was soon mingled with tears.

An hour later, she stood, stony-eyed, at the window. Below, she could see a throng of gentlemen entering. This was her business, and from now on, it would be her life. Tomorrow, she would hold a meeting with Nell and the girls to clear up any problems. Monday,

379

she would see to the hiring of new girls. At least five, she thought. The new cook would begin on Monday, releasing Maggie. Coldly, she juggled costs and income figures in her mind.

And there was something else. There was a new agency in town that claimed to do detective work. She must learn all she could, and quickly, about a man named George Hecker.

Chapter 22

On Monday, Tamsen, heavily veiled to hide her bruised face, set out to tend to her business dealings. She acquired two more girls from the Bella Union, incurring the wrath of its beautiful roulette croupier, the famous Madame Simone Jules. One of the girls was French and had been especially imported by Madame Jules. The other was Hawaiian.

Tamsen found a waif from Sydneytown, an Australian girl who had been deserted by her former lover. An English girl, who had been employed in a house in Portsmouth Square, was her next choice. Tamsen made her last call at Madame Ah Toy's, buying up the contract of an impish girl called Mei.

Mei was not too well-favored, her almond eyes being slightly crossed, but she was a born courtesan. In addition, she spoke fairly comprehensible English and would be able to translate for Ming Yee.

Tamsen's last chore of the day was a call to the office of Mr. Samuel Bunch. It was a hole in the wall with one battered desk on a dusty plank floor, and boxes of paper set about, and Mr. Bunch was a rat-faced little man, but he appeared to have a thriving business.

"I'd like to learn all there is to know about a local gentleman," she said. "Your research must be discreet, and without his knowledge. And I need the information soon."

The man hedged, insisting in a high, whiny voice that his agency handled missing person cases for the most part. Rich folks back East looking for runaway sons were willing to pay well.

The price Tamsen named brought him to the edge of the chair. Tentatively, he tried to raise it.

"That's my limit," she said, flatly. He would do what she required. She had seen it in his eyes.

She returned to her establishment exhausted, every muscle in her body trembling with fatigue. Removing her hat and veil, she studied her bruised features. The scratches were healing. In just a few more days, she'd be able to camouflage them with powder and paint. Now, she would rest.

Before Tamsen could lie down, Nell appeared at the door, her jowls trembling with irritation.

"Yuh gotta minute?"

Without waiting, she entered and sat on the bed, which sagged visibly beneath her weight. "We got us some problems."

Pushing her hair back with a weary hand, Tamsen listened as the woman's complaints flowed on. If she knew Nell, she would save the worst for last.

The problems were minor ones. The new girls were having to bunk in the attic until it could be partitioned off into private rooms. They didn't like it one bit. Katie, Carmen, Maggie, Belinda, and Sue were lording it over the newcomers. That Frenchie she got off Madame Jules was shook up some at being lumped in with a prostitute from Sydneytown.

"What about the new Chinese girl?"

"Hell, I don't know. Her 'n' that Ming Yee been jabbering away in Chink talk. Prob'ly figgerin' on knifin' me in th' back, fer all I know," Nell said gloomily.

Tamsen smiled. "Tell them all you're their new boss, that I gave you a free hand. You can handle them."

Nell scowled. "You betcher boots, I can. Now, there's somethin' else wrong—"

Here it comes, Tamsen thought.

"It's that there new cook I hired," Nell squinted. "Think we got us a bucket of worms."

"Can't she cook?"

"Hell, yes. That's where she had me fooled. But she's

382

the gawdamndest, meanest, cantankerous old bitch I ever did see. Told me t' git my butt out of the kitchen, first off. Said I wasn't th' boss around here, and she wasn't goin' t' take no orders from me. Thought she was goin' t' crown me with a skillet. So," Nell said, virtuously, "not wantin' to make any trouble, I vamoosed."

"I'll talk to her. If she can cook, we don't want to lose her. And maybe I'll sample her cooking while I'm at it. It has to be better than Maggie's."

"Well, watch out fer flyin' frypans when you walk in th' door," Nell growled.

As Tamsen walked down the stairway, she viewed her establishment with pride. It was early in the evening, too early for the trade. But the candles glimmering in the chandeliers reflected in the mirrored ceiling. The crystal prisms sparkled, sending shimmers of color against the silken walls.

It's mine, she thought, I created this setting. It was a lucrative business and growing more so. It was her life. She needed nothing else to feel complete.

The hollow feeling she'd had in her middle since leaving Em's was hunger. And that, she was about to satisfy.

She walked through the game room, touching the shining tables with approval, through the dining room, and into the kitchen at the back. There, she stopped dead. For the small figure that stood before the black iron stove, stirring something in a pot, was most familiar. As the ladle moved to one side of the kettle, the cook said, "Damn!" She stirred to the other side. "Hell!"

"Birdie!"

Birdie Faraday turned to face Tamsen. Her wiry white curls stood up in little corkscrews. Her cheeks were pink, her blue eyes shining with happiness.

"I was practicing cussing," she smiled.

Tamsen drew in a ragged breath. "What are you doing here?"

"Cooking," Birdie said, then after judicious thought, "and cussing."

"You followed me, didn't you?" Tamsen accused. "After I told you I wouldn't employ you. Birdie, this isn't a hotel! Do you know what this business is?"

"Sure do." She returned to her stirring.

"Birdie," Tamsen said, helplessly, "please believe me! You don't belong here. I'll find you another place—"

Mrs. Faraday dropped the spoon and turned, hands on hips. "Young lady, you're not going to tell me what I can or can't do! My daddy was a Baptist preacher. Watched me all the time, as if I was bound for hell! Found out for sure I was when I married myself a Methodist. Next, *he* thought I was goin' to hell because I was baptized Baptist. I figure since I'm goin' to hell anyway, I might as well have some fun while I'm a-gettin' there! So butt out!"

"I could fire you, Birdie."

The blue eyes that turned on Tamsen were defensive, a little watery with unshed tears. "You wouldn't do that, Miss Tamsen. Think on it for a minute. Up until I was fifteen, my daddy watched over me. Then I had a husband to boss me around. After that, I took care of the Aldens. The old lady was ten years sick abed. You might say I wasn't living!"

"But Birdie—"

"Oh, I know I don't belong here. But I've got a bump of curiosity about things. And I'm too old for any shenanigans. I wouldn't make any problems. Just as long as that foul-mouthed fat woman stays out of my kitchen!"

Tamsen smiled. "You can stay, Birdie." The woman was a jewel in the kitchen. Besides, Tamsen thought, I'm too tired to argue.

Birdie Faraday wrung her hands, swallowing back her tears. She had won! "Thank you," she said, with dignity. "Now, if you'll sit down, there's some pie."

Tamsen sat, and soon a piece of delectable dessert was placed before her, with a steaming cup of coffee. Mrs. Faraday was a welcome addition to the establishment, for sure.

"And I like the people here," the woman prattled on, "except for that one, of course. There's one man, a very nice English gentleman. I gave him a piece of that pie, earlier, and it's his favorite." She blushed pink.

Tamsen stopped, fork halfway to her mouth. English gentleman? Dusty? So Birdie Faraday was too old for shenanigans, was she! Now Tamsen knew the reason for the mutual dislike between Birdie and Nell.

When Tamsen returned to her room, she found Ming Yee and the new girl, Mei, waiting for her. Ming Yee's eyes were dancing with happiness as she pointed to her newfound friend, then to Tamsen.

The charming Mei, with her intriguing eyes, was smiling, too. "Ming Yee say you save her life. Much thank you. She love you."

Tamsen was overwhelmed at the girl's devotion. They exchanged polite words through their interpreter, and the girls turned to go. Ming Yee paused and, putting her hand on Mei's arm, added something.

"She sorrow that you are sad," Mei repeated. "She know your heart."

Then they were gone.

I'm not sad, Tamsen thought, angrily. I'm happier than I've ever been in my life! Now that I've come to terms with what I am! But she knew it wasn't true. It would be easier when she could go downstairs to entertain the clientele once more. Being cooped up in this room was destroying her.

Later that night, Nell puffed up the stairs again and entered, panting and grinning. "Got yerself some comp'ny," she panted. "Real ring-tailed doozie! Showed up without his coat 'n' tic, they wouldn't let him in, so he whupped hell outta th' feller on th' door. I got there jest in time t' save his gawdamn hide! Look who's here, wouldja?"

"Mike!" Tamsen came forward to meet the burly, bearded man, her hands outstretched. "Mike Dunnevant! You look wonderful."

Nell snickered, indicating the flannel shirt, the faded trousers, the dirty boots. "So wunnerful, I had to sneak him up th' back stairs," she said, happily. "He's gotta shiner too. You two match up purty good. Well, guess you two wanna gab. I'll go down an' pick up th' pieces."

When the door had closed behind her, Tamsen asked, "Mike, where have you been? You didn't come back before winter, and we were worried—"

"Struck it rich," he said, proudly. "Had to sit on it. Damn near starved and almost froze. But it was worth it." He frowned. "Been lookin' all over for you folks. Met Tallant and he said you were here. He didn't tell me what kind of place it was." His face reddened. "Didn't think to find you running a who—a *house*."

Something twisted inside Tamsen. Mike Dunnevant knew nothing of her cantina days. He knew only the girl he'd met on the trail and the widow Harper who sewed for a living.

"It—it's a money-making business," she said, feebly.

"Yeah." He didn't meet her eyes. "I guess it is." Then, with an attempt at light-heartedness, he said, "Where's your sister? And the kid?"

"Em's married. To a Senator Alden. They—they've adopted the baby."

His eyes asked what kind of a mother she was, to give up her child and take up an occupation like this, but he didn't put it into words.

"Figgered I'd make a pile and think about a family of my own." He grinned. "Damn near killed me, but I done it. That's why I'm in town. Gonna find that Katie girl and pop the question!"

He didn't know about Katie, either. She had only been a girl who worked at dressmaking. "Oh, Mike!"

"Something wrong?" His eyes were frightened. "Katie isn't married, is she? Or sick?"

Tamsen shook her head.

"Then do you know where I can find her?" Again, she shook her head. He mustn't find Katie here. She would talk to the girl, tell her that Mike had struck it rich, that he wanted to marry her. Then Katie could make up her own mind about him. She didn't think she'd be interested despite his wealth. Katie was dividing her attention between two men these days, Dan Tallant and Adam Wheeler. Right now, young Adam Wheeler seemed to have the edge.

From Mike Dunnevant's reaction at finding her here, Tamsen wasn't sure what he would do if he learned of Katie's true profession.

"I don't know where she is at the moment," she said. Mike's shoulders drooped.

"I'll keep on looking," he said, with a forced grin. "Guess I'd better get on with it."

Tamsen went with him to the door. "It was good to see you, Mike."

"You, too. Well—" His eyes widened. They were not alone in the hall. Katie and Adam Wheeler were coming up the stairs. His arm was about her waist, and they were both laughing.

"Katie!" The name burst from the big man's lips. For an instant, Katie looked stricken, then she tossed her head, defiantly.

"Hello, Mike. How are you? Wish I could stop to talk—but I have a customer."

Tamsen watched Mike Dunnevant crumple. For the first time, he seemed too small for his clothing. He turned dazed eyes to hers as Katie and Adam entered a room, and closed the door behind them.

"What's happened, Tamsen?" he asked in a halting, almost pleading tone. "Hell, you've all changed! I thought Katie—"

"You thought wrong. Come on in, Mike. I want to explain."

He stood tall once more, but his blue gaze was somber. "Not tonight," he said. "I think I've had about all I can take. Maybe tomorrow things will make more sense."

But Mike Dunnevant did not return on the morrow. He walked the streets of San Francisco where everything he saw increased his feeling that things had changed. The people, the city. Men in fine suits shouldered by him on the streets, buildings were going up, shop windows displayed an array of unfamiliar items.

387

One summer and winter he'd been gone. And everything had gone plumb to hell! He shook his shaggy head in bewilderment as he recalled the events of the night before. Tamsen McLeod—no, the Widow Harper —had turned into a madam. Madam Franklin, she called herself. And Katie! The dreams he had dreamed on the long winter nights on his claim died a hard, slow, agonizing death.

And Tamsen had given her little girl away. Maybe she had been right, he thought, miserably, what with Em married and respectable. A Senator's wife, too. Alden? That was the name.

A few well-placed questions, and Mike Dunnevant was directed to the Senator's home. Donald Alden was just leaving as his wife answered the door and he watched her greet a huge whiskery man with a cry of joy.

Alden stood astounded until Em disentangled herself from the stranger's bear-hug. Then she turned to him, her eyes sparkling.

"Donald, it's Mike! Mike Dunnevant! Remember, I told you about him! And Mike—my husband, Donald." She stressed the word husband with love and pride.

Alden put his portfolio down and gripped the man's hand. "Glad to meet you, Mr. Dunnevant. Are you going to be with us awhile?"

Mike's eyes darkened. Good heavens, the Senator thought, he looks like he might be going to cry! But the newcomer said, "I—I don't reckon so. I just needed to have a talk with—with your wife."

Em, too, had caught a hint of something wrong. She stood on tiptoe to kiss her husband's cheek. "Go on," she said, "or you'll be late for that appointment. I'll see you tonight."

When he had gone, she looked helplessly at Mike, who stood twisting his battered hat in his hands. Should she take him into the parlor? No, he would be uncomfortable there. "Let's go into the kitchen," she said, "and sit at the table. How about some coffee and cake?"

Sitting at the small kitchen table, Mike watched Em

as she bustled about, setting out refreshment. She looked so bright and happy, he thought. He guessed married life must agree with her.

Turning to find his gaze fixed on her, Em blushed, and Mike apologized. "Didn't mean to stare atcha. Hell, it's just good to find somebody that ain't changed around here."

"But I have changed," Em said candidly. "I'm happier than I've ever been in my life. I have my husband, my little girl—"

The kid that Tamsen dumped on her, Mike thought, like a stray cat. But if it made Em happy, it was none of his business. "Yeah," he said.

Em seated herself across from him, leaning forward to look into his morose features. "Mike, what is it? What's wrong?"

Clearing his throat, he told her the story he'd told Tamsen; of how he'd sweated it out on his claim and come back rich—to marry Katie.

"And Katie won't marry you?" Em guessed. "Is that the trouble?"

"Marry me, hell! Don't you know what Katie's doin'?"

"Why, she was—was working for Tamsen, the last I heard."

"Tamsen! Do you go along with what she's doin'?" His eyes held such an expression of dark disgust that Em felt her heart plunge. Tamsen had not come around since she'd moved out. Was it possible she was in some kind of trouble? She would have to go carefully, here.

"I—I'm not sure," she whispered.

"Not sure! Good God! I see Tallant and ask him where the hell all of you are, an' he sends me to this—this house! I have to fight my way inta th' joint, and Nell says, 'Oh, you want to see Madam Franklin.' Then I find out Tamsen's the madam, an' Katie—" he swallowed hard—"Katie don't have time to talk t' me. Hell, she had herself a customer!" And he smashed his fist down on the table.

Em sat transfixed, her face as white as milk. Donald had pointed out a brothel to her once, on a Sunday

389

drive, and explained what went on in a place like that. But Tamsen! Tamsen owned a small hotel! She worked nights on the desk!

Nights! Madam Franklin! That last name was too horribly familiar. Mike's story had to be true! Other things came to her mind; the way Tamsen had kept the fact that she worked from Donald; Sloan's innuendoes. They knew! But no one had told her.

"Sorry," Mike said, rubbing his hand and forcing a grin. "Never done nothin' like that before. Guess I had to git things off my chest—"

"It's all right, Mike," Em said, mechanically. "It's all right."

They chatted for a while, but both were too upset for a really good talk.

Later when Em saw him to the door, Mike turned and said, "I ain't givin' up without puttin' up a scrap. Say, them clothes yer husband was wearin'—I want to git me some like that. Could you tell me where t' go?"

Em gave him the address of her husband's tailor. She watched him go down the walk, then closed the door and leaned against it. The glass bubble of happiness that had enclosed her since her marriage seemed to shatter around her, falling into shards at her feet.

"Tamsen!" she said. "Dear God! Oh, dear God!"

Chapter 23

Mike Dunnevant left the Alden home on the hill and went directly to the Senator's tailor. The small Chinese man measured the big man's shoulders, shaking his head. This was something beyond his experience. It would take a while.

"Four day," he said, shrilly, holding up as many fingers. "Four day."

Mike Dunnevant picked up the suit on Saturday and made his next stop the barber's. Leaving there an out-sized, but most distinguished-looking gentleman, Mike made his way to Madam Franklin's Parlor. Entering unquestioned, he proceeded to become roaring drunk.

Tamsen had instructed everyone that the utmost decorum be maintained should they be paid a surprise visit by George Hecker and his citizens' committee so Nell went immediately for Tamsen when the stranger started carrying on.

"Big feller," she said, "dressed to the teeth. Throwin' gold around like it was water, tryin' t' pick a fight. Figgered I'd better get you."

Tamsen went down, reluctantly. This was to be the night of her return to the floor. She was dressed in a new and elegant gown, her makeup skillfully applied so that her bruises were almost invisible. She had planned to make an entrance, but this was an emergency.

She did not recognize the face, nor the clothing, but the voice was unmistakable, raised as it was in a bull-roar.

"Mike," she said, running toward him, snatching at his arm. "Mike!"

He threw her off, blindly, and turned back to the man he was threatening with a truculent air. Tamsen took his arm again and signaled to the men at the door. She hated doing it, but he had to be forcibly ejected. Suddenly, she felt him stiffen, as he turned his head to look toward the stairs.

Down those stairs glided Ming Yee, in her cheongsam of gold.

Straight toward Mike Dunnevant she came and touched his arm with her small golden hand. Mesmerized, he allowed her to lead him to a table, meek as a lamb.

"Well, I'll be damned," Nell said in Tamsen's ear.

"Me, too," said Tamsen, weakly. She had not seen that beatific expression on Mike Dunnevant's face since the day she hit him with a rock!

An hour or so later, Nell hurried to tell Tamsen that George Hecker had just come in. "Didn't ask to see you," Nell whispered, "so I reckon he figgers to see what the hell's goin' on, first."

Tamsen found a vantage point from which she could observe the gentleman who planned to close down her establishment. A stocky, balding man, middle-aged, with frizzy sideburns and a blue chin, he was staring lasciviously at Sue's ankles.

Tamsen smiled, thinking of the dossier she had in her office. Hecker was a minor merchant, his business subsidized by an Eastern wife who had just come out on a ship this year. Prior to her coming, he had been a notorious womanizer, but his wife's civilizing influence had turned him into a very moral man, a chairman of committees.

Her eyes, sweeping the room, approved of what they saw: a group of gentlemen enjoying themselves, their conversation quiet and refined. The girls that walked among them appeared only to be serving drinks.

Moving gracefully through the crowd, speaking to several men as she passed by, Tamsen approached the reformer.

"Mr. Hecker?" she asked, demurely. "I thought I

recognized you. You are quite well known, you know. I am Mrs. Franklin."

The man's mouth opened and closed, like that of a fish. Then he bowed with heavy gallantry. "I'm so glad to meet you. I've been wanting to talk with you—"

"It will have to wait," Tamsen smiled. "I'm so sorry, but it's time for me to sing."

She sang the song of the boy who had left home and gone wrong, whose mother died before he could seek forgiveness. A ballad of heartbreak, of loneliness. Above reproach.

Tamsen returned to George Hecker when she finished and suggested they talk in the dining room. They were served coffee and homemade cake by Birdie Faraday, a grandmotherly figure in black with a starched apron and a brooch at her collar of lace.

"Watch out for the coffee," she said, smiling, placing it before them. "It's fresh made—and very hot."

George Hecker was too enthralled to hear Birdie's words. The fact of being in the company of such a beautiful creature as Tamsen had driven all other thoughts from his head.

"You wanted to speak to me," Tamsen prompted him. "On business?"

Avoiding her eyes, red-faced, he launched into a prepared speech on the evils such places as her establishment presented to the public at large. He felt it only fair to inform her he must make a report, and that his committee planned to close such places.

"And what will your report say? Have you seen any signs of misbehavior? Or rowdiness? Did you not find the entertainment most dignified?"

"Oh, yes," he hastened to say. "Indeed. But the gambling. And what goes on upstairs."

"Gambling is not illegal. And what does go on upstairs?"

He knew the girls took men up there, he mumbled. He'd been told.

"Mr. Hecker, the girls who work here live there. I cannot deny them their private lives!"

"Maybe," he said, slyly, "if I could see one of those rooms?"

"Of course! I'll show you mine!" Then she hesitated, as though remembering something. "But I cannot. I fear I may have left personal belongings strewn about. Garments not for the—the eyes of a gentleman. Perhaps, if you'd come on Monday? Then I could be prepared—"

George Hecker was most happy to accept her invitation.

As soon as he left, Tamsen had a private talk with Nell and Dusty. "This," she said, "is what we're going to do." She outlined her plan. It would work. It had to.

On Monday night, Mike Dunnevant arrived at the Parlor, stone sober. He remained that way. And when Ming Yee finished her plaintive lute song, she gravitated to him immediately. Katie, who was on her way upstairs with Dan Tallant, made a careful appraisal of the new Mr. Dunnevant. Flirting with Mike at the dressmaking establishment had been a game with her. She hadn't realized he was such a good-looking man.

Once in the room with Tallant, she allowed her irritation free rein. "What is it with you, Dan? I'm getting sick of being used! You don't even look at me any more! What if I just stop now, keep my mouth shut—"

"You made a bargain, Katie. You're well paid."

"I thought there would be more than money," she said, sulkily.

"Ah, Katie!" He held out his arms to her, and she pushed him away.

"I don't want charity," she said, stiffly. "There are other men."

But when he had gone, she knew she lied. There was only one Dan Tallant in the world—

Tamsen, meanwhile, was setting out the props for the evening ahead. She did not intend to go downstairs until after George Hecker arrived and had been dealt with. In a delicate flowing robe of a semi-sheer material, she moved about the room, draping lacy undergarments where they would show to the best advantage. Nell had been given instructions, too.

394

George Hecker arrived and walked around the Parlor peering into the corners of the larger room, hoping to catch a sight of Madam Franklin. He fingered his new tie, bought especially for this occasion. It had a fine, red silken stripe. Elsie had no taste in men's ties, he told himself, thinking of the conservative colors he'd been forced to wear since her arrival. A man should look his best when he had a difficult task at hand.

There, the fat woman was approaching. He certainly hoped there was no delay, that Madam Franklin was not absent again.

"Lookin' fer somebody?" Nell asked.

He cleared his throat. "Madam Franklin, if you please."

"Upstairs. Third floor. First door to yer left. Jes' go on in."

Well, he thought to himself, a stirring in him. Perhaps he had made more of an impression on the lady than he'd thought. It would do her no good, of course. He must file his report. But surely this could be handled in a friendly fashion. Though his mind was intent on business, his body seemed to be pursuing its own course as he went up the stairs.

He paused for an instant, hand raised to knock, then thought better of it. The fat woman did say to go in. As he opened the door, the wave of emotion that struck him shut off his throat in the region of the red-striped tie. He could not manage a word of apology.

The girl who stood before him, clad in a diaphanous gown, had turned to look at him with startled eyes. Her long black hair swung to her waist like a wild horse's mane.

"Mister Hecker!" she said in a tone of horror, holding a very intimate garment before her, as if for concealment. "I didn't—Oh, dear! I didn't realize it was so *late*. I was just dressing!"

He mumbled something to the effect that he had been told to just walk in.

"My fault," she said. "I did leave that message downstairs. I've been looking forward so to—well, since you're already in—Please sit down. No, that chair's not too comfortable. If you don't mind the bed—"

George Hecker didn't. He sat down on the velvet, rumpled spread, his hat in his hands, oblivious to all but the gorgeous creature who swooped around, thrusting frilled items of personal clothing out of sight. "What you must think of me," she said. The scene was straight out of his adolescent dreams.

Tamsen clapped her hands to her cheeks. "And here I am," she whispered, "dressed like this! And I didn't even lower the shade!" She moved to the window to pull down the offending blind, then turned to face him.

Across the street, a dark figure observed her action, and moved silently toward the entrance of the house.

"Wouldn't you like a drink?" Tamsen asked the purple-faced man.

"I—I don't—" but it was too late. She had poured a large amount of whiskey into a glass. A few minutes later, a sound in the hall turned his face toward the door. He realized he was in an incriminating position for a family man, a member of the citizens' committee. He tried to get up just as Tamsen came toward him. She tripped, falling against him, spilling the contents of his glass over him as they sprawled together across the rumpled bed.

At the sound, the door flew open. A small man stood there. From hat to boots, he was dressed in conservatively cut gray. His blue eyes looked world-weary, blasé, and the mouth beneath his small mustache was drawn down in disapproval.

"Well, sir, I've caught you out. This lady here," he indicated Nell, behind him, "will serve as witness."

"Witness? What do you mean? This is blackmail!" George Hecker, whisky-scented, came boiling up from his prone position.

The small man's nose lifted. He sniffed. "Blackmail, sir? I represent a reputable agency. The Bunch Detective Agency. My credentials." He flashed a paper and put it into his pocket. "I have been employed by a Mrs. Elsie Hecker—"

"Elsie? Good God!" George Hecker sank back, his hands over his eyes.

"Now, wait a minute!" Tamsen stormed. "You have no right to break into my room! The evidence is misleading. This gentleman and I were having a conversation—"

"I have an obligation to my client."

"And you have an obligation to do the honest thing," Tamsen said. "Something like this could ruin the reputation of my business."

The man in gray grinned, slyly. "How much is your reputation worth to you? I just might change clients."

George Hecker listened as the woman bargained, desperately. At last, a sum of twenty thousand dollars was agreed upon. "Get the money out of the safe, Nell," Tamsen said, hands over her eyes. Then she turned on Hecker.

"Look what you've done," she said, furiously. "Get out of here, and don't come back! If you do, I'll send the man to your wife!"

George Hecker was only too glad to go. Once outside, however, he began to suspect that he'd been *had*. No matter, he dared not risk exposure.

Tearing off his whisky-soaked tie—the tie with its fine, red silken stripe—he threw it into the gutter and plodded home.

Upstairs, Tamsen threw her arms about Dusty's neck. "That was beautiful," she laughed. "You did just fine."

"Perhaps I should go into the detecting business," Dusty said. He smiled jauntily into Nell's admiring eyes, and they went downstairs.

When Tamsen finally came down the stairs, pausing for the applause that began when she appeared in her new gown, she was thinking of her checkered career. Farm girl, horse thief, cantina entertainer, dressmaker, madam, and now blackmailer. *Who am I really*, she wondered as she moved into the middle of the floor. Who am I?

Book Three

Castles In Spain

Chapter 1

The sun shone on Spain, a country of contrasts—ugliness and beauty, wealth and poverty—reigned over by a dissolute Queen with an impotent husband and a number of bastard children. Isabella had returned with her court to Madrid, and Lola Montez and her troupe had sailed for California. But Arabella remained with Juan. They lived at his home near Màlaga, and she was unutterably happy.

Arab looked down at her lover as he lay with one arm flung upward, his face soft with sleep. She caressed his amber brownness with loving eyes and marveled at her situation.

How far from Pennsylvania she had come! The room was flooded with sun. From the window, she could see the gardens, a Roman-style pool with white pillars where she and Juan often played like children.

Her eyes moved from the pool to the gardens where they walked, hand in hand; to a maze, filled with statuary, where they had happily lost themselves for a time. The gardens were terraced, their edges following the rocky terrain as it dropped to a beach of white sand framing the blue Mediterranean.

From another window, one would see Màlaga, parted by the Guadalmedina River, the Monte de Gibralfaro crowned by an age-old Morrocan fortress towering above it.

Arabella sighed with happiness. Slipping from bed, she drew on a leaf-green silken robe that enhanced the color of her eyes. Juan woke to a kiss, her cheek against his, and reached up to snatch a handful of sun-bright red-gold curls. "An oread, this morning," he said, lazily, "a mountain nymph!" He would have pulled her to him, but she drew away.

"Up with you, sir! This is a most important day. We have things to do."

Today they would visit Father Díaz, the one person who might aid them in what they wanted most in the world—to become man and wife.

As Arab dressed, a tap at the door announced that Lupe, the maid, was outside with a breakfast tray. The tray contained *churros*, a sort of fritter fried in olive oil; *café con leche*, a heavily sweetened half-milk, half-coffee drink; marmalade and honey, and thinly sliced Spanish oranges, dusted with powdered sugar.

"Thank you," Arabella said, smiling.

Lupe shrugged her shoulders, *"Por nada,"* she said, then, catching herself, "You . . . are . . . well . . . come, Mees."

Arabella beamed at Juan with love in her eyes. Lupe's presence had been another thoughtful gesture on his part. Arab had been a little frightened, felt alien in this country. So Juan had provided two servants with some small command of the English language—Lupe, who had worked for a representative from the United States, and Conchita, who had once cooked for a British Ambassador. Lupe, a little pigeon of a girl, Arab had liked on sight. Conchita, angular and with a harsh face, she wasn't so certain of. In the week they'd been in Màlaga, Arab had gotten the feeling that Conchita was spying on them.

But what was there to spy about? True, she and Juan were lovers, but they had announced their intention to marry. Of course, General Narváez, Juan's uncle, had sent a thundering communiqué when he learned of her presence here. *"Get rid of that woman!"* it had said, among other less-than-complimentary Spanish words referring to Arab's character.

Juan, incensed, had fired back a note stating their intentions to marry. The General had apparently wielded his influence with the Church, and they'd found no priest who would perform the ceremony, until Juan thought of Father Díaz.

Juan set his cup down, taking Arabella's hands in his. How handsome he looked in his white silk shirt, opened at the throat to display his brown chest. He kissed her fingertips and she brushed his cheek with her lips.

"I am not certain that we will meet with success— even with my old friend and teacher, Father Díaz," he said, somberly. "You know that?"

"Yes, I do."

"And if it is not to be, our marriage, it will make a difference?"

"No difference," Arab said, steadily, though she blinked back tears. "As long as we both feel we are husband and wife."

He drew in a ragged breath. "Then we shall seal the bargain, now, in the event we fail to convince my friend." He slid a ring on Arabella's finger, a matching one on his own. Rings of gold, woven into intricate lace, each with an emerald at its heart.

"My mother and father wore these," he said, his dark eyes filled with love, "and my father's parents before them. They have been in my family for a long time. A tradition. As long as we wear them, we will love and be true to one another."

He kissed her tears of happiness away.

They drove to the cathedral in the center of the old city behind a team of glossy black horses. Juan was very nervous. He talked to distract himself, describing the cathedral, begun in 1528 on the site of a mosque. He said the main facade, the interior, and one of the towers were completed in 1782, but that the second tower remained unfinished to this date. Something in his voice, however, made Arab apprehensive. Juan was obviously even more uncertain of the success of this errand than he had let on.

She told herself, looking down at the emerald ring, that it did not matter. With these rings, they *were* wed.

They found Father Díaz in the cathedral garden, his black robes flapping around his ankles as he dug dili-

403

gently at the base of a citrus tree. Juan called his name and the old man turned a wrinkled face with snapping black eyes toward them.

"Juan, my son!"

Then Juan was on his knees before the man, receiving a blessing. Arabella stood back, suddenly shy at the strong emotion that flowed between these two. When Father Díaz looked at her, listening to Juan's introduction, it was as if she were impaled on the sharp point of his hatred. Her heart sank.

Juan's old teacher muttered something in Spanish. Then, turning to Arab, he repeated it in English, "It will not do! It will not do!" Facing Juan again, he continued, "Your uncle will not allow it. You have been groomed for a position in the government of Spain—to counteract the influence of that harlot on the throne! She, who flouts the Church, who has brought hunger upon our people! Put this woman from you, my son!"

"I intend to take her as my wife," Juan said steadily.

"This woman is an entertainer. She has blinded your eyes!"

"I know all there is to know of her," Juan said. "All that is of importance. I am asking you to marry us. If you will not, then I must find someone else who will."

Arabella came out of the shocked state the old man's words had induced. General Narváez, she thought, wryly, had done his work well. But it didn't matter. Not as long as Juan believed in her. The priest's next words *did* matter, however.

"And what of the señorita Guzman? The lady to whom you are promised? Isleta was reared to stand at your side when you head the Cortes!"

Arabella felt faint. She turned a white, bewildered face toward the man she loved. Juan moved to stand beside her.

"When I head the Cortes, if that day comes, Arabella will stand at my side."

"It will not do! Her morals are no better than the Queen's! You will ruin yourself politically!"

"Then I will ruin myself."

"Don't be a fool," Father Díaz hissed fiercely. "You do not count. It is for the people—"

"I have long been of the opinion that it is the people who must free themselves," Juan said, slowly. "A leader cannot give freedom to them. They must change, or it is worth nothing."

"Do not abdicate your responsibilities. Spain needs you. The Church needs you. It would be heresy!"

"Then you refuse my request?" Juan saw his answer in his old teacher's bleak face. "I am sorry. Goodbye." Taking Arabella's arm, he said, "Come, my love."

Arab let him lead her back to the carriage. She felt numb as the conversation with the priest replayed in her head. Señorita Guzman, to whom he'd been promised! And political ruin! What had she done? The warm blue skies of Spain were suddenly alien, the music of street singers discordant on her ear, the man beside her a stranger—

"There are things one must explain," Juan said softly to her. He went on to tell her of a small boy who did not have a boyhood. His upbringing and education trained him for a position of power. Everything in his life had worked toward that end. A bargain had been struck between General Narváez and señor Guzman, one of the General's political allies. Juan and the Guzman daughter, Isleta, would marry. Isleta, too, had been carefully educated for her position. They were to build a new Spain together.

"And I have come along to spoil it all," Arabella said, forlornly. "I can't ruin your life, Juan."

"Ruin it?" He laughed with delight. "For the first time, little sweetheart, I am living. For the first time, I have something of my own! You are my life."

Arabella was silent, twisting the ring he had placed upon her finger. She loved Juan, more than anything else in the world. She loved their fairy-tale existence, too, but she would wear rags and live in a hovel with him if she had to. Passionately, she wished he were poor,

405

that he did not have a career to be weighed in the balance. In Spain, he was an important man—and she was nothing.

Even as she thought it, a ragged little urchin, his black hair sticking out in rebellious wisps, ran alongside the carriage, his round face split in a white grin as he shouted something in Spanish. Juan laughed and tossed him a coin which he caught adroitly before jumping away like a nimble monkey as the carriage rolled past.

"What did he say?" Arab asked, nervously.

"He said I must surely be a prince, since I am in the company of a lovely princess," Juan told her.

The compliment soothed her, gave her hope. She would do her best to live up to the image the boy had seen. Perhaps someday, General Narváez would see that she and Juan belonged together.

When they reached the gleaming marble casa they called home, Arababella went in search of Lupe. She asked, "Do you know anything about a señorita Isleta Guzman? How old she is, what she's like, if she's pretty?"

Little Lupe's face was blank, and she shook her head. But a voice behind Arab answered for her.

"The little Isleta? Ah, yes! She is young, most beautiful, most charming. She has the face of a Madonna, the bearing of royalty—"

Arabella, heart twisting with pain, turned to the speaker. "Thank you, Conchita. I was curious, that's all. I—I heard the name today."

"But I know her well. If you have questions—" There was triumph in the old woman's hooded eyes.

"I have no questions," Arab said. "But thank you." Head high, she turned and went in search of Juan.

Again they wandered in the garden, again they played by the pool, but tonight there seemed an air of transience about their relationship, as if it *were* only a dream. Arabella feared she would wake and find it vanished like the mist. She cherished each moment, fixing it in her memory. And later, as they made love, she savored it as if it might be their last time together.

When Juan finally slept, she lay awake beside him, frightened in a vague way. What was wrong with her? Was it a premonition? Was it all too beautiful to last?

She slept, finally, and dreamed. In her dream, she was not the regal creature she'd become, but a long-limbed child-woman, chained to a wagon frame, one ankle cuffed. And advancing toward her was the Reverend Smythe, his lips spread in an oily grin.

She screamed.

Juan held her to him, soothing, consoling, mingling liquid Spanish and English love words. Arab clung to him, feeling the smoothness of his shoulders, his long hard muscles, wanting to be closer, a part of him.

Hours later, when Juan slept again, drugged by love, Arab was still unable to close her eyes. The fragrance of the gardens wafted through the open window on the Mediterranean wind, while outside, small wind bells chimed. The surf on the beach below surged in and out with a lullaby sound, and the fountains tinkled with falling silver. The moon through the window touched their bodies, gilding them. Juan's was bronze, Arab's white-gold in its light.

Everything in the world was right. Yet, everything was wrong. Arabella's past stood over her, like the presence of Father Díaz. And across her happiness had fallen the shadow of señorita Isleta Guzman, the beautiful Spanish girl promised to Juan.

Chapter 2

Arabella, after her restless night, was still drugged with sleep when she woke in the morning. Instinctively, she moved toward the warmth of Juan's body, expecting his arms to encircle her. But he was not there. When her drowsy mind was able to accept the fact, she sat up, instantly awake. She wondered what had happened. Mornings were their favorite time together.

She looked toward the window. The skies did not smile. A murky atmosphere blotted out the sight of gardens and the sea. She waited, but Juan did not return.

Finally, she pulled the tasseled cord that would summon Lupe. Her brows were drawn into a puzzled frown as she put on her velvet robe. With Juan not at her side, and Lupe late in answering her summons, Arabella had an eerie feeling that she was alone in the house.

When a tap finally sounded at the door, she breathed a sigh of relief. "Lupe? Come in."

But it wasn't Lupe. This time, Conchita carried the tray—a single one, one cup, one plate. Was she to eat alone?

"The master has an early guest," Conchita said, dourly. "A gentleman who has come on business. He did not wish to disturb you. Lupe is serving them. She is *más guapa*—prettier than I."

"I see."

The woman set the tray down and was gone. Arabella suddenly had no appetite. Picking up her cup of *café con leche*, she wandered to the window to sip it. If she and Juan were truly married, she thought, moodily, she would be downstairs beside him, acting as hostess to

408

the visiting gentleman. The words of Father Díaz kept coming home to her. *"Her morals are no better than the Queen's. You will ruin yourself, politically."*

Please God, let him be proven wrong!

Her head felt strange, the seascape from her window seeming to tilt and blur. Arabella rubbed at her eyes. Nerves, she thought, or I am really ill. Perhaps it would be best to lie down until Juan's return.

She set her cup down, nearly missing the tray. Odd that her perspective should be so out of kilter! Her legs felt heavy, as though she were walking in sand, as she made her way toward the bed. She fell across it with a small moan.

Tired—so tired.

Moments later, Conchita entered with the white-faced Lupe. Together, they lifted Arabella's sleeping form into a more comfortable position.

"You did not poison the lady?" Lupe quavered in Spanish.

Conchita shook her head. "She is only sleeping for a little while. Now you may go. I will watch over her."

As Arabella slept, a carriage drew away from the house. In that carriage Juan Narváez, with his hands bound, sat between two of his old friends, neither of whom would meet his angry eyes.

"Rodrigo," he said, "Jose! What is this you are doing! Where am I being taken? I demand an explanation!"

"Only to your uncle," one of them said, placatingly. "He wishes to speak with you. You would not come to him."

"So I am being abducted?" Juan's voice was incredulous. "He knows where I live! He could have come to me! Come, Jose! Release me! This is insane!"

"We must obey orders," his friend said, guiltily. "The General commands and we obey. Pray, do not let this destroy our friendship—"

"If anything happens to Arabella in my absence," Juan said, "you need not think of friendship! I will have your heads!"

As the carriage moved along the road from Màlaga

409

to Sevilla, Juan thought of Arab. What would she think when she woke to find him gone? Conchita had awakened him this morning, whispering from the door that Rodrigo and Jose were downstairs. Thinking they had come as friends, to assure him that they were on his side in the affair with the girl he loved, he had dressed quietly and hastened down to greet them. Instead, he was met by Rodrigo who stood with a pistol in his hands while Jose tied Juan's hands. When both of them nodded beside him in the carriage, lulled by the long journey, he attempted to free his hands, but to no avail. He was trapped. A prisoner. Before he gave up Arabella, he would die!

In the house at Màlaga, above the sea, Arabella woke again in late afternoon. The murky sky had cleared. The golden eye of the sun shone down on a day that was still and hot. The fragrance from the garden was stifling as Arab stirred, uncomfortable and sticky with the humid heat. She sat upright, to see Conchita, looking like an emaciated vulture with her beaked nose and predatory eyes, rise from her chair and come toward her.

"Juan," Arabella said, faintly. "Where is he?"

"Then you do not remember? He came to say farewell, but he said you acted so strangely, he thought you must be ill—"

"I—I don't remember," Arab said, her hand going to her throbbing temples. "Farewell? But where was he going?"

. Conchita shrugged. "He did not confide in me. Business, I suppose, in some other city."

"Did he—when will he return?"

"He did not say."

Conchita, assured that Arabella was in her right senses, left the room. Arab got out of bed, but she did not feel well. She seemed overcome with lassitude, her limbs as heavy as her heart. If she'd been Juan's wife, he would not have departed without her. Or would he? This country was so different in its customs. She loved Juan, but did she know him?

She pushed the thoughts away. If Juan had gone, he
410

had a purpose in doing so. For in his eyes, she was his wife! She raised a hand to look at the ring he had given her.

The ring was gone.

She stood for a moment, stricken. Then she turned to the bed, tearing the sheets from it, throwing the pillows onto the floor. The ring had been a little large. It must have slipped off. When had she seen it last? When they had walked in the gardens? At the pool—

She searched the room, then called for Conchita and Lupe, directing them to search the grounds. Lupe only stared at her blankly, but Conchita looked puzzled.

"The master took the ring, milady. He said he wished to have it made into a smaller size."

Arabella said, "I see." But she did not. Juan could not have removed the ring from her finger without her knowledge. Yet, according to Conchita, he had bidden her farewell this morning and she did not remember that, either. Could she have been so drowsy that it hadn't registered in her mind? It was almost as if she had been drugged! But who would drug her, and why?

No, she had been ill, perhaps with some sickness peculiar to this climate. At least the ring was safe in Juan's possession. He would slip it back on her finger when he returned.

Days passed, days in which Arabella walked through the gardens alone, or languished by the pool, seeing another reflection beside her own in its depth. She waited for word from her lover, but none came.

And as she waited and worried, Juan faced his uncle, General Narváez, his face obstinately set. He had been ordered to give up the American dancer. He had refused. He had been bribed, and he had refused. Now, he was being punished. His bared brown shoulders had known the feel of the lash, wielded by the General's own hands.

General Narváez looked at the slender body before him, slashed and bleeding from the whip, and his granite features twisted in agony. "What can I do to convince you?" he cried. "You are like my own son!

411

You are the hope of Spain! And you would throw all this away for the sake of a woman of ill repute?"

"You do not know her, sir. And I do."

The General sighed. "Then keep her, but in some secluded place. After you are married to Isleta—"

"You are suggesting I take her as a mistress?" Juan's eyes were hot with anger. "That I will not do! I do not intend to marry anyone else, I have told you!"

"Then you leave me no alternative. If something should happen to the girl—" There was a threat in the General's voice.

"If anything should happen to Arabella, then you have lost me. I will go to the Queen and divulge your plans."

Fear shot through General Narváez. The young puppy might do just that! Besides, the general had no heart for doing injury to a woman. There had to be another way. Perhaps the girl could be driven to leave through her own free will? Then this puppy who had grown fangs might be brought to heel!

"Take him away," the General ordered. "Put him into the dungeons to cool his temper for a time."

The place Juan Narváez was taken to was more of an apartment than a cell. It had once housed a king. It was lavishly furnished, but the stone walls dripped with dampness, and there was a scent of decay. Rodrigo and Jose accompanied Juan to his prison room, both red with guilt at the humiliation of their friend.

"I will attend to your wounds," Jose said, awkwardly.

"I do not intend to be contaminated by your touch," Juan answered, his voice fierce with fury.

The two left him, talking in whispers as they ascended the worn stone steps that led upward to the light.

"I do not like this," Jose said, troubled, to Rodrigo.

"Nor do I. In this, the General is wrong. But what can we do?"

"Perhaps Juan might escape," Jose said. Rodrigo looked at him, his eyes lighting.

"It would take some doing," he said, "but it might be done."

As Juan's friends connived, a messenger approached the house in Màlaga. Conchita took the message, a verbal one, and conveyed it to Arabella in the garden. Purportedly from Juan, the message stated that Juan had been delayed, but that General Narváez, along with members of his retinue, would be arriving at Màlaga within the week. He asked Arabella to prepare for them, and to make them welcome.

No words of love, but he would not have sent such a message to be delivered verbally, anyway. Why had he not sent a note? Arab pushed her disappointment away. It didn't matter. For now she knew where he had gone—to make peace with his uncle, to assure his acceptance of her as his wife! Otherwise, General Narváez would not be coming to visit. Maybe Juan would be with him, and there would be a wedding. Her heart was full to overflowing with excited happiness.

Within the week, he'd said. And the whole house must be turned out, polished and shining. Foods must be cooked, rooms prepared for the guests—so much to be done!

She drove the servants unmercifully, managing to infect the round-cheeked Lupe with some of her own enthusiasm. Occasionally, however, she caught Conchita looking at her with something that resembled pity in her harsh features.

Four days later, on a bright morning, the General's coach arrived. All was in readiness, including Arabella. Wearing a green morning gown, one of Juan's favorites, she descended the stairs as Conchita answered the door.

The General, looking up, understood his nephew just a little, for this was a lovely creature that smiled down upon him, eyes the color of her dress, hair like sunshine glowing against the marble wall. Her neckline was cut low, revealing the whiteness of her throat and the tops of her breasts. He could see the pulsation of her heart as she spoke the Spanish word she'd practiced.

"Bienvenida."

"Your 'ospitality is most appreciated," he said in his rusty English, bowing.

Then Arabella saw the girl behind him. A small, dark, elfin creature, with wide dark eyes in a smooth-skinned olive face, clad in ruby velvet, her hair piled high, with a Spanish comb.

Arabella faltered for a moment, then walked down the stairs to greet her waiting guests. The General kissed her hand. The girl behind him removed a glove and extended a graceful hand to be touched in the American way.

Arabella stopped, stricken, her eyes dark with pain as she looked into the girl's face. For on that extended hand was a ring. A twin to that which Juan had given her to plight their troth. A twin—or the ring itself!

"And this," the General was saying, "is señorita Isleta Guzman, who is almost a daughter to me."

"I am happy to meet you," Arabella said, mechanically.

"And I, you," the girl replied in flawless English. "We have much to talk about, you and I."

The General broke in, introducing the other guests; señorita Guzman's duenna, señora Hernandez; and an aide and friend, Rodrigo Miranda. The latter studied her face as though to memorize it. Her cheeks grew hot beneath his gaze.

Like a puppet, she managed to put herself through the correct social procedures, to say the right things.

"I know you must be tired after your journey. Would you like refreshment now? Or do you prefer to be shown to your rooms?"

"Our rooms, if you please," the General answered for them all, "and perhaps something cold on trays, if it is not too much trouble. Then this evening, if you are free, I should like to engage a few moments of your time."

"Of course," Arabella said through stiff lips. "Lupe, will you attend the ladies? Conchita, the gentlemen?"

After they had gone, she stood dazed, fists clenched

at her sides. This visit! What did it mean? And the ring! Surely there were not duplicates!

"I told you she was beautiful, did I not?"

Arabella whirled to see Conchita standing behind her, returned from her errand upstairs.

"Please prepare trays for our guests," she said, coldly. "I'm sure that you know their preferences."

"I do," the old woman chuckled like a rusty hinge. "Indeed I do."

Arabella fled the house and went into the garden. She went to the pool and leaned against one of the pillars there, listening to the falling waters of the fountain as she had in happier times. Her heart was racing out of control as she held her hands tightly to her breast. Juan, she thought, oh, Juan, what's happening? What are you—they—doing to me?

"Oh," a small breathless voice said behind her, "Forgive me! I do not intend to intrude."

Arabella turned to face Isleta, a Spanish beauty who belonged in a Spanish garden. "It is quite all right," she said. "You are a guest here."

"Thank you." The dark girl moved forward and dropped to her knees, gracefully, placing slim fingers in the water. Then, raising shining liquid eyes to Arab, she said, "This is my favorite place. It has such memories." She stood, laughing, flicking the water from her damp hand, the gold-and-emerald ring shining in the sun.

"It is my favorite place, too," Arabella said.

"How nice that we share so many of the same likes and dislikes," Isleta cooed.

There was no mistaking the girl's insinuations. Arab barely repressed her fury as she forced herself to speak calmly. "Even to jewelry," she said. "I have a ring quite similar to the one you're wearing."

"Oh, but you couldn't! There are only two like this in all of Spain. Juan has one, of course. And mine was only given to me recently." She smiled down at the emerald on her slim finger.

"If you will excuse me," Arabella said in a smothered tone, "I have duties in the house."

She stumbled blindly into the castle-like structure that had been her home with Juan. These people had come to torture her. She must learn the truth. She went straight to the door of the room assigned General Narváez and knocked.

The man who answered her knock did not appear to be military at all. He was just a tired old man, tucking his shirt into his trousers. His eyes registered surprise at her appearance.

"My dear—"

"Where is Juan?"

He spread his hands. "I intended to speak with you later, after I have rested. I'm afraid I'm not up to discussing a delicate subject at this time."

"Where is Juan?" The haunted green eyes in her white face showed that they would consider no delay. General Narváez sighed. It was true that, like Juan, this girl believed herself to be in love. But love was not something one happened on. Love was orderly, planned, a part of living. His own marriage had been arranged, and it had been a satisfactory one, had it not? Still, he felt uncomfortable in his errand.

"Juan is away. He has commissioned me to speak for him. My nephew is a charming rascal, but he is young, inclined to rush headlong into affairs. But he has not the courage to end them when they have gone too far—"

"You are lying! I don't know what you and that girl are up to, but believe me—!"

He raised a soothing hand. "Young woman! Please comport yourself with dignity! Juan does not wish to rid himself of you. He has sent me to you with a proposition. He discussed the situation with Isleta when he gave her his ring. She does not object to his having a mistress, so long as his affair is discreet."

She looked at him with angry, frightened eyes, her voice faltering a little. Isleta did have the ring; the memory of the emerald on the girl's small hand was burned into her mind. "Juan would not make such a proposal," she said faintly.

"Juan is a Spaniard. His attitudes may differ greatly from those of the men in your country, I do not know. Perhaps you have taken him too seriously."

"I cannot believe it," she said, numbly. "I cannot believe it." Her green eyes were huge and bright with tears as she turned, stumbling, toward the door.

The General's hand caught her arm, supporting her. "I am sorry," he said, "even though I know Juan's marriage to Isleta is best for Spain. I do not like to see you hurt. So I will make a counter-proposal to my nephew's. If you wish, I will find a place on the first ship, and send you back to your own country."

Arabella shut her eyes, remembering the farm in Pennsylvania, a little girl with red curls who lay in a flower-filled meadow, dreaming of romance, of a prince charming, of castles in Spain. Now the dream was over and she had been wakened most cruelly.

"Thank you," she said, dully, "I will go home."

Chapter 3

The next morning, Arabella rose early. True to his word, the General had procured passage for her on a sailing vessel. She planned to be gone before her guests awoke. She dressed, and began packing her things in a small chest, taking only those things that she had brought with her. The gowns Juan had purchased remained in the wardrobe. With a quiver of pain at the memories those purchases invoked, she caressed the silks, satins, and velvets before she reluctantly closed the wardrobe door.

The jewels he'd given her rested in a velvet-lined box upon his pillow—except for the ring. She could not return what had been taken away. Atop the box was a note that said, simply, *"Juan, I love you. I always will."*

It was true, she thought as she turned to the window. She would always love the Juan with whom she'd lived and whom she thought of as her husband, despite his betrayal. The Juan who had drugged her, taken the ring and sent his uncle to speak for him was a stranger.

She looked down at the pool with its Roman pillars, its purity sullied for her now, and blinked back tears.

"The carriage ees waiting," Lupe called from the doorway. Arabella took a deep breath, set her chin, and turned.

"Thank you," she said, "I'm ready."

Picking up the small chest, she went downstairs and out into a morning filled with a wavering lemony light. She would not look back. Arab climbed into the waiting coach while Lupe stood outside giving the driver instructions.

418

In the household, there was another early riser. The lovely Isleta Guzman had spent a wakeful night. An ambitious girl, she looked forward to occupying a high place in the land along with Juan Narváez as her husband. Though she had never felt the stirring of love toward any man, she knew the handsome nephew of the General was infinitely superior to the elderly señor Mendez, another friend of her father's who had been casting eyes in her direction.

Isleta had come here at the General's direction, prepared to do anything to eliminate her rival. Tucked between her breasts was a small vial of poisonous liquid. She intended only to use it as a last resort, since it might create an awkward situation. But in case she must, and the girl's death was considered suspicious, she intended to drop the empty vial in Lupe's pocket. Or perhaps she could leave it in Rodrigo's room. She sensed Juan's friend was not happy with their errand.

She stood at the window, her mind on murder, her eyes on a gypsy wagon drawn up at the roadside. Two gaudily dressed young men were cooking their breakfast over a fire of twigs. They both looked up, their attention caught by a departing coach. Isleta leaned forward, her face partially concealed by the draperies, to see Arabella departing.

She felt a thrill of satisfaction. It was done! The ship was not due to depart for two days, but the girl had left to go on board. They had done their job well. She stood for a long time, her face fierce with exultation. Then, noticing a lone horseman coming from the other direction, her look changed to one of horror.

Por Dios! Juan!

Her mind whirled. She must alert the General. No, first she must go to the Arab-woman's room, see if she had left a note! There was so little time.

She hurried through the halls, in her tiny red-heeled shoes, to the room Arabella had shared with Juan. Lupe was straightening up, but Isleta ignored her as she searched, opening doors, pulling out drawers. The woman had left her jewels, she saw, opening the box

419

and studying them covetously. But there was no note or letter.

She pushed past Lupe on her way down to the General's room. Lupe held her hand clutched to her breast where Arabella's note lay safely hidden. She didn't know what was taking place, but she intended to see that the missive was delivered to its rightful recipient.

Isleta heard the clatter of boots upon the marble stairs and stepped hastily into an unoccupied room, leaving the door ajar. She heard Juan's anguished call for Arabella, then his hiss of indrawn breath when he discovered her room to be empty. "Where is she?" he shouted at Lupe. "Where is she?"

"She is gone to board a ship," the girl quavered. "Though it does not sail for two days. She left a message—"

Isleta frowned at the rustle of paper. So there had been a note! That vixen of a maid!

Juan made a choking sound, and Lupe added, "The General Narváez is here, señor, and the señorita Guzman."

"Show me to my uncle's room." Juan's voice was flat and ugly with hatred. Through the crack in the door, Isleta saw him pass. He was dirty, his clothing torn, his hair rumpled, the dark eyes agate-hard in his drawn face.

He looks like a *gitano,* Isleta thought. One of the gypsies.

When she thought he'd had time to reach General Narváez's room, Isleta followed, pressing her ear against the door. Dios! Juan was threatening to kill him!

Finally, the General spoke. "Perhaps I have been wrong in what I tried to do. I am an old man. I will fight you no longer—"

Isleta breathed an ugly curse in Spanish. She could not allow this! Why hadn't she poisoned the girl yesterday? The gitana who had brewed the poison for her had said—

The gypsies!

Isleta fled down the stairs, out of the house and up

420

the dusty road that curved to a hill. When one of the red heels broke from her shoe, she kicked both of them off. Hair flying, barefoot, she looked like a gypsy herself as she approached the wagon, now ready to leave.

"*Gitano*," she called out. "Gitano!"

The two rough-haired young men in their colored neckerchiefs looked at her in amusement. A pretty wench, to be sure. In search of a moment of dalliance? Their eyes widened as she slipped a jewelled necklace from her throat, bracelets from her arms. "These are yours," she said, "if you will attend to some business for me—and quickly. There is a girl—"

As Isleta explained her errand to the gypsy men, Arabella's carriage was approaching the harbor. The ship was moored in the distance, and the men who handled small craft were still not in from their fishing. She needed someone to row her, with her luggage, to the vessel on which she would leave Màlaga. With gestures, she dispatched Luis, who drove Juan's carriage, to find such a man.

When he had gone, she waited in the shadow of a building, unaware that the single finger of sun that slanted down to touch her hair would be her undoing.

Numb with despair, her eyes on the ground, she saw the man's grubby boots first. She raised her eyes to see a slim, rather insolent face. "Señorita," the man said, then rattled off a string of words she did not understand. Was this the boatman Luis had found for her? He did not look like one.

"I'm sorry," she said, uncertainly, "but I do not understand—"

She did not finish her sentence. For as she spoke, she was grabbed from behind, her arms pinioned. The man who had approached her had pulled off his neckerchief and gagged her with it. She fought, fruitlessly twisting her head and moaning as the filthy thing was forced between her lips.

"Please, God," she prayed, "stop them! Someone—!"

Then she found herself dumped into the rear of a wagon and covered over with a scattering of straw. One of her attackers shouted to the horses, and the wheels of the rickety vehicle began to turn.

Juan Narváez, riding full-tilt on his lathered horse, passed the gypsy wagon but paid it no notice. It was not unusual for gypsies to haunt the waterfront in the early dawn, meeting the fishing boats as they came in, scavenging and bargaining for their breakfast. And Juan's mind was on the girl he loved. He would find her and take her home where she belonged. Nothing would ever separate them again!

He found only old Luis, standing beside Arabella's chest, scratching his unshaven chin. He had left the señorita here, and when he returned, she was gone. But why did she not take her possessions with her?

Juan knelt beside the chest, where he recognized prints in the dust of the narrow aristocratic feet he'd admired so much. All about the spot, the sand was scuffed, as if a struggle had taken place. His heart pounded with fear for Arabella.

Setting Luis to search the harbor area, Juan found a small craft to row him out to the sailing vessel. Arabella was not aboard.

When he'd exhausted all possibilities in his search, Juan returned, tight-lipped, to confront his uncle with what he'd found. The older man was clearly shaken by the news that the girl had disappeared.

"I had nothing to do with it," he said. "I swear it on my Faith! She must have been attacked by thieves, Gitanos—"

A dim memory stirred in Juan's mind. The gypsy wagon. But no, there had only been two men. And if she'd been set upon by robbers, why did they not take the chest?

"I will get Rodrigo," the General said, rising, "and call for more men. We will continue the search for the girl."

The day was spent seeking Arabella. The hunt was unsuccessful. That night, Juan went to the pool in the garden, to sit beside it, head in hands. Perhaps if he looked up quickly, he would see her there, in the water, a white goddess, her lovely body dewed with crystal drops.

A hand touched his hair, and he looked up, his eyes filled with hope. But it was Isleta he saw.

"They will find her, Juanito. The General should not have led her to believe we were to be married. It was naughty of him. But perhaps some good will come of it. Knowing she could not have you, she has possibly found herself some other man. Then your conscience will be free."

As he stood, shaking off Isleta's caressing hand, he saw the ring she wore for the first time. Her part in all this was falling into place.

"Take off my ring," he demanded. "Now!"

"But Juanito, I cannot," she pouted, prettily. "See, it fits so tightly now that it has been made small for me."

"Then I shall have to take the finger along with the ring," he said. "Remove it, or I shall remove it for you."

The expression in his eyes frightened her and she pulled the ring off, tossed it in his direction, and fled.

Bending, he picked it up. The symbol of love and fidelity, twin to the one he wore. He put it into a pocket, along with a note that said, *"I love you, I always will."*

He would find his sun-haired green-eyed lady, if it took him the rest of his life.

Arabella lay on a dirty blanket beneath the stars. The gypsies had encamped for the night in a small wooded grove, a full day's drive from Màlaga. As a concession to their isolation, they had removed the gag, but her hands and feet were still bound. All attempts to speak to the two men had been unavailing. They only stared at her blankly. *"Soy Americano,"* she said, desperately, *"Inglés!"*

The gypsies had identified themselves. Pepe was the thin-faced youth who had accosted her. Pablo was shorter, bull-strong, with a round face and drooping mustache. They appeared to be brothers. And she did not like the way they looked at her.

"Please," she begged, "tell me why you brought me

423

here. Were you paid to do it? General Narváez? Juan Narváez? Isleta Guzman?"

The men exchanged glances at the mention of names and began speaking to each other in Spanish as if she had triggered a reaction.

"I was right," Pepe told the other, "she is a personage of importance. Someone will pay for her return. And she must be in good condition. Forget your plans for having her until we have spoken to Lazaro. He knows her language, and he will know what to do."

Pablo spread his hands. "But, brother, I am a man, and in need. Did the lady not say to dispose of her? And she paid us well."

Pepe punched his brother's shoulder, affectionately. "And what will your Rita say to this, eh? Do you always do as ladies wish? I think not! As for being paid, I have a feeling here," he touched his heart, "that this young lady's ransom will bring us wealth beyond our wildest dreams. No, we must seek Lazaro's counsel. We must do her no harm."

Pablo scowled, but he set to work building a small fire from twigs. Over it, he roasted a trapped hare. When it was done, Pepe broke a loaf of hard, crusty bread into pieces, and scooping the center out of each bit, he filled them with a spoonful or two of olive oil. He untied Arab's hands for a moment to allow her to eat. The meal was ended with manchega, a sturdy hard cheese made of goat's milk, washed down with a Spanish wine.

Pablo squatted before Arabella, staring at her, making it hard for her to swallow as she wondered what was in his mind. "Her flesh is as white as a flower, is it not?" he asked Pepe. Then, his eyes glinting wickedly, "I wonder if she is white all over. Now that would do no harm, just looking."

"No," Pepe grinned. "That would do no harm."

As Juan dreamed of his white-skinned water nymph at the side of the pool, rough hands tore at Arabella's gown. Not knowing their intent, she fought them until she could fight no longer, then closed her eyes.

After all, what difference did it make? She had no

reason to care any more about anything. Betrayed by David when he ran away from the scene of their love-making; betrayed by Tamsen who gave her into the hands of the Reverend Smythe; betrayed by Juan—worst of all—Juan. Perhaps that was all life was, one long betrayal.

Chapter 4

Arabella had lost track of time. Had it been three days, four? How long since she had stood on the wharf waiting for a small boat to carry her and her possessions to the waiting ship? It seemed that she had lain forever in the back of a gypsy cart, listening to the little bells on the harness tinkle, the creaking of the wheels. Did they actually have a destination? she wondered. Or was this to be her life from now on—the bells, the wheels, the nights beneath the stars. Last night had been so humiliating, though the men had not actually raped her.

She woke, slept, woke again. Perhaps the waking hours were preferable, for when she slept, she dreamed. She dreamed of Juan, of Isleta in his arms.

The wagon stopped, and Pablo came around to the back where she lay. He carefully checked her bonds and returned the gag to her mouth. By now, she knew this meant they were entering a town or city.

"Guadix," he said, repeating it three times. Apparently it was the name of the place. It did her no good to know. She had no idea of its distance from Màlaga, nor what direction they had taken. Lying beneath the straw, she heard the sounds of a small market town as the wagon jingled through. Then she fought to maintain her position, bound as she was, as the vehicle seemed to be climbing steeply upward. Soon it reached the crest and tipped downward once more.

Pepe called to the horses, reining them in, and Pablo was bending over her once more. He removed the gag and untied her bonds, assisting her to sit up as he indicated their surroundings. A hot, spiralling wind was blowing. Arabella's eyes were filled with grit and sand. A dreadful stench assailed her nostrils, the smell of many people living without sanitation.

She blinked her eyes clean and was amazed at what she saw. They were in the center of a city of caves, hollowed out of natural dolomite formations circling the hillside like an amphitheater. The caves had whitewashed fronts, their roofs were whitewashed, and they had whitewashed chimneys. And on the paths below, children swarmed in the funnels of blowing dust— ragged youngsters with shaggy heads. People lived in those dwellings! Children played in this atmosphere of foul odors and disease!

"Barrio de Santiago," Pablo said, proudly.

Arabella's heart sank. This was their destination! Pablo had come home.

As the wagon creaked down the path to the center of the village, people began to pour from the narrow dark holes that served as openings, running to greet the new arrivals, laughing and shouting. One girl, dressed in a rainbow of red and yellows, was shrieking "Pablo!" at the top of her lungs. Pablo reached up and swung Arabella to the ground. A filthy little girl, with black, snake-like locks, pawed at her gown, pulling loose a length of ribbon.

"Please," Arabella whispered, "oh, please." She backed until she was pressed against the wagon. Then a path was cleared for someone who was clearly a person of authority, a wiry youth in tight black trousers and a red silken shirt.

"*Hola*, Lazaro," Pablo shouted cheerfully.

The newcomer gestured toward her, apparently demanding an explanation for her presence. As Pablo answered, Lazaro studied Arab, his eyes approving what he saw. He indicated that she was to be taken into one of the caves.

Stumbling along between Pablo and Pepe, followed by an evidently irate girl Pablo called Rita, Arabella climbed up the steep path. Then from one of the holes that served as a door, a boy burst forth, waving flabby hands before Arab's eyes as he babbled wildly. Clad only in a sack, he was an idiot whose lips hung loose and grinning.

Arabella fainted.

She came to to find herself in a strange round room. At its perimeter, small cell-like apertures had been hollowed out. Each contained a straw mattress, such as the one that she was lying upon. She sat up, her skin crawling, but the room seemed to be clean. A wool rug covered the earthen floor.

Pablo's face appeared in the open doorway, and she shrank back. But he only turned away, calling, "Lazaro!"

The wiry figure of the young man entered with a jingling sound. She noted that he wore sleek black boots and huge, cruel-looking silver spurs. Timorously, she raised her eyes to his. He was smiling.

"You are awake?"

He was speaking English! Perhaps she could discover why she was brought here! A wave of relief brought a spate of tears.

"I—I'm sorry," she whispered finally. "I didn't know anyone here could speak—could speak—"

"English?" His grin widened. "I am the best horse-trainer in the world," he boasted. "All *gitanos* are good, but I am the best. I was taken at the age of fifteen to tend an Englishman's animals. And now I have returned, rich." He indicated the room around them.

"This is your home?"

"Mine, my brothers', my brother's woman. I believe in sharing. That, too, is a *gitano* trait."

"Then Pepe and Pablo are your brothers?"

He shrugged. "We have the same mother. Their father, I think, was a jackass."

"Can you tell me," she asked, her eyes pleading, "why they have brought me here?"

He squatted on his haunches, spat on a bandana, and began to polish his boots. "I thought you might tell me that."

"You mean—they had no reason?"

428

"They were stopped by a señorita, a most beautiful señorita, who gave them jewels to dispose of you."

"Isleta Guzman."

He shrugged. "If she is your enemy. It is an affair of the heart? You have taken her lover?"

"You might say," Arabella said, flatly, "that she has taken mine."

His eyes were fixed on her now, admiringly. She grew hot beneath his gaze. "I think that would be most difficult to do," he said. "She must be most beautiful, indeed!"

"You said *dispose*," Arabella said. "Do you mean they intend to—"

"To murder you?" He laughed. "That is not the *gitano*'s way. The lady paid to have you taken far away. Now, who will pay to have you returned safely?"

Arabella gazed into the dark fox-face with its small brilliant eyes as she thought—who? No one. General Narváez would be glad to have her out of the way. Juan, too, perhaps. "There is no one who will pay," she said, "not in Spain. I have no one at all."

Lazaro frowned. "Perhaps you will think of someone. I dare not tell them this. It is your protection."

"My protection?"

"You arrived here unmolested, did you not? One does not molest the goose that will lay the golden egg. So I beg you to think for a time. Though Rita, Pablo's woman, will be of some protection. She is most angry with him for bringing such a lovely señorita home. So make yourself at home. *¡Està su casa!* And think much on what I have told you. I will talk to them." With an admiring look at his shined boots, he was gone.

Arabella sank back on the bed, forgetting that it might be filled with creeping things. In this whole country, she had no friends. She and Juan had been sufficient to themselves. And now she was dependent upon the good will of a strutting peacock of a man, whose claim to leadership was based upon his career as a stableboy in England.

She could hear his voice at the cookfire outside as

429

he spoke to his assembled family, but she did not know what he was saying. "This girl," he was telling them in his *gitano* Spanish, "is a most important person. She is frightened now, unable to tell me who will pay the most for her freedom. You must give her some time."

"I will give her the point of my knife," the gypsy girl said as she spat. "And if Pablo looks at her, I will make a woman of him!"

"You will treat her well, or you will find yourself back in that hole you lived in!" Lazaro growled. "All she represents to any of us is the ransom she will bring. Is that understood?" He frowned around at them. "And no man here is to touch her! Pepe! Pablo! Anyone!"

I have gained a little time for the señorita, he thought, casting an anxious glance through the door of the cave. Then he grinned. "Lazaro," he told himself, "of all the *gitanos*, you are the best liar in the world!"

That night, having dined on an acrid soup and hard bread and cheese, Arabella finally slept. She was so weary that she was oblivious to the crowded sleepers all around her. But beneath her, the bed seemed to swing rhythmically to the sound of creaking wheels and tinkling bells.

She did not even know that Pablo rose and came to stare down at her. Or that Rita had raised herself upon an elbow to watch with hatred in her eyes.

Chapter 5

Protected by Lazaro's edict, Arabella was free to wander through the village at will. The place resembled a giant, teeming anthill, she decided. She recalled the big red ants near Magoffinville. They had carried Pecos diamonds, soft six-sided crystals, from their excavations, and the circular areas surrounding their homes glittered in the sun.

Here, too, were things of beauty. For despite the blowing dust, the suffocating heat, the filth, these people were artisans. They lived by the things they made with their hands: colorful woven baskets, cloth made on crude looms, crudely carved semblances of religious figures to decorate some household shrine. These were to be taken to the *feria* during Easter week. The *gitanos* would set up booths at Triana, the gypsy suburb of Sevilla where their wares would be sold.

Lazaro was at work on a wagon, a two-wheeled cart with a towering roof of canvas, draped, decorated, and festooned until it was like a bower. This, he explained, he intended to transport to Sevilla, using horses. There, he would rent oxen and drive in the parade of the Romeria del Rocio, a procession moving through Sevilla to Triana.

While he was gone, Arab thought, she would be left at the mercy of Pablo—and Rita. She did not know which one frightened her more.

"Take me with you," Arab pleaded one morning as she watched Lazaro's clever hands at work. "Please, I beg of you!" She placed a hand on his arm, feeling his muscles tense beneath the bright shirt. She had sensed

431

his interest in her, though he treated her in an offhand, lordly way.

"He travels fastest who travels alone," he said, a little sullenly. Then, boastfully, "Only in the procession will there be a woman in this wagon. They will fight, in Sevilla, to be the *maja* who rides beside me."

A gust of wind clouded them in a swirl of dust. Arab wiped her face with her hand and licked her gritty lips. She felt so dirty. Since she was taken from the wharf, she had worn this soiled gown day and night. Her hair was dull with grime. The notion that had flickered through her mind, that she might seduce this man, bribing him to take her from this place, was gone. She felt utterly hopeless.

"And what would you do if I did take you?" he inquired in a more gentle tone. "You tell me you have no one. Perhaps a priest might aid you, but you are not of the faith. You would be alone in a country where you do not speak the tongue. Here, you have Lazaro! And have I not protected you? Provided for you well?"

She tried to smile. He was so proud of his accomplishments. It would not do to anger him. "Indeed you have," she said. "But I cannot remain here."

"You must." His tone was final. "At the fire at night, the talk is of your ransom, how the money will be spent. They are sure that at the next *Romeria*, Pablo and Pepe will have their own wagons in which to ride; Rita will have a new gown and bangles for her arms. They will not let you go."

"This cannot go on forever. Soon they will discover I am no one." Arabella was forlorn. She was fighting back tears.

"I will think of something." His words sounded less than certain, and he camouflaged them with a quick smile. "Look," he bragged. "Look at my wagon. There will be none so beautiful as this at the *feria*. And when it is finished, we shall have a fiesta in honor of the occasion, before I go. Yes?"

Leaving him, Arab walked slowly back to the cave-house. Rita waited there, impatiently. Handing her a goatskin waterbag, she gestured toward the cistern-like well the *gitanos* used in common. Arab went to fill the bag, feeling Rita's cruel eyes at her back. The girl would enslave her, once Lazaro was gone.

At the well, Arabella looked at the closed dark faces of the women around her. Her eyes filled with tears of pain as one tawny hand flashed out and pulled at her hair. These women hated her. They hated her for being different, for drawing the eyes of their men. Lazaro could not protect her from the women, but she was thankful that he could protect her from the men.

She would not have been so certain if she had heard the conversation taking place in a small group of men who watched the women at the well.

"She is white all over," one *gitano* was saying. "Pablo and Pepe swear to it."

"I should like to see," a toothless old man snickered.

"Perhaps we shall," the first speaker shrugged. "Pablo says he thinks Lazaro is lying. He says many of the wealthy employ foreigners to teach their children in the big houses. Perhaps this is such a case, and this girl cast eyes upon the master of the house. And the mistress is well rid of her, and wishes to remain so. If it is not resolved before Lazaro's departure, Pablo will take matters into his own hands."

"But why would Lazaro lie?"

"He has eyes for the pale one. Have you not seen?"

The old man cackled. "If Pablo has designs, the red-hair may not keep her beauty for long. That Rita is a she-cat where he is concerned."

They laughed, and something in the sound made Arab hurry her footsteps toward the cave where Rita waited. The gypsy girl took the waterbag from her and made another gesture, this time toward the fire. Arabella began gathering twigs and set the cookpot over the flames.

That night Arabella was restless. She had grown accustomed to the round beehive of a house with its many occupants, to the sight of other sleepers in the flickering firelight, to the sounds that emanated from the bed-alcove of Pablo and Rita. But she could not sleep for worrying about when Lazaro would be gone. There would be no one here who could speak her language. Only for a couple of weeks, he'd promised. But those weeks stretched before her in a nightmare of imaginings.

What difference did it make? She would be just as alone in Sevilla, unless she could find some compatriot, which was unlikely. As Lazaro had said, if she were Catholic she could go to a priest for aid.

Suddenly she realized that there was one who might help her! Father Díaz! He disliked her, it was true, considering her of low character, but she was certain he would not condone what had been done to her. And he, of all people, would be glad to help her escape from Spain! If only she could persuade Lazaro to take her to Màlaga!

She found him putting the finishing touches to his wagon. She had thought of someone who would help her, she said.

Lazaro listened, frowning. He did not know of this priest, but he knew his Order. He would be a poor man, unable to pay—

"Pay!" Arabella said, shrilly. "Do you think of anything but money? I'm hoping he can get me on a ship, send me home!" She began to cry, and Lazaro, shaken, licked his lips nervously.

"I cannot steal you away," he said hoarsely. "We are watched. If they knew I helped you to escape, I could not return—"

"I thought you were the high and mighty leader here," she flung at him through her tears. "I thought you had only to speak, and they would do as you say!"

His face turned a dull red. "It is true," he said, "but I cannot betray my people."

"Then you will betray me." The tears had stopped now, burned away by anger and hopelessness. She stared at him for a moment, then turned to walk away.

"Wait," he called, "wait!" He ran after her, catching her arm. "My wagon will be finished this night. There

434

will be a fiesta to celebrate tomorrow, as I told you. And for you, I have a gift. A surprise!"

She shook off the brown hand and walked on, alone.

The next evening, a fire burned high in the center of the anthill village. Arab watched as the villagers gathered around the fire to admire Lazaro's wagon. Wild guitar music drifted up to assail her ears. They were out there, Pablo and Rita, Pepe, Lazaro . . .

She turned listlessly toward her bed. It would be cooler out there beneath the stars. She thought of a pool with Roman columns, the tinkling of a fountain, of Juan—

"Señorita?"

She jumped. It had sounded like Juan's voice. For a moment, she thought he had materialized. She whirled to face the person who addressed her.

Lazaro. Dressed in black and silver, a grin on his face. Draped over his arm lay a gypsy dress of bright colors, each of its ruffles trimmed with a braid of silver.

He had bought it for the lucky *gitana* he would choose to accompany him in the procession, but it was a nothing. There were other gowns to be had, he bragged. If she would wear it, he would be pleased to accompany her to the fiesta. He bowed as graciously as any Spanish gentleman.

The words of refusal died on her lips. Why not, she asked herself. If she were to be trapped by these people, why not share the good times as well as the work? And Pablo's Rita would be livid with jealousy!

"I would be pleased to accept your invitation," she said, coolly. "If you will give me a few moments to dress."

As he waited outside, she took down the goatskin bag, splashing its contents into a bowl. Rita guarded the water supply with an iron hand. Water was for drinking and cooking, not for washing. It was a precious item in the gypsies' way of life. Arabella washed her dirt-encrusted face and, running the damp cloth through her hair, felt the red curls grow damp and spring to life.

435

Then she slipped into the gown and put on the silver earloops Lazaro had given her. She would go barefoot, as the *gitanas* did. Her fiery red hair hung down to her waist, and she even managed a smile as she walked toward Lazaro.

"*Dios,*" he said fervently at sight of her. "Ah, *Dios! Bonita!*" He crooked an arm for her hand, and they strolled down toward the enormous fire with its leaping flames. As they pushed through the crowd, the exuberant gypsies fell silent; the music dwindled to a single guitar. A few castanets clicked as the people turned to stare, stunned, at the red-haired gypsy who had entered their midst.

Arabella stood, uncomfortable in the stillness her presence had evoked, feeling more alien than ever beneath the gaze of so many dark, unfriendly eyes. Then Rita moved into the firelight, arms curved above her head, castanets clicking.

"*Seguidilla!*" she cried.

The music and laughter began again. The area was full of jostling bodies as the gypsies threw themselves, with renewed passion, into the dance.

Arab watched, forgetting the squalor of the *gitano* existence. Rita was a whirling flame, her slim brown legs bared as skirts and petticoats flew.

"She is beautiful," Arab whispered to Lazaro.

"Not so beautiful as you," he answered, a bemused expression on his face that reminded her of Juan. Her heart twisted, and she turned away from him.

The dancing stopped, and suddenly Rita was standing there, hands on hips, before Arabella. She said something in a mocking voice that carried clearly, her compatriots having fallen silent to hear this confrontation.

Arabella turned to Lazaro, bewildered. "What does she say?"

"She asks why you do not dance, since you are dressed as one of us."

Arabella flushed. "Tell her I do not know these dances. The steps are strange to me."

436

Rita spoke again, a spate of words that hardened Lazaro's face, tightened his lips.

Arab grimaced. "What did she say? Tell me!"

"She says she does not think that is the reason," he said reluctantly. "It is that you believe you are too exalted a lady to join in our poor fiesta. This Rita is a troublemaker. I shall ask Pablo to take her to the cave."

Arab put a staying hand on his arm. "Don't do that. I will show her."

She moved into the firelight, looking back toward Lazaro. "I will sing. Translate for me."

Her head thrown back, her hair a fiery cascade in the light of the bonfire, she began to sing one of the songs she had sung to entertain the Queen. Lazaro, his voice filled with laughter, translated each line as she paused, for the benefit of a delighted audience. The guitars picked up the tune, and the castanets soon joined in. And then Arabella danced, as she had so many times with the Montez troupe.

Encore followed encore. When at last Arabella and Lazaro made their way back to the cave-home, the cool night air felt good. She was flushed with dancing, wine, and a heady sense of triumph. Lazaro was silent.

"Did you not enjoy your own fiesta?" Arab teased.

The gypsy looked at her somberly. This was not a girl, but a witch. Tonight her beauty had mesmerized him. And not only himself, but every man in the Barrio de Santiago. Even toothless old Franco's eyes had nearly popped out of his head! He began to fear for her safety in his absence. How he wished she were not regarded as an item of value. He would ask her to be his *novia*. But he dared not interfere. His hold over the gypsy village was tenuous at best.

"I had a good time," he said soberly. "But while I am away—take care."

Several hours later, when the gypsies were all abed, Arabella rose and tiptoed to the hole that served as doorway. Stepping outside, she looked down into the center of the encampment, where the embers of the fire still burned. The sky was lightening to a pearly cast. The wind had not yet risen, and the smells of the place were subdued.

The shadowy figure creeping up behind her suddenly lunged. Two great arms closed about her as a hand shut off her scream.

Pablo!

Arabella fought him as he pulled at the gypsy gown she wore. He swore as she sank her teeth into his palm, and he stumbled backward, drunkenly, to fall in a heap.

Arabella, panting, whirled to face a new menace. Pablo's woman, Rita, had appeared in the doorway. Her face was twisted into a mask of hate and fury as she moved toward Arab, her arm upraised.

A knife! Arab backed away from her, terrified. "Please," she said, "I didn't—"

There was a shrill outpouring of Spanish as the girl lunged, the knife drawn back to thrust. Arab closed her eyes, then opened them as Rita screamed.

Lazaro held the girl's wrist, twisting it. The knife clattered down the dusty hillside to the rooftop of the cave below. Leaving the gypsy girl sobbing, Lazaro led Arabella back into the cave.

His heart was heavy. Now something would have to be done. He was a person of importance here. The *gitanos* deferred to him because of his wealth and his travels. But his power was not enough to protect the red-haired girl. He must do what he had to do.

An hour later, the wagon with its fluttering canvas was ready to travel. Arabella would be with him, and Pepe too, to ensure that Lazaro carried out his errand. For he had told them the girl, frightened at her close call at Rita's hands, had spoken at last. She was a princess, he told them, from a land called California. A ship in the harbor at Màlaga awaited her return; a ship laden with gold, silver, jewels, enough to make them all rich. In Màlaga, she was guest to a great house, where the wife of the owner, jealous of her beauty and wealth, had conspired in the kidnapping.

The princess had finally promised to see that much of

438

the wealth fell into *gitano* hands, if she were returned to the ship.

As the wagon moved out, Arabella was bound and gagged once more. For Lazaro had not told her of his plans. The cart moved up and over the hill, then descended the steep slope on the other side. Again she heard the market sounds of the little city of Guadix. The wagon creaked onward. Beyond the city, the wagon halted once more. Pepe came to check her bonds.

As he bent over her, fingers testing the strength of the knots, there was a thudding sound. He fell across her, knocking her breath from her for a moment. Then other hands released her bound arms, her feet, and at last the gag that covered her mouth.

"I did not mean to hit him so hard," Lazaro's voice said cheerfully, "but his head is hard, since his father was a jackass. Here, help me tie him."

When the vehicle moved again, Arabella was beside Lazaro on the seat. Pepe lay beneath the straw in the back trussed like a chicken. And Lazaro told the girl his plans. He intended to deliver her to Màlaga where she could go to the priest she had told him about.

Pepe was to be left at the home of a friend of Lazaro's with instructions that he not be released for three days. Thus, they would avoid pursuit.

"But *you*," Arabella gasped. "What will they do to you when you return?"

"I will think of something," he said modestly. "It is not for nothing that I am the great Lazaro."

Chapter 6

The last night on the road, a day's drive from Màlaga, Lazaro halted his team in the little grove where Arabella had suffered her humiliation at the hands of Pepe and Pablo. Tonight, there was a cold wind, a sprinkling of stars that shone through the lacy trees. They drank at the cool, sweet spring.

Here, Lazaro set to work preparing a dye from herbs he had obtained at the house where Pepe had been left as a prisoner. First, Arabella's lustrous locks were dyed a *gitana* black. Next, Lazaro applied color to her face and arms. Though the coloring was not smooth, it had the desired effect—she looked like a gypsy girl with an unwashed face. The gown he had given her, torn in her struggle with Pablo, was now travel-worn and covered with dust, suiting her new appearance.

Lazaro felt a wild surge of emotion as he applied the coloring to her pale skin, exclaiming over its beauty, caressing it with trembling fingers.

Arab, too, felt a stirring within her. But Lazaro hastened to finish the job, his eyes lowered, not daring to look at her face. Finally, he stood and said harshly, "You will do. You are even more beautiful now." Then he fled.

Arabella was surprised. The great Lazaro, when he wasn't flanked by his admiring followers, was shy.

They ate a cold meal that night, having built only a small fire for comfort. As Arab stared into the flames, the memories of other campfires came to mind; those along the trail to Saint Louis, when Papa was with them; the campfires during the trek toward Santa Fe, when they lost him; campfires along the way to Magoffinville; those she had been forced to prepare for the Reverend Smythe. . . .

She shivered, and Lazaro reached to take her hand. "You are cold?"

"No. Just thinking." She had been thinking of the past, when it was the present which should concern her. "Lazaro, tell me again what I am to do tomorrow."

His voice was patient. "It will be late when we arrive. I will pause some distance from the cathedral, and you will jump from the wagon and disappear into the Holy Week crowds. So if anyone has followed us, you will be safe."

She was to leave him and make her way through the thronged streets of Màlaga alone. From there, all would depend upon Father Díaz. She felt a cold chill of fear as she contemplated the prospect.

"Come with me," she pleaded.

"I cannot. After I leave you, I will go on to Sevilla, to Triana. There, I will try to find an Englishman who comes there for the horses each year. He will be glad to take me back to England with him. After all," he grinned crookedly, "am I not the greatest horse-trainer in the world?"

"Then you can't go back home—to the Barrio de Santiago?"

He shook his head. "Gypsy vengeance is not a pretty thing."

Arabella's eyes sparked with tears. "Lazaro, I am so sorry!" Impulsively, she reached out both hands to him. "Lazaro," she said with a sob.

"My beautiful lady," he said, "oh, my beautiful lady!" Then she was in his arms.

It was not Lazaro she loved so passionately that night, her body straining against his, hands sliding over the tawny shoulders, her mouth afire beneath his lips. For in the darkness, he was Juan. His hands were rough, calloused with hard labor, but they were gentle, loving.

The black eyes that looked down into hers were dark pools in which she sank and drowned.

"Stay with me," he begged at last. "We will find a way to hide, to be together—"

Though she wept with loss, she knew that she could not. In the morning, he would not be Juan, but Lazaro. It would not be fair to him. Though she lay in Lazaro's arms, answering his bursts of passion that sent the stars reeling in the skies above her, she loved only one man—always.

How she wished she were what she appeared to be, a soiled and tattered gypsy girl who had never known Juan.

In the morning, Lazaro rose before her. She woke to the scent of *churros* frying over a small fire. He brought coffee to her, thick, without milk, but sweet with honey, presenting it as one would offer a gift.

"I thank you for last night," he said humbly. "It is a night to remember."

She touched his cheek with affectionate fingers. "I will remember it, too," she promised.

His face lit up. "That is because Lazaro is a great lover," he boasted. "The greatest!"

They both burst into laughter.

It was a long and dreary trek to Màlaga. When the Monte de Gibralfaro, crowned by its ancient fortress, came into view, Arabella closed her eyes in sudden pain, recalling her first sight of it with the man she loved. She had known that love for such a brief time, but there were so many memories.

The wagon creaked into the outskirts of the city, long after dusk. In Màlaga, strange figures, robed, with towering conical hoods, thronged the streets. Arab shrank back with a cry of terror.

"Hush," Lazaro whispered. "It is only the *cofradia*." He went on to explain that the hooded men were members of parish churches who had come to arrange the Holy Week processions. Each *cofradia* or confraternity could be identified by its colors. "*Sangre*," he said, pointing to a group in scarlet tunics and hoods, with white cloaks. "*Armagura*," he identified those in white gowns and violet or purple. *Soledad*, all in blue; and the most frightening of all, *Sepulchro*, black shadows in the night.

They rode past floats that held tall images of the Virgin in crimson, apple-green, or ivory robes. One, with a jewelled dagger in her breast, wept real pearls instead of tears. Lazaro identified her as the *Virgen del Gran Dolor*.

The carnival atmosphere, weird and unreal, was made more eerie by the deepening night. Arabella suppressed a desire to cling to Lazaro, to beg him once more not to leave her. She did not want to walk through these streets alone.

The moment of parting came too soon. "I will pause near that building," Lazaro said into her ear. "You must jump from the cart and run into its shadow. Remain there until I am out of sight, then go to the cathedral. Now!"

"May God go with you," he whispered as she jumped and ran toward the structure he had indicated. He whipped his horses, hastening from the town. His vehicle was not followed, he thought. Not yet. And he must get to Triana to seek the Englishman's protection. It was hard to give up his life in the gypsy caves outside Guadix. There he had been a king. But it had been worth the price. For he had spent the night in the arms of the most beautiful señorita in all the world. It would be a thing to think on when he was a horse-trainer in the chilly country of England.

"The *greatest* horse-trainer in England," he amended. He began to whistle a gypsy tune as he drove toward Sevilla, but his whistling had a sad and lonely sound.

Arabella watched the wagon disappear into the darkness as she huddled in the shadow of the building where she'd taken shelter. A group of the *Sepulchro* passed. They spoke among themselves with the voices of men, but they resembled gaunt specters of death. Arab stood frozen, long after they had gone. She tried to will her legs to move, but they would not.

443

I am not Arabella McLeod, she told herself. I am a gypsy. If someone sees me hiding here, it will attract attention. I must do as Lazaro directed. She moved into the street, walking slowly, trying to seem as unobtrusive as possible. Her courage began to come back, and then she felt a sudden rush of fear.

Here was an event Lazaro had not prepared her for.

Two young *gitanos* came down the street, singing, arm in arm. They were dressed in their most colorful finery, and were warm with wine and the fiesta atmosphere. One pulled at the other, pointing. Here was a *gitana*! One of their own kind. Bedraggled, to be sure, but she was *muy bonita*—and alone.

Arabella cowered as they came toward her, shouting what appeared to be compliments and pleasantries. She could not understand what they were saying. She could not help but give herself away. And gypsy messages seemed to flash from place to place with lightning speed. She would be returned to the vengeance Lazaro had spoken of. Her mouth was dry, and she moistened her lips with her tongue.

It gave her an idea.

She turned her back on the approaching youths. Then one reached out to grab her arm, to turn her to face him. He shrank back.

"Madre de Dios," he whispered in horror as he crossed himself. His friend followed suit, and they took to their heels.

For the face that Arabella had turned toward him was that of the imbecile boy of the Barrio de Santiago; her eyes slitted to hide their color, lips wet and gaping, the blank expression of idiocy. Her training as an entertainer had not been for nothing.

But her courage was shattered now and she began to run. Luckily, in the melee of preparations for the Holy Week processions, one small, very dirty *gitana* went unnoticed.

As she reached the cathedral, she slowed to a walk. The doors at the entrance were open, and groups of opulently dressed Spaniards were moving through them. Apparently some sort of Holy Week service had begun.

She crouched back against the wall, shivering. When a gentleman and his lady spoke to her, she looked at them blankly. "Perhaps she is a deaf-mute, poor little thing," the señora said to her husband.

The man looked at Arab with pity. There were so many street beggars in Màlaga these days, but this one seemed deserving. He flipped a coin toward the girl. It struck her gown and fell, tinkling, to the pavement. She stood for a moment, as if blind, then bent to retrieve the money.

"You are right," the man said to his wife. "She is quite deaf. These poor unfortunates."

Arabella didn't understand his words, but she recognized the tone. He had thought her a beggar, an object of charity. She tilted her chin. She would keep the coin. It would buy *churros* from a stall in the morning—if she were unsuccessful in her errand.

The church door closed and the sound of chanting began within. Arab searched the walls about the structure. She and Juan had entered through a wrought-iron gate. When she found it at last, the gate was closed and locked. She studied the gate, wondering if she could scale it.

Carefully, she fitted one foot into its ornate design, then another until she reached the top. Her gown caught on a spear-like point and ripped as she climbed down the other side. Holding her torn skirts together, Arab moved along the walkway to where she and Juan had stood that day. The little citrus tree was in bloom, sweetly scented. The ground at its base showed signs of infinite care.

Arab sat at the foot of the tree, huddled in her skirts to keep warm, praying that Father Díaz tended his garden as faithfully as he served his God—that he would be the one to find her in the morning.

She fell asleep to dream of hooded figures who removed their masks one by one, becoming Juan, Lazaro, Rita, Pablo, Tamsen, Em, Papa. . . .

It was a confused girl who awoke to see the shocked features of Father Díaz looking down at her. And the priest, in turn, was most confused to find that a dirty, ragged gypsy girl had invaded his monastic garden.

Chapter 7

It had not been a good morning for Father Díaz. He was growing old. The service last night had taken its toll. The bell had rung late for morning prayers, and somehow a cat had gotten into the cathedral, invading the holy places. He had trapped it behind the altar, where it spat at him and stared up with slitted green eyes—eyes such as those of this gypsy girl, here where she had no business being.

Out of breath, and a little out of sorts, he frowned down at her. "What are you doing here?" he asked in Spanish. "This is Church property, you know. Are you hiding? In trouble?"

Arabella's confusion faded. This was not a dream. She rose to her feet, unmindful of her torn gown. Stretching her hands to him, pleading, she said, "Father Díaz, please help me."

The gaunt old priest took a backward step, his face a study in bewilderment. A ragged gypsy girl, a beggar, no doubt, but speaking in English! "My child, I do not understand—"

"Don't you know me?" Arabella looked down at her ragged clothing. Of course he didn't! When he had first met her, her hair, with its natural color, was piled high, and she had worn an elegant gown. "I am the girl who came with Juan Narváez. We wished to marry—"

Father Díaz hastily crossed himself, calling on the name of his Lord. This could not be!

Her words tumbled over each other as Arab spilled out her story; of Juan's betrayal, the General's visit, her decision to return to America. He listened closely, his hard black eyes giving no indication of the turmoil in his mind. She continued, telling him of the kidnapping engineered by Isleta Guzman, of her days in the gypsy caves behind Guadix, her rescue by Lazaro, her coming here.

"And what do you want of me?"

Her eyes filled with tears. Ascetic though he was, he could not help marveling at her beauty. "I want to go home," she wept. "Back to my own country. There is nothing for me here, and if I must stay—I fear for my life. There is no one to whom I can go for help. I have no money for passage—"

"I cannot help you. I have nothing of my own." He paused, noticing the fever in her cheeks, the too-bright eyes that betrayed her condition. The child was ill. He sighed. He was old, too old to be confronted with so many problems at the beginning of Holy Week. "It will take some thought," he said slowly, "and I shall require some time. Come, I will take you to the Good Sisters."

Father Díaz handed Arabella over to a grim-faced nun, who seemed more shocked at the girl's soiled and ragged condition than the fact that she spoke in a foreign tongue. Then he returned to his small cell to meditate and pray.

General Narváez was his old friend, Juan his pupil almost from birth. He had also played a part in the plan for Juan's future in order to help build a new Spain. It was not only for his country, but for his Church. In 1836, under the Constitution of Cadiz, the Church lands had been taken away and sold to profiteers. The reign of Isabella II was insupportable. Spain was now ruled by the army, with *pronunciamientos,* a conservative General seizing control, then a liberal; plots and counterplots were hatched while Isabella passed from lover to lover.

A new Spain was the only hope. The years grooming young Narváez for his position must not be lost. But what to do?

He pondered the problem. The story Arabella had

told him did not ring true. Juan Narváez would not have deserted her in such a cowardly manner, leaving it to his uncle to break the news of his marriage to the Guzman girl. It must have been the General's plan, and so going to Juan was out of the question. Should he approach General Narváez, himself? Or had he been in league with the Guzman girl and the kidnapping? Father Díaz definitely did not approve of such methods. Sending the girl from the country was one thing, kidnapping was cruel and evil.

If he could not speak with Juan or the General, where would he obtain funds for the girl's passage? It could not be managed without money.

California. That was where the girl wished to go. How far was that? He had no idea, having been no farther than he could travel by muleback from his blessed church. He drew his brows together in a frown as he thought of the name of the place. He had heard it mentioned recently . . . somewhere. . . .

Ah! The priest's harsh features cracked into a rare smile. Going to the rear of his quarters, he called to a ragged, teenage boy.

"Trini, I have an errand for you."

Two hours later, his messenger ushered a man into the garden where the priest puttered around the small citrus tree. "You sent for me, Father?"

Father Díaz looked up. "Ah! Captain Lascal!"

The captain, turning his hat in his hands, looked terrified, for he captained what was known as a "bad ship." Many times the priest had been called to give last rites to his ailing crew members when they reached port. This time had been no exception.

Now, the stinking little vessel he owned was heading for California, with a cargo of oil and cheeses. The priest had given him a scolding the last time he was aboard, ordering him to take casks of vinegar for scurvy, to fill his casks with fresh water before he was out of sight of land, to check his tins of salted beef. What more did the priest want?

449

"I have complied with your instructions, Father," the man said, his voice trembling.

"Good." The priest's voice was abstracted, as if he hadn't heard. Then he fixed his fierce dark eyes on the man in a manner that made him quail.

"You are a good Catholic? You wish to perform a service for your God and your country?"

"Yes, Father," Lascal stammered.

"And you wish my blessing? My prayers for a safe journey?"

The captain nodded silently.

"Then you will take a passenger. There is a woman who is in danger here, a political thing; you need not know the details, only that you will aid in her escape."

"Women are bad luck aboard ship," the captain said sullenly. "And there is only one cabin. My own. The sailors sleep in the hold, or on deck."

"Then you will join them. As for bad luck, it cannot exist if God is with you."

Lascal's eyes flickered. There was fear in them. He was a poor and ignorant man, trying to propitiate at least the religious injunctions that would not cost him money.

"Yes, Father."

"When do you sail?"

"I sail in the morning, with the tide."

The old priest nodded. "Then prepare your cabin. The lady with be brought aboard tonight, under cover of darkness."

The next morning, Arab stood at the railing of the small vessel that was to carry her home, ignoring the hubbub of weighing anchor and setting sail. Because she was the only woman aboard, she had been timid about setting foot on deck. But her desire to take one last look at Màlaga, the place where she had known so much happiness and sadness in so short a time, had won over her fears. She gazed at the old city with its Moorish and Spanish influences all so evident. She knew this place would be burned into her memory forever.

The house where she had lived with Juan was out of sight, around a point of land. Straining her eyes, she hoped to glimpse its roof of Spanish tile one more time.

It was just as well that she couldn't, she thought wearily. She must begin to forget Juan.

Juan had not forgotten her. The previous night he had sent his servants away for the evening. He prowled the garden and waited at the pool, feeling that Arabella might suddenly appear. When she did not come, he cursed himself for believing in intuition. For the first time since her disappearance, he had felt that she was near. At last, he went to the room they'd shared together and knelt beside the bed, his face buried in the pillow where the scent of her hair still lingered. He wept for the first time since he was a little boy.

This morning, while Conchita was serving him his breakfast, Lupe had appeared at the door of his room. Her face was white, and she cast a frightened glance behind her as she requested permission to speak.

"Come in," he said. "Shut the door if you wish."

She entered, took a deep breath, and launched into her story. "I have an aunt," she said, "who is a nun." She had gone only this morning to ask for her prayers. And she had learned something most strange. Father Díaz had placed a ragged, dirty gypsy girl in the Good Sisters' care. The sisters had fed her, bathed her, then the priest had taken her away.

"And what is so strange about that? It was an act of kindness."

"This girl," said Lupe, "was not a true *gitana*. My aunt said that her hair and skin were colored with dyes. She spoke English and her eyes were green, like grass."

Juan leaped from his bed, overturning the tray, his mind suddenly alive with hope. "Leave the tray," he said to Lupe. "Find my boots!" *Oh, God*, he prayed, *let me find her with Father Díaz!* At the door, he turned to plant a kiss on Lupe's plump and blushing cheek.

Father Díaz was alone in his garden when Juan found him. God help me, he thought as he saw his beloved

451

pupil approach. So soon! He wondered if the vessel were clear of the harbor.

"Ah, my son! It is a delight to see you. Look at my small tree, how straight it grows."

"Where is she?"

Time, Father Díaz thought wearily, I need time. He paused for a moment, shutting out the angry young face before him, calculating the tide. He could only delay, for it was not in him to lie.

"Where is she?" Juan shouted angrily.

The priest turned his piercing gaze on Juan in reproof. "If you do not have respect for my age, my son, at least, have respect for my calling!"

"I am sorry, Father."

The old man smiled, recalling the rebellious boy he'd tutored through his youth. How many times the lad had said those words. But his smile faded as he looked into Juan's determined face. He was no longer a boy. He sighed.

"You are speaking of the young woman you wished to marry?"

"Arabella." Juan was bursting with impatience. "I know she is here."

Father Díaz turned away from Juan's agonized eyes. Putting out his hand, he touched his little tree. Some things grew as one wished them to.

"She is gone. She is on a ship that sailed this morning with the tide."

At the priest's words, Juan ran across the garden, through the gates, to his waiting horse. Father Díaz heard the thunder of its hooves as it headed toward the harbor.

The priest fell to his knees beside his little citrus tree, praying that he had done the right thing.

Juan Narváez arrived at the harbor in time to see the white tip of a sail disappear in the distance. His love was gone, and he knew what he was going to do.

Aboard that ship, Arabella had waited at the rail until she could no longer see the land. As she turned to go below, she knew that her thoughts of Juan and the

452

sights and scents of Spain would burn deep and long in her memory.

Even now, she thought she could smell the fragrance of almonds, carnations, and beeswax wafting across the water from the shore.

Chapter 8

As fall approached in San Francisco, the inhabitants agreed that this year they'd had the finest weather ever. The streets were dry, and the dust raised by the teeming commerce was preferable to the usual mud. One bright day followed another, and the citizens seemed to be trying to soak up enough sun to last through the rainy season.

Em and Donald Alden were no exception. One morning, as Donald pushed back his chair from the breakfast table, he suggested a picnic. He would not go to the office until afternoon.

Though she had a dinner party to prepare for in the evening, Em was delighted. She had not seen enough of her husband recently. And it would be good for little Martha to have an outing. There was no discussion about where they would go, for invariably, their excursions led them to the site above the sea where they would build their new home.

Today was no exception. Alden halted the carriage on the bluff where he had proposed to Em, and Em cried out with delight. Never had the sky seemed so clear, nor the sea so blue. Martha didn't give them much time to enjoy the view. She wanted down from the carriage, and once down, she began to run, a small bright figure against the wheat-colored fall grass.

Alden followed her with long strides, picking her up when she fell headlong, soothing her hurts, releasing her to run again.

Em watched, suffused with love. In the grass, she spread a cloth and set out the food she'd managed to put together hastily. Sensing that the meal was ready, Martha switched directions and came running back to eat.

A beautiful day, Em thought, watching her husband and child. She felt warm, relaxed, and drowsy with love and sunshine.

They ran and tumbled and laughed, taking full advantage of the day and of each other's happiness.

When it was time to leave, Em and Donald followed a path leading down to the sand. For a little while, they let Martha run barefoot near the water. The child was bubbling over with enthusiasm as she ran, searching for shells, then squatting to dig holes near the water, watching them fill up, giggling as she did so.

Em leaned her head against Donald's shoulder. "I wish we never had to go home," she said, passionately. "I wish we could stay here forever. You've been so busy, lately. I've missed you!"

"And I've missed you," he said, reflectively. "Em, what would you say if I said I was thinking about retiring?"

"Retiring!" She stared at him. "But you're so young!"

He laughed. "Retiring from politics, I mean. You know how I've been working with Gadsden on that purchase from Mexico. I think the deal will be completed before long. As for building a transcontinental railroad through that territory—well, it's enough to know I helped lay the groundwork. Let someone else do the building."

"But what would you do?"

"Build the house. Perhaps raise blooded horses. Plant a vineyard. Make love to my wife. Have more children—"

She hugged him. "You!" she said, affectionately. "But what brings this up now?"

"I need more time with you," he said, soberly. "I have all the money I need. And a man with a political career must have no scandals that may be used against him. That young hell-raiser, Adam! Well, you know what he's been up to."

"Yes," Em whispered. Adam Wheeler seemed bent on smashing Donald's reputation. The gossip about Tamsen hadn't helped it any, either. Em had not seen Tamsen since Mike Dunnevant told her that Tamsen operated a brothel. Tamsen made no attempt to call, and Em was upset and confused enough to be unable to make a move.

"It's Tamsen, too," she said, her voice hard. "She's spoiling things for you, isn't she? I—I don't think I can ever forgive her."

Alden gave her a little shake. "That's not like you, Em! Not like the girl I married at all! And you'd better remember that if it hadn't been for your sister we might never have met!"

"I know," she said quietly, "but what she's doing is so wrong!"

"I don't like it, either," he admitted. "But Tamsen is responsible for her own life, just as we are for ours. And it isn't against California law. The thing I can't figure is how she got involved in this without your knowledge. Living right there in the same house—"

"I think I knew," Em said in a choked voice. "But I didn't want to know. I didn't want to see anything that would disturb me. But I didn't guess how bad it was— that it could be anything like this! Donald, I know she owns the place, but do you think that she—that she—"

"No," Alden said firmly, "I don't think she does. From what I've gathered she just runs the place and sings occasionally. In any case, I think we should ignore the past, have her over to Sunday dinner. She's part of our family, after all."

"I'm sorry," Em said. "I can't. Not yet."

"Just keep one thing in mind. Tamsen's behavior has no bearing on my decision to retire. Nor does Adam's, for that matter, though I hoped I might be able to groom him to take my place. All I want to do is live happily with you forever. Isn't that enough?"

She pressed her cheek against his shoulder. "Enough," she said, dreamily.

456

At home, with Martha napping upstairs, Em hurried into the kitchen. Donald had wanted her to employ a cook, but she couldn't bring herself to do it. She had relented enough to let Lin serve, but the cooking was her own province. This evening she wanted Donald to be especially proud of her efforts.

Turning to her work, she crimped the edges of a pie, trimmed the crust, and slid it into the oven. The pastry had felt right. Mr. Stanton was a man for pie, as was Mr. Crocker.

Em smiled as she worked, for she knew all her efforts would be wasted. When these men got together and started talking railroad, they ate without noticing what was on their plates.

At last, everything was ready; the table set with the gold-rimmed china service; the crystal wine glasses and decanter on the sideboard; Em was perfumed and dressed. The gown she'd chosen was a new one, simple, softly draped, in a blue material that matched her eyes. Descending the stairs, she knew it was a good choice when she saw her husband's face.

"I have to be married to the most beautiful woman in the world," the Senator said, smiling proudly.

Em turned pink with pleasure. "I always felt so plain," she confessed. "I could never hold a candle to Tamsen or Arabella."

"You were wrong," he said, still studying her. "And what's strange is that you're far lovelier than you were when we married. I don't know what it is. A sort of serene maturity—"

It's just being loved, she thought as she went to answer the door. That, and gaining the self-confidence to make her own decisions. Growing up.

This is a part of it, too, she thought as Lin served one delicious course after another. The food placed before the guests was rapidly being devoured, though, just as she had suspected, the men were too excited by their conversation to appreciate what they were eating.

Mr. Crocker pointed his fork at the Senator. "Those

people up north are going to fight dirty," he warned. "They want that railroad someplace else, and they'll do anything to get it!"

"I don't think so," Stanford argued. "After all, this is to the whole country's advantage."

"Now wait a minute," another of the guests joined in. "If you think—"

Em smiled to herself, letting the conversation flow over her. She had heard it all so many times before. She sat in her place at the table, but let her mind wander, carrying her back to the morning, there on the sand by the sea. The way Donald held her in his arms; the way Martha looked running on the beach.

"Missee." Lin was standing at her shoulder. He bent to whisper in her ear. She looked up quickly. His face wore a worried expression. Trouble in the kitchen? The dessert was prepared—

"Yes?"

"A little missee in kitchen. Say must see you. No wait."

"Who is it? Did she give her name?"

"No, missee. Velly dirty. Look sick. Hungly."

"Ask her to wait. I'll be free in a few minutes."

"Yes, missee."

No sooner had he gone than they heard his voice raised in anger. He backed from the kitchen, waving his arms, trying to halt the figure that was pushing past him. Em rose. "It's all right. I will handle this—"

She stopped short, staring at the intruder—a tall girl, bone-thin, dressed in rags. From beneath a tangled, dirty mop of hair that was red at the roots, haunted green eyes stared at them. Her face was as white as milk. Only a spot of red on each cheekbone indicated the fever that consumed her.

When she saw the assembled guests, her dull eyes filled with embarrassment. "I'm sorry, Em," she mumbled, swaying on her feet. "I didn't mean to interrupt—"

"Arab," Em gasped. "Arab! Oh, dear God!" As she whirled from her place, her sweeping skirts caught her chair, sending it crashing to the floor as she rushed to

458

take her sister in her arms. "Oh, Donald! She's ill! Help me!"

Donald Alden moved to his wife's side. Taking one of the newcomer's arms in his, he helped Em support her as she looked at him, uncomprehending.

"Gentlemen," he said to the shocked faces at the table, "I would like to present my sister-in-law, Miss Arabella McLeod. Now, if you will excuse us for a moment—"

Leaving their stunned guests, Donald and Em helped Arabella up the stairs. As they led her into a bedroom, Arab burst into tears. "I didn't know, Em. I didn't know you were married. I was desperate! I guess I've spoiled things."

Donald Alden's mouth curved in a smile of sweet tenderness as he looked at his wife, and then back to her. "How could it spoil anything," he asked, "when the little sister my wife has been so worried about comes home?"

Home. That was the word that stayed in Arabella's mind long after the other two were in bed. The mattress she lay upon was soft, the sheets were clean, smelling of sunshine. Em had brought hot water for her to bathe. For the first time in a long while, Arab felt clean. Em's nightdress felt like silk against her skin. Her hair had been washed, the dyed ends cropped. A small fire burned in the fireplace to guard her against chill.

Home, after castles in Spain, the caves back of Guadix, Juan and Lazaro, after the gruelling trip on a small, dirty ship that was tossed about by storms; after the shortage of rations and a mutinous crew. Em had entreated her to tell of her travels, to tell what had brought her to this condition, but Arab had only turned her face away. "I don't want to talk about it," she'd whispered. "I don't want to think about it. Please, Em."

And Em, understanding and loving Em, tucked her in for the night and left her with her thoughts.

It was a long time before she slept.

The next day, she had two visitors. The first was a brown-eyed imp of a child, sitting at the foot of her bed when she woke, staring at her gravely. With a shock, Arabella saw that the little girl looked like Tamsen.

"Hello," the little one said.

"Hello, yourself," Arabella answered.

Then the tot was off and running, screaming, "Mom-eee." Em had said that she'd married Donald Alden last Christmas Day, but the child was older than that. Arabella was sitting up, a puzzled look on her face, when Em entered with a breakfast tray.

"Em, the little girl——"

"Her name is Martha." Em's cheeks were red.

"But whose child is she? I don't understand."

"She is mine."

"But you haven't been married long. Not long enough for——," Arab's eyes lit with a new knowledge. "She's Tamsen's, isn't she? Tamsen got herself in trouble, and foisted her baby off on you. That's it, isn't it?"

Em's face was still flushed, but with anger now. "You are wrong, Arab. Martha is mine. And my husband has adopted her. Perhaps I'll tell you the whole story, some-day, but not right now. There are things I don't want to talk about, or to think about. I, too, am entitled to privacy."

Arabella's eyes filled with tears. "I'm so sorry, Em. I didn't mean to pry. It was just that I was surprised."

"It's all right," Em said, laying a cool hand on Arab's forehead. "You're still feverish," she said with some alarm.

"I've been ill for some time," Arab confessed. "I contracted a cold some months ago, and I haven't been able to rid myself of it. I've been so . . . tired." Tears washed her eyes again and she blinked them away.

"Eat your breakfast," Em said. "Then you're going to sleep. I'm going to the apothecary to get some herbs for that cough of yours. No," she waved away Arabella's protestations, "I insist. Then we'll have a good long talk after I dose you properly and you get some rest."

Arabella was alone in the house when the second

visitor came. She heard a door shut downstairs and thought it was Em returning from the apothecary. Then she heard footsteps on the stairs, but they did not sound like Em's. Senator Alden? The steps stopped at her door and she sat up, pulling the coverlet to her throat as the door opened.

The young man who stood there was just as surprised as she to face a stranger. Then a dimple flickered in his cheek and his blue eyes danced.

"I'm sorry," he said, ruefully, "I seem to have intruded. This is my room when I stay overnight, and I left—," he paused. "I'm Adam Wheeler, the Senator's stepbrother. May I ask . . . ?"

"I'm Arabella McLeod, Em's sister," she answered.

He studied her for a moment, wondering at the cropped curls, not missing the curves of the figure beneath the covers. Too thin for his taste, but he had a notion she was made for love. More like Tamsen, he imagined, than Em. It would be exciting to see if there were any fire in this girl.

"Do you mind if I come in, then?" Again, that charming, crooked smile. "Since it's all in the family, after all. I left my jacket here."

She nodded her head, and he went to the wardrobe, taking down the coat he'd mentioned.

"Where have they been hiding you?" he asked.

"I've just returned from—from an ocean voyage. Last night, in fact. I've been ill."

"Then you must hurry and get well so we can become better acquainted," he said turning toward the door. "Trust old Donald to find himself a wife with *two* pretty sisters."

He was gone, and she lay back to dream. Adam Wheeler was very nice-looking. He probably had many traits in common with his brother. It might be nice to have someone like him around.

She frowned, recalling his conversation. *Two pretty sisters.* Then he knew Tamsen. Where was Tamsen? Em had taken care to avoid mention of her name. Arab

461

did not wish to see her, but Em might have told her where she was living and what she was doing. Was she alive and well? She felt a sudden twist of pain at the thought that there might be something wrong.

Ridiculous! Tamsen was like a cat, always landing on her feet. Tamsen was indestructible!

Chapter 9

Tamsen was alive and well at her establishment, where business was thriving. The only thorn in her rose garden was Adam Wheeler, though his visits had become less frequent of late. Most of her clientele were decorous in their manner toward the girls, and she had heard nothing from the citizens' committee since George Hecker's hasty departure. Thinking of it brought a smile to Tamsen's face.

She was sitting before her mirror, brushing her hair, and that sudden smile surprised her. It had been a long time since Tamsen had felt amused by anything. Since the uncomfortable visit with Sloan, she had thrown herself into her work, thinking of nothing else.

Did it show in her face? She put a tentative hand to her smooth, unlined olive cheeks. Was there a hardness about her eyes? She thought of other madams she had met whose profession showed in their features. It was not an easy business, she thought glumly—keeping the girls satisfied, settling petty disputes and jealousies, maintaining order in the Parlor at night, keeping an eye out for those who imbibed too freely.

It was worth it, though, when she appeared on the floor and received applause, adulation even. It was worth it, knowing she kept a clean and very profitable house. Men admired her brains as well as her body, for she had made it her business to become informed on all the issues of the day. Many a business deal was consummated in Madam Franklin's Parlor.

Why then, was there so little to smile over?

A light tap at the door ended her musings. At first,

Tamsen wasn't certain anyone was there, the knock had been as soft as the brush of a butterfly's wing. The door opened to reveal Ming Yee's small ivory face.

"Soo-plise," the girl enunciated, carefully. "Soo-plise."

Tamsen stared at her. What was she trying to say? Surprise? "Ming Yee! I can't believe it! You're speaking English!"

"I learn," the girl boasted, smiling her delicate porcelain smile. "Pletty damgood, hunh?"

Tamsen swallowed her laughter. "It is a surprise! Who taught you?"

"Who th' hell d'ya think?" Nell's face beamed around the door frame. "This here gal helped some, a'course." She jerked a thumb toward Mei, who had joined her.

"Ming Yee, I'm proud of you. And I'm really happy for you!" Tamsen said.

"I ploud, too," the doll-like creature said. "Happy rike hell!"

"Don't git stuck-up over it," Nell said. "She didn't do it fer *you*. What a woman won't do fer some gawdamn feller!"

"For Mike," Ming Yee nodded, pleased. "Learn for Mike."

Tamsen hugged her. "Whatever the reason, I'm glad," she said. But after they had gone, she wondered. The language barrier had kept Ming Yee safe. Tamsen she had always explained to those who approached her for the girl that she was an entertainer and did not go upstairs. But what would happen if Ming Yee should express her own preferences? It was clear that she was attracted to Mike Dunnevant. But Mike had been hurt by Katie. Suppose he just used the girl, and then moved on?

Tamsen turned listlessly back to brushing her hair. The door opened behind her and the mirror revealed Em standing in the doorway.

Tamsen was unable to suppress a little cry of delight as she rose and turned to face her sister. Her pleasure at seeing her after all these months faded at Em's expression. Hatted, gloved, as befitted her social position, Em wore the look of one forced to make a rather distasteful duty call. Tamsen was conscious of how she must appear, with her hair loose, robe opened, and bare shoulders. She pulled the robe together, and pushed back her locks with a nervous hand.

"I'm glad to see you, Em," she said quietly.

"And I am glad to see you." Em's voice was sincere, but her face turned pink as she said, "Though it is most difficult for me to come here. I would prefer other surroundings."

Tamsen lowered her eyes before her sister's, which were both loving and condemning. "I'm sorry," Tamsen said. "I suppose we might have met someplace else."

Em moved toward her, impulsively. "Tamsen, I can't bear this! Talking to each other this way! Like strangers!"

Tamsen moved to a chair, taking hold of its back to steady her trembling. "If you are here," she said, coolly, "there is a reason. I trust Martha is well."

"It isn't Martha I've come about. It's Arab. Arab is home."

"H—home?" Tamsen stammered.

"She is staying with us. Something happened to her in Spain. I don't know what it was, since she won't discuss it. When she came, she was ill and dressed in filthy rags and her hair was dyed." Em's eyes filled with tears. "And, oh Tam, she's different. So sad and melancholy—I thought just being home would help, but it's been two weeks—"

"I want to see her," Tamsen blurted.

Em didn't think that was wise. She and Arabella had discussed it and agreed that Tamsen should know she was home and safe, for her own peace of mind, but Arab was not eager to see Tamsen yet. She still felt Tamsen was responsible for the things that had happened to her, but perhaps some day she might soften.

"I see," Tamsen said. "Very well, Em, thank you for coming."

Tamsen walked to the door and opened it. Again, Em

465

put out her hand, pleading, "Please, Tamsen! Can't you understand what it does to me to see you living like this? It's not too late! If Papa were here—"

"But Papa is not here. This is my life. I chose it. I can take care of myself, and I do not appreciate your interference."

Then Em, hurt by her sister's harsh words, left the room. Tamsen returned to her mirror, looking into it dully. She envisioned a scene far back in her memory. Papa had the grippe, and was concerned that he might die, leaving his precious daughters.

Reaching to touch Tamsen's hair, he'd said, "You can't imagine how I depend on you, girl! Em is so frail, born to be protected, and Arabella's a wild one, don't know where she came by it—"

Tamsen closed her eyes, smelling the scent of a Pennsylvania afternoon; the odor of rich black loam, freshly turned, of baking bread wafting from the kitchen where Mrs. Goodson was at work.

And she could hear her own voice saying, "Don't worry, Papa! I'll take care of them. But it's just the grippe, you'll be all right!"

"You're my good right arm. I'd hoped you'd turn out to be a boy. You're named after my father, you know. His name was Thomas."

Tamsen after Thomas. She was not a boy, but a woman destined to live in a woman's body, with a woman's weakness, a woman's desires, with only marriage as a standard of success. And now, because she'd done the best she could with what she had to work with, she was the wild one. It was a joke! A most unfunny joke! A ragged laugh cut at her throat like a knife as it turned into a sob.

Angrily, she dressed and went downstairs.

Em, too, was angry as she hurried home. But she was angry at herself. How self-righteous she had sounded! How prissy! She and Tamsen had once been so close. She could not talk to her now. Tamsen had changed, Arab had changed. But perhaps she had changed most of all.

466

There was another change, too. One that Em and Donald discussed that evening as they sat before the parlor fire. Looking up from her needlework, Em watched lovingly as the Senator filled his pipe.

"Have you noticed," he asked, finally, "the effect that young sister of yours is having on Adam? The scamp has become most respectable these days. Perhaps what he's needed all along is something like this. How does she feel about him, do you know?"

"I think she likes him," Em said, honestly. "I don't know if it could become more than that. She's had some sort of experience that's left its mark. I imagine it involved a man."

"She seems to be recovering from it, I would say."

Perhaps he was right. But he had not known Arabella before—the laughing, sunny Arab with her penchant for mischief. The thin, pale girl with serious eyes seemed almost a stranger to Em. Her exuberance was gone, her zest for living absent. Arab seemed to endure each day with a dogged acceptance.

"She's very different," Em hedged.

"And so is Adam." Donald Alden puffed at his pipe, smiling through its smoke at the woman who was so dear to him. "I think I've been too quick to criticize where Adam is concerned. He says I treat him like a kid, and I suppose I do. Now that he seems to be reforming, I have an idea that it might be a good thing to give him a little more responsibility, let him sit in on a few confidential meetings, build up his self-confidence. What do you think?"

Em had not lost her distrust of Adam. His reformation had been too sudden. "Your work is so important," she said, troubled. "If anything should go wrong—"

"The boy's changed," his stepbrother insisted. "Em, he came to see me at the office this afternoon. We had a long talk."

"I'm glad, for your sake," Em said. "You know, I've been thinking of having some sort of affair to welcome Arabella home. A garden party perhaps, before the weather changes."

467

"Good idea." Senator Alden picked up a late copy of the *Alta California*, looking at her over the paper. "And Adam can be her escort. They make a handsome couple, don't you think?"

Adam Wheeler was thinking the very same thing. He'd been attracted to the girl at first sight, challenged by her air of diffidence. He'd called often after that morning, playing the gentleman. Arab had begun to take a place in his plans, especially after the talk with Donald this afternoon.

Adam laughed as he entered the door of Madam Franklin's Parlor. The information he'd sought to gain by spying on his brother was being handed to him on a silver platter. He would woo the fair Arabella, a part of his work that he regarded as a pleasure. In the meantime, he didn't intend to let business completely take over his life. He was looking forward to Katie's attentions.

He looked around the room, which was empty at this early hour, and saw that the red-haired object of his search was in conversation with Dan Tallant. Adam Wheeler beckoned to Katie, and she turned from Tallant immediately. The gesture made Adam feel very important. He could take Katie away from any man, any time. She would not be sorry that she favored him, for he would soon be a wealthy man. Even though he was marrying Arab, he felt that he was man enough to handle them both.

Tamsen, who passed the couple on the stairs, was startled by the knowing smirk Adam gave her. He was up to something, she was certain of that. She only hoped that it didn't have anything to do with her or the Parlor.

Chapter 10

The California weather was on Em's side the day of the garden party in honor of Arabella. The evening was warm, and a soft breeze flowed through the small garden at the rear of the Alden mansion, which was strung with Chinese lanterns and decorated with flowers. Em's guests had not disappointed her, either. There had been no rejections from the socially elite of San Francisco.

There were gentlemen in evening suits, gentlemen in storekeeper's clothing, executives, sea captains, and men newly rich from the gold fields. They made a rather motley-appearing group. The ladies showed even greater disparity. Some were garbed like peacocks, bonnets towering with plumes. Others were dressed in sober daytime attire. The newly prosperous types arrived escorting women of rather dubious backgrounds. These were overdressed and stiff in their manners as they viewed their surroundings with awe.

"Such a hodgepodge of people," Em whispered to her husband when they found a moment alone. "I can't believe it!"

Donald Alden grinned. "Haven't you heard the story of how the elite of San Francisco are chosen? One draws the line between wholesale and retail. It is said that if a man sells soap and candles by the box, he's socially acceptable, if he sells it by the pound, he's outside the pale."

"Then some of our guests must be meeting socially for the first time," Em giggled. "Oh, and Donald—Dan Tallant hasn't arrived. You did invite him!"

"I did, but he sent his regrets. What about Tamsen?"

469

"I didn't ask her," Em said in a small voice. "Not because of her profession, Donald, so don't frown! I just thought it might not be the right time. I want Arabella to be happy tonight."

"She certainly seems to be." Senator Alden looked at the young couple standing away from the crowd, near the tiny fountain. Adam and Arab stood close. "Look at her face," Alden said. "You can see!"

It was true, Em thought. Arabella looked so beautiful! Green was her best color, but she had refused to have a single gown of that shade in the new wardrobe Em had provided for her. Still, that soft gold was perfect in the light of the paper lanterns. She looked like a princess, Em decided—Sleeping Beauty—the way her face was lifted to the stars with that odd, bemused expression. Surely Adam had not inspired that look.

Indeed, Adam Wheeler had not. For while she listened to the silver fall of water in the fountain, Arabella had been transported to Spain. She wandered in gardens that stretched to the edge of the land, tumbling down terraces to the sea. The fragrance of remembered flowers filled the air. The polite chatting of the guests ebbed and flowed like a sound of waves touching the shore. If she turned quickly enough, her prince would be there.

"Miss Arabella?" Adam's voice was amused. "Where are your thoughts? Certainly not with me!"

She turned, her face still dreaming. The look of enchantment faded and her green eyes dulled. "I'm sorry, Adam. I don't know where my mind was. What is it?"

"I have spoken with my stepbrother," he said, clearing his throat, "and also with my dear sister-in-law. They both approve of a question I wish to ask you. This," he indicated the teeming garden, "is not the place nor the time. I would like permission to call on you tomorrow, and to ask that you think seriously on what you surely know I intend to say."

Arab moved away a little, putting her hand to the fountain's edge. This was not unexpected. Em had been making little conspiratorial remarks for several weeks. "Don't you think you should change for the evening,

470

Arab? Adam's coming to dinner." Then, "Adam's such a changed man these days. Donald is so pleased."

Sighing, Arab turned toward Adam. She saw a very earnest young man, stone sober, respectably dressed; this Adam bore no resemblance to the scapegrace she knew he'd once been. With Adam, at least, she would not feel the qualms about marrying him that she would feel if she were wedding a man who expected virginity in his bride.

"You haven't answered me," he said, quietly.

"Tomorrow, then," she finally managed to say.

He took her arm in a proprietary manner. "I must not keep you from your guests," he said. "After all, you are the guest of honor. I will be here shortly after ten in the morning. And we will talk, here, in the garden."

As they rejoined the group, Arab could tell that both Em and Donald were aware of what had taken place. It was almost as if the whole thing had been staged—the script written, the setting provided. She smiled humorlessly. Now, all she had to do was be the actress she really was, marry a man she didn't love, and pretend all the rest of her life.

After the guests had gone, Arab stood at her window looking down at the garden below. Tomorrow's setting for the proposal.

She had to face the fact that Juan was lost to her. She had to try to build some kind of acceptable life for herself—a life including a husband and children. There would be no rapture, but neither would there be depths of degradation. She had certainly reached both ends of the scale.

Her answer to Adam would be yes. It had to be.

Tamsen learned of Arab's upcoming marriage through an item in the *Alta California*. The paper was brought to her by Nell. "Dusty said you oughta see this," she grumbled. "Wouldn't say what th' hell was in it." She squinted her eyes as she put the paper in Tamsen's hand. "Jes' can't read th' fine print," she said. "Whyncha read it out loud?"

471

Tamsen smiled at Nell's excuse, then her smile faded. Dusty had marked the item. *"Senator Donald Alden and his lady are pleased to announce . . ."*

"Dear God!" Tamsen breathed. "Oh, no!"

"Well, what is it? Somethin' wrong?"

"My sister Arabella is getting married next Sunday."

"Hell, what's wrong with that?"

"To Adam Wheeler."

"Wheeler? That no-good sonofabitch?" Nell's face was apoplectic. "Don't know your little sis, but if she's anything like Em, she's making one helluva mistake! Maybe you oughta put a bug in her ear!"

"She's not like Em. To tell the truth, I don't know what she's like now. She wouldn't listen to me, anyway."

Nell snorted and left. Tamsen sat for a long time holding the paper in her hand. Young Adam was charming on the surface, but beneath his charm was a streak of weakness and cruelty. Of all the girls in the house, only Katie seemed to be able to stand him. The same feeling about him seemed to exist among the other patrons. The only men Adam consorted with were those who operated just on the fringes of legality.

Nell was right. She must talk to Arab and to Em, tell them what she knew of Adam Wheeler. Tamsen half-rose, then sank into her chair again. After all, she had been the one who talked the family into heading west, and Papa had died. She had been the cause of the attack on Em, and was the one who had sent Arabella with Reverend Smythe; she was the source of embarrassment to the Alden family. Why should anyone think her advice worth considering?

Tamsen read the newspaper article again in its entirety. It was to be a garden wedding. The bride, Miss Arabella McLeod, sister of Mrs. Alden, had returned recently from a trip abroad. The groom, stepbrother to the Senator, was being taken into his legal firm as an associate.

Perhaps it will work, Tamsen thought, trying to reassure herself. If Adam really loves her, he might settle down.

472

A memory of Em's wedding appeared in her mind. How beautiful Em had been in her happiness. Perhaps it would be the same for Arab. She certainly hoped so.

Feeling very empty and alone, Tamsen rose to survey her little kingdom. The girls were either resting or getting dressed for the night. Downstairs, Nell and Dusty were polishing glasses at the bar. Their heads were close together, their faces flushed. It was clear they both had their minds on a more romantic occupation.

With a forced smile in their direction, Tamsen continued into the kitchen, where Birdie Faraday was cutting peaches for a half-dozen pies. At the metal sink, elbow deep in suds, was Ben Lavery, a new and unpaid addition to the kitchen.

"Hello, Ben," Tamsen said, smiling. "Birdie put you to work?" She liked the old man. Huge, with a white mustache and a mass of hair that curled on his shoulders, he had small twinkling eyes and a rumbling laugh. He hadn't come to the Parlor for the girls, he admitted frankly on their first meeting, but for the pies. And once he met the cook, the old reprobate moved into the kitchen.

"Works th' pants offa me," he admitted. Then he added with a leer, "But I figger that's what she wants."

"Shut up, you old fool," Birdie's mouth prissed, though the glance she sent him held a deep affection. "And get them dishes clean, you hear?"

"Make 'em sparkle like yer eyes, fer a kiss," he rumbled.

"You'll settle for a piece of pie," Birdie sniffed, "and that's all!"

He sighed. "I'm a patient man."

Feeling like an intruder on their peculiar courtship, Tamsen hurried to her office and busied herself with counting the previous night's receipts. Thus engaged, she looked up to see a red-faced Mike Dunnevant standing with a blushing Ming Yee beside him.

"Tamsen," Mike said, awkwardly, "we—we gotta talk to you, Ming Yee and me."

473

Bit by bit, he stated his errand, stammering with embarrassment. He wanted to buy up Ming Yee's contract. He would pay what Tamsen thought fair, double it if she wanted more.

Tamsen looked at the little Chinese girl. She had appointed herself the child's protectress and was uneasy at the thought of giving her into anyone else's hands. She would not approve if Mike thought he could enjoy her for a while and then sell her services to someone else.

"It depends upon your reasons, Mike. Are you planning on going into the profession?"

"Hell, no!" Mike roared. "I love her! I want to marry the girl!" The look he turned on Ming Yee had such love in it that Tamsen's heart turned over.

"Ming Yee," she asked, "is this what you want?"

The fragile creature beamed, her perfect lips opening. "Hell, yes," she said. "Gawdamn right!"

Tamsen reached into a file, withdrew the girl's contract, and tore it up. "Ming Yee has always been free, Mike. I intended doing this any time she wished to leave."

"I can't let you do that," he said awkwardly, "I'll pay—"

"Call it a wedding present. And speaking of weddings, I'd like to have a real celebration. You can be married here—"

"I'm sorry," he bumbled, his face redder than ever, "but I kinda thought it's a good idea t' git started off right. Em—Mrs. Alden says we can have it in her garden, after this other weddin's all over an' done."

"I see. Well, then," she said with forced enthusiasm, "I suppose congratulations are in order. You're a lucky man, Mike."

"I know." His tone was reverent as he smiled down at his ivory-tinted, doll-like bride-to-be.

When they had gone, Tamsen put her hands to her hot cheeks. Mike was quite correct. She was a fool to think they'd want to be married here—in a brothel. Even though they'd met here, and Mike had courted her

474

in this atmosphere, he could not consider it a place for marriage. It was a measure of his serious intentions that he wanted to, as he'd said, get started off right. There would be enough strikes against them, with the California attitude toward Chinese.

Yet it rankled, somehow, that he had gone to Em. Em would think Tamsen had actually bought the girl to enslave her, when she heard his story. And it was Em who would provide the wedding. Well, let her! When the minister asked, "Do you take this man . . . ," the Aldens would be in for a small surprise!

Ming Yee would most probably answer, enthusiastically, "Hell, yes! Gawdamn right!"

Em and Donald Alden. Nell and Dusty. Birdie and Ben. Arab and Adam. And now, Mike and Ming Yee. Everybody had somebody—except Tamsen.

It didn't help her to feel any more cheerful, when she went downstairs that night, to hear Dan Tallant's voice and Katie's giggle behind one of the closed doors along the hall. When Tamsen had finished her turn in the entertainment, she found herself snatching at every compliment, thrilling a little at the touch of any man's hand.

When Charles Cannon, a handsome, wealthy newcomer from the East remained at her side all evening, she felt herself drawn to him, despite her policy of remaining uninvolved.

"I enjoy your company," she told him, honestly, "but I'm afraid I'm keeping you to myself. Would you like an introduction to the girls who work here? There's Sue, now—"

"I can't see anyone but you, ma'am," the tall man whispered. "You're the most beautiful woman I've ever met." Cannon looked down on Tamsen's masses of dark hair that his fingers itched to caress, on the slender body in apricot silk, on the blush that tinted her cheeks at his touch.

"I don't suppose we could have some time alone?" He nodded toward the stairs.

Tamsen had learned the art of evasion well, and had

a dozen stock answers to discourage ardent admirers, but tonight those answers did not reach her lips.

"Not—not now," she said, stammering a little. "Perhaps another night."

She hated herself for saying that, just as she hated being alone. I suppose, she thought, eventually I'll go up those stairs with some man who attracts me, through sheer loneliness. After the first man, it'll be easier. There will be more men, then more—until I am old and sick and used up, the way Madam Foster was.

She made an excuse to leave and fled to her room. When Dusty came looking for her later, he found her with her face buried in her pillow. She sat up at his call, and he could see that she had been crying.

"There's someone downstairs who wishes to speak with you," he said. "A gentleman."

Charles Cannon? He did not give up easily! "Please tell him that I'm indisposed; I have a migraine. Perhaps another time."

Dusty shook his head. "I would advise you to see this man. He won't take no for an answer." His eyes were twinkling, with a look of slightly tipsy conspiracy. "I'll tell him to come on up."

Before Tamsen could stop him Dusty was gone.

A tap sounded at the door. She drew a deep breath and opened the door, smiling brightly. "Come in," she said.

Her welcome turned to a gasp as she stared at the man who filled the doorway.

Sam Larabee!

Chapter 11

Tamsen's first impulse was to throw herself into Sam Larabee's arms, but the expression on his face stopped her. She caught herself and stepped back, beckoning him in.

"Well, Sam!" she said. "You're looking good!"

It was true. The man's tall body had filled out. He looked cared for.

Sam entered her room reluctantly, as if he would prefer to be anywhere else. His face reddened as he looked at his surroundings, glanced at Tamsen's bare shoulders above the apricot gown. He mumbled something about how nice it was to see her, and she gestured toward a chair.

"Won't you sit down?"

Finally, he exploded. "Hell, no! This isn't any damn social visit—or anything else, either!" His cheeks burned as he looked toward the bed with its silk sheets and obvious purpose. "What I want to know is what th' hell you're doin' in a place like this! A girl like you! A lady!"

Tamsen poured a drink and handed it to him. "You were wrong about me, Sam. I never was a lady. I run this place, and I make a pretty good profit, I might add."

He took a stiff swallow and stared at her over the rim of the glass. His eyes were troubled. "It isn't because I went off and left you, is it?"

"No, Sam. I knew you were going away all along," she said, rather sadly. "How did you find me, and what are you doing in San Francisco? Are you here on business?"

Sam shook his head. He'd gone to Hawaii, he told

477

her. There he had met a girl, a pretty Eurasian, Josette. She looked a lot like Tamsen, he said, flushing. They were married and now she was in a family way, and it had got him to thinking about that night with Tamsen. He had wondered—

"No problems," Tamsen assured him. "But I thought you were a man who didn't want ties. What happened?"

He grinned. "Dunno. But Josie's a damn good girl. She takes me for what I am."

"I'm glad, Sam," Tamsen said, impulsively. "You deserve to be happy! I wish—!" She stopped short. She must not let him glimpse her present depression.

"I am," he said, his voice sober, a little awed. "That's why I couldn't leave any loose ends. I had to know what happened to you. I went to this detective agency, and they put me on to this place. Almost slugged the sneaky little sonofabitch. Thought he was lying, sending me on a wild-goose chase—"

"Well, now you know the truth."

Sam Larabee was quiet for a moment, then he drained his glass and looked at the girl he'd once loved. "I have to know how you got here, Tamsen," he said, slowly. "You've been standin' between me an' Josie ever since we got married. I want to go home not feelin' guilty about nothin'. So maybe we better clear this up so I can get th' hell outta here." He looked around him with distaste. "It ain't that I been so lily-white, myself, but—"

"Sam," Tamsen said, "I want to tell you the story."

She began back with Pennsylvania, telling him about dull Will Franklin, about the way Em was jilted a week before her wedding, about Arabella's escapades, and Papa's drinking. She explained how she had persuaded everyone to make the move that sent them out on a wagon train to Texas.

She told of Scott McLeod's death on the trail, of the way she'd stolen Dan Tallant's horses, the trek to Magoffinville, the cantina.

"My God," Sam interrupted. "You poor little kid!"

Tamsen shrugged, smiling crookedly. "You're wrong,

478

Sam. I found out that I loved my work. When I won the place in a card game, I felt a sense of power. I guess I'm ambitious. Maybe I should have been a man."

Looking at the small figure, a candle flame in her apricot velvet, Sam thought, ruefuelly, that he would argue that point. If he'd ever seen a real woman this was one—in spite of the fact that she was only pint-sized!

He listened as Tamsen went on with her tale, describing the trek to California, Em's giving birth to Martha as a result of that terrible night in Magoffinville.

Sam's face was a study in bewilderment. "I thought the kid was yours! My God, why didn't you tell me?"

"I took her as mine. I didn't think Em would be able to take care of the baby, she was so awfully ill! I'm not a widow, Sam. I never was."

Before he could say more, she continued. "You know about the sewing shop, the fire. I was trying to build a respectable life. But there were so many of us, and the fire finished that."

She told how she had taken his money, using it to buy this establishment. She even told him how she had blackmailed Dan Tallant for the remainder, letting him think Martha belonged to the two of them.

"I suppose he had reason to think so?" Sam's face was livid.

"Yes, he did." Tamsen did not intend to go into details about her relationship with Dan. She just wanted to let Sam know there had been other men.

When she finished, Sam did not meet her eyes. "This Tallant feller," he growled, "must be one helluva guy."

"I suppose he is," she admitted. He had come to her rescue more than once.

"His name's *Dan*. Reckon I get th' picture, now. He still around?"

"Yes." She blushed. Let Sam think what he would!

"Then I'm offa th' hook." He stood up, looking at her a little uneasily. "You sure this kinda life's what you want?"

"I'm sure."

"Sam!" He had turned to leave, and she ran toward

479

him, flinging herself into his arms, crying as if her heart would break. He smoothed her hair gently, murmuring words that had a consoling sound. But in a moment, she felt him begin to tremble against her, his virility asserting itself, and she knew that he was on the brink of forgetting the purpose of his visit.

She pushed away from him. "I'm sorry, Sam. I don't know what got into me. But you mustn't go before we talk business. The money that went into this place is yours. I've got enough to repay you, now——"

He shook his head, still breathing a little heavily. "It's yours," he said. "Keep it, if you want. Don't look like it's made you a helluva lot happier than it done me. Got Josie, a shack on th' beach, food grows on th' trees where we live. Hell, what do I need money for?"

Turning at the door, he said, "Tell that Tallant feller he's got him a great little girl." Then he was gone.

Tamsen felt a bubble of hysterical laughter rising in her throat. Tallant had a great little girl, all right. Katie Ryan. And he probably had a great many more besides. But let Sam go away thinking she had someone she loved, someone to watch over her. Let him go back to his Josie with a free mind. Josie, who loved him for what he was.

On Friday afternoon, Arabella stood at her bedroom window looking out over the garden. Trellises of white latticework had been set up, and they shone in the slanting sunlight like bare bones. Sunday morning they would be wreathed with flowers, making a bower for the bride and groom. Her gaze wandered to the fountain. She had not wanted the wedding in the garden, but Em was so delighted with the idea.

She closed her eyes, imagining herself standing in a bower with Juan, taking her vows to the sound of the fountain's music. It seemed so real. . . .

As Arab daydreamed, Adam walked into her room with an air of ownership. He pulled her into his arms and kissed her roughly.

480

Twisting her head away from the scent of liquor on his breath, Arab said, "Adam! You've been drinking again!"

His dimples flashed. "An' you don' like me when I'm drinking. Right? Only when I'm a sh—sober citizen."

"It's not that, Adam. It's just that you promised!"

He ducked his head, like a scolded child. "And now I'm a naughty boy. I'm sorry. Forgive me?"

"You know I do." He moved toward her again, and she backed from him. "Please, Adam, you know we agreed to wait."

"But I don' want to!" His face was set in stubborn lines. "C'mon. Jus' a little kiss—to celebrate."

She forced a laugh. "To celebrate what? What are you talking about?"

"Your husband's going to be a rish—a rich man! We're going to show brother Donald, aren't we? I don't need him! And it's all set! And I did it! Me!"

"Adam, you *are* drunk! You aren't making sense!" Something in his face stirred a vague alarm. "Suppose you explain what you mean!"

He stopped short, his boyish expression changing to one of tipsy slyness. "You're not going to get me to talk! I won't tell!"

She sighed. "All right, keep your secrets. But why don't you have some black coffee? You remember Donald's having important guests, tonight. You'll want to be sober—"

"You don't look like Donald," he said, plaintively, "but you sound like him. Don't worry about me, I can handle myself. And tonight promises to be a memorable occasion."

"Remember that coffee," she warned, as he left her. He promised that he would.

After he had gone, Arabella stood for a while, wondering if this were to be her life, worrying about a husband who was little more than a wayward boy, making excuses for him. If he did anything to disgrace Donald before the people who were coming for dinner, it would

481

be dreadful. Ruefully, she admitted it was possible. Adam seemed to be possessed of a terrible jealousy where Donald Alden was concerned.

Arab went down to the kitchen where Em was busy. But Adam had not gone there for coffee. When Arab expressed her fears, Em frowned, but tried to reassure her sister. "He'll be all right. Just a case of wedding nerves."

Adam Wheeler had gone to a bar. He was just sober enough to be angry at himself for almost spilling the beans. But he hadn't, he told himself. He could handle his liquor. It was her fault. That green-eyed girl with her made-for-love body and her indifference toward him was driving him wild. It wouldn't have been so bad, if he hadn't had to make a pretense of being on the straight and narrow—even staying away from Katie.

With Arab's looks, if she had Katie's skill—

He had a drink, then another. Soon, the thought of Katie was too much to resist. He peered, owlishly, at his watch. Madam Franklin's Parlor opened at five-thirty. Donald's dinner guests would not reach the mansion for dinner until eight. He'd have some time for Katie and still get there for the fireworks. The word he used, mentally, made him laugh aloud. It was most appropriate. But he had time. And surely, with the deal he'd pulled off he should have someone to celebrate with.

Adam left the bar, weaving a little as he made his way through the streets toward Madam Franklin's. Katie would understand him, he thought, summoning a few drunken tears. She was one helluva woman! Not like Arabella, who sounded like an echo of old Donald!

When Adam entered the Parlor, Tamsen saw him and stiffened. She gave him a look of disapproval and disgust. But Katie ran to meet him.

"Hello, sweetheart," she said in her husky voice, "I've missed you."

"Had—had to see you," he slurred, smiling tipsily at her. "Gotta—gotta shober up. Big deal, tonight."

"Come upstairs with me," she tucked her arm
482

through his, "and tell me about it. I'll have Mrs. Faraday fix some black coffee, later."

In an upstairs room, Katie pressed her mouth to Adam's as she unbuttoned his shirt. Her practiced fingers moved to his belt, while his eager hands roved over her body.

"This big deal," she pouted, "what is it? Some other girl?"

He put one finger solemnly to the side of his nose. "Shecrut," he said.

"I've got a secret, too," she laughed.

"Tell it to me." He reached for her, and she evaded him, skipping to the other side of the bed. "You little she-devil," he panted, trying to catch her. "What is it? Tell me!"

She stopped. "I'll tell you my secret if you'll tell me yours!" She watched him, head tilted to one side as he pondered. At last, his dimple flashed.

"You firsht."

She stood on tiptoe to whisper in his ear, her hands caressing him, making him tremble with desire.

"I love you," she said. "Now it's your turn." She backed from him. "Tell me—or I'll go downstairs!"

For a moment, his face was dark. Then he laughed. "Hell, you're on my shide. Why not? You got a drink up here? Less sh—celebrate."

He dropped, half-clad, into a chair and watched lazily as she brought out a bottle and a glass, then pulled her down on his lap. "All right," he said, "Heresh what's going to happen tonight. Lish—listen—"

Downstairs, Tamsen paced back and forth. Adam had been the first arrival, and the place was empty as yet. She kept raising her eyes to the upper floor, thinking of Arab's husband-to-be up there with Katie—and the wedding was on Sunday.

Perhaps if she sent for Em and Donald, let them see what was going on up there, they would either halt the marriage plans or bring Adam's indiscretions to a halt.

Probably, she thought, with a twist of pain, they

483

would blame her. After all, this was her establishment. She provided the wares sold here.

No, all she could do was wait and hope that the wedding would make a man of the scoundrel!

There was one remedy she would take, however. Katie had gone up with him knowing full well that he would be marrying Arab the day after tomorrow. It was clear that she would consider herself available even after that marriage.

Tonight, Tamsen thought fiercely, would be their last time together. Tomorrow, she intended to rid herself of the Irish girl. Tamsen would pay Katie off and send her back to Magoffinville. Katie would have no choice. For, if she didn't go, Tamsen would see that she was blacklisted in every brothel in town.

Chapter 12

Tamsen was aware that all her employees knew of Arab's coming marriage and of the groom-to-be's defection. Nell asked a question regarding whisky supplies in hushed tones, her black eyes expressing sympathy. Dusty brought Tamsen a glass of tea, all she drank these nights at work. He proffered it with an I-know-how-you-feel air. Only a few gentlemen had come in as yet, and there was not enough to keep her busy.

"Give the gentlemen drinks on the house," Tamsen told Dusty. "I have some business to attend to."

She went upstairs, wanting to throw open the door to the room Katie and Adam occupied and denounce them both. Gritting her teeth in anger, she went to her own chamber. There, she took out a drawing she'd been working on, a plan to tie her house and the one next door together.

The sound of the door opening and closing behind her brought her whirling about. Her eyes narrowed as she saw Katie, disheveled, a robe drawn hastily about her naked body. The girl looked desperate, terrified.

"Well?" The word was like ice in the air between them.

"Is Dan Tallant downstairs?" Katie asked, looking furtively toward the closed door as if she expected someone to burst in.

"Why should that concern you? You have a customer, do you not?" Tamsen's tone was frosty. "Or do you prefer two at a time?"

Katie ruffled her hair with one hand, her face weary

485

but determined. "All right, Tamsen. I know you don't like me. And the feeling is mutual! But this is an emergency. A matter of life or death! Believe me! You've got to believe me!"

"Dan Tallant is not here. I just came upstairs. Now, if you will excuse me—"

"I will *not*!" Katie cried hotly. "If you want to be so high and mighty, I ought to walk out of here. But I'm not going to! I'm going to have to trust you! I can't warn them! They'd never let me in—!"

"Katie, I haven't the slightest idea what you are talking about! Warn whom? Who won't let you in?"

"Senator Alden, that's who! Somebody's going to be killed—!"

Tamsen was on her feet, her eyes wide with fear. "Who? For God's sake, Katie, explain!"

Tamsen heard her out, then shoved past her, running down the stairs and out into the night. Once outside, she stopped in a moment's indecision. Should she go back in, tell Dusty to saddle a horse or ready her carriage? That would take time, and there was no time to spare.

Fate intervened as a carriage drew up before her establishment and a gentleman stepped out. She recognized him as one of her patrons. He, in turn, was struck dumb by the sight of the beautiful madam here in the street in her low-cut crimson gown.

She ran toward him. "I must borrow your carriage," she gasped. "Emergency!" Before he could answer, she had swung herself up and was tapping the driver's shoulder.

"Do you know where Senator Alden's home is? Then drive there! Hurry!"

The dispossessed owner looked after them ruefully. His vehicle was well-known on the streets of San Francisco. He hoped his wife didn't hear about this! Shaking his head, he entered the Parlor.

In the carriage, Tamsen leaned forward, as if her posture could lend wings to the horses feet. It was a frightening story that Katie had told her.

486

James Gadsden, Minister to Mexico, was to meet with local merchants interested in a transcontinental railroad along the southern route at a secret dinner-meeting in Senator Alden's home. Em's home!

Adam Wheeler, the Senator's own stepbrother, was in league with Northern interests who saw it to their advantage to build the railroad farther north. They were willing to use any means to achieve that end.

Tonight, when Gadsden entered the Alden house, there would be a sniper stationed across the road and Gadsden would be shot. His death would end his influence in Mexico and foil the purchase of the lands the southern-planned route would follow.

Adam Wheeler had set the whole thing up! He had betrayed his own brother!

"Dear God," Tamsen whispered, "let me get there in time!"

Holding tightly to the seat as the carriage swerved around corners, Tamsen thought of Dan Tallant. Katie had told her of his role in all this.

An agent for the government, Dan was doing a secret study of transportation deals and people with illegal influence. It had been his job to keep people like Wheeler under surveillance. And Katie had helped him.

Katie had tossed her head, scornfully. "I'm nothing, so don't get any ideas. Like I said, I like my job and I'm good at it. But I keep my eyes and ears open, and I get paid for passing along what I hear. What happens to that information is none of my business. But I don't think that your sister is going to like having a man murdered on her doorstep."

Em! What if she were shot when she opened the door to greet her doomed guest? Or Arab!

The carriage had stopped, and Tamsen was down the step in a flash and running up the walk.

She pounded at the door.

Inside, the family awaited their guests. Donald Alden was looking over a packet of papers in his study. Tonight, he wanted to have all the facts and figures on the proposed railroad route fresh in his mind.

Leaving him to his work, Em and Arabella checked the table to see if they had overlooked any details. It was set beautifully with a blue damask cloth and Wedgewood imported from England; some of Em's late-blooming roses were arranged in an elegant centerpiece.

"One would think we were having the President to dinner," Arabella said.

"Perhaps this is more important," Em told her. "This has to do with the future of California, a whole continent. Can you imagine being linked with the East? With home?"

"You still get homesick for Pennsylvania, don't you, Em?"

"Not for the place," Em said, wistfully. "For the people, I suppose. For the way we were—"

"Papa—and Tamsen?"

Em blinked away tears. "I suppose so."

"I miss Papa," Arabella's chin was set stubbornly, "but I don't care if I never see Tamsen again."

Em wisely changed the subject. She had suggested, almost pleaded, that Tamsen be invited to the wedding, but Arab had been adamant. This was no time to start another argument. The dinner, tonight, was a business meeting really. She and Arab had already eaten and were about to retire upstairs, now that their preparations were finished. The pounding startled Em.

"It appears someone has come a bit early," she said. "Lin's in the kitchen. I suppose I'd better get the door."

The door opened to reveal Tamsen, her black hair windblown, looking every inch the madam in her crimson gown.

Em gave a startled exclamation. Tamsen didn't wait for an invitation, but pushed her way in. Em stood before her, lovely in her blue velvet gown, but it was the girl in gold behind her that Tamsen's eyes were fastened upon. Arabella, now grown into womanhood—Arab, whose heart she was about to break.

There was no time to think of the consequences to Arabella! No time! "Em," she gasped, "your husband!

488

Where is he? Someone—someone is going to be killed! Murdered!"

Em was still in a state of shock at seeing Tamsen and her mind refused to accept Tamsen's words. Em gestured toward the study, and Tamsen whirled in that direction.

Senator Alden rose to his feet as she entered. His mouth opened in surprise, the papers still clutched in his hand. "Why, Tamsen," he said, his eyes taking in her disheveled condition, "how nice to see you! This is a surprise, Em will be—"

His voice trailed off as she closed the door, leaning against it, panting to regain her breath. Her eyes were fixed upon him with a look of desperation that amounted almost to madness.

"What is it, my dear?" He was alarmed at her condition. He walked toward her, offering his arm. "Come, let me take you to Em," he coaxed. "I'm expecting guests—"

"Em knows I'm here," she gasped. "James Gadsden! Gadsden—"

He flinched at her mention of the name. That had been a closely guarded secret. No one knew he was to be here tonight.

"James Gadsden," she said again, on a ragged sob, "is to be shot as he reaches your door!"

"My God!" It was a low sound, almost a groan as he stared at her, seeing by her face that she spoke the truth. He reached her in one stride, taking her by the arm, leading her to his desk where he poured a thimble of brandy. "Drink that! Now, tell me, where did you learn this? Who is planning this assassination?"

When Tamsen just stared at him blindly, he set the glass down again, sensing that she was in shock. "You've got to tell me, Tamsen!" At last, he shook her until her hair swung back from her pale face. "Talk, girl!"

"Your stepbrother," she said, numbly. "Adam Wheeler."

"She's lying!"

489

Donald Alden turned to see his stepbrother wavering in the doorway. His eyes looked sober, but the flush along his cheekbones belied them. He had clearly been drinking. Alden stared at him, and his gaze slid evasively away.

"All right, Adam, then what is this all about?"

"Haven't the slightest idea," Adam said with attempted nonchalance. "Say, you got any more of that brandy?" His eyes fastened on the decanter, and Donald Alden moved in front of it.

"*You're* lying, Adam." Alden's eyes were narrowed. He knew all the signs. By God, he'd been a fool to let Adam take him in like this. Only Adam, outside of his normal group, knew that Gadsden was coming here.

"I'm lying? You mean you're going to take her word against mine? A little tramp like that?" Adam smiled his charming smile, but his eyes were frightened—guilty.

"Where a man's life is concerned," Alden said, grimly, "it's better to be safe than sorry. So, at the moment, I intend to believe the lady. I'm going to ride out to meet Gadsden and the others and stop them until we're sure the premises are clear."

"Donald!" Em's voice sounded, tremulous, from the doorway. Behind her, Alden saw Arab, the girl who was to marry his stepbrother on the morrow.

"Em," he said, abruptly, "take care of your sister." He indicated Tamsen. "She's been through a bad experience. Arabella—Arabella, I'm sorry." His apology held a deeper meaning. "I'm sorry my brother is what he is," was what he wanted to say.

He turned from the women to his desk, and taking a pistol from it, began to load it. He placed it on the desktop as Em came toward him, throwing her arms about him.

"Donald, please don't go out. I couldn't bear it if—"

Tamsen gave a small cry. Adam Wheeler had snatched the gun up and was holding it to Tamsen's back, gripping her arm cruelly. When he spoke, his voice was nervous, high, almost at the edge of hysteria.

"I'm only trying to save your life, brother. If you

490

walk out there, you might get mistaken for Gadsden in the fog. Maybe we'd all better think this over."

Arabella, standing behind Em, found she had clenched her fists until her nails cut into her palms. Seeing Tamsen again, in danger and helpless in Adam Wheeler's hands, she knew nothing had changed. Tamsen was still her sister—bossy, but dearly beloved.

"Adam!" Arab's voice rang clear in the parlor. "Adam, put that gun down! Now!"

His eyes focused on her blearily. "The little bride. Trying to henpeck me, already. Don't like that, Arab. *Katie* wouldn't—"

"Adam!" Arabella moved toward him. "Adam, we don't want any trouble tonight. Remember? We're getting married tomorrow. Here, give that to me." Backing a little, he brandished the gun in her direction.

"Stay away from me. Back against the wall, Arab. You, too, Em, Donald. We'll all wait right here until it's over. I'm sorry to discommode you ladies, but it'll only be a little while—"

Arab didn't move. "And then what, Adam? Don't you realize that if Gadsden is shot, you'll be a murderer? You'll go to prison?"

He laughed again. "I'll have money enough to go wherever I want! It's all fixed. And nobody would have known I was even involved if it hadn't been for this snoopy little bitch!" He turned malevolent eyes toward Tamsen again, the gun wavering back in her direction.

Arab moved forward, her hand outstretched, and he whirled to face her. "Let me alone," he shouted. "I'll shoot!"

"He will," Tamsen said, grimly. "He means it, Arab. He'd do anything to save his own skin." She'd known so many of Wheeler's kind before. If he has to shoot anyone, she thought, let it be me. Then maybe Donald might be able to disarm him.

"If you're going to fire that thing," Donald Alden said, "you'd better aim it in my direction. Because if you hurt anybody in this room, I intend to see that justice is done. All your life, I've been pulling you out of one

491

scrape after another! Trying to make myself believe there was some good in you. Well, by God, I'm through. Right now, I could kill you myself—with my bare hands!"

"Big brother," Adam sneered. "Always so kind and good! Doling out the cash a little at a time, to keep little brother out of trouble. Well, I don't need you any more. I'm getting paid well for setting this thing up. And after it's over, I'm getting out." He grinned at Arab. "And maybe I'll just take you along with me."

Alden lunged forward, his face scarlet with anger, and Em caught at his arm. "Please, Donald," she gasped. "Oh, please! He's dangerous."

Adam laughed again, his high-pitched nervous giggle. "You have a smart little woman there, Donald, old boy. I—"

He stopped short. From the outside of the house came the sound of a gunshot, flat and ugly. Adam Wheeler slumped in relief, dropping the gun to his side. "There!" His voice was rich with satisfaction. "Now—"

There was another shot, and his eyes widened. The explosion was followed by the shouts of angry men and the sound of running feet. A tremor ran through the hand that clutched Tamsen's arm. Adam released her and she moved away.

"There was only supposed to be one gun." His voice cracked. "A rifle. Those were pistol shots. Something went wrong."

"I hope for your sake that it has," Alden said. His face had gone death-white. "By God, if Gadsden's dead—"

"He isn't, Senator."

Tamsen whirled toward the doorway. Dan Tallant! Oh, dear God! Dan! Her knees went weak with relief. But Dan did not see her. He was looking beyond her, at Adam Wheeler.

"I don't know how much you know, Senator," he said with a somber expression, "but there was a plot to kill Gadsden tonight. The man who planned to shoot

492

him is dead. But he had a confederate, I'm sorry to tell you that it's your brother."

The gun that had been hanging from Wheeler's limp fingers came up in the man's trembling fingers. It pointed, waveringly, at Dan Tallant's heart. And Tamsen screamed.

"Look out! He's got a gun!"

She flung herself forward to shield the man in the door.

At the same moment, Donald Alden moved, throwing himself against his brother in an attempt to wrest the weapon from his grip. He was too late.

The gun exploded beneath Wheeler's nervous trigger finger. Tamsen felt a blow that sent her reeling. She stood for a moment looking into Dan Tallant's startled eyes. Then with a whimper, she sank to the floor.

Tallant caught her and held her gently, staring at the blood that welled from her gunshot wound. "Tamsen," he said in a broken voice, "oh, my God!"

Then Em and Arab were beside him, weeping as they tried to stanch the wound. Tallant stood looking at the white-faced Wheeler. Then, in a single movement, he reached the boy and struck him a blow that knocked him backward against the desk.

"I didn't mean to shoot her," Adam whined. "Listen, we can talk this over. I can explain! It was Donald's fault. I can explain—"

Tallant knocked him down again.

The room filled with people. Gadsden, Crocker, Stanford, all the men who had been invited to confer over dinner. It took their combined efforts to separate the two struggling men. "You'll kill him, man!" Gadsden was saying in his soft, Southern drawl. "Let him be. Let him stand trial. The important thing now is to get a doctor for the girl—"

Tallant shook his head to clear his senses. For a while there, he had been out of his mind with anger. But Tamsen mustn't die! She mustn't die!

With the words running through his mind like a

prayer, he picked the girl up, and carried her to an upstairs room. His eyes were wet as he put her down carefully on the bed.

"Donald told Lin to go for the doctor," Em said. "Dan, if you don't mind——," she waved a hand toward the door.

He looked at her blankly, then said, "Yes, of course. I'll wait in the hall."

Outside the door, Dan Tallant paced the hall, half out of his mind with fear. That was Tamsen in there! Tamsen's blood on his hands. He looked at them in disbelief. Tamsen, so tiny, but of such tough fiber. She couldn't die! She couldn't!

He put a hand to the knob, and drew it back, cursing the job that had taken him away from her in Magoffinville, cursing his own stubborn bullheadedness that had kept him from seeing that he loved her.

"I love her!" he thought in surprise. "I've always loved her! God, what a fool I've been!"

She had flung herself in front of him, to protect him. And now she might die!

He struck the wall with a doubled fist, savoring the pain.

As Tallant walked the floor above, Senator Alden held a gun on his brother. He had asked his guests to retire to the dining room and give him a moment alone with Adam.

"I ought to kill you," he said. "If Em's sister dies, I will."

Adam didn't believe him. Donald had always come to his aid. He would help him find a way out of this jam.

"I didn't mean to shoot her," he whined. His face was white, dripping with sweat. The boyish charm that was his chief attraction was gone.

"Look, Donald, I've thought of a way we can make this thing look good. That girl has been an embarrassment to you. Everyone knows what she is. We can say she engineered this whole thing tonight. That she was holding you at gunpoint when I came in. Then—well— I tried to take the gun away from her, and she got shot.

494

Tallant doesn't *know* anything. He's only guessing. And the man who was to do the shooting can't talk. He's dead."

The contempt in his brother's eyes made him shift his own. "This way, it won't reflect on you, you see. Em will go along with the deal to protect your name. And Arabella won't let anything happen to her future husband. She doesn't have any use for her sister, I know that. The wedding can go on as planned—"

Adam halted before the Senator's expression of loathing. "I'm trying to remember," Donald Alden grated, "that I'm a civilized human being—that I believe in law and order. But I warn you, I'm on the verge of forgetting!"

Charles Crocker stood in the doorway. "I thought you might like to know the doctor has arrived."

"Thank you. Now, I wonder if you'd mind taking my place to guard this—this garbage—while I go up to check on my sister-in-law and my wife."

Leaving his friend to stand guard, Alden went upstairs.

When the doctor emerged from Tamsen's room, Em preceded him. Flinging herself into her husband's arms, she wept with happiness. "Tamsen's going to be all right," she cried. "Oh, Donald, she's going to live." Holding his sobbing wife in one arm, the Senator reached out to touch an equally tearstained Arabella with the other.

Dan Tallant watched for a moment, then went back downstairs to the parlor. There was something he had to do.

"Senator Alden asked me to relieve you for a while," he said to Crocker, drawing his own gun. Seeing the dark eyes that burned like coals in Tallant's bleak face, Crocker hesitated. Then he thought, what the hell! Justice is justice. He left the room.

Tallant prodded the boy at gunpoint out into the reception hall and through the door. Wheeler whimpered as he was forced into the waiting darkness. "You can't do this," he said. "My brother will—"

"Your brother will do nothing." Tallant's voice was flat, deadly. "Walk!"

"But where are you taking me?" Wheeler blubbered. He was crying now, and it made Tallant sick inside. He sounded as Wally Knight had, that night so long ago. Two of a kind, he thought, contemptuously. Then he laughed, a grating sound. For Adam Wheeler had given him an idea.

"Keep walking," he said.

He herded him in the direction of the wharf. For a way, Wheeler kept up his snivelling. But at last he quieted. It took all his strength to stagger along in front of the implacable enemy who surely intended to kill him. The only sound was that of their footsteps in the quiet night.

Reaching the waterfront, Tallant put his gun in its holster, removed the belt that held it, and draped it over a post at the end of the pier. "Now," he said, "let's see if you can fight like a man."

It was nearly dawn when Dan Tallant returned to the Alden household. He grinned to himself as he neared his destination. A battered Adam Wheeler had been placed aboard a vessel bound for Australia, where he would find company of his own type.

As for Tallant, he had his work cut out for him. For while he and Alden had waited outside Tamsen's door for the doctor's report, the Senator had asked Dan to escort Gadsden back to Mexico and stay there until the purchase was safely concluded.

It was just as well, Tallant thought, his eyes shadowed with sadness. He and Tamsen seemed to bring each other nothing but trouble.

Chapter 13

In an upstairs room of the Alden mansion, Tamsen McLeod drifted in and out of delirium. *"Thomas, Tamsen,"* she kept repeating in a little singsong voice as Em and Arabella looked anxiously at each other across the slight figure on the bed.

"She's burning with fever," Arabella said. "Oh, Em, do you think—"

"It's just the grippe," Tamsen muttered. *"You'll be all right, Papa. I'll take care of the girls."*

Em's eyes were wet with tears as she bathed the feverish forehead with cool water. "She'll be all right," she assured Arab, though she was beginning to be terrified herself. Tamsen had suffered severe shock, the doctor said. The wound had developed an infection, and she was on the verge of pneumonia.

"Em—what she just said—she *has* taken care of us. I—I didn't realize it until I saw her again! I guess I made her into some kind of monster in my mind!" Arabella was frankly weeping. "She pulled us through on the trail! She did a man's work, while I acted like a child!"

"And I sat back, remembering I was a lady," Em said, slowly. "Don't blame yourself too much, Arab. I was wrong, too."

"Arab," Tamsen babbled in her fever. *"I've got to find Arab!"*

Arabella knelt beside the bed, putting her tearstained cheek against Tamsen's burning one. "I'm here, Tamsen," she wept. "Oh, Tam, I'm here! I'll never go away from you again!"

"But everybody goes away," Tamsen confided, clutching at Arab with burning hands. "Everybody goes away."

Em turned away, her hands to her face. "I can't bear it," she said. "Oh, Arab, I can't bear what I've done to her! I've been so cold, so unforgiving—"

And so have I, Arab thought, tucking the small hand she held beneath the counterpane. And so have I.

Nights were the worst. At night, Tamsen would start up, screaming, and it took both sisters to hold the frail figure on the bed. She relived the night of the shooting over and over in her mind. "Dan!" she would shriek. "Watch out, Dan! He's got a gun!" She babbled of Martha's kidnapping, talked to Nell, telling her that, even though this was a brothel, it must be respectable.

Then there were the hours she was in another place, another time. "Sh-h," she would whisper, "Em and Carmela will hear." Then, "Those men! You killed them?"

"She's talking about that night in Magoffinville," Em said. "The men Tallant went after—"

"Sh-h . . . Listen, Em!"

Tamsen's arms reached out as if to clasp an invisible lover. "Please, Dan," she said with a sobbing cry, "love me!"

Her face was beautiful for a moment, then it twisted in fury. "Go to Katie," she raged. "Go!"

Arab looked at Em, questioningly. "I don't know anything about it. She never confided in me," Em said. "I guess I never knew Tamsen at all, never understood her."

"I think I do," Arab said slowly. "All our lives, Tamsen was Papa's right hand. We let her be responsible for all of us. I think this Poppy Franklin was inside her all the time and just didn't have a chance to get out. Em," she looked at her sister, defiantly. "I think I like Poppy Franklin."

But Tamsen was speaking again, from her dream. "Dan," she was saying once more, "love me."

Her sisters sat silent. Em thought of Donald, who also

498

needed comforting, but who waited patiently. Arab thought of Juan, who had not waited at all.

And finally, Tamsen said, in a child's voice, "Em . . . ? Arab . . . ? My arm hurts. Where's Papa?"

Bending to soothe her, Em looked up, eyes alight. "Her fever seems to have broken, Arab! I think she's going to be all right!"

At last, certain that Tamsen was sleeping a natural sleep, Arabella prevailed upon Em to go to bed. The wakeful nights had taken a toll of both of them, and downstairs, Donald Alden waited.

"Just for a little while," Em said. "But call me, if—"

"I will."

So it was Arabella that Tamsen saw when she opened her eyes. "Arab?" she said, weakly, "Was Dan . . . ?"

"He's all right. He had to leave for Mexico with James Gadsden. He wasn't hurt."

Tamsen was silent for a long time, then she asked, "And . . . Adam?"

"He's gone." Arabella's eyes were hard. "And good riddance."

"I'm sorry," Tamsen said, slow tears beginning to roll down her fever-parched cheeks. "I'm sorry about everything. I seem to spoil everything I touch—"

"You've spoiled nothing! You saved a man's life, perhaps two lives!"

Tamsen stirred restlessly against the pillow. "What happened? How did Dan get here?"

"A girl named Katie Ryan. I understand she's the one who warned you. It seems that when she left Adam to go to you, he became suspicious and when she returned, he beat her pretty badly. But she managed to get word to Dan Tallant, who—"

Tamsen heard no more. She drifted off to sleep again. Dan was safe and she was here, Arabella's hand clinging to hers. All was well.

Waking again after a long, restful sleep, Tamsen felt a moment of bewilderment. What was she doing here in her old room in the Alden house? She lived at the Parlor now.

She tried to sit up, but the pain in her shoulder reminded her of what had happened. Lifting her good arm, she brushed her hair back from her face. She recalled the shooting, but what had happened afterwards? She had a dim memory of Dan lifting her in his arms, of Em and Arab hovering about her, murmuring words of affection. And there had also been terrible dreams.

What was real and what had been a figment of delirium?

Em entered and called to Arab, and suddenly Tamsen was engulfed in loving arms. They were together again. And all was as it should be.

Not everything, Tamsen thought later. They had told her about everything that had occurred during her illness, and among the bits of information they imparted was that Dan Tallant had returned to Mexico with James Gadsden.

What had she expected? she wondered. That he would come to her, fall to his knees before her, just because she'd done the right thing for once in her life? She might have guessed he'd go.

Despite herself, she began weaving a dream. A dream in which Dan would come to her. Her wound would be healed by then, and he would hold her close. He would say that he hadn't wanted to leave, but it was his duty. That he'd only been counting the days. And they would lie in each other's arms, reliving that night in Magoffinville, but with a happier ending.

As the days slipped by, Tamsen spent the hours embellishing her fantasy, thinking of what they would say and do. And then, when Nell visited, her beautiful bubble burst. She fell headlong down the dark tunnel of reality.

Nell was visibly uncomfortable. "Figgered I wouldn't be welcome here," she confessed, eyeing her surroundings with suspicion. "Then I thought, hell, it's Tamsen. She might want t' see an' ol' buzzard like me."

"I'm delighted, Nell." Tamsen touched her hand affectionately.

"Well, don't blubber about it." Nell's eyes were suspiciously moist. "We miss you. It's like a gawdamn graveyard over t' th' place."

"I miss you, too." Tamsen was surprised to find how true her words were. "I've been wanting to see you. And I'd like to see Katie, to thank her."

Now it was Nell's turn to look surprised. "Didn't nobody tell you?" she asked incredulously. "Katie's gone. Run out on us th' night after this here all happened."

Tamsen felt a hollow in her middle, an ache of premonition. "You mean—she just left? Where did she go?"

"Didn't say. Got a note from th' Tallant feller, an' took off."

"You don't know what the note said?" Tamsen's hand plucked at the coverlet. She studied her fingers as if she hadn't seen them before, not looking at Nell.

"I kept th' gawdamn thing," Nell said. "Figgered yuh'd want t' take a gander at it. Katie left it layin' on th' desk." Reaching into her capacious reticule, she pulled out a crumpled slip of paper.

"*Katie, darlin*'," it read, "*It's all set up. What you've always wanted is about to happen. Get yourself ready for a trip. I'll pick you up in a couple of hours.*" It was signed with Dan Tallant's name.

"Then she went with Dan." Tamsen said in a monotone.

The big woman shrugged, irritably. "Hell, I dunno. Didn't find th' note 'til later. She run upstairs an' when Tallant showed up, she was all packed. Come downstairs, run over an' give me a big smack, says, 'Oh, Nell, I'm so happy,' an' skedaddled. No warnin' at all. With you down an' Katie gone, things is shot plumb t' hell."

"Find someone to replace her," Tamsen said. "And I'll be back soon, Nell. I'll be back."

Her promise was not kept. For several weeks, Tamsen seemed so wan and exhausted that Em and Arab feared she was suffering a relapse. Then, gradually, she began to improve. She had come to terms with what had happened, and the love of her sisters served as a cushion

501

against her hurts. They spent long afternoons talking of other days that were happier ones for Tamsen and Arab. It was good to laugh in loving companionship; good to have Martha, now a little mischief of a girl with sparkling eyes, playing beside her bed and chattering away.

But in spite of her inertia, Tamsen began to grow restless, not even knowing why. Caught in a limbo, halfway between her old life and the new, she knew the day would come when she would have to return to the Parlor. But for now, the doctor had ordered that she remain quiet.

Then one day there was a flurry of activity below. Em and Arab came to her room, wearing conspiratorial smiles. They had guests. Tamsen was to dress and come down. They had come to help her.

"Please, I would rather not," Tamsen began. Her sisters hushed her protests, making much of which gown she should choose, how she would wear her hair. "But who is it?" she demanded. "Someone I know?"

They still maintained their air of mystery.

Tamsen's heart began to bump in her chest. Dan Tallant! Could it possibly be Dan? Though she knew it was impossible, since he was surely on his way to Mexico, a longing began to swell inside her.

"There," Em said, "you look beautiful!"

Tamsen looked at herself in the mirror. Her olive complexion was wan, her eyes huge and haunted in a pointed little face. Her illness had taken its toll. She looked fragile, breakable, like a stranger.

Donald Alden came to lend her his arm. As they descended the stairs, Tamsen saw a sea of familiar faces.

Nell! Dusty! The girls! Birdie and Ben!

Half-laughing, half-crying, she said, "What a lovely surprise!"

"This isn't the only surprise," Alden said, smiling. He led her to a chair, without giving her a chance to greet the assembled friends, pointing to the wedding bower that had been set up in the middle of the room.

A wedding? As if in answer to her unspoken question, the minister came in, taking his place. He was followed by a very pale, very nervous young man, extremely conscious of his great size.

Mike! Mike Dunnevant! She would attend his wedding after all!

All eyes turned toward the stairs, to watch the bride as she moved down the steps on tiny feet. Ming Yee wore an embroidered Chinese wedding gown that enhanced her doll-like perfection. A misty veil was fitted to her hair with a circlet of flowers. Her eyes saw only the big man who waited for her, with love in his heart.

As the couple stood in the little bower and exchanged their vows, Tamsen thought of Dan, and pain wrenched at her heart. She had finally come to terms with her feelings for him. She could not love another man, not in the same way. She blinked back tears of self-pity, then turned at a sound from Arabella.

Arabella was openly crying, her face soft with yearning. And Tamsen recalled with horror that, except for that awful night, Arabella would have been married to Adam. Perhaps she *had* loved him and was suffering more than she and Em had guessed. Unable to bear her sister's expression of naked sorrow, Tamsen looked away.

The ceremony was short and soon over. Ming Yee had apparently been coached well in her answers to the minister's questions. They had been proper and most sincere. At the strains of the recessional, both bride and groom went straight to Tamsen's chair.

"We waited until you were well enough to come," Mike said, simply. "We wanted all our friends."

"Thank you, Mike." Tamsen's eyes misted. "I wouldn't have missed this for anything."

He bent and kissed her, shyly, clumsily, making some joking reference to stealing horses to cover his sentimental gesture. Tamsen reached up to touch his cheek, thinking how different things would be between them now. The old, daredevil, carefree Mike was no more. He was a husband, now, and Tamsen had a hunch he would be steadfast and faithful to his little Chinese bride.

One by one, Tamsen greeted her friends. Carmen, Maggie, Dusty. She had a hug for each of them. And finally, Nell, who had been standing back, scowling fiercely, approached her.

"Lissen, honey, when ya comin' back?"

"I don't know. Are things going all right?"

"Fine as frog-hair."

"Then I think I'll wait awhile," Tamsen said in a low voice. "I need a vacation." But, as Nell started to leave, she called out, "Nell—wait!"

Nell stopped, and Tamsen pulled her down beside her. "I want to ask you something, Nell. Something that's really none of my business."

Nell frowned. "Shoot."

"You and Dusty. I know you . . . you are fond of each other. Why haven't you two married?"

Nell's eyes were glassy for a moment, then she said, "I guess it's because we're kinda romantic. If we got hitched, it'd prob'ly ruin everthing. Hell, he might find out I'm just a fat old fool." She shook off the disclaiming hand Tamsen touched to her arm. "An' me, I might just ketch on that he's a whisky-soaked little runt. Thisaway, we both figger the other'n's young an' goodlookin'. See?"

Coming from anyone else, Nell's explanation might have been laughable. Instead, it touched Tamsen deeply. Nell and Dusty, two misfits who had found each other, had between them something deeper, more fulfilling than the love most people would ever know.

"I envy you, Nell," Tamsen whispered.

Nell flushed with pleasure. "Hell, honey, you got nothin' t' envy me for!" She smacked her on the shoulder with a ham-like hand. "Now, you getcher self all th' rest y' need. I better go find Dusty before he drownds in the punchbowl. Be seein' ya."

When all the guests had gone, Donald Alden offered to carry Tamsen upstairs. As soon as she thought she was alone, she gave way to tears.

But Arabella's hand on her shoulder brought her up with a jerk. "Are you all right, Tamsen?"

"Yes. It was a beautiful wedding, wasn't it?"

"I enjoyed meeting your friends. I liked them. They all seem very fond of you."

"I suppose."

"Tam, there's a man, isn't there? Something that didn't work out?"

Tamsen flinched at her sister's words. Was it there on her face for everyone to see?

"Don't settle for second-best," Arab said in a forlorn, small voice. "I tried that, Tam. And you know what happened. I never loved Adam Wheeler. Don't ever settle for second-best."

Tamsen thought of Arabella's face while the wedding was in progress. "Then there's someone else for you?" Tamsen's voice was hoarse.

Arabella sank to the floor beside Tamsen's bed. Today she was dressed in soft yellow. Her skirts billowed about her as she put her head against her folded arms. For a moment, she was the small Arabella, come to Tamsen with a problem.

"We've been away from each other so long," she said, "and I want you to know about my life and what's happened to me. I . . . I couldn't bear to talk about it before."

There, with a soft wind coming through the open window, a wind that carried the sound of a tinkling fountain and the scent of late-blooming flowers, Arabella told Tamsen about Juan and the love they had had.

Chapter 14

On the first of March, in the middle of the night, someone pounded on the door of the Alden home. As Senator Alden took up the loaded gun he kept at his bedside and went to answer it, Em looked down fearfully from the top of the stairs.

Their caller was a mud-spattered man. He thrust a paper into the Senator's hand, and was gone. But Donald Alden's excited shout brought all the members of the household down to the entry hall.

"We've done it!" he yelled enthusiastically, grabbing Em and whirling her in a little dance. "Oh, Em!"

The arrival of Tamsen and Arabella brought him to his senses. He looked down at his nightshirt and flushed. Thrusting the paper into Em's hand, he said, "Read it. I'm going up to dress! Then bring out the champagne. We're going to celebrate."

Em read the contents of the message aloud. It was from James Gadsden, delivered by courier. Gadsden had concluded a treaty with Santa Anna in which Mexico would give up the Mesilla valley and would cede nineteen million acres south of the Gila River. The proposed transcontinental railroad was now a possibility.

Donald Alden returned, now properly attired for the company of ladies, and they sat before the roaring fire in the parlor to discuss the situation.

"Nobody but Gadsden could bring it off," he said. "Thank God he was there to do it."

The others knew that Donald was remembering the night Gadsden was almost killed on this very doorstep, and that his own stepbrother had a hand in the plot.

506

Donald raised his glass to the light, looking at the bubbles in it, but it was an unconscious gesture. His mind was elsewhere. "Of course, it has to be ratified by the United States Senate," he mused, "and there will be hell to pay. The Northerners don't want the railroad to come to California. They are using their fear of the expansion of slavery as an excuse—"

"Do you mean it isn't over? That you can't retire?" Em looked at him with troubled eyes.

He smiled at her. "It won't be long, sweetheart. We can break ground for the foundations of our house by the sea right now."

Arabella and Tamsen exchanged glances across the room.

Later, as Tamsen prepared to go back to bed, Arabella tapped at her door. Arab took such a long way about in her request that it was a full minute before Tamsen realized Arab was asking for a job at the Parlor.

"I can sing, dance, entertain," she said. "Please, Tamsen."

Tamsen agreed to think it over, but she felt sick inside at the thought. Why, she wondered, dully, did she think it was all right for her to own the establishment, to entertain there, yet feel that it was so wrong for Arab? Perhaps because Arabella was more or less forced into the decision. It was either that or live on the Aldens' charity. Arab had been on the stage—still, it was a far cry from the stage to a brothel.

I don't want to go back, either, she thought. It had been good here, wrapped in love and attention like a warm blanket, with no Wally Knights to contend with, no George Heckers. What *did* she want from life? The slow tears came, as they seemed to so easily these days. If she wanted a home, she could find some man to marry who, unlike Cleve Sommers, would take her as she was.

There was no sense in dreaming that Dan Tallant would return. She knew in her heart that he'd taken Katie with him.

But the dream stayed with Tamsen through March

and April. A dream that she'd been wrong about Katie and that someday, Dan would knock on the door of the Alden home and she would open the door to see the face of a man in love.

When that knock came, it wasn't the man for whom she'd been waiting.

A ship docked in the harbor one April morning. Having made the crossing through wintry seas, it was jury-rigged, its sails hanging in tatters. Its horde of ragged sailors swarmed ashore, ravenous for fresh food, fresh water, and after that, the girls. They had been a long time at sea.

Among their ranks was a tall young man, face burned almost black by the winds that had buffeted his ship. His shirt, buttonless, was tied at his lean waist; taut muscles showed through the ripped sleeve on one arm. He looked like a pirate, but he had the bearing of a gentleman.

Normally, men of business drew aside from people of his ilk, fearing robbery or worse. But something about this sailor compelled them to stop, to listen, to answer his questions. He was looking for a house on a hill where he believed the most beautiful woman in California lived. There would be three sisters there, named McLeod. No one knew them.

Then perhaps they would know of the house itself. It must be very grand, since it had belonged to a statesman. A Senator—Al-den?

Supplied with directions, he set off toward the Alden mansion.

That day, Em and Donald had taken the baby and set off in the carriage for a picnic at the site of their new home. Arab and Tamsen were invited but refused because they felt the family needed some time alone.

Tamsen almost rued her decision. It was lovely out, the sky like blue silk, the sun warm on her face as she stood at the window. She had gone to join Arabella in the garden, but found the girl sitting beside the fountain, lost in a dream. So Tamsen had slipped away, an inner sense telling her to leave Arab alone.

Then the knock came at the door and she opened it to see a ragged, rakish-looking fellow. The man's face, lit with a glow of anticipation, changed at sight of her. Tamsen frowned.

"You are—Em?" the stranger inquired, turning one palm upward in an engaging gesture.

"Mrs. Alden isn't here at the moment," Tamsen said, stiffly, wondering at this person who used her sister's first name.

"And you are—?"

"Tamsen McLeod." There was no need to use the name Harper now.

"But there is another. Arabella? She is here?" The man's voice trembled, his eyes beseeched her to say yes.

"She's here, but—?" Tamsen stopped as his face seemed to break up for a moment. Surely this grown man was not going to cry! And what did he want? Why didn't he state his business?

She gave a startled cry as he pushed past her, his eyes roving over the parts of the house he could see. "*Dios*," he said, huskily. "God, I thank you! Where is she?" He turned on Tamsen with an intensity that stopped her protests. "Where is she? Tell me!"

"In the garden, but—"

"Which way?" He started in the direction she indicated, but she called after him, furiously, "Stop! What do you want? Does Arabella know you?"

The smile he gave her was beautiful in its tender happiness. "Forgive me," he said simply, "I have forgotten my manners in my joy that she is here. I am Juan Narváez."

Arabella had dressed this morning in a checked yellow cotton gown, made along peasant lines, that was cool and fresh and made for the California sun. Donning it, she had wished Juan could see her in it, then pushed the thought away. All her waking moments were colored by having known him, and she had no rest from him in her dreams.

Too restless to remain in the house after the Aldens had gone, Arab had wandered to the garden, seating

509

herself on a low wall beneath a willow tree in view of the fountain. The long trailing fronds of green drooped over her shoulders. She reached out a hand, absently, to run her fingers over the lace-like leaves, remembering.

The small fountain, sparkling in the sun, became a larger one, cascading into a pool of azure, surrounded by Roman pillars. The perfume of the blooms in Em's garden mingled with the remembered scent of more exotic plants. If she only turned her head, just a little, Juan would be there, a prince in his crimson uniform—

She turned, uttering a choked cry at the man who stood before her, smiling. A man with a face burned black by sun and wind, in ragged, tattered sailor's garb. For a moment, she was frozen in shock, unable to move.

"A dryad," he said.

Then she was in his arms, laughing, crying, trying to get close enough.

It was a long time before Arabella came to her senses. Then she looked up at him with dazed eyes. "How did you find me?" she asked. "I thought you were to marry Isleta. Your uncle said—"

"My uncle lied," he said, somberly. "You were very badly treated by my people. Can you find it in your heart to forgive me?"

Forgive him! "I love you," she said in a small voice.

Taking her in the circle of his arm, he led her back to the wall beneath the willow. There, he told her his story, how he had arrived at the harbor when her ship was moving over the horizon, the way he'd been kept virtually a prisoner for some time after she left. He had finally escaped, taking nothing but the clothes he stood in, and worked his way to San Francisco as a sailor.

That explained the hard, calloused hands, the whip-cord muscles of his once-smooth body.

"I brought one thing with me," he said, "something which seems to have been mislaid for a time. I hope you will accept it—again."

On her ring finger, he slipped a circlet of intricately woven lace with an emerald at its heart.

"It has been worn by someone else, but I did not put

510

it on her finger," he said. "I remained true to my vows."

Arabella shrank from him. She had not. She had been with Lazaro through choice, that night before reaching Màlaga. And she had nearly married Adam Wheeler for the sake of expediency.

"I can't take the ring," she said, weeping, "until I have told you the things that have happened to me. I've remained true to you in my heart, but—"

He put a finger to her lips. "I know all I need to know. You were lied to, sent away, kidnapped, and taken to the gypsy caves at Guadix. When you escaped, you went to Father Díaz, who helped you to reach this country."

"But that isn't all."

"It is enough. Now we will begin a new life in my new country. I feel it only fair to tell you that I have nothing. I cannot give you a house like this—," he indicated the Alden mansion "—perhaps anything but my love."

That, thought Arabella, would be enough.

He touched his lips to hers, and they were lost in an embrace oblivious to the birdsong in the willow above them or the small fountain's tinkling accompaniment to the music of springtime.

When Em, Donald, and little Martha returned from their outing, Tamsen met them at the front door, her eyes strangely bright. "I wanted to warn you," she said in a little rush. "Don't go into the garden. Arab has a guest, Juan—"

Em read the identity of that man in Tamsen's eyes. "Her prince," she breathed, "from Spain."

"I suppose so," Tamsen said, wryly, "though he looks more like a pirate to me. Oh, Em! I think you're going to have another wedding to prepare for!"

Em burst into tears of happiness. "This is one wedding I'll be only too happy to have," she said, throwing her arms about Tamsen's neck. "Oh, Tamsen, I've prayed! It's like a miracle!"

Behind her, Donald Alden stood holding the sleeping Martha with one arm and a picnic basket in his other hand, waiting patiently. At last he said, "Would you girls mind postponing the nuptials for a few moments to lend me a hand? At this point, it might not be a good idea for this fellow to find out what he's in for!"

When the young couple came in, drifting in a haze of ecstasy at being together once more, Donald Alden studied Juan, who told his story in a straightforward manner. Alden liked Juan. Apparently he'd had a great amount of legal education, which was all to the good. As the girls chattered, making wedding plans, Donald Alden was formulating some plans of his own. He would broach them in a day or two, he thought, puffing at his pipe contentedly.

Only Tamsen felt a sense of not belonging. Em, driven by intuition, looked in on her that night before retiring and saw she had been crying.

"I've made up my mind to go back to the Parlor," Tamsen said, defensively. "I've been here long enough. I'm quite well now."

It was true, Em thought, but something made her plead that Tamsen stay just a little longer, until after the wedding, which would be soon.

Tamsen finally agreed. But after Em left, she thought of her sisters and their happiness, and of Dan Tallant, the man she feared she would never see again.

Chapter 15

On Arabella's wedding day, the sun rose in a blaze of glory, its light seeming to concentrate on the garden that was to be the scene of Arab's marriage to Juan. There was no trellised, artificial bower today. The bride and groom elected to stand near the fountain, using a willow as background.

Looking down on the scene from Em's window, in the room where the girls had gathered to wait for proceedings to begin, Tamsen thought she had never seen the garden so beautiful. The grass was a soft and velvet shade of green, the willow in full leaf, flowers blooming. It had rained lightly, the previous day, and the whole world seemed washed new and clean.

Turning from the window, Tamsen smiled at Arab and Em. They both looked so lovely, Arab regal in the gown Em had worn at her own wedding, her shining hair a red-gold crown, and Em, dressed in a shade of sapphire that enhanced the blueness of her eyes. She was proud of them. And so happy for Arab.

"The guests seem to have all arrived," Tamsen said. "I suppose we should go down and take our places."

Carefully, Tamsen placed the bouquet of lilies and orange blossoms in Arab's arms, completing the picture of a perfect bride. Em had white roses, intermingled with babies' breath. Tamsen lifted her own bouquet, adjusting the trailing ribbons, looking to her sisters for approval of her appearance.

Tamsen, a diminutive figure in a rose gown, held a spray of talisman roses, golden, their hearts touched with crimson. There was even a touch of color along

513

her cheekbones. But it was the expression in her eyes that caught her sisters' attention. Huge and dark, warm with love, there was still a depth of underlying tragedy.

"Tamsen," Arabella said, impulsively, "there will be a day like this for you—"

Tamsen swayed a little, her eyes filling. Then the sound of music from below came to her rescue. The music announced that the wedding was about to begin.

The sisters went silently down the stairs, Arabella's heart bursting with joy, Em reliving her own wedding. As they walked to the garden, Tamsen uttered a silent prayer of thanks. Everything had turned out well for Arab and Em.

The music changed. It was Arab's cue. She stepped out into the sun, an ethereal figure in clouds of white, and moved toward the willow where the minister stood. Juan Narváez waited, tall, with a royal bearing. Alden stood at his side. The birds singing in the trees were a trilling accompaniment to the bridal music. One bird darted like a flash of blue fire to perch on the fountain's brim, despite the crowd of assembled people.

Dan Tallant, felt his heart turn over. He had returned to San Francisco two days before. His mind was on only one thing, seeing Tamsen. First, he had attended to his duty, going straight to Alden's office to deliver dispatches from Gadsden.

During that visit, he'd made a damn fool of himself, telling the Senator that he'd fallen in love with this stubborn-mule-headed girl. He confessed that he seemed to rub her fur the wrong way every time he got around her, and that he was trying to get up enough nerve to propose.

Alden suggested that Tallant stay out of sight until the wedding. If he were to plead his case at such an appropriate time, perhaps he would have better luck.

Seeing Tamsen now, so small, so fragile, Dan decided he'd been wrong about her willful nature. Maybe the fault had always been his. And maybe, today, in this romantic atmosphere, he might be able to get across what he wanted to say—that he loved her, always had and always would, ever since he first saw her bending over her campfire, her dark hair framing her beautiful serious face.

Right now, he'd like to go up there, grab her, and kiss her until she couldn't breathe. The memory of her slim dark body was so strong in his mind that he was having difficulty breathing. He ran his finger along the inside of his collar. Dammit, she looked so poised up there, like a golden butterfly. Couldn't she feel his presence? Hear the tumult of his thoughts?

The minister spoke, and Arabella and Juan answered in low, love-hypnotized voices. Finally, a plain gold band joined Juan's family ring on his bride's finger.

As Juan's dark face bent to Arabella's, the sweetness of their yearning kiss touched Tamsen with a searing pain. Then the music began, triumphal and joyous. Arabella and Juan were one.

Bride and groom led the way to the house. Tamsen and Em followed. And midway across the lawn, Tamsen looked up to meet a man's compelling gaze fixed upon her. She stumbled, almost losing step.

Dan! Dear God, Dan! And he was alone. Katie wasn't with him.

She had to get her wits together. She didn't trust herself to talk to him. Not just yet. Not with every nerve quivering at the shock of seeing him.

Murmuring something about seeing to things in the kitchen, she pushed past Arab and Juan, who had paused at the door to receive congratulations from the guests. It was a dim excuse, but all she could think of at the moment. She hurried into the Senator's study and closed the door. She stood there, leaning against it, her heart pounding in her ears until she couldn't think.

How long she stood in that spot she didn't know. She was brought out of her state at the sound of voices. Charles Crocker?

"I'm certain I saw her go in here," he said. And the voice that answered him was Dan's.

"I've got to find her," Dan said, distractedly. "There's something I must tell her."

She ducked back as the door swung open, standing behind it, her mouth dry.

"Well," Crocker said cheerfully, "looks like I was wrong. If she isn't upstairs or downstairs, I guess the lady's disappeared. I must say its good to see you again. I've been wanting to talk to you. I understand Gadsden's negotiations went off without a hitch."

"Yes, they did." Tallant's voice was impatient.

"And what do you intend to do now? I understand you have a new assignment."

"The United States is taking a good long look at Alaska. One of these days, we might just buy us another piece of land."

"And you're being sent there?" Crocker whistled. "Into Russian territory? Look, Dan, everybody's after a piece of Alaska. This could be a dangerous undertaking."

Dan's voice had a smile in it. "This is different. This time, I'm an envoy of this country. I'll be consulting with the Russians about transportation problems. My reports to our own government will be the end result. There'll be no undercover stuff. And now," Tallant's tone took on an embarrassed note of enthusiasm, "now, I'll be able to take my wife."

"Congratulations," Crocker said. "Who's the lucky lady?"

"It's a secret for now. I'll let Alden tell you after I go."

"And when do you leave?"

"Tomorrow morning, by ship."

"I envy you." Their voices faded as they moved out of the room. Tamsen stood rigid. Then she thought, I can't stand here forever, and I can't run away. I have to go out there. She moved into the dining room, where Juan and Arab stood at the wedding-bedecked table, preparing to cut the cake.

"There you are," Dan's voice was husky in her ear. "I've been looking for you."

"And I've been looking for you," Tamsen lied. "To

516

offer you congratulations. Be sure to pass them along to Katie."

The smile with which he had greeted her faded. He looked bewildered. "I don't know what the hell you're talking about. Tamsen, I've got to talk to you—"

"Excuse me," she said, pulling away. "There's someone I wish to speak to."

She pressed into a crowded group, joining in the conversation. There! That would take care of him. He wouldn't dare make a scene at Arab's reception. She guessed what he wanted to discuss. Like Sam Larabee, he wanted to cut all ties clean. He probably figured he owed her something for moving between him and Adam's gun that night. He didn't. Now they were even. He had his life, and she had his money. Pretty fair exchange.

Arabella, as she had planned, tossed her bouquet straight into Tamsen's arms. Tamsen could do nothing but receive it. But as soon as the bridal couple climbed into their carriage in a shower of rice and good wishes, Tamsen ran to her room.

Em found her there, minutes later, sitting on the edge of the bed, Arab's flowers beside her.

"I saw you leave. Dan Tallant's looking for you. Are you ill?"

"No, but, Em, I do want to be alone right now. I think I have had enough family for a while. I am going to pack a few things and move back to the Parlor today."

"Why?" Em pleaded with Tamsen to remain with her and Donald until she was sure that she wanted to return to that life.

"Please, let's talk about it another time." Tamsen was on the verge of tears.

"At least talk to Dan Tallant, see what he has to say," Em asked.

Tamsen turned on her sister, her eyes ablaze. "Dan Tallant wants to tell me that he has married Katie and that they are going to Alaska!" Angrily Tamsen pulled

517

down her single piece of luggage and began throwing clothes into it.

Em was confused. Dan hadn't exactly said what he wanted to speak to Tamsen about, but Em was pretty sure that it had nothing to do with his marrying Katie. Still, Tamsen was in no mood to discuss things calmly. Em decided that she would just find Tallant and ask him what it was all about. She left Tamsen packing her clothes furiously and went down to get Tallant.

Tam changed into the brocade that she had worn for Em's wedding and picked up the suitcase. She would go down the back stairs and, if one of the guests were leaving the wedding in a carriage, she could ask for a lift to the Parlor.

She could hardly believe her luck when, as she got out to the road, Charles Crocker's carriage came along beside her. Accepting the hand held out to assist her by the man in the driver's seat, she looked up into a familiar face.

Dan!

Dan jumped down and before Tamsen could move out of his reach, he picked her up by the waist and placed her on the carriage seat. Tossing her bag up after her, he climbed aboard and quickly flicked the reins across the horses' backs. They were off, running pell-mell through the streets of San Fancisco.

"You're going to sit there," he said through gritted teeth, "until you've listened to what I've got to say!"

Chapter 16

Whatever Dan Tallant had to say, he seemed in no hurry to get to the point. Instead, he concentrated on driving. The carriage rocked and careened around corners, scattering people on foot from its path.

Tamsen sat huddled at the far edge of the vehicle, her hands clasped tightly in her lap. Her anger at being abducted faded. She felt only the overwhelming sensation of Dan's presence beside her and a dry-mouthed fear that she might make a fool of herself over this man once more.

"All right?" Tallant asked as the carriage swayed, throwing Tamsen forward.

Tamsen righted herself and closed her lips stubbornly, refusing to answer. Then she thought, drearily, there's no sense in prolonging this. Let him say what he's got on his mind—clear the air between us. Then he can go his way, and I can go mine.

She reached out a hand to touch his arm and hastily drew it back again. "There's no reason for going any farther, Dan. Whatever you want to discuss, let's get it over with. I have to get back."

"Do you think you're being fair to everyone, running out like that?" he asked Tamsen.

She didn't answer, and he sighed. "Very well. We'll change the subject. Look." He pointed with his carriage whip toward the sky above. A scattering of stars was beginning to appear in the early night. A small breeze had sprung up, carrying the sweet fragrance of green and summer flowers. They were far from the heart of the city, high in the hills.

And they were alone.

Tamsen was acutely conscious of that fact as Dan turned off the narrow cart path and drew the horses to a halt. She twisted her hands nervously in her lap. "You —you have something to say. Say it."

"Not here." Tallant climbed down from the carriage and came around it, extending his hand to Tamsen, who sat still. Wings of panic beat in her brain, blocking out coherent thought.

"Get down," Dan said.

"We can talk here. I don't think—"

"Get down." It was not a request, but a quiet command.

Mechanically, Tamsen obeyed. He helped her to the ground and she flinched away from the hand that seemed to burn on hers, moving a few steps away to stand poised for flight.

"Tamsen."

His voice held a deep compelling note that made her start. Then he spoke again.

"Tamsen!" All the love and yearning that had been building inside him sounded in the name that issued from his lips. "Tamsen, come here."

She moved toward him, hypnotized by the urgency in his tone. She stopped within his reach, but he didn't touch her for a moment—just looked at her, his dark eyes deep with some indefinable emotion.

Then his hands went to her hair, loosening the pins that held it in place. It fell to her waist in a silken cloud, her face pale against its darkness. He stroked it for a moment, feeling the strands cling to his fingers.

"We're begining all over," he said, huskily. "Let's pretend," he indicated the carriage, "that this is a wagon. And over there," he pointed to a flat stone, "is the campfire. I've just come along, and there you are. And I know right away you're the girl I love—will always love. Then I say, 'I'm going to Alaska in the morning, come with me.'" He shrugged, grinning crookedly. "That's as far as I can go, without knowing what you say—"

Tamsen was stunned by his words; all her fantasies had come true. She looked at him with the eyes of a sleepwalker until he spread his hands and asked, "Well?"

"I will," she said in a small voice that sounded like that of a stranger in her ears. "I—I will."

"Tamsen," Tallant said in a rough whisper, "Oh, Tamsen, my God! I want you! I need you! Please!"

His arms went around her, lifting her, crushing her against his body. Then she was molding herself to him, meeting his kisses with a passion that matched his own. It was he who came to his senses, putting her away from him.

"Not like this," he said. "Like this—"

He lifted her gently and carried her to a grassy spot beneath a tree. Then he lay beside her, propped on an elbow, one finger tracing her eyes, her cheekbones, the oval of her face.

"Getting to know you," he said softly. "I'm courting you, Tamsen. We don't have much time here—but I don't want to miss anything. Now, you're supposed to ask me something. Like if there's another woman in my life—"

"Is there?" Katie! She'd forgotten Katie!

"If there were, if I were married to someone I didn't love—would it make any difference? You'd still go with me?"

It would make a difference, Tamsen thought, but . . . "I would still go."

"I have a weakness for fallen women," Dan said, teasingly. "Unfortunately, we won't be able to live in sin. Katie's gone, Tamsen. I sent her to New York the night after the shooting. She earned enough in the Gadsden affair to pay her fare there and to bring the rest of her family from Ireland to be with her."

Tamsen burst into tears. "I thought—"

"I know what you thought. But eavesdroppers never hear the whole story. I told Crocker I intended to take my wife, but I didn't tell him I hadn't asked the lady yet."

521

"Em told you!"

"She did." Tallant brushed the tears from Tamsen's lashes, touched his lips to her eyes, then his mouth to hers, his own tasting a little of salt.

"I'm glad," she said faintly. "Oh, Dan, I'm so glad!"

"And so am I," he said, his fingers unbuttoning the high collar of her virginal gown, drawing it back to reveal the curve of a white shoulder.

"Forget everything else, sweetheart. I want you to think of nothing except that—we're here, and we've found each other." His voice grew unsteady as he said, "You're so beautiful in the moonlight. Sort of a creamy gold, like a flower." His lips touched her throat, her shoulder, and she lay dazed with the wonder of it all.

This was what real love was like. It was tenderness; big hands that were surprisingly gentle; a hard mouth that softened on hers and grew exceedingly sweet. Love was tenderness and it was need. Love was passion and, at last, fulfillment. Love was lying on the grass beneath a tree, seeing a scattering of stars through its branches. Love was cradling the dark head of the only man in the world. A man who loved her.

And Tamsen smiled a secret smile; this time, it had been he who said *please*.

It was a night that lasted forever and was at the same time much too short. False dawn tinted the sky with a hint of pearly opalescence, and a bird stirred in the tree above. Dan sat up. His ship sailed at dawn. It was time to go.

Tamsen composed herself, searching in vain for the pins that held her hair.

"Leave them," Dan said. "I like it down this way."

Before they left the spot, they stood, arms about each other, looking down at the city below. Here and there, lights winked on as early risers left their beds. And Tamsen felt an overwhelming love for the city she was about to leave.

"I'd like to stay here forever," she whispered. "Dan, do you realize I feel truly married now? That this is our true wedding night?"

"About our wedding," he said, an odd note in his voice, "there won't be time for——"

She put her finger to his lips. "It doesn't matter, not as long as we feel married. It's just that I don't want this night to ever end."

He bent to kiss her, and they walked reluctantly back to the carriage that would take them to the harbor where their long journey would begin.

Tamsen leaned against Dan contentedly as he guided the team from the spot where they had really found each other at last. It would stay in her mind forever, this high hill with a soft night wind, the scent of grass, a sky full of stars that watched over them.

I lied, she thought, a little forlornly. She had wanted a wedding. Not because the words said or the vows taken would change their relationship. She wanted Em and Arab there. She wanted them to share in her happiness.

But there was so little time. And this was Arab's wedding night. She would be lying in Juan's arms. And Em, weary after the preparations for Arab's wedding, would be abed beside Donald. Tamsen would send them a message from the docks before she boarded the ship. They would be happy for her, she knew.

We all have someone now, she thought. We all have someone.

She cuddled close in the circle of Dan's arm, letting his words engulf her in a warm wave as he described the life they would live in the far north among the Russians, the Eskimos, the Aleuts, and the Indians. They would dwell like royalty in a small replica of the Russian court among the more adventurous aristocracy. But there would be long treks, via dogsled, the two of them beneath fur robes, alone in the long night.

And one day, the new country would have shops, offices, all the things that would make up a city—like San Francisco. Her eyes widened at a sudden thought. There might be a fortune to be made!

As if he were reading her mind, Dan gave her a little shake. "There's one thing I want you to remember.

Your only responsibility is to love me. From this time forward, I'm going to take care of you! Understand?"

Tamsen looked up into the dark face that was now the boundary of her whole world and said, "Yes, Dan! Oh, Dan, I love you!"

It was good to lean against him, to delight in his strength. The streets were tunnels of silence as they moved through the sleeping city. And at last they neared the harbor. Tamsen could see the shadows of two carriages drawn up near the dock's edge. Other passengers waiting to board a ship, no doubt. She felt a twinge of regret. She and Dan would no longer be alone.

Apparently he felt the same way, for he drew the carriage to an abrupt halt.

"Tamsen," he said in a nervous tone, "there's something I want to tell you. Please, don't be angry—"

Tamsen stared at him, wondering at the note in his voice. He's still a little afraid of me, she thought, suppressing a smile. This lean, hard man, so sure of himself, now sounded most uncertain!

"Yes?" she asked.

"I don't want you to think I took too much for granted," he floundered, miserably, "but after I talked to Em, I took the liberty—"

His voice faded in her ears as Tamsen caught sight of the figures alighting from the carriages on the wharf, running toward them. Figures she recognized.

Arabella! Em!

She leaped from her own vehicle and ran to meet them and was swept away by loving arms, greeted with ecstatic voices that hovered between laughter and tears. Soon Donald and Juan joined them, pumping Dan's hand, offering congratulations. And there was someone else—

"We brought the minister," Em bubbled, "just as you said, Dan."

"And I've brought the veil," Arab laughed. "Em and I wore it, and now you—"

Numbly, Tamsen looked at Dan. His cheekbones were flushed with color. He *had* taken a lot for granted.

524

And knowing her stubborn nature, he'd probably been in agony as to how she would take this!

Smiling, she moved to his side. They were well-matched, she and this virile, strong-willed man who would love her forever, watch over her, protect her—and who could still be reduced to this state of boyish uncertainty at her moods.

Then she stepped forward to let Arab arrange the veil over her long, dark hair.

The wedding took place on the wharf, in the silence of a night turning into morning. Tamsen stood beside Dan, fragile and virginal in her white brocade, lost in the minister's sonorous words. For music there was only the lapping of the waves below.

A pink glow appeared in the east as the minister said, "I now pronounce you man and wife."

Tamsen turned to Dan, lifting her face. And as he bent to her, the watchers seemed caught in a silent tableau, unable to move, to speak, their hearts stopping at the beauty of the scene. No one wanted to break the mood the ceremony had induced.

Tallant took Tamsen's arm. Wordlessly, they moved toward the waiting boat that would carry them to their ship. Its oars cut through the lace-frothed waters, lifted in a spray of silver. Then those on the wharf could see only the silhouette of two people standing in its bow, their shadows becoming one.

"Look," Arab whispered.

The taller of the shadows had raised an arm and was pointing toward the last faint star lingering in the lightening sky.

The North Star.

Em was the only one not to feel the magic of the setting. Weddings were supposed to be performed in churches, in homes, and in gardens. Somehow, a ceremony performed on a wharf in the hour between night and morning didn't seem quite legal.

"It isn't right," she said, forlornly. "I wanted Tamsen to have a real wedding, like yours, Arab, and mine."

Arab put a consoling arm around her. "It was a real

525

wedding," she said, her voice still hushed at the wonder of it. "The most beautiful one I've ever seen. And it suited Tamsen. Tamsen's . . . different."

As Donald led Em toward his carriage, Arabella met Juan's eyes. She felt again that sense of timelessness, of being enclosed in a world that was all her own.

He smiled and said, "Let's go home."

As they left the wharf, Arabella turned for one last look. Her hand fingered the gift Tamsen had given her before the ceremony, now plunged deep in the pocket of her cloak. It was the family Bible, which held a sprig of their mother's forsythia pressed between its pages—the symbol of a journey ended, a journey begun.

SARA

Brian Cleeve

*A spellbinding Regency novel
from Warner Books*

*When Captain Joshua Pownall of His Majesty's
Secret Service found Sara in 1809, she was a terrified ten-year-old, the sole survivor of a Spanish
village utterly destroyed by the French. For five
years Pownall and Sara traveled together as he continued his undercover work; sleeping sometimes in
caves, in barns, on the ground rolled up in their
traveling cloaks. Then he brought her to live with
his sisters in Sussex, expecting her to grow up into
a decorous young Englishwoman. But Sara was born
for adventure, and found it even in the serene
British countryside . . .*

"Mrs. Goatlake just come by," Molly whispered.
"Oh, Sara, I'm so feared of her, what'll we do?
Why'd you make me go with you t'other night? I
must ha' bin mad, stark mad."

"What are you talking about? What did she say?"

Molly stared at her. "She knows. She knows I told
you 'bout the poachin'. My dad told her you come
with me t'other night an' she's so angry with me for
tellin' she wants to kill me, she said. She said you'll
tell—you'll tell the captain, an' they'll all go to jail.
What'll we do?"

"You know I won't tell."

"But she don't. She don't believe it, she says you
belong to them an' you'll tell Dr. Newall. An' if my
dad do go to jail, what'll become of Marthy and
Willum? Oh, Sara, I could—— Why'd you make me

do it? I must a' bin mad out of my mind to tell you anything. An' then go bringin' you. I just thought he'd laugh, just have a good laugh at you—an' now—"

"I'll tell her myself. Where is she?"

"She's gone now, but you can tell her a'right. She wants us to come back to my dad's cottage again an' take our oath on it. Tonight, after dark again. If we don't, she says she'll put her eye on us, make us wither up."

"You don't believe that stuff!"

Molly twisted her hands in her apron in a rage of impatience.

"You're so mortal clever you don't believe nothin' till it come up an' hit you bang on the head. What d'you know about what she can do?" She looked away, her mouth trembling.

"Nobody can do that." But her voice trailed. Doña Ana had had the eye. Although only for enemies. "Nobody can," she whispered.

"Then you won't mind comin' tonight?" But Molly was too frightened to be bitter; she gripped Sara's arm with both hands, beseeching. "You got to come. If you don't she'll be sure you're tellin'."

"Of course I'll come."

Peg opened the kitchen door, looked at them. "There's some as has little enough to do, it seems. Miss Susannah's wanting you, Miss Sara. You get on with them bottles, Molly."

It was close to eleven before they could slip out of the darkened, sleeping house. The night fine and cold. A rag of cloud black-edged against the moon. A dog barking somewhere. A ruffle of wind as they climbed the ridge towards Over Thaxstone before turning away towards the marsh.

"We'll just tell her," Sara said. "She's got to believe me." She drew in deep breaths of the night air, was glad to be out in it, the tremor of fear that she had caught from Molly gone with the excitement of escaping from the house, creeping down the stairs, sliding the bolts they'd greased with butter after Mrs. Hobhouse and Peg had gone to bed.

But Molly was still afraid. Not saying anything as they trotted up the path, turned down the far side of the ridge, past the edge of Masham's farm. Now and then catching her breath at something, gripping Sara's arm, making her hurry and then seeming no longer to want to hurry, falling back into a walk. They came to the spongy marsh edge, trodden by Mr. Masham's cattle into deep, sodden holes, the grass becoming sedge, reeds. Followed the path that wound from hummock to reed bank and up onto the island. The oiled paper of the cottage window a small square of dull yellow tonight, a crack of light round the door. Other crevices of light where the walls were splitting. A thin plume of greyish smoke from the hole in the low roof.

"If she looks at me I'll die," Molly whispered. "You promise her, promise her everything she asks."

"I'll promise." She felt her own heart beating. The dark. The silence. Molly touching the door, not knocking, just touching. Then her fingers tapping on it, her voice whispering, "It's us. We've come."

A man's face, dark and twisted, the nose flattened. Beckoning them in, his smile as twisted as his face and nose, thin and savage.

She went in slowly, the same choking smell, worse with the warmth of the fire, the people there. Molly's father sitting on the stone that served as another stool. His face gaunt bones, jutting, full of shadows. The woman opposite, crouched on the one wooden stool, her skirt spread, blackish green in the firelight, her face stooped downwards, only her eyes raised—one eye drifting sideways, staring, showing the white. Looking at them from under black eyebrows, black hair, her face walnut dark, the same thin, twisted shape as her son's. Mrs. Goatlake. Her son, Joseph, looked at them. The three children hidden in the rag bed.

The fire crackled, a heap of stolen wood beside it,

beside Mrs. Goatlake. She lifted a stick, held the end of it in the fire, still saying nothing.

"We've come," Sara said. Tried not to be afraid. She felt Molly shaking beside her. Molly's father, Henry Bone, turned his gaunt, slow head, put up one huge, clumsy hand to his chin, rasped at it.

"So you did," Joseph Goatlake said. "And now, what you goin' to tell us?"

"That we—I won't say anything. I promise. I won't say a word to anyone. Never. She didn't mean —she just told me—by accident."

"We don't like accidents, do we, Ma? Accidents is bad for folk." He had taken a knife out of his pocket, opened the blade. He touched the point of it to his thumb, tried the edge, seemed intent only on it. The firelight, the candle glittered on the steel, and it held Sara's eye as though it was threatening her.

Mrs. Goatlake turned her head, as slow as Henry Bone's, the eye drifting, sliding downwards, looking at the floor while her other eye looked straight at Sara, turned to Molly. Sara felt her mouth dry with terror in case the drifting eye should look at her. The dreadful whiteness of it, as though it was coming out of its socket. The old woman drew the stick out of the fire, its end already burning, held the flame up between the two of them so that her eye shone. Like a white stone. Then it stared straight at Sara, as black and malignant as the other.

"What a pretty one," she whispered. She held the stick closer to Sara's face, smiled, her teeth broken, the stumps the same colour as her skirt, greenish black, sickening. "Een't she handsome, Joseph? What a pity if she got spoiled. An' Molly Bone . . ."

She looked at Molly. Sara heard Molly's breath catching, thought she could hear her heart thudding.

". . . An' our Molly Bone grown so fine an' big. All that good feedin', eh, Joseph?" Her voice rustling, like something dragging in wet, rough grass.

"Maybe she do have forgotten what 'tis like to be hungry. Eh, Molly?" The stick, its end still smouldering, darting towards Molly's face, almost touching. Molly swaying her head back, staggering, her hair brushing the roof, the rough underside of the turf that covered it, ragged, dirt-crusted, like thick cobwebs. Joseph Goatlake reached out and grabbed her wrist so she couldn't back farther away. The burning stick close to her eyes.

"Let go of her!" Sara whispered, tried to shout, to move.

"Oh, oh," Mrs. Goatlake said. "This een't the time for givin' orders, this een't Lavender Cottage with gentle folk sittin' about. This is here. What you been tellin' that captain of yours? About us? About what Molly here been tellin' you?" She moved the stick, quickly, like a snake darting. The heat of it against Sara's cheek. "What you been tellin'?"

"Nothing. I swear, nothing."

"An' what you goin' to tell? Dr. Newall comes to take tea with your ladies an' says, 'Them poachers, them wicked poachers, I do wish I could have 'um took up an' sent to jail.' What'll you say then, sittin' an' listenin'? 'I do know who they are, I do know where they go and when, with their faces painted black; I do know how they sells their gainin's. 'Cause Molly Bone did tell me.' Is that what you'll say?"

"No. No."

"Give us your oath on that, eh? You oath me now you won't tell?"

"I swear I won't."

"Oh, not lady's swearin', not Bible oath. My oath. That I'll give you. Will you swear that?" She lowered the stick, the end of it now no more than a dull eye of red, dying. Her own eye swerving away to the fire, showing the white glisten, blind.

She breathed, "Yes, I'll swear." Her own eyes fastened on that whiteness. Beside his mother, squatting on his heels, Joseph Goatlake slowly honed the blade of his knife against the heel of his palm. Henry Bone said nothing, his hands like slabs of knotted wood hanging again between his knees, his face expressionless.

"You kneel in front of me," Mrs. Goatlake whispered. "The two o' you. Say this after me. 'If I tell what I knows of Mrs. Goatlake, or any of hers, or any of her doings.' You say that after me now. 'If I tell . . .'"

Kneeling. Not wanting to obey. But kneeling as if she had no will. Whispering the words after her. Their two voices.

". . . may my throat close an' leave me dumb . . ."

". . . leave me dumb . . ." Molly's voice almost crying, thin with fear.

". . . may my eyes be blinded . . ."

"No!"

"You say it after me, Molly Bone, both of you say it."

". . . may my eyes be blinded . . ."

". . . like hot coals of fire, an' may my heart wither in me till I drags about blind an' fumbling my path. Say it."

The fire burning. And yet the hut cold. ". . . my path."

". . . and here's my blood on it, for my solemn oath."

". . . my solemn oath."

And before she could move, the knife had touched her wrist, cut skin and flesh. Hers, Molly's. Joseph held both their wrists; the knife dropped on the earth floor. A thin ooze of blood on her skin. And he put his mouth to her wrist, his lips wet, cold wet, sucking, like a toad. Her wrist, Molly's. Her whole body shuddering from the cold wetness of his mouth, the shock of the knife blade. He picked up the knife again, a red smear of blood on the tip, mixed with dirt. He put it against his tongue, licked it clean, his eyes still watching. Molly's breath crying in her throat.

"An' that een't the end of it," Mrs. Goatlake whispered. "I'll be watchin' over you, day an' night. The eye swivelled, stared full. "You hear li'l tappings at your window in the dark, I'm there, I'm there. I'll know if you tells. Such pretty ones. Such a pity to go blind, eh? Eh? You feel your eyes a bit sandy, your throat go sore a bit—then you think of me, eh? You say to each other, 'She's thinkin' on us, she's watchin' over us.' You do that, an' you won't be tempted to tell stories. Jus' a li'l pain'll come to you, an' you'll think, 'They took my blood, they took it, for an oath, an' she's workin' on it, workin' to do me harm.' Now you 'member all that an' go 'long back to them nice warm beds of yourns. But don't look round too quick as you go, 'case I'm follyin'—" She cackled with a sharp, cold laughter, showed the blackened stumps, the red throat, the whitish lump of tongue, reached up her hand with its black fingernails, earth-coloured fingers, to touch Sara's arm, her body. "Such a pretty one. Send 'um away now, Joseph." She stood up, reached out, touched Sara's eyes and throat. "Blind an' dumb," she whispered. "You 'member that. Blind an' dumb an' fumblin' about in the dark forever. Just you 'member. An' my eye'll be on you to keep you a' mind on it."

They stumbled to their feet, out the door into the moonlight, Joseph behind them, his hand at Sara's neck, on her shoulder. "You 'member," he whispered. The knife in front of them, point upwards, the moonlight on the blade. Then they were running, their breath gasping until it hurt to breathe, and the sweat ran into their eyes, stinging.

"I cain't go no more," Molly gasped, fell on her knees in the grass, lay flat. Sara knelt beside her, tried to pull her up again.

"We've got to get home."

They got home at last, holding their breaths, to the familiar dark of the kitchen. Up the stairs.

"Can I stay in with you?"

Lying in the narrow bed, holding each other, long shivers of fear running down Molly's body, as though nothing would warm her. Sara lying awake, listening, now shutting her eyes against the moonlight, and then opening them quickly as she heard a sound, the creak of timbers, the rustling of a mouse, something. "It's all lies," she whispered. "She can't do anything." Molly's arms tightening round her, clenching, half asleep in nightmare.

Almost asleep herself, Sara saw the old woman's white, staring eye like the moon, her skirt spreading black across the room, over her. Pushing out her arms against it, against the dark. The clock striking four. Was she asleep? One minute yes, then awake again, listening. Half asleep. The nightmare of the bone-white eye. Mixing with other nightmares, screaming. The sound of screaming, the soldiers—

"Wha'—wha'—"

Both of them sitting up. Dark. The moonlight gone. Pitch dark.

"I cain't see," Molly whispered. "I cain't see."

* * * *

The sky hung livid, a sickly, leaden colour, threatening ill weather. Autumn had become winter overnight and the leaves of Great Wood were already blackened. They ran, hugging their parcels, two stolen bottles of claret wine, a pudding that should have been delivered to Mrs. Grimmer.

"Wait for me," Sara called, Molly ahead of her. "Wait for me." Still trying not to believe in Mrs. Goatlake of last night, in Mrs. Talbot, whom they were going to see now. "Will it be enough? What we're bringing?"

"It'll have to be, it'll have to be. An' we can promise her money from when we gets it. Come on."

Along the ridge, the dark mass of Lord Southcott's Great Wood on their left, like a wall, and the marsh to their right, below them. Flat, sullen, stretching to the far horizon. Steel-shimmering of water. Black reeds, black mud, the vivid green of marsh holes gathering the remains of daylight into them, a skein of birds far out, black arrowheads. The horizon already threatening night. No wind blowing. A heavy stillness, cold falling from the air, settling.

"There it is," Molly whispered. "She do live down there all alone with no one. Just her cat."

Mrs. Talbot. Just a name in Lavender Cottage, not well thought of, but just a name. Old John the gardener's half-sister.

"Oh, no more than gossip, child," the captain had said. "A poor old woman who lives alone, there's always some sort of gossip."

A tongue of land below them, pushing out into the marsh. Lapped on three sides by water, mud banks, the water shallow, green with weeds and cresses, one thin stream of blacker, deeper water twisting among the reeds, touching the narrow point of land. And there, built almost on the water, the cottage.

They went down the path, not running now, slower and slower as they came near. A cat sitting on one of the posts. A large tabby cat with amber, narrowed eyes watching them come down the path towards him.

"That's him," Molly whispered, and made a kind of bend of her knee, a ducking of her head as she went by, pretending to be settling her parcel under one arm before she knocked at the door. And as she knocked, the door opened, an old, tall woman was standing there, staring at them. As tall as Molly. Thin. Her hair snow white under a black satin cap. Her nose thin and straight, her eyes grey and commanding, her whole bearing one of command. Staring at them as though she knew who they were, why they had come, everything.

"We—brought you somethin'," Molly whispered. Held out her parcel. "We got somethin' to—ask you.

Oh, please, you got to help us, we're in such trouble, we—we don't know what to do."

The old woman still said nothing. But she stood aside and they went in. Molly so slowly Sara needed to press her forward in case it seemed rude. A smell of herbs, of tar. A candle burning, the soft hiss and whisper of the fire. Like last night. But nothing else the same; even the fire was of sea coal, not of wood, the flames whispering, content. The candle in a pewter candlestick, set on a table. The floor swept. A chair. Spectacles lying on the table, and a book. And behind the table, shelves full of china jars, glass bottles. Bundles of brown herbs were hanging from nails in the black timber walls. The light caught the green glass shoulders of the bottles, the white china.

The old woman went behind the table, stood there still looking at them, waiting. Molly set her parcel down, and Sara hers. Not knowing whether to open it.

"Just some wine," Molly whispered. "An'—an' a puddin'. An' a bit of money. It een't much, but we'll . . ."

"Tell me what is the matter." Her voice sounded harsh and at the same time educated. Nothing like Molly's voice. Or Old John's. The gossip that she was Lord Southcott's half-sister, by Old John's mother. The old lord's daughter.

Beside her on the wall the shape of a bat, pinned against the timber. A real bat. Mouse head, sharp, papery brown wings. Bead eyes. She couldn't look away from it. Forced herself. And in a clear glass jar behind the old woman's head two snakes were coiling. The fire brightened, turned them to jewels, blue, silver, amber.

"Mrs. Goatlake," Molly was whispering, "she told us—" Whispering the story. Stumbling. Repeating. And the old woman listening, her face showing nothing, her eyes fixed on Molly, turning once or twice to Sara.

"Show me your wrists," the old woman said. Her fingers were cool, like ivory, and yet the tips of them were rough. Drawing their wrists towards the candlelight. She had put on her spectacles, bent her head a little to see the small cuts of Joseph's knife, no more than red lines a half inch long across the blue veins. Molly's hand, red from scrubbing, large, powerful. Sara's, thin and brown, her fingers as long as Mrs. Talbot's.

The old woman let go of Molly's hand, spread Sara's out until it lay flat, the fingers bending backwards. She traced the lines on it with her forefinger, closed the fingers up, reopened them, said nothing. Took Molly's and did the same thing with it. Spread it out, tried to make the fingers lie flat as Sara's. But they curled upwards, made a cup with the palm.

"You have strange hands, the pair of you. Many things will happen to you both." She sat down, looked at them unsmilingly. "Why should I help you? Why should I make an enemy of Mrs. Goatlake for the sake of—" She made a gesture of such contempt towards their offerings that Sara felt her face burn. "If you keep your promises, she'll not harm you."

"She will, she will!" Molly cried, leaned over the table towards her. "I feel it already." She half lifted her hand towards her throat, her face, and took it down again as though even the gesture might bring evil.

Mrs. Talbot sat for a long time, no longer looking at them, seeming to be considering, looking at something far away.

"If I should help you," she said, "there would be a price. But not in money."

"Anything!"

The old woman looked at Sara.

"What sort of price?"

"I do not know yet. Do you want me to help you?"

"Yes, yes. Oh, please, missus, please. We'll give anything, anything."

"And will she?"

"Yes, oh, yes. Tell her Sara, say you will."

"If I can," Sara whispered.

The old woman smiled at that, and was suddenly beautiful, as she must have been long ago. "That is a good answer," she said. "Show me your wrists again."

She held them, peered close at wrists and hands through her spectacles. Her own hands somehow courteous, touching delicately and yet very strong. "It will hurt you," she said. "Those scratches must be burned away. Will you be able to stand that? And to bring the burns back to me untouched?"

"Burned?"

"Yes. With a hot iron. Are you brave?"

"I don't know."

"I een't brave, but I'll do anything, anything if it do—if it—"

"Go tomorrow to the smith, to Mr. Lightharness. He'll know why you've come. But you'll have to be very brave." She took the shillings that Molly had laid down on the table beside the wine. "Take two of these, one each, and give them to him before he begins."

"What will he do?"

"I told you you must be brave. He will burn your scars away with iron."

Molly staring at her wrist, her throat working, swallowing. Sara standing beside her, the cottage, the old woman, seeming a long way away, the sharp smell of the herbs catching her breath, choking. The warmth of the fire. To burn the scar away with iron. She tried to imagine it, wanted to shut her eyes against the thought of it. And saw the bone white of Mrs. Goatlake's eye, felt Joseph's mouth on her skin. As though he had put poison there and she could feel it working. Her wrist throbbing. It had throbbed this morning, the skin reddened around the scratch. She looked down at it. Angry red.

"Will you go?"

She nodded, tried to say yes.

"An' tonight?" Molly breathed. "If she do know we ha' come to you—an' een't safe yet? Please, een't there nothing you can give us for tonight?"

The old woman stood up, reached down a bunch of herbs, and another, tore off a part of each, put the parts together, and re-divided them. "Keep these close by you," she said. "Under your pillows. And lay this on your window-sill and this by your door. You will be safe. She cannot reach you across these tonight." She gave them the small sprigs of dried brown grasses, dried flowers. Stood up. "Run home now. And come to me tomorrow night."

*   *   *   *

The forge was like a black cave, full of the noise of hammering, the hiss of white-hot iron in water, smoke from the charcoal fire. The smell of iron, harsh as blood. The smith's face dark, sweating, the sweat rolling in silver snail paths onto his naked throat, onto his enormous chest, itself sweating, the black hairs curling above the ragged, greasy edge of his leather apron.

"Only a li'l burn it'll be," Molly whispered. "Like touchin' a coal. That's all it'll be." Her hand trembling.

The smith beckoned them, his eye red as the fire. The bellows-boy looked at them and looked away, as though he too knew why they had come. He had a strange, soft, foolish smile that he turned on everything—the bellows, the fire, anyone who came—as though all were one to him. He was deaf and dumb, and simple.

Slowly, and then with a quick movement that almost spilled the coins onto the black earth floor, Molly put their shillings down, side by side on the anvil, bright as white eyes in the dark, the firelight. The smith nodded to the boy, who took the shillings, dropped them into a pocket of his leather apron, smiled, at Molly, at Sara, at the dark. The smith made a gesture with his fingers, and the boy took two horseshoe nails from a box and laid them where the coins had been. When he had done that, he went out into the road.

"He'll tell us if someone comes," the smith said. " 'Twon't take long."

He took the nails in the long pincers, held them as delicately as finger-tips could, thrust them into the fire. They watched, Sara's mouth growing dry, her throat closing with the terror, the charcoal fumes, as the smith worked the bellows with his lame foot, his shortened leg, pumping them up and down, up and down, the flames hissing, the nails reddening, glowing, becoming as crimson as the fire itself. Sara wanted to close her eyes against it and was afraid to, could not look away, could not breathe.

The nails grew white, burned with a white light in the fire, unbearable. And still she could not look away from them. The smith took smaller tongs, a smaller hammer, and with an extraordinary swiftness gripped one nail, began to beat it with quick, short blows, the hammer dancing on the burning iron, curving it, curving it, until the nail became a ring, the white glow dulled to red, began to blacken, was re-plunged in the fire and grew white again, was hammered, hammered, laid aside, and the second ring formed as swiftly, white glow dulling to red and blackening, burned white again, laid with the first, and then both heated red, smouldering and dull like burning eyes on the black surface of the anvil, where the white shillings had laid.

"Do ye still want them?" the smith said.

Sara swallowed, managed to whisper, "Yes."

"Hold out your arm, girl." He came close, grew huge, black as midnight, and she shut her eyes against him, holding out her arm. And there was a sudden pain in her wrist, on the inside, where Joseph Goatlake's knife had cut, the pain terrible. She tried to shriek, her throat locked with the agony, with the burning could only gasp and feel her knees giving, Molly gripping her, the smith's hand closing on her wrist, dragging it down, plunging it into the bucket of water beside the anvil. There was a hissing sound, and the ring was in the bucket with her hand, burned her knuckles as it sank, turned black instantly, sent a curl of steam up from the shimmering surface of the water.

Molly whispered, "Hold me, Sara, hold me," and Sara threw her arms round her, hid her own eyes against the sight of Molly's bared wrist, the second ring. She felt Molly's body shiver with the pain, heard her gasp in her throat, her jaws clenched against crying out, and then whimpering, "Oooh, oooh," as the smith bent her forward, plunged her hand and wrist into the water.

They stood shaking, holding each other, and the smith took up the two rings, tossed them on the horn of his palm. "You take them wrists to her tonight," he said. "An' don't you show 'em to no one till you do. Nor these." He gave them the still warm rings, made them close the fingers of their hands over them, held their hands tight in his. Stared into their faces. "You've got friends now," he whispered. "Will have, when you do with those as she tells you. Against her you're afeared of and else besides. So long as you don't talk." He held their hands so tight that Sara thought her fist was crushed, the ring driven into her flesh. The furnace whispered, the charcoal seemed to have its own soft language as it burned and glowed. The dark of the forge closed round them, there was no daylight, there was no day outside. Only the forge and the black shape of the smith and his eyes, like glass, red-burning with the firelight.

Then he let go of their hands, said harshly, "Keep them wrists covered, mind. And get to her quick as you can or 'twill be no more than a burn, an' all for naught. Get along home now."

It was midnight before they reached Mrs. Talbot's

cottage, panting against the gusts of wind, with the fear of being missed from the house, of what they were doing. Their wrists still hurt with a sharp, raw pain as their sleeves touched the burns. They had twisted rags round them, but the rags kept slipping down as they ran, and in the end they had thrown them away. They had their rings tied tight in their handkerchiefs, and gripped them against the shadows, the sounds of the night. The weight of shadow of the Great Wood, an owl drifting overhead, the desolate crying of a night bird in the marshes ahead.

They were over the ridge, and below them they could see the light of a candle in Mrs. Talbot's window, the black shadow of the rook against the water.

"So it's done, eh?" Mrs. Talbot said, drawing them in, a subtle difference about her manner from the previous day. She examined their burns by the candlelight, pursed her lips over them and took a small earthenware jar from the table, opened it. "This will hurt too, mind. Just for a moment and then you'll feel no more of it." She put her forefinger into the dark red ointment, paused for a second. "After this," she said, "the mark won't leave you. Ever."

And shortly after, witchmarked and beautiful, Sara found herself in London of the Regency—a city of forbidden delights and dangerous temptations, including the bold men who loved her to the edge of obsession . . . and beyond.

THE BEST OF THE BESTSELLERS
FROM WARNER BOOKS!

MORE LIVES THAN ONE?   (89-372, $1.95)
by Jeffrey Iverson
More Lives Than One? reads like a detective story and
is the most thorough attempt to authenticate experiences of
"previous incarnation." **8 pages of photographs.**

THIS LOVING TORMENT   (82-694, $2.25)
by Valerie Sherwood
Perhaps she was too beautiful! Perhaps the brawling colonies
would have been safer for a plainer girl, one more demure
and less accomplished in language and manner. But Charity
Woodstock was gloriously beautiful with pale gold hair and
topaz eyes—and she was headed for trouble.

A STRANGER IN THE MIRROR   (89-204, $1.95)
by Sidney Sheldon
This is the story of Toby Temple, superstar and super bastard,
adored by his vast TV and movie public, but isolated from
real human contact by his own suspicion and distrust. It is also
the story of Jill Castle, who came to Hollywood to be a star
and discovered she had to buy her way with her body. When
these two married, their love was so strong it was—**terrifying!**

Ⓦ A Warner Communications Company

Please send me the books I have checked.

Enclose check or money order only, no cash please. Plus 35¢
per copy to cover postage and handling. N.Y. State residents
add applicable sales tax.

Please allow 2 weeks for delivery.

WARNER BOOKS
P.O. Box 690
New York, N.Y. 10019

Name ....

Address ....

City .... State .... Zip ....

—— Please send me your free mail order catalog.